Books by V

LOST STAF ⎯⎯⎯
The Lost Starship
The Lost Command

DOOM STAR SERIES
Star Soldier
Bio Weapon
Battle Pod
Cyborg Assault
Planet Wrecker
Star Fortress
Task Force 7 (Novella)

EXTINCTION WARS SERIES
Assault Troopers
Planet Strike
Star Viking

Visit www.Vaughnheppner.com for more
information.

The Lost Command

(Lost Starship Series 2)

By Vaughn Heppner

ISBN-13: 978-1507755297
ISBN-10: 1507755295
BISAC: Fiction / Science Fiction / Military

FROM:
OFFICE OF THE LORD HIGH ADMIRAL
STAR WATCH SUPREME COMMAND
PLANS AND OPERATIONS DIVISION

TO:
BATTLE GROUP COMMANDERS
SITUATION ALERT
TOP SECRET

Captain Maddox has returned from the Beyond on a secret Intelligence mission to locate an ancient alien starship. He has delivered this ship to the Oort cloud in the Solar System. [Star Watch experts continue to examine the alien vessel, searching for superior weaponry.] Several weeks after the captain's return, the New Men invaded the Commonwealth.

Supreme Command believes the two events are related. The New Men conceivably wish to defeat the Commonwealth before we can discover and use the ancient technology to shift the balance of power.

The attack started on the rim of "C" Quadrant. In the last seven months, the New Men have annihilated four Star Watch battle groups and an allied flotilla of rim system warships. There are unconfirmed reports the enemy has bombarded habitable colony worlds with nuclear warheads.

Two and a half months ago, Supreme Command sent the augmented Fifth Fleet to "C" Quadrant. [Half the warships carry the new wave harmonics shielding.] Admiral Fletcher's orders are to engage in battle under favorable conditions. Otherwise, Fifth Fleet must practice a fighting withdraw, slowing down the enemy but keeping the fleet intact.

Detailed *Combat Studies* in the Strategy Council suggests that Star Watch must commit to maximum mobilization. Henceforth, all leaves are canceled until further notice. The New Men represent a category one emergency. The personnel of Star Watch must respond with utmost vigor in what might be the very existence of the human race.

CARIA 323, "C" QUADRANT

-1-

The senior officers of Star Watch's Fifth Fleet sat in the conference chamber of Flagship *Antietam*. Most of them looked worried. They had a right to be.

"It's definite," Admiral Fletcher said. He was a big man with harsh features, sitting at the head of the table. "Commander Guderian came through the Laumer-Point an hour ago. She spotted the enemy in the Lamia System. The New Men could be here in three days, maybe less."

That caused a visible stir among the officers. The fear intensified in a few. Others looked more determined.

The admiral understood both emotions. He felt them himself.

"How many star cruisers did Guderian see?" Rear Admiral Blake asked.

Blake was thin and balding with pinched features, an officer with a mathematical bent of mind. The rear admiral commanded nine monitors: big, slow-moving vessels with dense shields and heavy-mount lasers. The monitors were almost the equal of the older generation battleships, lacking the *Bismarck*-class's speed and space marine pods.

"Over twenty star cruisers," Fletcher said. "The New Men were jamming, of course. There could have been more.

3

Guderian's *Osprey* is a Patrol craft and has excellent sensors, but the enemy—"

"Excuse me, Admiral," Blake said, interrupting. "Did the New Men spot the *Osprey*?"

"We can't know for sure," Fletcher said, "but we must assume they did."

Blake glanced at the others before saying, "The New Men know the Fifth Fleet is here, Admiral. They know we're waiting for them."

"It's possible," Fletcher conceded, "although I doubt it."

Blake laughed bleakly. "These are the New Men we're talking about. Their technology has trumped ours at every turn. Their beams bypass our shields and drill through our hull armor with ease. On the reverse, their deflector shields shrug off our heaviest lasers, and whatever alloy they use for armor resists our best efforts. With all due respect, sir, we've brought our fleet too far forward. We should retreat and consolidate as per orders, gathering greater reinforcements."

"I don't agree," Commodore Garcia said. She sat across the table from Blake. The small woman was old, with dark eyes and hunched shoulders. Many considered her the cleverest tactician among them. She ran Taskforce 31, which was the highest-rated in the fleet.

"No one has faced the New Men and survived," Blake told her. "Why are we going to be any different?"

"For one thing," Garcia said, "many of our vessels have the new wave harmonics that changes a shield's frequency at high-speed. That should stop the enemy beams for a time, a new and critical advantage for us."

"Let me point out that only *half* our ships have these new shields," Blake said. "And if the shields are any better than the old ones, no one knows that yet. But even if they are, that means *half* our ships are still criminally exposed to the enemy beams, including all nine of my monitors." The rear admiral paused, as if letting that sink in. Then he added, "I've said it before and I'll say it again. We should retreat and refit *all* our ships before thinking to face the high-tech star cruisers."

"No," Fletcher said in a low voice.

The senior officers gave the admiral their attention.

4

"We're Star Watch," Fletcher said. "We've sworn an oath to protect the people of the Commonwealth. That includes the five hundred million souls on Caria Prime. If we pull out, the New Men might bombard the planet, maybe annihilating everyone."

"I agree that's a war atrocity of the first order," Blake said. "Caria 323 is also the pivotal star system of "C" Quadrant. If there's any place to face the New Men out here on the rim, it's this system. The Commonwealth has poured vast sums of money into strengthening it. I refer to the star base guarding Laumer-Point Alpha."

Faster-than-light travel mandated tramlines, or as some called them "wormholes" or "jump routes." A ship with a Laumer Drive opened a Laumer-Point and jumped along the route, traveling the many light-years connecting the two star systems in a matter of seconds. Once in the new star system, a ship had to travel the ordinary way to the next Laumer-Point. The journey across a system often took a week or more before the ship could jump again.

Caria 323 was a critical rim system, particularly as it was now the last easy route from the Commonwealth to the Wahhabi Caliphate.

"Star Base Alpha has collapsium hull armor," Blake was saying. "I happen to know that beggared the treasury fifteen years ago when they installed it."

Fletcher was aware of all that. Star Base Alpha guarded Laumer-Point Alpha near the system's G-class star. Laumer-Point Beta was way out here on the edge of the system, near the last gas giant. Caria Prime, the inhabited world, had its own star base, making this the most heavily defended system of "C" Quadrant.

"We can't let the New Men capture such a collapsium-armored star base," Commodore Garcia said. "As the admiral has pointed out, we can't just leave Caria Prime to its fate."

"Don't you see yet?" Blake asked, his voice rising. "Don't any of you understand? The New Men have deliberately left this star system alone because it's so valuable to us. They *wanted* to lure us out here. They want to catch our main fleet and destroy it so they can continue the invasion at their leisure.

It's like Napoleon's invasion of Russia in 1812. Napoleon needed to defeat the Tsar's armies early, in the Russian provinces nearest Europe. Instead, as we should do, the Russians marched their armies deep into the motherland, luring Napoleon to his doom far from his home base."

"We can defeat the New Men here," Garcia said.

"Where is the evidence of that?" Blake asked. "We must be coldly rational in this. The survival of the human race could be at stake. No. My thought is that whatever the enemy wants, we should avoid. That means we should use the Fifth Fleet as the kernel to creating a *gigantic* armada."

"Where are these extra ships that will make up your super fleet?" Garcia asked.

"I'll tell you," Blake said, pointing at her. "We must add the Wahhabi Navy to ours; do everything in our power to convince them to join us. Then we must add the Spacer Forces and those of the Windsor League as well. If the enemy has superior technology, we must match it by overwhelming numbers."

Fletcher had heard just about enough. He'd hoped to win Blake and his adherents over to the plan. If the Fifth Fleet were going to beat the enemy, they needed unity.

"Admiral," Blake said. "You have the right idea. You've gathered every remnant from the defeated battle groups, keeping everything together. But this is too little too soon to face the enemy's superior technology. Instead of losing Caria Prime with its five hundred million people, you're risking the billions upon billions of the entire Commonwealth."

"You call this too little?" Commander Musgrave asked. He was a red-haired officer with wild eyes who ran a flotilla of heavy cruisers.

"I most certainly do," Blake said. "I've given each star cruiser a numeric value in relation to its combat power, and I have computed the same for our vessels. Despite the fact that we will have more ships, they will have the superior force."

Musgrave slapped the table. "We have seventy-four capital ships, *seventy-four* of the finest vessels of Star Watch."

"I'm aware of how many ships the admiral commands," Blake said, dryly.

6

So was Fletcher. It still awed him. There were seventeen *Bismarck* and *Gettysburg*-class battleships, thirteen motherships, nine monitors and thirty-five heavy cruisers. It's true he had fewer destroyers than he would have liked. The enemy often used speed and flanking maneuvers. Masses of destroyers would have aided against that. Instead, Fletcher had missile boats and escort vessels. Despite those numbers, he'd also emptied a dozen troop transports of their space marines. The transports now bristled with the latest electronic gear, turning them into highly expensive decoys.

"According to my calculations," Blake said, "we have enough ships to make our losses critical, but not enough to hurt the New Men, to say nothing of defeating their invasion fleet."

"Wait a minute," Musgrave said. "You think the enemy knows how many ships we have and that we're stationed here?"

Blake took a deep breath. "I know what you're thinking, all of you: that I'm a defeatist. But I've studied the enemy. The New Men are smarter than we are. They're stronger, quicker, *better* in every way. Unless we are very, very careful, they will make monkeys out of us."

In the ensuing silence, Admiral Fletcher picked up a clicker. He turned on a holoimage that appeared above the center of the table.

Everyone could see the ships of the Fifth Fleet. They waited behind the last gas giant of the system, a blue Jovian world with Saturn-like rings. Laumer-Point Beta was on one side of the planet, the fleet was on the other side. That was by design.

Just like Blake, Fletcher understood the enemy's superiorities over them. But even New Men experienced Jump Lag when coming out of a Laumer-Point. Jump Lag was a temporary, but often debilitating, effect of "jumping" that people experienced in a variety of ways. Some people vomited. Some had blurry vision. A few had even died. Computer systems also suffered most of the time. The duration of the effects varied, but these disturbances could be critical.

Therefore, jumping through a tramline under combat conditions called for a strict procedure. One first sent through nuclear warheads. They used a timer and a spring, which were impervious to Jump Lag. The thermonuclear explosions cleared away any nearby defenders. That allowed the invader time for Jump Lag recovery.

Fletcher, with Garcia's help, had developed a plan to defeat the enemy. When the New Men sent thermonuclear warheads through Laumer-Point Beta, the blasts would strike the gas giant and its rings, but do nothing to the fleet waiting behind the planet. The explosions would be the signal. Fletcher would order his battleships, monitors and long-range-firing heavy cruisers to swing around the planet. As the New Men appeared, disoriented from Jump Lag, he would destroy them as mercilessly as they had destroyed previous Star Watch battle groups and allied rim warships.

"I appreciate your concerns, Rear Admiral," Fletcher said. "They have merit. But let us suppose the New Men come through with double the number of star cruisers Guderian counted. We will still heavily outnumber them. What's more, we will have the advantage. Yes, they have better shields and beams. But we will catch them at the worst possible moment for them. It will mean a resounding victory for us. It's possible we can even end this war."

"What if the enemy doesn't come through?" Blake asked. "What if he stays in the Lamia System?"

"Why would he?" Fletcher asked.

Blake looked distressed. "I don't know, sir. I'm just worried we may have overlooked something."

"Maybe this will put you at ease," Fletcher said. "I suspect the New Men have something I call 'victory disease.' They have beaten us every time, often decisively. It is my belief they have come to view us with contempt. Instead of worrying about their so-called invincibility, we should see this as a golden opportunity to catch them with their pants down."

Blake frowned thoughtfully.

"The New Men will come through," Fletcher said. "Of that, I have no doubt. They will trust their star cruisers to defeat us as they have defeated everyone else. Do you doubt we can defeat them if they appear?" he asked Blake.

"If they come through exactly as you expect..." Blake put his small hands on the table, his eyes unfocused, thinking. He looked up with resignation in his eyes. "If they come through as you say, we should defeat them."

"You truly agree with that?" Fletcher asked, surprised at the concession.

Blake looked around before staring up at the admiral. "If they come through as you say, yes. But I'm betting that's a mighty big if, sir."

Fletcher felt his temper slipping. He reminded himself he'd called the meeting to sound out his senior officers. Well, he had what he wanted: their real opinions. Now it was time to wrap this up.

"We can't win a war if we grant the enemy supernatural abilities," Fletcher said. "Maybe the New Men are smarter than us, but even geniuses can make mistakes. This time, they're walking into a trap. The tactical situation at the jump point will nullify their normal advantages."

Rear Admiral Blake looked as if he wanted to say more, but he held his tongue.

Fletcher could live with that. Blake was scared, and maybe the man had a right to be. The legend of the New Men's invincibility had been growing for some time. Here in the Caria 323 System, they were going to shatter that idea and smash the invasion fleet for good. Later, they could search the Beyond for the New Men's homeworld, and end the war.

The admiral gazed at his senior officers. It was good to let his people air their differences, as long as they could come to a working consensus in the end. He just hoped Blake's nerve held for a few more days.

"It's time to get back to your ships and get your people ready," Fletcher said. "The great battle is only a few more days away."

-2-

Three days and sixteen hours after Commander Guderian had informed the fleet about the New Men, Admiral Fletcher settled back into his command chair. He sipped a steaming mug of coffee, watching his officers at their consoles. The regular buzz of noise told him everything was in order.

An officer informed him there were still no signals from the picket ships watching the Tannish System.

Fletcher nodded.

The Tannish System was closer in terms of distance than Lamia, less than a light-year away. Since no wormholes linked Tannish directly with Caria 323, a journey from one to the other would take at least six months at sub-light speeds.

In anticipation of an enemy trick, Fletcher had put pickets on watch. They searched for any enemy-launched missiles from the Tannish System. For such drones to reach here at this time, the New Men would have needed to send the missiles months ago.

As Blake had said, the New Men were clever, impossibly so. Fletcher recognized that. It's why he left nothing to chance.

"There's a message for you from the *Schlieffen*, Admiral," his comm officer said. "It's from Commodore Garcia."

"Put her on holoimage," Fletcher said.

Seconds later, a hologram face appeared before Fletcher.

"Admiral," Garcia said. "My people are receiving strange transmissions from Star Base Alpha."

"Alpha?" Fletcher asked. The base protected the Ember-Caria Tramline in the inner system. A cold worm of fear wriggled in his heart. Could Rear Admiral Blake have been right? Fletcher asked quietly, "Are you informing me the New Men are coming through there?"

"No, Admiral. I'm saying Star Base Alpha has transmitted strange patterns—" Garcia put a hand to her right ear. "Excuse me, Admiral. I need to take this call."

Fletcher frowned, waiting, wondering what the other person said to the Commodore.

"Sir," Garcia said in a weak voice.

"What's wrong?" Fletcher asked.

"I can't believe this, sir. It—it doesn't make any sense. I'm transmitting you a visual. I think you should see this for yourself."

Garcia's holoimage vanished. In its place appeared Star Base Alpha.

To Fletcher's horror, what must have been an interior eruption occurred within the star base. In a funnel shape of intense white light, collapsium plating blew off the hull. A second eruption blew another section into the void. Then several explosions blew more away. Finally, a titanic blast of nova white light shredded debris in all directions, some of it down onto the Mercury-like planet below the star base.

Garcia's face reappeared. "Sir, my people are verifying the authenticity of the image. We're seeing what happened. Since the star base is five billion kilometers from us, this already happened over four and a half hours ago."

Fletcher could only stare at her.

"It must be sabotage, sir," Garcia said.

Fletcher forced himself to think. Yes, sabotage was the most obvious reason. Yet that would imply the New Men had agents in the star system. There was another problem, though. Why would the enemy destroy Star Base Alpha?

"Commodore," Fletcher said, "what's happening at Laumer-Point Alpha?"

"Sir, I'm—I'm transmitting the images to you."

Fletcher sat rigidly in his chair, watching.

Garcia's face disappeared. In its place appeared a holoimage of Laumer-Point Alpha. The jump point near the star shimmered. An enemy cruiser slid into existence.

"No," Fletcher whispered.

He recognized the triangular shape. It was like a thick slice of pie, with turrets and nods studded everywhere and big engine nozzles in back. Another star cruiser slid into existence, and then a third and a fourth.

"It looks as if their main battle fleet is coming through the Ember-Caria Tramline," Garcia said.

Fletcher rubbed his tired eyes. They felt gritty. Worse, a hollow feeling grew in his gut. How could the enemy have swung around to enter there? That would imply weeks of traveling in a detour of jump routes. It would mean the New Men had anticipated Fifth Fleet just as Rear Admiral Blake had suggested.

"Sir," Garcia said. "This, this, this— I don't understand, sir. Up until now, the New Men have always kept their fleet together. They've done that for the last seven months. Guderian was explicit. *Osprey* counted at least twenty star cruisers in the Lamia System."

"The New Men have divided their fleet in the face of the enemy," Fletcher said. "Militarily, that's a bad idea. Here's an example of their overconfidence."

"Unless…"

"What?" Fletcher asked. "Talk to me, Commodore."

"Maybe Guderian only *thought* she saw their starships in the Lamia System. Maybe those were all decoys."

Fletcher thought about the troop transports he intended to use as decoys. Perhaps the enemy was using the same tactic.

This was bad, but he still had the Fifth Fleet under his command. What was the right answer? Had Guderian seen decoys in the Lamia System? It would be foolish for the New Men to come into the outer system with a mere twenty star cruisers. One thing everyone knew: the New Men didn't make stupid mistakes. Yet, if they were going to come in at Laumer-Point Beta and he left the gas giant…

What should I do?

"Sir," Garcia said. "The New Men in the inner system will likely head for Caria Prime."

Fletcher nodded. Caria Prime was much closer to the enemy fleet than the Fifth Fleet was out here. The planet's star base might hold out for a little while. Afterward, the enemy might begin a planetary bombardment. He had to defend Caria Prime.

"Commodore," Fletcher said, speaking crisply. "You will get your taskforce in order. We're moving out at 0300 hours."

"Sir?"

"We're going to head in-system and destroy the enemy. We have many more vessels than he does, and we have our new wave harmonic shields. Look at their numbers: I'm counting thirty-one star cruisers. We're far more than double that. We can destroy them. We're going to have to."

Garcia took several seconds. Then, she straightened and nodded. "Yes, sir, I agree."

Fletcher approved of her confidence. The New Men had snookered him. He wasn't too proud to see the obvious. Using treachery and speed, the New Men had managed to enter the star system intact. He wouldn't get to play his trick on them out here at the gas giant. So be it.

A half-hour later, the Fifth Fleet began acceleration. The blue gas giant with its rainbow-colored rings slowly dwindled in size. Seventy-four capital ships with accompanying destroyers, escorts and troop transports continued an intense burn for an entire day as they continued to head in-system against the enemy.

Rear Admiral Blake's massive monitors dropped farther and farther behind. The nine monster defenders simply didn't have the engine power to keep up with the rest of the fleet.

Fletcher sat in his ready room, hunched over his tactical display. He didn't like leaving the monitors behind. But if he was going to reach Caria Prime in time to save the planet, he couldn't afford to travel at the slower monitor speed. The planet's star base could only hold out for so long.

"Sir!" an aide shouted, pounding on the door of his ready room. "Sir, there's an emergency!"

Open," Fletcher said.

The door slid open, and a wild-eyed major staggered inside the office.

"What's the meaning of this?" Fletcher demanded.

"Sir, it's a ruse, a trick."

"What is?" Fletcher said, his stomach knotting up.

"The enemy fleet approaching Caria Prime, sir, it's false, fake, a decoy."

"Make sense, man," Fletcher demanded.

The major's eyes bulged outward and sweat slicked his face. "The fleet we saw coming through the Ember-Caria Tramline is nothing but decoy images. They're not real, sir."

"What?" Fletcher said. "That's impossible. Why would the New Men have sabotaged Star Base Alpha then?"

The admiral knew the answer before the major told him. The New Men had snookered him twice. They had played their military jiu jitsu on him, and he had fallen for it just as everyone else had.

"I have reports of thermonuclear explosions outside Laumer-Point Beta, sir," the major said.

"Where we just were twenty-four hours ago," Fletcher whispered.

"Yes, sir. The enemy fleet is coming through by the gas giant, sir."

Fletcher thought he understood. It was much easier slipping a commando force, as it were, in the long detour route to reach Laumer-Point Alpha. Then, the New Men would have used their advanced electronic decoys. Combined with the sabotage of Star Base Alpha, the enemy must have been certain he would rush to save Caria Prime. Now, the real fleet was coming through Laumer-Point Beta just as Commander Guderian had said they would. The *Osprey* had seen real star cruisers after all.

Fletcher lurched to his feet. With an oath, he rushed past the dazed major. The New Men had stolen a march on him. With these maneuvers, the enemy had separated the Fifth Fleet before a laser cannon had been fired. It was unbelievably clever.

Gritting his teeth, the admiral determined to fight his way out of this. What other choice did he have?

-3-

Fletcher's stomach seethed, and the skin on his face was stretched with worry. He sat in his command chair, clutching a cold mug of coffee.

The nine monitors accelerated. The rest of the Fifth Fleet braked hard, slowing the velocity they had gained in the past twenty-four hours. It would take time for the two unequal bodies to converge with each other.

As Fletcher tried to reunite his fleet, the New Men accelerated impossibly fast. They had already left the gas giant far behind. Did they have superior gravity-dampeners or could they simply take greater G-forces for a longer amount of time than regular humans could?

The enemy had forty-eight starships. As they accelerated, they moved together, merging into a cone formation. It was impressive. The perfectly positioned star cruisers acted as one.

Fletcher envied them that. What's more, every enemy ship was alike. He had to take into account the different capabilities of his various classes of vessels: battleships, heavy cruisers, motherships, monitors, destroyers and missile boats. Look at them. The star cruisers were packed much more closely together than Star Watch vessels would ever dare. They acted like an elite wing of strikefighters.

Why, they must have aligned themselves screen to screen. It's uncanny.

Shaking his head, Fletcher handed the coffee mug to an aide. He stood and walked toward the main viewing screen.

The enemy had forty-eight capital ships. He had seventy-four, plus a host of lesser craft. Space combat was relatively easy to comprehend. The goal was to hammer a single enemy ship with three or four of your own vessels. Concentration of effort won the day. With a deadlier and longer-ranged beam, and in their cone formation, the New Men would be able to strike his vessels one right after another. Such concentration of force would knock down a ship's screen in minutes, burn through the hull armor and chew the insides to nothing.

I have to get my battlewagons close to them. The question is how do I do that in time?

Fletcher closed his eyes. A lot of good men and women were going to die. Many excellent vessels would vanish. Why had he fallen for the enemy's tricks so easily? Maybe he should have listened more closely to Blake.

You need ice in your veins, Fletcher. You have to make the hard decisions and live with them for the rest of your life. Are you ready?

The admiral exhaled, and it felt as if his strength deflated with his breath.

You can't bail out, Admiral. Are you a coward?

Silently, with his eyes still closed, Fletcher shook his head.

Then start acting like a commander. Give clear orders, and set your face like flint. This is it. Humanity's fate rests on your puny shoulders. Don't let them down, Admiral.

Fletcher's eyes snapped open. They were shiny with moisture. Even so, an iron resolve began to mold his features.

"Comm," he said, in a rough voice.

"Here, Admiral," a man said.

"Patch me through to Rear Admiral Blake."

"I have him online, sir."

"Good," Fletcher said. "Put him on the screen."

The comm officer did so.

Admiral Fletcher raised his head and began to issues orders.

***

Behind the monitors, the rest of the fleet began to spread out like a net. The troop transports anchored the left. The decoy

16

equipment transmitted electronic impulses, sending out signals as if they were battleships.

Fletcher had to get his ships close to the enemy to do heavy damage. Would the New Men take the bait, the twelve troop transport decoys? Even if the enemy's electronic warfare pods failed to pierce the decoys' disguise, there was a fifty percent chance of failure. The New Men might go after the real battleships, leaving the decoys for later.

It's like flipping a coin. Heads I win, tails I lose.

The one thing Fletcher knew the New Men wouldn't do was fly straight in at the middle of the net formation. The greatest feat any space commander could achieve was to encircle the enemy formation in a vast globe. That meant, logically, the enemy would concentrate on one of the wings. Fletcher's plan counted on giving the New Men one flank to kill, hopefully the fake battleships, and hitting the enemy vessels later with everything once the cone formation was close enough.

"Sir," the weapons officer said. "Our monitors are in enemy range."

It has begun, Fletcher thought. *I'm sorry, Blake, I should have listened to you more closely.*

Each of the nine monitors was perfectly round except for the attached warfare pods. Every inch of space was devoted to its massive engines that supplied the beam power and gave energy to the deflector shields. Those engines weren't rigged for fast maneuvering, though. The monitors had one of the longest-ranged Star Watch beams.

The star cruisers beamed their horrid rays. Forty-eight lances of destructive energy leapt from the cone, spearing at the speed of light. From farther away than any Star Watch laser could reach, the massed beam reached the first monitor's deflector shield.

The targeted Star Watch vessel lacked the new wave harmonics. The giant beam bypassed the shield as if it didn't exist. With this critical technological advancement, the enemy trumped the monitor's greatest strength: its normally heavy deflector shield.

With indescribable fury, the combined ray hit the thick hull armor. Reinforced tungsten boiled away as globules of wet metal wobbled from the stricken monitor. The massive beam chewed through armor, causing a metallic vapor to appear and burn away almost as fast. The beam struck vitals, obliterating laser coils, turning crewmembers into disembodied molecules and striking the fusion core. Interior explosions added to the mayhem. Bulkheads blew down, a food processing center melted and munitions vaporized. The entire monitor shuddered, loosening armor plates and igniting fireballs everywhere.

The giant beam smashed through the SWS monitor, beaming into space. Then the ray sliced sideways, cutting the vessel in half as the giant beam traveled to the next monitor in line.

"Sir," the weapons officer addressed Fletcher.

"Tell the monitors to fire."

"The New Men are still out of monitor range, sir."

"Hit the enemy!" Fletcher said. "Blind their sensors, if nothing else. Take some of those bastards down with them."

The weapons officer stared at the admiral.

"Give the order," Fletcher said. "The monitors aren't going to be alive much longer."

The weapons officer turned pale. Facing his console, he relayed the order.

Space battle wasn't like fighting on Earth. The extreme distances meant greater time delays. A commander set his course and awaited the outcome as his ships closed with the enemy. It could be maddening.

Watching the monitors die in rapid succession stole Fletcher's strength. The defenders beamed back at the New Men, but to absolutely no effect. It was worse than a joke. Then the nine monitors were nothing but drifting debris in space.

It all happened so fast as the cone formation kept bearing down on the remainder of the fleet.

The admiral's knees weakened. He staggered back to his command chair and found himself sitting in it. Rear Admiral Blake was dead. It shouldn't have happened so easily. The man must have known he was going to die.

Fletcher swallowed as guilt filled him.

Time passed. Slowly, the cone formation bore to the left, aiming at the troop transports. The distances meant this was going to take a while.

Seeing this—the enemy going for the fake battleships—helped revive Fletcher.

"We're going to get our chance," he told the bridge crew. The New Men were heading for the decoys. Finally, something went his way.

A half-hour later, the weapons officer said, "Missiles, Admiral. The enemy is launching a blizzard at our right flank."

"They want to keep us busy over here while they annihilate the left side," Fletcher said. "Well, let's not make this too easy on them, or the New Men might get suspicious. Launch a missile barrage."

A minute later, Flagship *Antietam* shuddered as *Titan*-class missiles left the tubes. Other big missiles the size of destroyers burned with hard acceleration for the enemy.

During the next hour and a half, electronic countermeasures, jamming, hot flares, decoy buoys and other technological marvels attempted to protect and pierce the various missile barrages. This was a contest for computers. The New Men's were better, but sometimes mass and numbers counted too.

In time, counter-missile-lasers flashed from the ships. Mines exploded, surges burned out targeting warheads. Then, thermonuclear explosions from each side's missiles threatened to create a permanent sensor whiteout between the fleets. Fortunately, the warheads had ignited too far away. Still, over one hundred shields turned red as they protected the crews from the thermonuclear warheads' gamma and X-rays that finally reached the fleet.

Afterward, as the shields lost their color, the whiteouts faded back into normal space.

More time passed.

Fletcher accepted a steaming mug of coffee. He slurped it absentmindedly, hardly noticing that it burned his lower lip.

"The other flank is in star cruiser range, sir," the weapon's officer said grimly.

Two hundred thousand kilometers separated the two fleets. That meant the New Men could fire. Deadly enemy beams began to slice into the first troop transport, the first decoy vessel.

Fletcher stood, striding toward the crew. He yearned to hit back at the New Men with an almost physical need.

"This is a day to remember, gentlemen," the admiral said. "Yes, the enemy has hurt us, but we're going to hit back very soon now."

The New Men's ultra-beams chewed through the transports in short order. Twelve big troop ships died, leaving a field of expanding debris. The enemy must have recognized something was wrong. Big Star Watch battleships didn't go down as easily as that.

"Look, sir," the weapons officer said.

The cone began to come apart. Individual star cruisers became more apparent. Enemy vessels rotated. Seconds passed, minutes. Beams fired from the turrets, hitting SWS heavy cruisers in the center of the Fifth Fleet.

Soon, five heavy cruisers no longer existed. More died all the time.

Relentlessly, the New Men moved toward the Star Watch fleet. Fletcher's ships had finally halted the velocity taking them in-system. The Fifth Fleet headed out-system now, beginning to build up momentum as it headed toward the faster-moving enemy ships coming at them.

Fortunately, the laws of motion meant the enemy ships finally came within Star Watch range. The New Men had built up their velocity high enough that they couldn't turn away that easily.

"Now!" shouted Fletcher. "Let's start pounding their ships!"

A loud *thrum* vibrated the deck plates under Fletcher's feet. Battleship *Antietam's* engines revved at full power, giving the laser coils the needed wattage. The main cannons targeted a star cruiser. A new whiny sound indicated the first shot.

On the viewing screen, heavy lasers speared into space. More joined in from other Star Watch vessels.

The Fifth Fleet still possessed all seventeen *Bismarck* and *Gettysburg*-class battleships. They were substantially bigger than the enemy's star cruisers. They used powerful heavy-mount lasers.

As the two fleets closed, it quickly became apparent that the New Men's shields were fantastically better than Star Watch's wave harmonics deflectors.

Fletcher watched with growing despair. He made a fist with his right hand, his fingernails digging into the meat of his palm.

Antietam's heavy lasers struck an enemy shield. They turned it red as the shield attempted to dissipate the incredible energy. The enemy shield darkened and then became black. Finally, the enemy shield went down.

"Yes!" Fletcher said.

Antietam's lasers burned into the star cruiser's hull armor. The battleship's interior engine *thrum* aboard the flagship made the deck plates shiver. The hot lasers burned through layer after armored layer.

"We're going to kill it, sir," the weapons officer said.

Then the New Men practiced a hateful and deceitful maneuver. Fletcher could hardly believe it. The hit star cruiser shifted its position within the enemy fleet. It pulled nearer another star cruiser. As they advanced on the Fifth Fleet, an unhurt star cruiser interposed itself between the *Antietam's* lasers and the hurt star cruiser.

It was incredible piloting. Worse, it meant the battleship failed to annihilate the stricken enemy vessel.

Dully, Fletcher realized the New Men did the same thing up and down their semi-loose formation. The enemy was killing Star Watch vessels and only taking wounds in return.

The two fleets had almost merged. In minutes, they would be at their closest point. Then the two fleets would pass and move away from each other, the New Men heading in-system and what remained of the Fifth Fleet going outward.

A holoimage appeared before Fletcher.

It was Commander Musgrave of the Heavy Cruiser *Canada.*

"I'm dead anyway, Admiral," Musgrave snarled. The man's eyes blazed with heat. "Before that happens, I'm going to blow a hole they can't repair."

"What are you talking about?" Fletcher asked.

"Get ready, sir, and remember my crew."

"Musgrave, make sense," Fletcher said. The man had always been a hothead.

As the two fleets merged, Heavy Cruiser *Canada* took the brunt of four New Men beams on its upgraded deflector shield.

"Sir," *Antietam's* weapons officer said. "Heavy Cruiser *Canada* is going critical."

"You mean its new antimatter core?" Fletcher asked. It was the latest in starship engine construction. Only a few heavy cruisers had it.

Before the weapons officer could answer, a titanic explosion took place out there.

Heavy Cruiser *Canada* ignited. Musgrave's engineers managed to funnel the obliterating antimatter blast at the nearest star cruisers. The raving energy knocked down one New Men shield after another.

Finally, it dawned on Fletcher what Musgrave had meant. "Everyone," the admiral shouted on wide-beam, "concentrate your beams on the stricken star cruisers."

Other SWS battlewagons turned their lasers on the enemy star cruisers, those lacking any kind of shielding. The *Canada's* antimatter blast gave them a rare opportunity. The Earth ships took it.

Lasers dug into enemy hull armor, digging ever so slowly toward the innards. The New Men tried their trick of darting behind a fresh star cruiser. This time, the enemy didn't move fast enough.

A star cruiser exploded in violent fury. The energy struck other New Men shields and vessels.

"Hit and kill!" Fletcher roared. He finally witnessed a star cruiser die to his dwindling fleet. Thank God for Musgrave's brave sacrifice.

Maybe this came too late in the fight for them to win, but it wasn't the last dead enemy vessel. More star cruisers perished as every Star Watch warship beamed its lasers at nearly point blank range. Missile boats added their cargoes. Escort ships poured weaker laser fire at the passing enemy ships. SWS destroyers used every watt of power to inflict damage upon the New Men.

The Fifth Fleet made almost all its kills in these brief moments. Then, the two fleets passed each other. The antimatter-stricken ships were gone. Now, the New Men began to use their old trick to protect damaged star cruisers.

At that point, the New Men began braking, slowing their velocity. No doubt, they meant to annihilate the now fleeing Fifth Fleet.

The two sides continued to fire beams and launch missiles at each other. Time passed. More Star Watch vessels exploded or drifted away as burnt-out hulks. The Fifth Fleet struck back, killing another star cruiser and wounding others in the process. Finally, though, both formations pulled away out of firing range.

The first round of the Battle of Caria 323 was over.

-4-

"Damage report," Fletcher said, staring at the viewing screen.

The bridge crew worked fast, giving him the numbers within minutes.

A paltry seven enemy star cruisers were drifting hulks or floating masses of loose debris. Fourteen of the New Men's vessels appeared to have sustained damage. That left twenty-seven of their hateful ships intact or forty-one altogether.

For the Fifth Fleet, it was much worse. All nine of Blake's monitors were gone, and all the troop transports had vanished. Out of seventeen battleships, Fletcher had ten left. Out of thirty-five heavy cruisers, he had seventeen remaining. Nine motherships remained intact, but he only had enough strikefighters and bombers to arm four of them. Most of the destroyers were gone, although the majority of the depleted missile boats remained. That meant out of a beginning seventy-four capital ships, he had thirty-six left.

He'd lost half his fleet for seven enemy ships destroyed. Would the New Men lose any of the fourteen damaged star cruisers before this was over? If not, how long would the stricken vessels be out of commission? A month, six months, a year?

"Admiral," the comm officer said in a strained voice. "I'm picking up a transmission from an enemy star cruiser. Sir, it's their fleet commander. He's calling himself Oran Rva. He's wishes to speak with you, sir."

24

"He's calling for me by name?" Fletcher asked.

"Yes, sir," the comm officer said, his eyes large and staring.

Fletcher knew that the New Men seldom said anything to Star Watch personnel. If they did, "Surrender or die," were the usual words. Regardless, Fletcher decided it would be good to speak to the enemy. If nothing else, the psychologists could study the video later to help get a better picture of the New Men's character. They knew so little about the enemy.

"Yes," Fletcher said. "Put him...put him on the main screen."

The admiral didn't know if that was wise or not. If he put the New Man on the holoimage, everyone on the bridge would be trying to overhear and likely get the message wrong. They might create rumors worse than the actual message. He decided to let them see the enemy and what they were up against.

The main screen wavered as the stars disappeared. In their place, a golden-skinned New Man appeared, standing on what must have been his bridge. Oran Rva wore a silver suit with a single purple emblem on his right pectoral. He had a weapon belt around his slender waist with a holstered blaster.

The man had long, inflexible features. He was tall with a dark pelt of hair. The eyes were like swirling black ink, the skin like golden ivory. He seemed the very image of arrogance.

"Surrender, Admiral Fletcher," the New Man said. He spoke with a deep and confident voice.

"You're Oran Rva?" Fletcher asked.

"I am your conqueror. Therefore, it is unseemly that you question me. Do you not know that the inferior either waits in silence or answers direct queries? Any other actions bring swift punishment or death. I speak to you today to offer life. It would be foolish of you to squander this unique opportunity through bad manners."

"You're the fool," Fletcher said with heat. "You won the first round only. We'll see about the second."

"No. There will be no second round. There will only be butchery if you persist to speak ignorantly."

"Why did you call me?" Fletcher snapped.

Oran Rva's eyes swirled with power.

"I sully myself speaking to one of the untamed," the New Man said, "but there is a reason. I desire your remaining ships intact. Therefore, I have broken protocol and will give you a choice. Surrender your vessels, and you, along with your crews, shall live out your days in peace."

"As your slaves?" Fletcher sneered.

"Do not worry on that account," Oran Rva said. "You are too set in your unrefined status for us to trouble with retraining. Experience shows that would prove too tiresome. Therefore, we will let you roam on the smallest continent on Caria Prime."

"Roam like wild horses?" Fletcher asked.

"You are stretching my graciousness, Admiral, asking these unseemly questions. Grasp at life instead of death. Recognize the futility of fighting your superiors."

Fletcher stared at the New Men. Did Oran Rva think these were convincing arguments? The New Men were supposed to be unbelievably smart. Yet the golden-skinned man talking to him seemed to believe he was acting mercifully.

"It is you who called me," Fletcher said. "Not the other way around. Or have you forgotten that you want my ships intact?"

The ivory-like skin seemed to tighten on Oran Rva's face. The New Man studied Fletcher's features as if he could burn them into his memory.

"You would live as hunter-gatherers," Oran Rva said, "free to indulge your lust-driven appetites for as long as you found game or grazed upon the plant life."

"You have an amazingly high opinion of yourselves," Fletcher said.

"That is incorrect and insulting," Oran Rva said. "We deal in realities, seeing the universe as it is, not engaging in the half-dazed fantasies that you of the lower orders are accustomed to. Perhaps this will goad you to a correct solution. Continue in your vain resistance, and I shall annihilate the population of Caria Prime."

The threat stole Fletcher's breath. The New Man spoke about killing five hundred million humans as one would swat a fly. Slowly, the admiral shook his head. Humanity could never surrender to the New Men. Star Watch must fight to the end, if that's what it came to.

"Your stubbornness has sealed your fate, Admiral Fletcher, and sealed the fate of your doomed fleet and the lives of those on Caria Prime. If by chance you survive the battle, I will hand you over to the teacher. Then you will wish you died in the destruction of your antiquated vessels."

Oran Rva waved a long-fingered hand, ending the connection.

Fletcher blinked several times, and he felt heat flush his face. He wasn't used to anyone talking to him like that. It was unnerving, galling and angering. He wished there was some way to destroy the star cruisers.

Fletcher scowled. He hated this helplessness. With a slow step, he returned to his command chair and sat down.

"Sir," the comm officer said.

Fletcher raised his head. "What is it now?"

"Commodore Garcia wishes to speak with you, sir."

"Oh," the admiral said. "Yes. Put her on holoimage."

Garcia had the thousand-meter stare. She seemed badly shaken. Had she seen that?

"You wish to speak with me?" Fletcher asked.

"We must run," she said.

Run? Where did she want to run to?

"The New Men are braking," Garcia said. "They mean to come after us and finish the fight."

"We can get to the gas giant before they reach us," Fletcher said.

"Do you mean to use Laumer-Point Beta to slip into the Lamia System?" she asked.

"What?" Fletcher asked. "No. I mean to circle the gas giant and finish them if I can. Commander Musgrave showed us what we have to do. Using the Jovian planet, we'll slip near them and explode some of our vessels that use the new antimatter engines. Then we beam those of the star cruisers we can before we all die."

After listening to Oran Rva, Fletcher realized he would use any expedient he could, short of surrendering his ships, to save the people of Caria Prime.

Garcia was shaking her head. "We dealt them a heavier blow than I ever thought possible, sir."

"Seven measly ships?" Fletcher asked in disbelief.

"Twenty-one of their star cruisers sustained damage or died."

"At a cost of over half our fleet," Fletcher said. "I meant to annihilate them."

"They'll annihilate us if we try to face them again," Garcia said. "The numbers have improved drastically in their favor."

"I'm well aware of that. I'm also certain they have a few star cruisers waiting for us in the Lamia System. If we were foolish enough to try to jump, they would obliterate our Jump Lagged fleet at no more cost to themselves."

"Then we're doomed," Garcia said, flatly. "The Commonwealth will be open to even greater assaults than before."

As Fletcher thought about Caria Prime and the rest of the Commonwealth, he felt uselessness bubble up in his chest. He loathed the feeling. He couldn't believe this. Blake had been right after all. He'd been so sure he could defeat the enemy. Now, hatred for the New Men consumed his thoughts.

"Sir," Garcia said.

"We bloodied them. Because of Musgrave, we must have hurt the New Men more than they believed we could. I think we'll have slowed their invasion some."

"By a few months only," Garcia said.

"That's something at least."

Garcia became earnest. "Admiral, we have to save our fleet. We dealt the New Men more damage than anyone thought possible. Your trick with the decoys helped. The new wave harmonics also made a difference, and we can't forget Musgrave's sacrifice."

"Running to Laumer-Point Beta isn't going to change anything," Fletcher said. "We will use the gas giant as a pivoting post. Yes, the enemy is going to decimate us now, but we can still take a few more with us."

"Sir, there's another answer. I implore you to—"

"What other answer?" Fletcher asked.

Garcia licked her lips. "Sir, we could run for the Tannish System. It's close enough."

It took Fletcher a second to understand her meaning. "In case you haven't noticed," he said, "there's no direct tramline from Caria to Tannish."

"Exactly," Garcia said. "We would cross the void at sub-light speeds."

"And get to the Tannish System in six months or more," Fletcher said. "How would that help us? The New Men would be waiting at Tannish, using the tramlines to get there a few weeks from now. What's worse, in six months their damaged ships might be fully repaired."

"I realize all that," Garcia said. "But it will give our side six months to do something creative."

"Bah," Fletcher said, waving his hand. "Do you yearn for life as a beaten foe that much?"

"No," she said. "But the maneuver gives us something greater than what we can get any other way. If we run for Tannish, we're giving Star Watch six months longer to figure out something to do."

"I don't follow your reasoning," he said.

"If we flee into the void, heading to Tannish at sub-light velocity, the Lord High Admiral might be able to convince the leaders of the Wahhabi Caliphate to ally with us against the New Men. Or maybe Star Watch can figure out how to make the alien super-ship work for us."

"Captain Maddox's vessel?" Fletcher asked.

"Yes, Admiral," Garcia said.

Fletcher shook his head. "Don't put any faith in that ancient starship."

"We'd better find some other way to face the New Men, sir. At least the ancient vessel gives us a ray of hope. We can trust the Wahhabi princes to come to their senses and join us. Six months is a long time, Admiral."

Fletcher looked away. If they ran, would Oran Rva nuke Caria Prime? Maybe the New Men wouldn't have time to do it right away.

"We have to maintain hope," Garcia said. "Otherwise, we might as well surrender to the New Men now and get it over with."

Fletcher sat up, scowling at her. "I will never surrender to them."

"Then race into the void and buy us more time, sir."

"The New Men might follow us into the void and finish us there."

"Good!" Garcia said. "Let them follow us. That means their fleet is out of the tramlines for four months or more. That could be critical. But I doubt they'll follow us. They'll likely head to Tannish through the tramlines to wait for us."

Fletcher drummed his thick fingers on the armrest of his chair.

Garcia's features grew intent. "Admiral, you have hurt the enemy. No one has destroyed as many New Men vessels as you just did today. It cost us, but we hit back and made it count to the tune of seven destroyed star cruisers. Use that against them. Buy our side more time. We have to try to gain some sort of advantage. Otherwise, they've won. I know you don't want that, sir."

Maybe that's why Oran Rva had called, even though it was against New Men protocols. Fifth Fleet had destroyed seven star cruisers.

Fletcher rose wearily. He didn't relish running away. Yet, the commodore had an interesting point. No one had hurt the New Men as hard as he had here today. He had destroyed enemy vessels. That was a new feat. Could the leaders of Star Watch budge the stubborn caliphate to take up arms against the New Men? Surely, the sheiks would see the danger in doing nothing.

"If we're going to try this, sir," Garcia said, "we're going to have to run at full acceleration right away. We have to build up velocity as soon as possible. Otherwise, the New Men might catch us before we can get deep enough into the void."

Fletcher stared at her. Oran Rva had outmaneuvered and outfought him. If he ran...it would mean the hated enemy couldn't declare victory right away. And, he would keep Fifth Fleet alive a little longer. If he lost the fleet now to no good effect, the war was lost. This gave humanity a slim chance in the future, where now there was none.

"Yes," the admiral said. "We have to try. We can't give up until we're dead. Commodore, see to your people. I have some calls to make. Then, we're going to try something different and see if we can make these New Men lose a little sleep at least."

An hour later, the surviving warships of Fifth Fleet increased velocity, turning toward the Tannish System less than a light-year away. The race for survival had begun.

EARTH

-1-

On Earth, events moved normally. It was true people knew about the golden-skinned invaders of "C" Quadrant. That ruckus had been going on for months already. Military law had gone into effect throughout the Commonwealth, but that hadn't really changed things all that much here on the homeworld.

The common consensus was that it couldn't be as bad as the newscasters claimed it to be. The Wahhabi Caliphate would come to its senses any day now, throwing their vessels into the conflict. The Windsor League readied its fleets, and the Spacers would have to do something. The people who said the Spacers would simply go elsewhere didn't have a clue. Spacers might live in giant spaceships and move around like nomads, but they made their living off trade.

So sure, the New Men were bad, but the Star Watch would take care of it, right?

There had been shows about Admiral Fletcher taking heavy reinforcements to "C" Quadrant. He was a fighting admiral, a bloodthirsty SOB who would take care of business.

Besides, the fighting was taking place out on the rim, far from most of the settled worlds. It would take the New Men endless jumps to reach Earth. The enemy didn't have enough warships for that. If nothing else, attrition would wear the New Men down.

Maybe a few commenters were over-worried about the situation. But come on, it took *weeks* for mail ships to bring news from "C" Quadrant. That was the fastest messages could travel, and so far, no one had heard anything upsetting about Admiral Fletcher.

Therefore, despite martial law on Earth and throughout the rest of the Commonwealth, life pretty much went on as it always did. People worried about the pebble in their shoe, not about a war hundreds of light-years away.

Well, most of the people didn't care. Those of Star Watch Intelligence worked harder than ever so others could sleep the peace of the innocent.

-2-

In the darkness, the enemy agent gasped as he died, with blood leaking from his suit. He lay between two huge storage containers in New York City Spaceport. With a supreme effort, the dying man reached for his coat pocket.

Reluctantly, Captain Maddox of Star Watch Intelligence aimed his long-barreled gun. He wore night-vision glasses, which looked remarkably like sunglasses. With a soft sound, he fired his suppressed gun for the second time tonight.

The enemy agent jerked, shivered a final time and died, with his face thumping against pavement.

Seconds passed, a half-minute. Finally, Maddox rose from his location behind stacked steel crates.

Sergeant Riker did likewise, with his gun trained on the dead agent.

The sergeant was an older man with leathery skin. He had a bionic eye and a fully bionic arm. The man had lost the eye and arm in a blast many years ago on a desperate mission on Altair III. In fact, the sergeant had received *many* wounds in his years in Star Watch. He was an old dog, handy with a gun, possessing a cunning tactical eye and fierce loyalty to the service. In a word, the man was a soldier.

With Riker at his back, the captain approached the corpse. Maddox was tall and lean. He moved with the lethality of a large jungle cat. He wore his uniform, tucking the night-vision glasses in a side pocket. Around them, spaceport lights began to come on.

Maddox wished he could have captured the man alive. The enemy agent had refused to surrender, though, drawing a gun against them. Whatever else one could say about the enemy, his people were brave.

"Be careful," Riker whispered. "You never know, sir."

Maddox hardly heard the words. The enemy agent was dead, but this was still a break, perhaps an important one. Despite Brigadier O'Hara's worry, the tip had proven correct, and that was rare in this deadly game of espionage against a superior foe.

Even as the New Men invaded "C" Quadrant, the enemy's secret service continued to infiltrate Earth's government and the military, finding traitors among humanity. In reality, the enemy had been here a long time, decades, in fact. This time, however, Star Watch Intelligence had gotten the jump on one of them.

Maddox stared at the corpse, wondering if the New Men had tampered with the agent when alive and if so in what manner. Expectantly, he crouched beside the corpse.

Interestingly, the New Men had begun their invasion a few weeks after Maddox had brought back the ancient, alien super-ship. In their secret service attempts to stop the ship, the New Men had revealed some of their hidden hand. Now, in the Oort cloud, while surrounded by a Star Watch taskforce, scientists studied the alien vessel. Humanity needed the ancient technologies to help defend themselves against the onslaught of the New Men.

The captain continued to watch the corpse. What had the agent had been trying to reach before dying? It was time to find out.

"Let me do that, sir," Riker said from behind. "I'm expendable, you're not."

"Keep back," Maddox said. "Let me concentrate."

The captain's long fingers brushed the pocket's cloth as he felt within. There was something cool and thin here. With his heart hammering, Maddox pulled out a communicator. He twisted it around, looking at the glowing screen. It had a single phrase: *Begin Operation Odysseus.*

Had the agent sent the message, or had he been trying to erase it? What did the message mean?

I should search the files.

Before Maddox could begin, the words began to flash and the communicator to vibrate.

A premonition caused Maddox to hurl the device from him. It exploded in midair, the blast knocking him down.

"Captain," Riker said, crouching over him. "Are you hurt, sir?"

Maddox blinked at the sergeant. He was more surprised than hurt. "I'm fine," he whispered, his throat dry. Then his forehead furrowed.

Begin Operation Odysseus. What are the New Men trying to do now?

-3-

Two days after Maddox shot the enemy agent, Meta sat in her apartment in New York City. She fingered the locket the captain had bought her several months ago.

Meta sat before a mirror, wearing a tight party dress of shimmering Neptunian sequins. They glittered from hot pink to cherry red as she moved, and they clung to her voluptuous figure, revealing far too much cleavage and thigh.

Meta hadn't worn something like this since assassinating Baron Chabot, the owner of the Rouen Colony. She'd been born on the two G mining world, modified for strength like all the other indentured workers there. In her childhood, the leader of the Resistance had decided to use Meta's already obvious beauty. Her secret training had begun then, and it had been thorough and difficult.

As Meta stroked the locket pressed against her throat, conflicting emotions raced through her. Throughout her short life, she'd used her beauty to enter places others couldn't. When she closed her eyes at night, she could still see the baron's tongue protruding out of his slack mouth. In his bedroom, she'd choked the man to death, digging her strong fingers into his flesh.

Even though the baron had deserved to die, assassinating him had turned her already hard heart into unrelenting stone.

Meta swallowed uneasily. Releasing the locket, she picked up a brush and drew her platinum blonde hair to one side so it draped over her left shoulder and down over a breast.

Several months ago, she and Captain Maddox had had a terrible fight. Well, she had done all the shouting. He had grown quiet and watchful, with his lips pressed together. It had been the only sign of his emotions. The captain liked to believe he was cool and collected. Meta knew better. A fire raged in his heart, but he didn't let anyone else know.

Meta sighed wistfully.

After endless months of tension and battle in the Beyond—bringing the alien super-ship to the Commonwealth—they had finally reached Earth, spending several glorious weeks together in New York City. Meta had tried to become someone she wasn't, acting carefree, enjoying the company of the handsome captain.

Meta set down the brush. She had a secret that only a few people knew. She was damaged goods, a killer who had used good people, and sex, to achieve her deadly ends. Yet what had she accomplished? The Rouen Colony still belonged to the consortium. Her family back home slaved in the mines while she frolicked on Earth.

Biting her lower lip, Meta considered a truth about her. Men loved to stare at her body. She knew that and had often used it to her advantage.

Meta stared into her eyes in the mirror. She had to leave the Commonwealth and return to the Rouen Colony. She had to finish what she'd started as an eighteen-year-old assassin.

Standing, Meta ran her palms over her hips, brushing the Neptunian sequins. They were soft to the touch. Maddox had bought her the dress when they returned to Earth, but he'd never seen her in it except for the one glimpse in the store. They had fought afterward, and that had been the end of their relationship.

The trouble was that Captain Maddox had called this afternoon. After all this time he was coming over, no doubt to try to patch things up between them. What had changed his mind?

Could she go back to those carefree nights they'd enjoyed together? To help her decide, she'd put on the dress. She still felt an attraction to the captain. Yet in her heart, she knew one of them would eventually hurt the other. She didn't want to be that person.

I have to leave. I should have left months ago already. I don't know why I lingered.

She could board a space liner tonight, working her way to the distant Rouen Colony. It was far from "C" Quadrant and the mysterious New Men. Part of her wanted to stay and explain all this to Maddox. The other half wanted to be long gone before he arrived.

Meta shook her head. *I don't deserve love. If Maddox really understood what I did in order to reach the baron, he would turn away from me in disgust.*

It hurt to realize the truth. She would leave the dress for him. It had cost him too many credits that he could ill afford. She'd wanted to see what she looked like in it one more time, but she couldn't go through with this. That's why they'd had the fight in the first place.

Sitting down, Meta reached for a pad and stylus. She'd leave a note for him with the dress. If she didn't go now, the captain might convince her to stay. That might turn into another week, a month, and then who knew what. No. She needed to run while she had the resolve to go.

Picking up the stylus, Meta wrote quickly, almost completing the note before a soft noise alerted her. She paused and raised her head, listening.

"Maddox?" she called, with a thrill of fear coursing through her. She couldn't let him see her like this. It would be like the captain to try to surprise her.

There was nothing, though, just silence. Then a new sensation settled onto Meta. It felt as if someone held his breath, waiting for her to relax.

Meta frowned. In these situations, she trusted her instincts. Setting down the pad and stylus, she stood up slowly. Someone was in the apartment, which seemed incredible. Security was tight here, and behind them were Star Watch surveillance teams. Would Maddox continue to sneak around once she'd called his name?

It was possible. He had an arrogant side that both attracted and repelled her.

In the mirror, Meta glanced at the glittering gown, how it hiked far too high on her thighs, clinging with promise. She had to change. Otherwise, the captain would get ideas. He was already too aggressive. That was part of the problem.

Purposefully, she moved to the bedroom door to shut and lock it. She had to get out of the dress. Damn Maddox, why had he shown up? Why couldn't he have left things alone?

Her hand closed around the knob. Before she could push the door closed, a man stepped into view. Meta had an instant of shock. The man wore a black leather jacket, had short, bristly hair and a silver stud in his tongue. He certainly wasn't Maddox.

With the creak of his leather coat, the thug shoved the door open. With a *thump*, the edge struck Meta against the face. Her nose exploded with agony, and her head snapped back. She stumbled backward as tears welled in her eyes. The back of her right foot tripped over a high-heeled shoe. She fell, sprawling onto the carpet, the back of her head hitting the side of the bed.

The Neptunian sequins slipped up over her hips, revealing her nakedness beneath it.

The man looked down at her, and his eyebrows rose. A second later, he grinned with appreciation. Then he chuckled in a growly way, a man who obviously smoked too many stimsticks.

Like a volcano ready to explode, anger boiled in Meta.

"You're tempting me to take a dip, sister," he said.

A sharp retort weighed down Meta's tongue: she was ready to tell him the extreme extent of his mistake. However, her ears picked up other sounds in the apartment. There were more home invaders, backup for Mr. Black Leather Jacket. That stilled her tongue as her mind shifted into overdrive.

Why would thugs break into her apartment? This was a super-deluxe suite in one of the most expensive high rises in New York City. It was supposed to have fantastic security, as many rich people lived here. Were the invaders rapists? No. The leering pig had just said he was tempted. That meant it hadn't been his original intention.

Even though her nose throbbed, Meta managed to smile in a frightened way as she covered her nakedness. It was time to lure the man to his doom.

"Please don't hurt me," she said, trying to sound scared.

Chuckling, the man let a shock rod slide out of his sleeve into his waiting hand. "Nice try, sister, but I happen to know you're a tough bitch. Maybe I'll do you later, once they're through questioning you. Would you like that?"

The words galvanized Meta. As he approached, she scrambled to her feet. The hard eyes told her he liked to give pain. Meta had no more time for reflection. As he swung the shock rod, she stepped toward him.

The man was fast, but Meta proved faster. Her muscles were dense from life on a two G planet, and her infighting technique was perfect from years of martial arts training. The sharp twist of her hips added power to the punch as her fist slammed against his jaw. The lower bone slid away from the blow, one end popping out of the jaw-joint. The man's eyelids fluttered. Unfortunately for Meta, the shock rod caressed her forearm.

Several actions occurred at once then. Despite his toughness, the man collapsed onto the floor, unconscious. Meta bit back a groan of agony. The energy jolt flared with intensity, reaching her shoulder. Her arm swung down, numbed and useless. Lastly, the shock rod slipped from the man's nerveless fingers, rolling onto the carpet, making sizzling sounds as it zapped once more.

"Jacques?" a man called from the hall.

Gritting her teeth because she didn't have time to let pain slow her down, Meta crouched, scooping up the shock rod with her left hand. The right wouldn't work for a few minutes, at least.

Heavy boots thudded on the hallway flooring. Another black-clad man appeared in the doorway.

Meta lunged, striking with the tip of the rod as if she was a fencer. The end sizzled against his face. He cried out, jerking away, stumbling from the door. Meta followed, swatting the side of his head, knowing such a blow could induce brain damage. The jolt rocked him. In his effort to escape, the man

41

flew against a wall, catapulting off it. A third time, Meta stroked him with the rod. The device must have overheated, discharging a thin ribbon of smoke. The man thudded onto the floor, as unconscious as the first invader in her bedroom.

At least one more man was in the house. Meta heard him. She knew that in these instances taking the fight to the enemy often made the best sense. That's exactly what she did now.

Fast and barefoot, in her shimmering sequined gown, with Captain Maddox's locket against her throat, Meta burst into the living room.

Two men waited. One held a stubby, shotgun-like weapon in his hands. She recognized it as a tangler. Neither of the men wore black jackets. The gunman was medium-sized with pale hair and paler features. The other was big.

A retired wrestler, Meta thought.

The man had gray hair, and it seemed as if a bleak sculptor had chiseled his body out of flat slabs of muscle. What's more, his gray clothes were so conservative they might have been a uniform. The only flashy thing about him was a big black ring that glittered with a circle of diamonds.

The tangler discharged. A small black capsule popped out of the weapon and struck Meta. It exploded, shooting clinging strands around her thighs, arms and torso. Immediately, the sticky strands contracted. Meta was strong, and she fought back, struggling, but she tripped for the second time tonight.

Remorselessly, the tangle web tightened until she could barely breathe on the floor.

The gunman glanced at the big man. "Should I check on the others, Mr. Kane?"

With the seeming force of a glacier, the big man turned his head to stare at the speaker. The gunman nodded in acknowledgment of the silent order, hurrying into the hallway.

Mr. Kane advanced on Meta, causing the floorboards to creak. How much did he weigh? He tugged at his trousers, pulling up the fabric. It almost seemed impossible that such a blocky man could bend. Yet he did, crouching before her.

Arching her neck, Meta looked up at him. If the first invader had hard eyes, Mr. Kane's were like chips of granite.

He had wide features with a stone-chiseled quality. The lips managed to frown thoughtfully.

Meta said nothing, just studied him, trying to figure out why they had done this to her. His eyes were cold. He was a killer, a dangerous man.

Kane stood, treading his way into the hallway, maybe to hurry the others.

With him gone, Meta began to test her bonds. That proved to be a bad idea. The more she struggled, the tighter the tangle strands constricted. The trick was to relax.

She tried that, willing herself to go slack. Captain Maddox was coming. Should she play for time? No. If she couldn't handle them, Maddox wouldn't be able to either. What had happened to Dempsey Tower security or the Star Watch teams providing backup?

Shortly, the two men in black leather jackets stumbled into the room. They looked dazed and confused. The tangler-man followed, with his weapon broken open in half. He slid another capsule into the firing chamber. Lastly, Kane appeared.

The big man in the gray suit approached Meta from behind, crouching again. With his thick fingers, he tugged the dress down over her naked butt, covering it.

"The note," he said from her back. "Maddox is coming over. We thought he was finished with you."

Kane didn't phrase his statement as a question, yet she had the feeling he wanted confirmation. She would not comply.

"The boss would love to question Captain Maddox," the tangler-man said, snapping his weapon back into one piece.

Kane said nothing.

"Ambushing Maddox here would be easy," the tangler-man added.

"You are wrong," Kane rumbled. "No." He patted Meta's bottom. "I prefer your goodbye letter. I will leave that for the captain to find. You would like that, yes?"

Meta twisted around to stare at Kane crouched behind her. He held a tiny can in his hand.

Kane depressed a nozzle, the diamonds in his ring glittering. A fine aerosol mist sprayed from the can. Meta tried to hold her breath, but it didn't help. Seconds after he sprayed, she slumped into unconsciousness. Thus, she never felt Kane gather her in his arms, carrying her to a cleaning lady's dolly, depositing her into a large laundry bag. Seconds later, the men rolled the dolly into the hallway, taking Meta with them.

-4-

Captain Maddox strode down a New York City sidewalk. He wore his uniform tonight, as he had a meeting later this evening with Brigadier O'Hara. The Iron Lady said it was important.

The captain carried a dozen roses in his right hand, with a heart-shaped box of chocolates tucked under his left.

Sergeant Riker had suggested the items. The man waited in an air-car on a nearby skyscraper landing-pad.

Maddox looked up at the blaze of lights. Tall buildings surrounded him. Ground vehicles swept past on the street. Hundreds of people shared the sidewalk with him, noisy crowds in search of entertainment. He understood that many sought the nightlife because no one knew how much longer mankind could play these mindless games.

He had begun to wonder that himself. Maybe that's why he'd called Meta. He wasn't sure. Maybe it was watching the enemy agent die, leaking blood onto the spaceport's paving. That made him wonder how much longer until he did the bleeding. Was that too morbid? In truth, he had enjoyed his short vacation with Meta in the Big Apple after the debriefing from *Victory*.

Meta was an unusual woman. It was a pity they had gotten into that argument. Perhaps it had been inevitable. Meta was strong-willed, and she insisted on carrying her sorrows deep inside her.

Maddox frowned. He had his own…loneliness. Yes, that was the right word. The nature of his birth had set him apart from others. He was a hybrid, a half-breed. Alcohol failed to make him drunk. He had a slightly higher core temperature than regular humans. His reflexes were phenomenal, and he was stronger than he looked. The fear of his life was that he was part New Man. What else could he be? He dreaded the idea that he had any connection with the supermen invading the Commonwealth of Planets, the entire *Oikumene* or Human Space.

Maddox's fingers tightened around the rose stems, making the clear plastic crinkle.

Whatever had happened to his mother, she escaped from the Beyond, birthing him on a Windsor League planet. From there, she had taken him to Earth and died afterward. Using his analytical talents and a flair for detective work, he had discovered these truths several years ago.

Maddox wanted to know the truth about his birth, but he was also afraid of it. It frankly surprised him that Star Watch still trusted him. That trust had a lot to do with Brigadier Mary O'Hara.

Inhaling the brisk New York air, Maddox headed for Meta's building.

Several months ago, she had unleashed on him. Her fury had shocked him. He had endured, though. It was a storm, but given enough time, it would pass. Yet, he had found himself that night on his bed brooding about her accusations. Maybe he should have called the next day. He'd decided to let her stew…for several months now.

On a whim, he had called this afternoon. Her guarded voice decided it for him. He *would* win her back. Meta was different from other women. There was strength in her, a steely core. Maybe that's what he needed in a woman. Otherwise, he would just bulldoze over her.

He passed the building's security check and entered the interior plaza. Dempsey Tower was a skyscraper like all the others around it.

In the lobby, a gorgeous woman with red curls smiled at him. Her escort was impassive, but Maddox had the impression the man didn't care for her smiling at another man. Something about the escort struck a chord in Maddox, and he studied the fellow out of the corner of his eye.

The gray-haired man was big and obviously strong, and he wore a severely conservative gray suit. He had a big black ring with a circle of diamonds. It looked like a professional sport champion's trophy ring.

Bodyguards flanked the pair. What's more, the gunmen noticed him but tried not to show it. That seemed odd. Usually, bodyguards gave perceived intruders a stare-down.

Maddox decided to ignore them. He was here to see Meta, to win her back. Besides, the big man was likely worth millions, maybe the owner of a professional sports franchise, maybe someone famous even. The ring indicated that. Such men didn't like to notice that their girlfriends looked at others their own age.

Maddox rode a spacious lift to Meta's floor. Star Watch had paid the tab for this apartment. Brigadier O'Hara had insisted Meta stay at the best apartment complex in the city. It had been the least humanity could do for one of its saviors.

Maddox grinned in appreciation. He knew how the Iron Lady worked. O'Hara wanted Meta in Star Watch Intelligence. The service was always in need of exceptional talent. The Iron Lady had given Meta a reward for her services with the alien super-ship, but she likely still hoped to persuade her to join Star Watch.

The lift stopped on the tenth floor. The elevator opened, and Maddox strode down the corridor. He felt like whistling. This was the right decision.

Finally, he came to Meta's door. Using his left hand, he rang the bell and waited for a long moment. Nothing happened, so he rang it again. More time passed, and the door remained closed.

Had she gone out? Even knowing he was coming over?

Pursing his lips, Maddox wondered what he should do. He had to meet the brigadier later. Maybe he should text Meta before he ran out of time.

A sly grin worked onto his face. *No. I'll surprise her.*

He set the chocolates and roses on the carpet beside the door. Taking out his wallet, he extracted a plastic card key. Meta had lent him a duplicate, and he'd forgotten to give it back. Maybe this was fortuitous.

He used the card in the lock-slot, watched the light blink and turned the handle. Using the toe of his shoe to keep the door open, he put the card back into his wallet, slid that into the back of his trousers, picked up the roses and tucked the chocolates under his left arm.

Smiling just in case Meta stood inside with her arms crossed—catching him in the act—he stepped inside the apartment.

Lights blazed everywhere, which was unusual if Meta had gone out. She always turned every light but one off. It must have been a habit ingrained during her childhood in the Rouen Colony. There, each watt of energy had taken grueling labor to pay off.

Maddox refrained from calling out. If he heard her, he'd retreat outside and ring the bell some more. He soaked up the room's ambiance to get a feel for the situation.

His smile drained away. There was something wrong here. Softly, he set the flowers and heart-shaped box on the floor. He still wasn't sure Meta had left the apartment, but in case she hadn't, he didn't want her to hear him yet.

Maddox straightened, concentrating, trying to figure out why he didn't like the apartment's feel.

There was a faint smell in the air, body odor perhaps. It most certainly didn't belong to Meta.

Maddox's head swiveled from right to left, taking in the living room. A cushion lay near the forward edge of the sofa, not pushed against the back with the others. Meta had proven meticulous about the cushions, complaining to him about it on one of their first nights. Afterward, when she wasn't looking, he had made a game of always setting a cushion out of place. Meta had noticed it every time and put the cushion back against the sofa.

As Maddox considered that, all humor left his face. He went into caution mode, undoing several buttons on his jacket.

He reached under it, unhooked the holster strap and withdrew his long-barreled gun.

Like a leopard stalking its prey, Maddox advanced across the hardwood floor, searching for clues.

He moved into the hallway and halted. There was another odor. His eyes narrowed as he tested the air. Someone had used a shock rod a short time ago.

There was a slight stain on the wall. Maddox rubbed a finger against it, noticing its moistness.

His throat constricted. He moved to the bedroom door. It stood ajar, and the lights were on. The room felt empty, though.

Swiftly, Maddox stepped into the bedroom, aiming the gun in several directions. The lights around the mirror shined brightly. Sniffing, Maddox smelled perfumes, several different odors. Meta must have been testing them earlier?

That meant Meta had been here only a short time ago. Scanning the room—

Maddox's heart thudded. He spied a pad propped on the bed's pillow. Cautiously, he approached it and read the message about her need to leave Earth. She'd ended abruptly in mid-sentence, which seemed strange. There weren't any explanations or anything about their time together. That struck Maddox as wrong.

He whirled around, moving to the mirror. He scanned the scant belongings there. He didn't see any perfume bottles. Going into the bathroom, he checked the cabinet and found nothing, not even a tube of toothpaste.

If Meta had left like this, would she have taken the perfume he'd specially bought her those many months ago? Suspicion flooded his eyes. Holstering the gun, Maddox hurried to the door. He needed to speak with the building's security chief.

***

A few minutes later, Maddox stood with the Dempsey Tower's security chief, a short, precise woman in a red blazer. Her brown hair was pulled back so tightly it seemed it might hurt her skull. On a large screen, they watched a video of the last half hour before Meta's door.

It showed an older couple passing the hidden camera, but nothing else except for Maddox entering the room.

"You had a key," the woman said.

"Never mind about that," Maddox said. "Run through the last hour."

The security chief tapped a panel. She had blunt, bare fingers, lacking any adornments. On the screen, time sped up. A Dempsey security agent walked past the door. He wore a red blazer. Then the older couple passed again and finally Maddox entered the apartment. By the timer, twelve and half minutes separated the Dempsey agent and the older couple.

Maddox considered what he saw. If Meta had left the apartment, and the odors in the room had persisted long enough for him to smell them, why hadn't he seen her leave? Surely, Meta wouldn't have crawled out the window to a waiting air-car.

"Make it two hours," Maddox said.

The security chief didn't even glance at him, but tapped the control.

During the recorded time, no one else passed or used the door.

That confirmed it for Maddox. "Someone tampered with the video," he said.

The security chief spoke in a quiet, controlled manner. "That would be impossible," she said.

Maddox eyed the woman. She stared back impassively. The nametag said *Beth Paris*. Maddox knew nothing about her, nor did he have a gut feeling yet.

"Is someone monitoring the Tower cameras?" he asked.

"Of course," she said. "We have a team in place. That is our standard procedure."

"I want to see the team."

Paris blinked slowly like a lizard.

That bothered Maddox. Until this moment, the woman had acted in a robotic manner. The blink seemed out of character for the severe security chief.

That set Maddox to thinking. Would someone want to kidnap Meta? Yes. The New Men would want her. They would desire to question anyone who had traveled on the alien super-ship. Could that have been the meaning of Operation Odysseus? That would be a grim coincidence. Maybe his subconscious had recognized the possibly all along.

The idea of that troubled Maddox. He'd thought he'd wanted to see Meta because of…he shook his head. It was time to concentrate on the problem at hand.

Could Beth Paris and the two monitors in the security room belong to the New Men's secret service operating on Earth? That seemed highly unlikely. Could the enemy's secret service have corrupted these three, forcing them to help? Clearly, they *could* have. Could and would, however, were two vastly different situations.

Paris seemed to come to a decision. The slow blinking stopped. She moved her lips in an approximation of a smile.

"Of course, Captain Maddox," she said. "If you'll come with me, I'll take you to our security quarters."

"Thank you," he said. "Give me a moment, please." He unhooked the comm-unit on his belt, clicking it on with his thumb.

Her shoulders tensed the tiniest fraction. That confirmed Maddox's hunch.

"Sergeant," Maddox said into the unit.

"Here, sir," Riker said.

"Call the brigadier," Maddox told him. "I want a combat team ready to move."

"Is there trouble, sir?" Riker asked.

Maddox glanced at the chief officer, who watched him. "Yes. Beth Paris of Dempsey Tower Security is withholding critical information regarding Meta's disappearance."

The security woman inhaled sharply becoming angry. It was the first time she'd shown emotion.

Maddox found that interesting. She didn't plead with him but—

Inwardly, he grinned. Outwardly, he raised a single eyebrow at Paris. She'd drawn a needler, aiming it at his midsection. Sometimes, applying pressure worked wonders. In this case, it had happened faster than he had expected and to his disadvantage.

"Sir," Riker said from the comm. "Do you want me to run a background check on Beth Paris?"

"That won't be necessary," Maddox said, as he stared into Paris's cold eyes.

"Are you certain, sir?" Riker asked.

"When I believe myself hard of hearing or indecisive, Sergeant, you shall be the first to learn of it."

There was a moment's pause before Riker asked, "Would an indecisive man make such a declaration, sir?"

"I suppose not," Maddox admitted.

Paris scowled, and she made a critical blunder. She waved the needler at Maddox, no doubt implying that he quit talking to the sergeant.

Reaction times were interesting things. Maddox's reflexes and ability to decide bordered on the miraculous, at least to those who had never witnessed them before. Before the call, he had already begun to suspect the chief security officer. The video hadn't shown Meta leaving her apartment. The lingering perfume and the shock rod discharge meant she couldn't have left two hours ago. It had to be within the last hour, and this video hadn't shown that.

In any case, Maddox's suspicion allowed him to react faster than he would have otherwise to Paris. The first time she waved the needler, Maddox made his decision to go for it. The second jerk to the left caused his right hand to come down faster than a striking rattlesnake. He released the comm-unit and caught the woman's gun-hand. At the same time, she pulled the trigger. Maddox twisted his wrist and yanked hers hard. The first steel needle punctured the muscle and fat of what should have been a love handle. Maddox was steely lean and lacked those, but his side still had a small deposit of fat there. The second and third needles missed his body and stuck the wall behind him.

Then, Paris screamed. Maddox twisted the weapon, catching her trigger finger in the trigger guard. He twisted hard until a distinct *snap* told of a broken finger bone.

A moment later, he pulled, taking the needler from her weakened grasp.

"Captain Maddox!" Riker shouted from the comm-unit on the floor.

Beth Paris, if that was her real name, didn't bother with her injury. Instead, she launched herself at Maddox. He was ready for that and thrust a knee against her chest. She grunted and flew backward. In the moment of contact, Maddox learned that Paris had the consistency of toughened leather and sinew. She was anything but normal. Her back struck the wall hard. Most people would have slid down at the blow. She remained standing. And, with her injured hand, she reached into an inner pocket of her Dempsey Tower blazer.

Maddox had no idea what she planned to pull out, nor did he intend to let her surprise him. He struck with precision, using his stiffened fingers to jab her in the throat.

Her eyes widened. She gagged, and purified hatred shined in her eyes. It's possible she would have spoken if she could. Instead, with great deliberation and unbelievable concentration, she sucked down air. Then, her jaw muscles tightened as she bit down on something in her mouth. There was a distinctive *cracking* sound.

Maddox struck harder than he had earlier. With full force, he hit her in the face. Likely, that saved his life. It seemed that Paris had planned to exhale sharply, spewing the air in her mouth. A vicious poison floated in there, released a second ago from the hollow tooth where she had kept it. Instead of blowing the substance at Maddox, she swallowed reflexively.

Maddox was already scrambling back, lunging for the door, hurling it open to escape the enclosed chamber.

As he did, the chief security officer of Dempsey Tower slumped dead onto the tiles, killed by the toxins released from her false tooth.

-5-

Maddox slammed the door shut, sealing the dead security officer inside. The problem was that he left the comm-unit in there as well.

Riker would have to make do for a few minutes. Yet, it meant that Maddox had cut himself off from his link to Star Watch Intelligence.

Maddox stood indecisively for several seconds. If Paris had planned to spew poison at him, had she intended to die no matter what the outcome? That had ominous implications. Rubbing his forehead, Maddox wondered if some of the toxin had seeped into his skin, slowing his reactions.

I have to reach the security monitors. I can't let them destroy the real recordings of Meta's apartment camera.

Right. Where was the recording chamber? He'd have to find another security agent and ask.

As if they had read his mind, two Dempsey Tower security personnel appeared. A man and a woman ran into sight, their faces contorted with anguish and determination. Each wore a red blazer with the tower crest on the right side. Each aimed a powerful stun gun at Maddox.

"I'm with Star Watch Intelligence," he said. "We have a situation on our hands."

"Do you have any ID?" the woman snapped. She had a buzz cut, a skewed nose and was too thin.

"I do," Maddox said, reaching into his uniform.

"Do it slowly," the woman warned. "We'll shoot you at the first sign of something odd."

"I understand." The captain slowly removed his official ID, flipping it open and holding it toward the Dempsey security people.

The man looked first while the woman continued to aim the stun gun at him. "It seems legit," the man said. He had thick shoulders and a scar on his broad forehead.

"I want to see it," the woman said.

The man shrugged, stepping back, aiming his stun gun at Maddox. "Sorry, sir, we have to be careful these days. The scare with the New Men—"

"No problem," Maddox said, wondering what they would do if they knew he might be part New Man himself.

The woman studied the ID, finally frowning at Maddox.

"The monitors called us," she said. "They said you struck our security chief."

"I did," Maddox said. "She's dead in there." He pointed at the closed door.

The woman lurched toward it, reaching for the knob.

"I wouldn't do that," Maddox said.

"Why not?" the woman snapped, angry again.

"Because your security chief just cracked a hollow tooth and tried to spew poison into my face," Maddox said.

"What?" the woman asked. "That's crazy. Spew poison? That would be suicide."

"Exactly," Maddox said. He waved his ID at them. "What Star Watch wants to know is who she is."

"Beth Paris," the woman said. She cocked her head. "Paris used to work for Star Watch Intelligence."

Maddox smiled faintly.

"What's so funny?" the woman demanded.

"I doubt very much she worked for the Iron Lady."

"Who?"

"Never mind," Maddox said. "Take me to the monitors, the video chamber. It's time to see if we can begin to unravel this mess."

He didn't say anything about Meta yet. Maddox wasn't sure how deep the rot went in Dempsey Security. He wanted a

Star Watch combat team on the scene before he revealed his hand.

"Do you have a communicator?" Maddox asked.

"Where's yours?" the woman demanded.

"In there with Paris. Do you want to get it?"

"Here," the man said, pulling out his comm-unit. "You can use mine."

Maddox took it, wondering if either of them would do something. He doubted it. If they were part of the rot, wouldn't they have done something already? He placed a call to Riker. Once he heard the sergeant's voice, and saw the thin security woman relax, he decided that maybe these two were exactly who they said they were. But who exactly was Beth Paris?

***

Two hours later, Maddox sat at a secured Dempsey Tower computer terminal as Riker guarded his back.

The Star Watch Old Guard had stuck the sergeant on him some time ago; the captain understood some upstairs in Intelligence wanted to temper what they considered as his *reckless impulses*. What the Old Guard didn't understand was the so-called impulses were part of his...*difference* from them. Maddox didn't want to think of it as his superiority. That would be thinking too much like a New Man.

In any case, to Maddox's chagrin, Riker had saved his life several times in the past few years. It seemed as if the sergeant enjoyed wedging himself into a quiet corner, with his gun on his lap. After everyone had forgotten about him, *bam*, Riker fired the critical shot that saved the day one more time.

Maddox and Riker had checked the Dempsey Tower monitors and their videos. The seeming originals didn't show Meta leaving her apartment. It appeared that Beth Paris had worked alone, which Maddox doubted.

A surface computer search had shown Maddox that the records indicated Beth Paris used to work for Star Watch Intelligence. Digging deeper, he found that was a lie. Beth Paris had actually worked for Maxwell Enterprises, a steel manufacturing company. Paris had run security over there. Before that, she'd worked for the Chabot Mining Consortium.

"Chabot," Maddox whispered, sitting up.

"Sir?" Riker asked.

"Nothing," the captain said at the terminal. "Carry on."

Thoughtfully, Maddox rubbed his lower lip. Meta had worked in the Rouen Colony mines. The Chabot Consortium owned the entire planet. Meta had assassinated *Baron* Chabot in her youth. Had the Chabot Consortium kidnapped Meta? Would they have sent agents all the way to Earth to do that? That seemed highly unlikely. How would they have known where to find Meta?

Maddox sat forward, using the terminal to keep digging. Time passed. He went from site to site, searching. Wait a minute. This was interesting. The consortium had a connection to Earth: the Cestus Space Hauling Company.

For the first time at the terminal, Maddox felt his pulse quicken. Two nights ago, the enemy agent he'd shot had used the *Cestus 9* Hauler to reach New York City. That would indicate a possible link with the Chabot Consortium.

Who owned the Cestus Space Hauling Company? Maddox clicked away, searching. Hello. He sat up, surprised. The Nerva Conglomerate owned the Cestus Space Hauling Company.

"Octavian Nerva," Maddox said to himself.

The captain quietly mulled that over. Before his voyage into the Beyond, he had fought a viper stick duel with *Caius* Nerva, Octavian's heir. Octavian just happened to be the richest man on Earth, one of the wealthiest in the Commonwealth. Caius had cheated during the duel by wearing a body suit. Worse, he'd attacked while Maddox's back had been turned. Riker had shot the heir with a stunner. Riker's blow had caused Caius to fall down, and his viper stick had landed on his face. The proton discharge had accidently killed Caius Nerva.

That night, Nerva man-hunters had almost kidnapped Maddox in his apartment. Octavian's revengeful nature was well known. Maddox's departure from Earth as he left on the mission into the Beyond had cut short any further repercussions concerning Caius' death. Had that now resurfaced to haunt him?

The captain pondered the Chabot-Nerva connection. Could Octavian have ordered Meta's kidnapping in order to get to him?

With a start, Maddox began to type. He searched for an hour before he found what he was looking for. He couldn't believe such an obvious clue.

It appeared Octavian had planted Beth Paris into Dempsey Tower security. The interesting thing was Octavian had done it two years ago. That would eliminate the possibly of Paris's posting in the Tower to grab Meta.

Why would Octavian plant an operative in the Dempsey Building? The answer was simple. Many of his major competitors lived in or used Dempsey Tower while vacationing in New York City.

Was this about industrial espionage? Maddox didn't think so. Octavian clearly had connections with the New Men. Nerva Conglomerate actions against him over a year ago made perfect sense now. Nerva hunters had not only tried to snatch him, but in orbit a conglomerate *Ventra*-class shuttle had launched drones at the *Geronimo*.

Naturally, on his return to Earth, Maddox had spoken with Nerva representatives concerning the shuttle. They had reported it missing weeks in advance of the assault. That held up under scrutiny. It looked now as if Octavian carefully covered his tracks.

Maddox sat back, trying to piece this together. Had Octavian only recently learned of Meta's stay in Dempsey Tower? With the enemy's secret service order to begin Operation Odysseus, had the tycoon decided to act? If Octavian had captured Meta and the man worked for the New Men…

Maddox nodded. That meant he had to act fast to save Meta. One of the enemy's greatest powers was the speed at which he moved. They would hurt Meta sooner rather than later in order to extract her usefulness.

If the New Men were involved, the enemy would have covered his tracks well. Notice how there wasn't any video evidence of Meta or her captors. That pointed to the enemy's secret service.

Maddox's eyes narrowed. If there was no way to track Meta...how could he rescue her? Maybe he could negotiate directly with Octavian Nerva. Clearly, the tycoon would deny all knowledge of this. Yet...

Shaking his head, Maddox knew what Brigadier O'Hara would say to his idea. He could hear her voice in his head.

"No, Captain, you're quite wrong about the link between Octavian and the New Men. It's all circumstantial evidence. We need concrete proof of their cooperation. Octavian has too many powerful friends in the government and the Star Watch for us to act in any other manner. We will have to move softly, searching for implicating clues. Just because Paris used to work for him won't sway any judges."

"Sergeant," Maddox said, standing. The captain had come to a decision. He would risk dealing directly with Octavian. "Is the air-car ready?"

"It's on the roof, sir," Riker told him.

"Then let's go. We have a long drive ahead of us."

"Where are we headed for, sir?" Riker asked.

"Monte Carlo," Maddox said.

"Sir?" Riker asked, surprised.

"Let's hurry, Sergeant. We have to move before they take Meta off Earth."

-6-

"Take us higher," Maddox said.

Sergeant Riker sat in the flitter's pilot seat, thinking about the bottle of Guinness beer waiting for him at home. He wanted to stretch out on the sofa and finish watching the hockey match between Japan and China that he'd started viewing earlier tonight while waiting for Maddox. The beer would help soothe him before going to bed.

"Did you hear me?" Maddox asked.

"What's that, sir?"

"Higher," Maddox asked. "Take us higher."

Riker piloted a flitter. It was a nifty model, identical to the vehicle Maddox had used to fly down to Loki Prime over a year ago. The sergeant didn't like to think about that episode. He still had nightmares about the place and the worse convicts. Loki Prime was the vilest prison planet in the Commonwealth. The air-car had a bubble canopy and a range that could take them several times around the planet before refueling.

Below, the lights of New York City spread out in a vast panorama with the dark Atlantic Ocean to their right.

"Sir," Riker pointed out. "Your apartment is only a few kilometers south in New Jersey. Shouldn't I go down instead of up?"

"I already told you. We're headed to Monte Carlo."

Riker knew the impetuous young agent better than most people did. The captain possessed uncanny abilities, with the strengths and weaknesses of youth. He was bold, clever and could storm his way through most troubles. He was also reckless and trusted his abilities far too much. For all that, Riker had come to appreciate the man's insights. The sergeant saw it as his task to shepherd the genius back to harbor, watching for the common sense troubles the "high-flyer" sometimes missed.

"Meta is in Monte Carlo?" Riker asked.

"As to that, I don't know yet. Octavian Nerva is, though. We're going to see him."

Riker hesitated. Loyalty was everything to him: first to the Star Watch and then to his companions in arms. They were the guardians keeping the wolves at bay. It was lonely work against a seemingly infinite supply of enemies. The truth was he found his worth serving Star Watch, knowing that he walked the ramparts to keep his nieces safe in Tau Ceti. He believed in Star Watch's code of honor and duty to humanity. The service was his home.

"It's quite simple," Maddox explained. "Meta knows more about Starship *Victory* than anyone else save for Doctor Dana Rich. The doctor is in the Oort cloud and quite untouchable. Meta was exposed. I believe the New Men desperately want that knowledge. We know the enemy acts fast. That is their normal mode of operation. What that means is that we have to free Meta tonight, or it might be too late."

"Shouldn't we tell the brigadier about this, sir?"

"No. O'Hara would likely order me to stay away from Monte Carlo. I don't feel the need yet to face an inquest."

"How are the two ideas related, sir?" Riker asked.

"I would have to disobey the brigadier's direct order if she told me to stay away. That's why we're headed there on our own."

Riker squeezed his fingers around the controls. "There's another possibility, sir. I wonder if you've thought about it." When Maddox didn't answer, Riker continued. "Maybe Octavian is acting alone for reasons that include hatred for the two of us. I'm the one who actually *shot* Caius Nerva. I'm the one who killed Octavian's son and heir. If he wishes to torture anyone more than you, sir, it's me."

"We can't let fear hinder our resolve," Maddox said.

61

Riker's back stiffened.

The captain must have noticed. "Your courage is well noted," Maddox said, a trifle grudgingly. "I owe my life to it on more than one occasion."

"I don't like it when you speak well of me, sir. It means you're going to ask me to do something incredibly foolhardy."

Maddox's lips thinned as he looked away. The captain sat like that for some time. Finally, as he stared out of the side canopy, he said, "If nothing else, Beth Paris has shown me I'd better have a partner for what I plan. I don't know who else to ask, Sergeant. I need your assistance for this little expedition."

It struck Riker that Maddox was worried about Meta. That surprised him. Maddox was a slick operator, normally cool and reserved with the ladies. There had been indications of a liaison aboard the starship on the journey home, but Riker had assumed it had been caused by Maddox's boredom. Now, he wasn't so sure.

"I still say we should call the brigadier," Riker said.

"No! The brigadier would be confident of tracking Meta down dead or alive. The Iron Lady is more concerned about the overall picture. I'm interested in getting to Meta while she's still alive."

"The war is more important than our personal interests, sir. Besides, did you ever think that Octavian might have special training? He will if he belongs to the New Men. We can't hope to barge in and rip Meta loose from Nerva. This will take careful preparation."

Maddox faced him with a soft smile on his lips. "I disagree completely. We must strike with furious resolve. We must match the enemy speed for speed. That means I must act tonight, because I'm the only one on our side who can react as fast as the enemy can. Meta's life is in our hands."

"What's your plan, sir?"

"A face to face meeting with Octavian Nerva," Maddox said.

"Octavian would only allow such a thing in complete safety," Riker said.

"True."

"He'd have his people strip us of our weapons and possibly bind us first."

"That does seem likely, I agree," Maddox said.

Riker shook his head. "I hope you're not suggesting you're going to overpower his bodyguards, take one of their guns, put it to Octavian's head and offer to trade his life for Meta's."

"The basic idea is right," Maddox admitted, "but wrong in a critical detail."

"One or two details won't make any difference, sir, as there is a gigantic flaw."

"Oh?"

Riker spoke with gravity. "If Octavian works for the New Men, it's more than possible they will have trained him in their advanced thinking."

"You've already mentioned that."

"If Octavian is acting on his own because of Caius' death, we should remember that he is one of the oldest of the Methuselah People. His advanced wisdom could trump your skills."

As Riker spoke, he studied the captain's face. The lad was so enamored with his unique skills that he often forgot others could possess unusual attributes.

Over two hundred and fifty years ago, scientist-explorers had discovered a breakthrough in longevity treatments known as the Methuselah Cure. The critical source came from New Australia, a world fifty-three light-years from Earth. A rare plant grew in the depths of the world's ocean. Dredging the plant in specially built submarines was dangerous and ultra-lucrative. So far, no one had been able to duplicate the growth process anywhere else.

Since that time, refinements in the Methuselah Treatments had broadened in scope. More people scraped together the vast sums of wealth needed to pay for the drugs and medical procedures. Octavian had been one of the first recipients of the treatment in the early days before the plant, making him one of the oldest or possibly *the* oldest person alive.

The man was nearly three hundred years old.

The Methuselah People had certain similarities with each other. Extreme age fossilized key personality traits. In

Octavian's case, it was bitter ruthlessness. Great age also brought about extreme caution. The elder Nerva protected himself with prejudice, having one of the best security details in existence. The man seldom took unnecessary risks, having long ago decided to model his operations on spiders. He sat in his web, only approaching those carefully trapped by his threads. Now, the captain thought he could get to Octavian? It was preposterous.

"Listen to me," Maddox said. "Octavian will have every advantage but one. I will exploit that weakness and free Meta."

"What could you possibly have over him, sir?" Riker asked.

"You won't like it," Maddox said.

"I don't even know what it is, and I already don't like it, but I must admit I'm curious."

"Right," Maddox said. "Octavian wants to live more than we do."

A cold feeling stabbed through Riker. "You're wrong, sir. I very much want to live."

"I'm speaking of ratios," Maddox said. "Octavian is one of the Methuselah People. Their guiding star is a marked desire for longevity. That is the fulcrum we'll use to lever Meta's freedom."

"I don't understand."

Maddox studied the stars. They were bright outside the canopy. "I'm going to ask you to do something difficult, Sergeant. I want you to trust me without knowing all the details."

"Can you be more specific?" Riker asked.

"I need your help. I need you with me on this one, but you can't ask too many questions."

"You want me to head straight into the lion's den, and you don't want to tell me your plan?"

Maddox appeared troubled and remained quiet for a time. Finally, he asked, "Do you know where that phrase originated?"

"What phrase?"

"Into the lion's den," Maddox said.

"No, sir, I have no idea. Why does it matter?"

64

"It doesn't matter, strictly speaking. I was simply curious." Maddox inhaled, saying, "Information is everything. The lion's den. Have you ever heard of a man named Daniel?"

"I'm not sure. Daniel who?"

"He wrote the ancient Book of Daniel."

Riker shook his head.

"It's in the Bible," Maddox said.

"Oh. No, sir, I would have no idea. I've never read the Bible."

"It's a curious tome," Maddox said. "In any case, Daniel was an old man at the time of the situation. His crime was that he prayed to God several times a day."

"Why would that be a crime?" Riker asked.

"Ah. Therein lies the tale. Certain nobles of the Persian Court hated old Daniel. Yet they couldn't find any corruption in him. So, they devised a law that would entrap the pious man. Daniel was a Jewish advisor to the Persian king, you understand, and the nobles resented his power. The court nobles persuaded the king to pass a decree that people could only pray to him. Once Daniel learned of the law, he refused to comply. The nobles informed the king and forced him to carry through his decree. They did it by telling the king no one would respect him if he didn't stand by his laws."

"Daniel died?" Riker asked, "Just as we're going to die? The nobles' hatred was like a den of lions?"

"On the contrary," Maddox said. "Daniel told the king not to worry. God could protect him. The guards lowered Daniel into the underground den of lions. Then they rolled a rock over the hole, sealing the entrance. The king went home and tossed all night, unable to sleep. In the morning, he raced to the den of lions and called out. Daniel answered him. He told the king that God had sent an angel to keep the lions' mouths shut all night."

As Riker piloted the flitter, he glanced at Maddox several times. That was it? "What angel is going to keep Octavian's men from shooting us, sir?"

"Afterward," Maddox said, as if he hadn't heard the question, "the king confronted the nobles who had urged him into making such a decree. The king had the offending nobles tossed into the lions' den. Oh, and he struck down the law."

"What happened to the nobles?"

"The lions ate the lot of them."

Riker mulled that over, finally saying, "You do realize we don't have an angel on our side, sir? It seems to me we're more like the nobles than Daniel."

"Maybe in our version of the story we're going into the lions' den in order to rescue the angel," Maddox said.

"Are you talking about Meta, sir?"

"Indeed," Maddox said.

"I've never seen an angel that can hit as hard as her, sir."

"No," Maddox said. "The point…" The captain stared up at the stars.

The point, Riker realized, was that sometimes a man had to live or die according to his convictions. The sergeant appreciated that. This Daniel could have belonged to the Star Watch. He hadn't deserted his post under pressure, but had remained faithful to his charge.

What should I do? One of the old team is in danger, and we're the ones who have to go in and rescue her. If anyone can do this, it's Captain Maddox. Can I let him go in alone? No. I have to bring him home in one piece. If I don't do that, I've failed in my duty.

There was a reason Maddox didn't want to tell him the details. Riker trusted this young genius, but it was hard to commit for the final kilometer.

The realization came upon the sergeant that he wasn't going to get to drink his beer tonight. It was another long night walking the rampart, trying to bring order out of chaos and protect the good people, like his two nieces in Tau Ceti.

"Okay, sir," Riker said in a low voice. "What do you need me to do?"

"Thank you," Maddox said softly, without looking at him.

Riker grunted.

Clearing his throat and wiping away any sentimentality from his features, Maddox said in his usual crisp voice, "We're headed for France, Sergeant. On the double, I might add. We will land in Dijon at Tenth and Second Streets. Afterward, we will hurry to Monte Carlo."

Riker muttered to himself quietly.

Maddox slouched lower in the seat. "Wake me up once we're in French air-space."

"Will do, sir."

Maddox folded his arms against his chest, resting his head against the canopy.

As Riker headed due east, he knew this was a long shot. The enemy had gone to ground with Meta, and the Earth was a vast place in which to hide someone. Instead of working from the bottom up in the normal Intelligence manner, they were going to the source and working down.

Could the captain beard Octavian in the tycoon's best-laid web? They would find out soon enough.

As Maddox began to breathe rhythmically, old Sergeant Riker raced the flitter across the vast Atlantic Ocean.

-7-

Meta blinked groggily. The last thing she remembered was a gray-haired wrestler spraying her in the face with something.

I've been unconscious, she realized. *He used a knockout gas on me.*

Fear coursed through her body. A second later, she suppressed it, letting her eyelids slide shut. She relaxed her muscles next. If someone watched her, let him think she almost came out of it but slipped back into unconsciousness.

I'm sitting in a chair. It's chilly in here. I feel like I'm in a basement or a meat locker.

Meta let that settle. After the knockout gas, Kane must have taken her somewhere else. She had no idea why or where.

That will come. They'll tell me. So, I don't need to worry about it just now.

"What's taking so long?" a man asked. "Why isn't she coming all the way out of it?"

"I'm unsure," another man said, one with a reedy voice.

The first man—Meta recognized his voice. He was the pale-skinned shooter, the one who had fired a tangler capsule at her. The second speaker—she had no idea who he was.

"We're supposed to work fast," the pale man said.

"Perhaps a stronger stimulant is needed," the other said.

"No! Slap her in the face. That will wake her up."

There was a half beat. Did the other man have to think about that? Before Meta could decide, she heard approaching footsteps. The charade was up, so she opened her eyes.

The pale man moved toward her with ugly intent. He was medium-sized, wore a sweater and had sparse blonde hair. As soon as he realized she saw him, the man retreated, disappearing out of sight.

That proved easy to do down here.

Meta sat in a metal chair with her ankles and wrists secured by steel bands. She still wore her sequined dress and was barefoot. Harsh lights in the ceiling blazed down. They limited her field of vision to what was directly before her. Behind the light, she heard movement and then whispering. The two men must be conferring on what to do next.

Meta tested the metal bands around her wrists. They didn't give her much play, and they would secure an ordinary person. Maybe if she had enough time she could break them. The metal chair felt sturdy, but she thought she felt a loose screw holding down one of the bands.

"Lower the light's intensity," the pale man said.

The overhead lights softened a fraction. It allowed Meta to see two men in black leather jackets, the ones she had stunned earlier in her apartment. They wheeled a large trolley toward her. It held a tubular machine. Behind them followed a thin man in a white lab coat.

The bigger of the two street thugs had dark circles around his eyes, and he moved sluggishly. That must be because she'd zapped his head several times with the shock rod. It told her she hadn't been unconscious that long. The smaller of the two—the original attacker in her bedroom—glowered at her. His mouth looked stiff. Someone must have popped his jaw back into place.

"I ain't forgotten you, sister," he said without moving his lips. Even so, pain creased his face.

The lab-coated doctor concentrated on the thug as if surprised. "No, no," the doctor said. He had the reedy voice. "You mustn't talk to her. Didn't I tell you that already?"

While avoiding the doctor's eyes, Mr. Black Leather Jacket nodded carefully. Meta believed his name was Jacques.

As the thugs latched the trolley's wheels, the doctor removed a penlight from his front breast pocket. He clicked it on and approached Meta, shining a blue light in her right eye.

"Hmm," the doctor said. He had a garlic odor and compressed his lips in a pinched manner. Switching to her other eye, he repeated the performance.

Clicking off the penlight, stepping back, he told Meta, "You are lucid."

"She's ready then?" asked the man hidden by the lights, the pale man.

The doctor turned around. He raised his voice, speaking into the brightness. "I still suggest we wait twenty minutes before we attempt the operation."

"You said she's lucid."

"Yes, yes," the doctor said, "we must first have that. The retardant Kane gave her earlier might interfere with the results if we attempt it too soon."

"What retardant?" the pale man asked.

"He means the knockout gas," Meta said.

Although they had restrained her, she could still talk. That meant it was possible to influence the outcome. Speech could be a weapon if wielded skillfully. In this situation, her chances of doing that were slim, but it was better than wilting and accepting fate. Far better to fight, no matter how weak the weapon she had at her disposable.

The doctor faced her. He appeared thoughtful. With his thumb and index finger, he pinched his lower lip. "You have a remarkable recovery time. That is interesting. Your cognitive abilities seem fully restored. Perhaps we could speed up the procedure without risk."

The idea that her talking had harmed rather than helped her made Meta angry. She yearned to hurt the doctor, if only to free a leg and kick him in the shin.

Maybe he recognized her desire. The doctor hastily stepped away from her.

"What's wrong?" asked the pale man.

"She has a high aggression quotient," the doctor said.

"Does that make any difference to the procedure?"

The doctor peered into the light. "No, why should it?"

"I'm wondering why you stepped back," the pale man said.

"Because he's afraid of me," Meta said. It was time to take a new approach. "You should be afraid too."

The doctor pinched his lower lip again, studying her as one would a wild beast.

Meta needed more information on the situation. "Is Kane gone?" she asked. "Is that why you can't decide what to do?"

Jacques the thug cracked his knuckles. "Leave me alone with her for a few minutes. She'll beg to tell us what you want to know."

Was Jacques the weak link? The street thug seemed easily goaded. Meta concentrated on him. "I doubt that," she said. "I think you'd faint again like you did in my bedroom."

"Now we see, eh, little sister?" Mr. Black Leather Jacket lurched toward her.

"Jacques!" the pale man said.

The thug stopped and peered into the light.

"Don't let her prod you," the pale man said.

"We should teach her better manners," Jacques said. Gingerly, he touched his jaw.

"No!" the pale man said. "We're here to extract information. Doctor, are you ready?"

"I've reconsidered," the doctor said. "We're proceeding too quickly."

"You said she was ready," the pale man said.

"I know, but..." The doctor shook his head.

"We have to get started."

The doctor raised his eyebrows. "Am I to understand you're unconcerned about her rationality afterward?"

The pale man spoke with bite to his words. "I'll tell you what. Let's call Kane and ask him."

"No need for that," the doctor said, sounding frightened.

Was Kane nearby or would they use a comm-unit to speak with him? Meta realized the wrestler scared his men, which was good to know. Why wasn't Kane down here? If kidnapping her was so important, it seemed like the leader should be here during the interrogation.

The doctor cleared his throat. "We will proceed on the assumption she should retain her sanity. That will make my task more difficult, however."

"You're unable to do what we need?" the pale man asked.

"Please," the doctor said, sounding offended. He stepped to the trolley, opening a slot, making small instruments jangle against each other.

Meta noticed that the tubular machine had cables with adhesive leads attached to the ends. That reminded her of the alien creature on the shuttle when they'd stormed *Victory*. Would the doctor hook the cables to her skin and shock her?

"Why are you doing this?" Meta asked. "What am I to any of you?"

With his hands in the machine's slot, the doctor looked up at her.

"You must begin at once," the pale man said. "Our time may be limited. You know that, right?"

The doctor withdrew a hypodermic syringe from the machine. He poked the sharp end into a beer-colored capsule. As he pulled the stopper back, a gloppy yellow sludge filled the needle. After removing the needle from the capsule, he approached Meta. He held the syringe up, with a glistening drop of sludge oozing from the tip.

Meta knew what she had to do. This was her only chance, and it would be slight indeed. First, she needed to lull them. The easiest way was to make them think she was frightened.

"Why not ask me what you want to know?" she said, with trembling in her voice. "I'll gladly tell you."

The doctor smiled, revealing stained teeth. "It should be obvious to you why not. You could spin fabrications."

"I won't lie," she promised. "Please, don't use the needle."

The doctor's eyes shined with enjoyment. He turned to the others, and he spoke with greater authority. "I need one of you to tie her upper arm. That will help me find the right vein."

"Jacques!" the pale man said.

"I ain't no nurse," Jacques complained.

"Would you like me to tell Kane that?" the pale man asked.

Jacques muttered under his breath as he shook his head.

"There is a rubber tie in the drawer," the doctor said.

"Wait a minute," Meta said breathlessly. "Please, tell me what you're going to do."

The doctor's smile grew. "Your hostility isn't quite so pronounced now, is it?"

Meta shook her head.

"No, not so hostile at *all*," the doctor said smugly.

What was in the needle? How could she find out? "Will I remember any of this?" Meta asked.

"I should seriously think not," the doctor said, lifting the needle. "I will inject you with Z-592. You won't remember a thing. Depending on your base obstinacy, a subconscious quotient, I will have to do this two or three more times. It might permanently damage your mind." He shrugged his narrow shoulders. "But I will most certainly learn what Mr. Kane desires to know."

"Kane scares me," she said. "Who is he really?"

Before the doctor could answer, Jacques stepped up with a length of rubber tubing in his hand.

"Tie it around her upper arm," the doctor said.

Jacques stared purposefully at Meta. She let her eyes drop as if frightened of him. Chuckling, he stepped closer, using his hands to slide the tubing around her arm.

Meta had been waiting for this moment. It would appear Jacques had been sufficiently lulled. No doubt, the thug believed himself tough and strong. With a bound woman before him, those feelings of superiority surely increased. Someone like Jacques failed to recognize that a fighter used whatever means in her power.

For the last minute, Meta had been concentrating, building up an inner martial arts essence or chi, readying herself for a feat of strength. Her years of training in the assassin's art had taught her to act explosively. Instead of straining harder and harder at a thing, she would use a multiple of power in a single moment of time.

Jacques bent his head nearer as he wrestled with her arm.

Gathering her chi and judging his position to a nicety, Meta said, "*Hey!*"

Jacques looked up. With an explosive movement, Meta struck. Her head snapped forward to smash against his nose. It was a perfect strike. The thug's nose crackled, flattening against his face as he screamed. His head snapped back, and his body followed. With a meaty thud, it connected against the doctor. The two men sprawled onto the floor in a tangled heap.

Meta shouted as she released her pent-up essence. Savagely, she twisted her right arm, concentrating all her considerable strength against the steel band. She didn't have any hope of tearing the steel itself. That was beyond her power. Rather, she strove to rip the screws from the holes bored into the chair.

"Doctor!" the pale man shouted.

With a screeching sound, Meta tore the screws loose. Her arm flew upward, as did the metal band.

"No!" the pale man shouted.

Meta used her right hand, gripping the other band, working her fingers between the steel and her flesh. For a tense moment, she gathered her resolve and strength. Then, once more, she concentrated all her effort into one second of time. The other steel band ripped loose from the chair. This one, however, didn't fly away. She kept hold of it to use as another weapon.

The pale man stepped out of the harsh light and into view. He aimed a gun at Meta. "Stop," he ordered.

Meta laughed wildly. She knew they feared Kane, that the wrestler wanted information from her.

"Go ahead," she said. "Shoot me. See what kind of information you get then. Tell Kane you had to kill me."

The pale man lowered his gun.

Meta threw the steel clutched in her right hand. It flew hard and fast, striking the man in the forehead. He collapsed onto the floor, groaning in agony. Blood flowed from his scalp.

From on the floor, Jacques snarled, pushing the doctor away from him.

Time was critical now. Meta panted from her efforts. Sweat glittered on her face, dripping from her chin. The knockout drug earlier had dulled her. The exertion had winded her already, and she had two more steel bands to go. She didn't know if she could summon the power to rip them out.

"I'm going to cut you, bitch!" Jacques hissed. "You broke my nose."

Blood poured from it down his chin, soaking the shirt under his leather jacket.

"Thanks," Meta hissed. His very real threat galvanized her. She bent down, grabbing the right band around her ankle, feeling the chi building in her stomach. With a shout, she ripped the band free.

Jacques was on his feet. Even though he trembled, he *clicked* and a switchblade swung into view. "Now we see, eh?"

"What will Kane do to you if you cut me?" Meta asked.

Fear entered Jacques eyes, making him hesitate.

Before he could change his mind, Meta hurled the new band, knocking him onto the floor. Jacques struck the doctor, who had been climbing to his feet. They both fell again. The released switchblade skittered across the floor.

Even though this was going much better than she had anticipated, Meta forced herself to think. Rather than ripping off the last restraint, she twisted around and found a button on the chair. Pushing it removed the last band.

The men were far from out, though. The last leather jacket-wearer seemed to shake off his daze. His upper lip curled, and he reached into his jacket.

Meta didn't give him time to pull anything out of the jacket. She engaged, crossing the distance separating them and hitting him in the face. He catapulted against the nearest wall, his eyes rolling up into his head as he hit the floor.

Meta whirled around, judging the situation. The three remaining men were confused and disorganized. Yet they were still dangerous and would fight with desperation. What's more, she was still outnumbered.

It forced Meta to play deadly. Scooping up the needle, she jabbed it into the doctor's chest. He screamed, flinging himself from her. Tripping against Jacques, the doctor twisted and fell onto the needle. Seconds later, the doctor began to thrash and shiver on the floor, maybe from a drug overdose. Compared to Meta, the man looked frail.

Even though Jacques scrambled for the switchblade, Meta beat him to it. With a fist, she clubbed him on the side of the head. He thudded onto the tiles. Then she hurled the knife across the room. The pale man had crawled toward the gun, reaching for it. The blade stuck in his wrist. For a second, he stared at it. Then the pale man howled in agony. With a trembling hand, he removed the knife from his flesh.

Meta skipped over Jacques' leg. The thug lay on the floor, using a French kicking technique to try to trip her. It failed. He scrambled to his feet, hissing at her.

Grabbing the gun, she turned and shot deliberately twice. Each bullet smashed one of Jacques' knees. The street thug crashed to the floor for the last time, sobbing in agony.

The pale man made his last play for her. Meta shot out his knees too. It took three shots, and then the gun clicked empty.

"What's wrong with you?" she stormed. "Why don't you carry more bullets?"

The pale man was in a ball, cradling his ruined knees, weeping softly.

I need to get out of here. I need to think, not just react.

Meta took a moment, breathing deeply. Then, she hurried across the room, exiting through the only door. She kept the useless gun in her left hand and the switchblade in her right. Maybe she'd come across more ammo.

She passed through an empty room. It had the smell of a storage locker. Afterward, she came to stairs leading up. Bounding up them three at a time, she burst into a larger room.

Kane sat in a chair. He put a small, flat device into his inner coat. He still wore his conservative gray suit.

"I'm impressed, Meta," he said in his deep voice.

The shock of seeing Kane made her indecisive. Why was he so calm? What impressed him about her? What had he put in his coat? She had the feeling it was a small video screen.

She raised the gun, aiming it at his head. "Lie on the floor," she said.

Kane stood to his feet. He was big, maybe six-five, six-six and what...four hundred pounds? There was an aura around him. It exuded strength, sheer power.

"You can't stop a bullet," she said.

"Let us see if you are correct or not. Go ahead. Shoot."

How did he know the gun was empty? "Have you been watching us?"

"Of course," he said.

"Why did you let me kill them?"

"You didn't kill any of them, which is unfortunate. Well, maybe the doctor will die."

"That doesn't answer my question as to why you allowed me to escape," she said.

"You are correct in that. I did not."

"Okay," Meta said, realizing she'd have to fight past Kane. She reversed her grip on the gun, holding the barrel so she could swing the butt like a club. With the switchblade held low in her other hand, she advanced on him.

"Excellent," he said.

His confidence bothered her. He seemed indifferent to her approach. He couldn't be that good. She had a knife. If she could cut him several times, she would play for time until he bled enough to weaken him. Then, she would either kill him or escape.

"This is better than I had anticipated," Kane said.

Meta shifted her manner of attack at the last minute. She swung the gun, aiming for his head. The knife would come in once he was distracted.

Kane moved faster than his size would warrant. He struck her wrist, numbing it, making the fingers open involuntarily. The gun clattered onto the floor. She stabbed for his stomach. He caught her striking wrist. The move amazed her. Then, he squeezed her wrist. The pressure proved terrific.

Before she cried out in pain, Meta struck with her left fist, punching him in the chest. It was like striking a tree trunk, having absolutely no effect on Kane, not even rocking him.

How much did the man weigh?

Meta cried out in agony. The switchblade fell from her nerveless fingers. Kane kicked the weapon the instant it landed on the floor.

"Are you human?" she whispered.

Those granite eyes stared into hers.

With his fingers, he began to grind her wrist bones together. Meta struggled, striking, kicking and trying to tear her wrist loose. She scratched the top of his hand, drawing a thin line of blood.

"Are you a cyborg with fake skin?" she shouted.

He released her, and she stumbled away.

"Don't be ridiculous," Kane said. "I'm quite normal, simple flesh and blood like you."

"I'm not normal," she said.

"True."

"That means you aren't either," she said.

"Also true," Kane admitted.

"Are you a New Man?" she asked.

"I'm afraid not."

"Why have you taken me captive?"

"You have knowledge I desire."

"What knowledge?"

Kane stared at her. "Tell me about Professor Ludendorff."

"What?" she asked. "I've never heard of him."

"You are a skilled liar, but not proficient enough in this case. You have been with Doctor Rich on Loki Prime, the prison planet. Oh yes, I know all about that. She must have told you many things about Ludendorff. Dana Rich is beyond my reach just now. So, you will tell me everything you know about the professor."

"Why should I?" Meta asked.

Kane's nostrils flared. "You have made this easier for me. What you did downstairs, it was priceless. However, time is still precious. We will continue this conversation later in a safer environment."

Meta took a martial arts stance. If he wanted to leave, she wasn't going anywhere.

Kane reached into a coat pocket as he advanced. She shouted, lashing out with a foot. Kane took the wheel kick against his side. He didn't even grunt. Instead, the hand in his pocket reached out. Meta tried to evade it, but he grabbed her shoulder, and the device in his hand discharged.

With a groan, Meta went rigid. A moment later, she slid to the floor. Her muscles refused to respond to her will.

Kane scooped her up in his arms. Then he headed for the stairs.

-8-

In the light of a continental mid-morning, the flitter lifted into the air, leaving the French city of Dijon behind.

Sitting in the passenger seat, Captain Maddox massaged his stomach. In Dijon, he had gone alone into a small shop on the corner of Tenth and Second streets. After a short conversation with the clerk, he'd followed her into the back. There, she withdrew a key from her front pocket and unlocked an old, ornate cabinet.

Selecting the needed item from the top shelf, Maddox had asked for a glass of water.

She gave him a bottle instead, telling him she didn't trust the tap water here.

He twisted off the cap, put the item on his tongue and filled his mouth with water. Swallowing carefully, Maddox forced the item down into his gut. Without another word, he left, soon joining Riker in the parked air-car.

They now flew toward Monte Carlo.

Earlier, the sergeant had taken a stim to keep awake. The older man was bleary-eyed and yawned too often. Otherwise, his gaze was flinty. He played the odds in his mind. They weren't good, but the old war-dog wasn't complaining. He'd given his word, and Maddox knew Riker would stay the course until the end.

Unfortunately, the captain knew the plan lacked finesse. Yes, it played upon Octavian's ruthlessness and a belief that the man enjoyed torturing his opponents. But what if Octavian interviewed him via screen? What if the New Men had placed restraints on Octavian's actions? Everything rested on the man coming in person. Maybe what Maddox disliked the most was giving himself into his enemy's hands. That bit against every grain in him. Yet he couldn't see a way around it.

Time passed as Maddox brooded. Finally, the towers of Monte Carlo rose on the horizon.

"It's time," Maddox said.

"I've been thinking, sir. Maybe the best thing is to find where Octavian is staying and ram our air-car straight down his throat. At least that way if we're wrong, we won't spend our last hours screaming on a torture frame."

Maddox glanced at the older man. "You've done a splendid job of piloting, and you're tired. I appreciate your letting me rest. I feel much better now, on top of my game, in fact."

"Is that supposed to cheer me, sir?"

"We're surprising them, Sergeant. That always has a way of unhinging the enemy. They will make mistakes, and we shall capitalize on them."

Riker gripped the controls tighter.

Maddox fiddled with the flitter's communicator, using a number that less than fifty people knew. The captain had liberated it from Star Watch Intelligence files some time ago. This was a restricted line to Nerva Headquarters in Monte Carlo.

The small screen in the dash flickered on. A pretty, red-haired receptionist looked out inquiringly.

"This is Captain Maddox of Star Watch Intelligence."

The receptionist raised her eyebrows. It was clear she'd heard of him, which would save time.

"Please inform Signor Nerva that I am about to land in Monte Carlo," Maddox said.

The receptionist stared at him, seemingly taken aback. "You're landing here?"

"Correct," Maddox said. "I wish to interview Signor Nerva."

"Captain," the receptionist said. "I'm not sure—"

"Inform Octavian I'm almost there," Maddox said flatly.

The receptionist paused for a second. Then her features tightened, and she nodded. "I will inform his Excellency, Captain Maddox." She moved a toggle. "I have pinpointed your craft and will give you clearance. I'm sure Signor Nerva will be...*interested* in having a face to face conference with you."

"Yes, I'm sure he will," Maddox said.

"You must come unarmed, you realize."

"I understand," Maddox said.

"Under those conditions," she said, "you may proceed."

"Thank you," Maddox said.

***

They flew fast toward the city, toward destiny.

Riker stirred in his seat. "It's taken me a while, sir. I've mulled the situation over all night, in fact. I'm thinking we should take a final precaution."

"I'm listening," Maddox said guardedly.

"You should send the brigadier a time-delayed message. If we fail—I know you think that's impossible—but if we fail, Star Watch needs to know what happened to us. If nothing else, they might recover Meta after we're gone."

"Yes. That's a good idea."

Maddox sat forward, and his fingers played upon the panel, setting up the message and transmitting it to a relay station. Afterward, he turned back, opened the flitter's armory and began to select a variety of weapons.

Riker watched, growing obviously more puzzled by the moment. "We can't fight our way in."

"I have no intention of doing such a thing."

"Then what's with all these weapons, sir? You must realize they'll search you."

"Of course," Maddox said, as he tightened an ankle hostler.

"Then I don't understand what you're doing."

"It's elementary. I'm giving them weapons to find. It will help put them at ease."

"How does breaking your word calm them?" Riker asked.

81

"Exactly my point," Maddox said. "They expect nothing less from me. If I don't deliver, they might become suspicious and look for the one item I don't want them to find."

"What you picked up in Dijon," Riker said.

Maddox gave Riker an enigmatic smile before snapping his fingers and pointing at the dash. "Please, Sergeant, pay attention to our path." The captain aimed at a blinking red light. "We're almost there."

Riker adjusted the air-car, following the Nerva beacon. It soon became apparent that they flew toward the largest tower in the city. It was a massive structure, fifty stories taller than the buildings around it."

Another beep sounded from the panel.

"Anti-air radar is tracking us," Riker informed the captain.

Maddox had already wrapped himself in an impenetrable air of unconcern. It was possible neither the sergeant nor he would come out of the venture alive. Yet, he could see no other way of freeing Meta. Either the New Men or Octavian wanted something from her. To cover their tracks, it seemed certain they would kill her after extracting the data.

"We're going to succeed," Maddox said. "I want you to believe that."

"I'll do my part," Riker said, his eyes hardening with determination. "You don't need to worry about me, sir."

With a jolt, the flitter slowed abruptly.

The sergeant checked the controls. "They're using a tractor beam, sir."

Maddox nodded. This was it. There was no turning back. He stared ahead with fixed resolve.

Remorselessly, the air-car headed for a landing garage halfway up the massive Nerva Tower. A second later, the flitter's panel shut down. As if moved by an invisible hand, the car slid past an opening and toward an inner landing pad. Several sleek air vehicles were parked down there. A knot of security people in black body armor waited.

"You're a good man, Sergeant."

Riker glanced at him in surprise. "I'm counting on you, lad. You outfox these bastards. Don't say die."

Glancing at the sergeant, Maddox nodded. The old dog would stick with him to the very end. He didn't deserve a friend like this, but by the stars, he was glad Riker had his back.

The flitter went down and thudded onto the floor. It shook Maddox out of his reverie. It was time to begin the play. With a click, the bubble canopy slid back.

Maddox didn't wait for instructions. With his hands on the side, he vaulted over the door, landing before the waiting guards. Five pitted gun barrels came up, training on his chest.

Riker used the flitter's door, leaving it ajar as he walked around to join the captain. Two other guards aimed their weapons at him.

"Search them both." The words came out of an amplifier perched on the shoulder of the largest bodyguard. The man stood seven feet tall. He was likely a clone specially bred for combat.

A normal-looking woman separated herself from the black-armored guards. Her hair was in a bun. She wore a suit and held a thin scanner.

With it beeping as she waved it over the captain's body, she proceeded to disarm Maddox. He divested himself of a force blade, gun, needler and one-shot nozzle, tossing the items onto a growing pile. After he pitched his ankle-gun onto the pile, she looked up into Maddox's face, giving him a reproving glance.

He gave her a cool smile in return. Just don't let her change the wand's setting. That's all he asked. This was the moment his ploy would sink or swim.

She ran the wand over his body again, without it making a sound. This was it. She brought the scanner to her chest, and it seemed as if she was about to switch settings. Instead, she moved beside Riker and waved it over him.

The old man wore his sidearm, but that was it. He unbuckled it, taking his time doing so. Trust Riker to play it out, making the others impatient; the curmudgeon did his part perfectly. Maddox could have cheered.

"Well?" the chief bodyguard asked. "The boss is waiting. Time is money."

"They're clean," the woman said, holstering the scanner at her side.

With the tip of his machine gun, the seven-foot bodyguard prodded Maddox in the back. "Let's get going. It's time to talk with his Excellency."

Maddox and Riker walked in front, followed by the powered-armored guards. Their boots clanked against the floor, proving the body armor had to weigh four to five times as much as a man. The woman with the scanner stayed behind.

Out of the corner of his eye, Maddox noticed that Riker walked stiffly, with his hands in the air. The captain cleared his throat.

The sergeant glanced at him. Maddox slapped his hands against his hips. Understanding flooded into Riker's eyes. He lowered his hands.

"You must try to relax," Maddox whispered.

"I need a Guinness for that, sir. I can almost taste the one I could have had last night."

"Quit your yapping," the giant told them. "And just in case you two don't know, if either of you attempts anything Signor Nerva dislikes, I'll put you down hard."

Maddox stopped and looked back at the guards. It was time to begin unnerving them. He would react oddly, against expectations. "I'd already assumed that to be the case."

Two of the guards traded glances with each other. The chief guard waved his repeater, obviously meaning for Maddox to keep walking.

"As you wish," Maddox said, resuming the march.

After turning a corner, they entered a large lift. It easily accommodated the lot of them. The door slid shut, and the elevator headed up instead of down. Maddox found that interesting. The greater safety lay on or in the earth. Octavian must feel perfectly at ease, an odd emotion for someone shaking his fist at Star Watch Intelligence during a time of martial law.

Soon, the lift slowed, the door opened and the power-armored guards prodded the pair. Maddox and Riker walked through a spacious chamber displaying several ancient and quite famous statues. Next, they passed old swords, spears and shields, obvious antiques.

"These are originals?" Maddox asked over his shoulder.

None of the bodyguards answered. Maybe they didn't know.

"If these are real," Maddox told Riker, "this is a more impressive collection than the items in the Louvre."

"Where's that?" Riker asked.

"Paris," Maddox said, as if the sergeant should know.

The old man shrugged.

The chamber turned into open space, maybe three floors in height. From the ceiling, a large disc lowered. A soft hum from the underside indicated antigravity generators. In a moment, the disc landed on the floor and the humming stopped. On the disc were several sofas and large chairs. A man in a dark suit sat on one of the chairs facing them.

The bodyguards came to attention, although they kept their weapons trained on Maddox and Riker.

The captain recognized the seated man as Octavian Nerva. Maddox had never met the tycoon, but he had seen plenty of pictures.

Although he was nearly three hundred years old, Octavian looked like a well-kept athlete in his sixties. He was regular-sized, with a full head of dark hair, intense brown eyes and a fierce manner. He stood and walked toward them, moving with greater flexibility than most men a quarter of his age.

"Sir," the guard leader said. "May I suggest—?"

"Benito," Octavian said, gently shaking his head.

The bodyguard fell silent.

Octavian halted several meters from Maddox, studying him. Then, the richest man on Earth glanced at Sergeant Riker.

"You're the bastard who shot my son in the chest, isn't that so?" Octavian asked.

"Uh, your Excellency," Riker said in a humble tone. "That was a terrible accident. I never intended your son any harm."

"Yet you shot him at full stun," Octavian said. "I've read the report. Clearly, you did intend to hurt him."

"Of course he did," Maddox said, with contempt in his voice. "Your son cheated during a viper stick duel. That's why he died such a useless death."

While switching his focus from Riker to Maddox, a grim smile edged onto Octavian's face. "Are you attempting nobility, Captain? Are you trying to enrage me in order to distract my attention away from your aide?"

"I should think that obvious," Maddox said.

"Benito," Octavian said sharply. "Put up your weapon and hold Captain Maddox's arms. Lucca. Do the same for Sergeant Riker. We don't want this to end too soon. I fear these murderers may attempt something foolhardy, forcing you men to shoot them."

"Not to worry, Sergeant," Maddox said calmly.

Octavian's smile became rigid. He watched Maddox as the seven-foot giant stepped close.

The fingers of the exo-powered gauntlets circled Maddox's upper arms. He knew the guard could pulp the flesh and crush the bones. These were the latest in exo-powered armor, better than the Odin space marines had used against the invading New Men over a year ago.

"Despite the captain's words," Octavian told Riker, "you have much to worry about. I am a vengeful man. Or did you believe the stories about me exaggerated?"

"I believe them with all my heart, your Excellency," Riker said.

"Then why did you willingly come here?" Octavian asked.

"He asked me to," Riker said, using his head to nod at Maddox.

Octavian frowned. "Am I to understand you're willing to die because he asked you to?"

Riker glanced at Maddox.

"It's fine, Sergeant," Maddox said. "You can tell him the truth. In fact, I prefer it. You belong to the Star Watch after all."

The sergeant stood a little taller. "Your Excellency, I'm a simple man. I do my job to the best of my ability. But no, I wouldn't jump to my death because Captain Maddox ordered me to. In the end, I came here because he assured me I would survive the encounter. So far, he's never been wrong about something like that."

"Your faith might be touching to someone else," Octavian said, "but not to me. Worse for you, though, is that your captain is quite wrong."

"I could argue the point," Maddox said. "Yet that seems futile. We'll let events judge the accuracy of my predications."

Octavian cocked his head as if puzzled. "One word from me, and the two of you will die on the spot."

"I seriously advise against that," Maddox said, "as that would seal your own death."

"Threats, Captain?" Octavian asked. "I had expected something more refined from you."

"No threats, Signor Nerva. I am simply informing you about the bomb in my stomach. It is quite powerful. If you move, I will ignite it."

Octavian glanced at Maddox's gut. The tycoon frowned and looked back up at the captain's face. "If you do such a thing, you'll die, too."

"That is correct," Maddox said, his eyes shining more brightly than before.

"Your sergeant would also die," Octavian pointed out.

"He has always expected to die in the line of duty defending his home. He is a soldier."

Octavian glanced at Riker. The sergeant stared straight ahead with his features fixed.

"No," Octavian said. "You're bluffing."

"If I must die," Maddox said, "my last act will help humanity in the bitter war against the New Men. I will rid our planet of a foul traitor."

Octavian's frown deepened, producing creases in his face. "You're working under false assumptions, Captain."

"No," Maddox said. "Your people kidnapped a former team member of mine named Meta last night in New York City."

"You're talking about the woman from the Rouen Colony?" Octavian asked. "Why would I bother with her?"

"Indeed," Maddox said. "That's what I'm here to find out."

Octavian studied the captain. After a time, he said, "I think you really believe what you're saying."

Maddox said nothing, although he noticed that Riker had twisted his head around to watch the bodyguards behind him. If one of them should silently raise his gun to shoot him Maddox trusted the sergeant would call out. Good old Riker, the sergeant did the little things that made the difference between winning and losing. Perhaps as important as the sergeant's diligence was that Octavian noticed it.

"Interesting," the magnate said, as he attempted to maintain his calm. "Well... Let us begin to brush away these illusions. The first is that you're able to threaten me. You have no bomb."

A wolfish grin spread across Maddox's face. "I will allow one of your bodyguards to get a scanner set for carbon."

Octavian shifted uncomfortably. His features had become stiff, and he spoke with a noticeable rasp to his voice. "You should first explain why."

"Because I have a highly charged carbon-based bomb in my stomach," Maddox said. "That's why your woman failed to find it."

Octavian swallowed uneasily.

"Perhaps I should warn you," Maddox said. "If you attempt to leave, I will detonate the device."

Octavian's gaze burned into the captain. The burr in his voice because more noticeable as he said, "I feel I should point out that Benito is pinning your arms."

"Not to worry," Maddox said. "I anticipated such an event, as you can well imagine. I can detonate the bomb at any time."

"How?"

"I merely need to tap my back molars together," Maddox said.

"Interesting," Octavian whispered, as a faint sheen of sweat appeared on his forehead. He swayed as if he felt dizzy. "Let us proceed as if what you say is true. I must inform you that it still doesn't help your situation, although it makes mine precarious."

Maddox cocked his head. "That doesn't make sense."

"Why yes, it does!" a man shouted from a balcony three stories up.

Maddox craned his neck, looking up. A man wearing a dark suit stood on the balcony. He had thick dark hair and intense brown eyes. In fact, he looked exactly like the Octavian Nerva standing before the captain.

Maddox looked at the perspiring man before him and then up at the one on the balcony. A sinking feeling settled in his belly. It appeared he had miscalculated.

"He's your clone?" the captain shouted up at the man.

"Yes," the man on the balcony said, using an amplifier.

"You are the real Octavian Nerva?" Maddox asked.

"That is so," the man on the balcony said. "Now go ahead, Captain Maddox, detonate your belly bomb."

Maddox thought quickly. None of his options were pleasing. Yet what if he could enlist the help of the bodyguards and clone? Surely, they wanted to live.

Suiting thought to action, Maddox called up, "If I ignite, that will kill Benito, Lucca and your body double."

"I will miss them," Octavian said. "But such are the events of life."

Perfect. The magnate had disowned his people. Maddox concentrated on the clone before him. "Do you want to die?" the captain whispered.

"No," the sweating man said.

"Then survive by helping me take him down," Maddox said.

The clone shook his head. "I am, of course, psychologically unable to commit any act that might harm the original Signor Nerva. The bodyguards have been similarly adjusted. We cannot help you."

"Check and mate," Octavian called down. "Do you have any last words, Captain Maddox, Sergeant Riker?"

Riker sighed deeply. "I had no idea this was your plan, sir. I admit, it could have worked, but not now. You'd better explode your bomb. I don't fancy spending my last days screaming in agony for Octavian's amusement."

Maddox looked up at the magnate. He had not anticipated body double clones. They were illegal and dangerous to the owner. Even with psychological blocks in place, the temptation for the clone to kill the original and take the man's place must be overwhelming.

The captain frowned. It appeared he had lost to the three hundred year old Methuselah Man. That bothered him. Could he dredge up a new advantage? He didn't see how. Still, he might as well play his hand as far as he could take it.

"Good-bye, Octavian Nerva!" Maddox shouted. He steeled himself and—

"Wait!" the man on the balcony shouted.

Around Maddox, the bodyguards stirred uneasily. The clone was pale, looking as if he might collapse. The man sweated copiously, stains appearing under his suit.

Maddox stared up at Octavian. It was hard to tell, but it seemed as if the tycoon appeared strained.

"This is an unusual situation," Octavian said. "You have intrigued me with your nerve, Captain. I also admit to some hesitation in having you ignite yourself. In truth, Benito's squad is my favorite. I don't appreciate losing their services. You are also speaking to my most trusted body double. As I'm sure you're aware, loyal people are hard to come by these days."

"Go on," Maddox said.

"Further, I admit that Caius cheated. My boy was lazy, always wanting to use shortcuts. I've begun to believe he would have squandered my fortune."

"Yet you sent man-hunters after me," Maddox said.

"No. I did not."

"Over a year ago," Maddox said. "In your dotage, can you have forgotten the order?"

The body double sucked in his breath, shaking his head. "Signor Nerva forgets nothing, sir. If he said he doesn't remember, it's because he didn't give such an order."

"What are you trying to suggest?" Octavian shouted down at Maddox.

"I had an apartment in Geneva," Maddox said. "Before my escape into the Beyond over a year ago, you sent a trio of hunters to kidnap me."

"I have told you I did not. Believe me. I would have remembered such a thing."

"Star Watch Intelligence did autopsies on the dead men," Maddox said. "The hunters belonged to the Nerva Conglomerate."

"Give me their names," Octavian snapped, almost sounding angry.

Maddox did so.

"Please, give me a moment," Octavian said. The man on the balcony took out a communicator. He spoke for several minutes. Finally, thoughtfully, he put away the unit.

"Why did you come to Monte Carlo?" Octavian asked. "I want the real reason."

Maddox wondered what the tycoon had found out over the comm-unit.

"Respectfully, sir," Riker said. "What can it hurt to say?"

Maddox focused on Riker. "You're doing well, Sergeant. Maintain your vigilance. This is far from over."

Riker looked into his eyes. After a moment, the sergeant's lips firmed. "Yes, sir," the old man said.

Maddox shouted up at Octavian, "I came here because of Beth Paris."

"The head of security in Dempsey Tower?" Octavian asked over his amplifier.

"The same, signor. Star Watch knows she worked for you."

"It's true she did several years ago," Octavian said. "So what?"

"Then you admit she was your plant?" Maddox asked.

"Of course," Octavian said. "Who doesn't have spies in enemy territory? At my level, it is one of the costs of doing business."

"Last night your plant Paris committed suicide while trying to kill me."

"How?" Octavian asked, sounding angry.

"She used a hollow tooth, swallowing poison. In fact, her use of the tooth gave me my idea for triggering my bomb."

"No," Octavian said. "That makes no sense. I do not rig my employees for suicide. It's the wrong sort of motivation. I can't understand why she would do something so foolish."

Maddox was impressed with Octavian's ability to lie. The tycoon sounded sincere. Then a worm of doubt filled the captain. Could he have misjudged the situation? Could the magnate be telling the truth? There were certain elements that weren't adding up. Given that possibly, Maddox told Octavian about Meta's disappearance and the altered Dempsey security videos.

The magnate cursed explosively in Italian. He took out his communicator. His actions indicated this was a surprise to him. The tycoon spoke longer this time. Afterward, he put away the comm-unit, staring down at Maddox.

"You have a choice, Captain," Octavian called down. "You can explode your bomb, or you can allow Benito to take you to a holding cell. There, you will speak to my chief of security."

"Why should I do that?" Maddox asked.

"In the interest of humanity," Octavian said.

"How have you come to such a conclusion?"

"As I'm sure must be clear to you by now," Octavian said, "I think the New Men may have infiltrated my security organization. Given little clues here and there, I've been wondering about that for some time. If I didn't order Meta's kidnapping, who did? Who would have the organization and cleverness to use my people without my knowledge? The only group I can conceive would be the New Men. They are your enemy, Captain. You desire Meta's freedom, and you want to thwart the terrible menace to Earth. I am giving you that opportunity. By using your perceptions, my security chief may be able to locate the breach and help plug it."

"This is a trick, sir," Riker whispered. "Explode the bomb before they disarm you."

Maddox ignored his sergeant as he concentrated on the possibilities. Could Octavian be telling the truth? If any group should be able to withstand the New Men, it would be the Methuselah People. Age brought wisdom, didn't it? Unfortunately, there was also a chance Octavian told him all this to try to save his body double and guards.

"I'll agree to this on one condition," Maddox said.

"Yes?" Octavian asked.

"You free us afterward."

Riker groaned, shaking his head. "You can't trust the man," the sergeant whispered. "He's trying to trick you, sir."

"I'm sorry," Octavian said. "I can't give you such a guarantee. You did kill my son, after all. Despite his laziness, I loved Caius."

"His death was an accident," Maddox said. "You must come to terms with that."

"Do you want this Meta freed or not?" Octavian asked sharply.

Sergeant Riker dipped his head. "No," he muttered. "Tell him no, and detonate your bomb. Don't let him torture us, sir."

Maddox stared up at Octavian. "If I sense you trying to gas us, I will ignite."

"I have already presumed that much," Octavian said.

"A mere tap of my molars..."

"Come, come, signor," Octavian said. "Is it a deal or not?"

"Yes," Maddox said. "I will speak to your security chief. Let Benito take us to the holding cell."

Riker shook his head.

The body double standing before the captain exhaled with relief. The clone stepped closer. "Thank you, signor. Thank you indeed." The clone shook the captain's hand. Then the body double hurried away to safety.

-9-

Maddox sat on a chair, waiting. Beside him, Riker paced back and forth. The captain appreciated the sergeant's silence. The older man could have been accusatory. Instead, Riker bled off his frustrations the best he could.

"I'll let you in on a secret," Maddox said. "This has gone even better than I anticipated."

Riker halted and peered questioningly at the captain.

Maddox slid his gaze upward, signaling.

The sergeant glanced around the room, searching.

"They're well hidden," Maddox said, referring to Nerva Security microphones. Riker knew that the others listened to them. It was time to get started, to let them understand none of this bothered him. "If it puts you at ease," Maddox added, "notice the far wall. They're watching us through it."

Riker faced the wall. "How can you tell, sir?"

Raising his right arm, Maddox snapped his fingers. "Let us proceed," he said toward the wall. "I believe you've studied us long enough."

A moment passed, and then the wall changed texture, becoming clear. On the other side, a bent man in a suit peered within. He held onto a cane with a quivering, wrinkled hand. His head seemed too heavy for his frail frame. The skin looked waxy as if it belonged to a mannequin. The blue eyes belied that. They were alive with burning curiosity.

"Call me Strand," the man said in a creaky voice. "I run Nerva Security."

"You are a Methuselah Man?" Maddox asked.

The dry lips peeled back. "I have a rare disease. It means I maintain a terrible vitality even as my body withers on the frame. It will no doubt surprise you to learn that I am one hundred and sixty-three years old."

"Half of Octavian's age," Maddox noted.

"A little *over* half," Strand corrected.

"The conclusion is obvious then," Maddox said. "You must be good at your job. Otherwise, Octavian wouldn't spend the fortune he must to keep you alive."

"Any idiot could have guessed that by looking at me," Strand said. "That's what I think you are, Captain Maddox, a fool."

"Thank you," Maddox said. "It's good to know where one stands with his captor."

"You pretend to be at ease, which I reject out of hand. Despite your idiocy, you must realize that you're on the edge of an excruciating future."

"I see," Maddox said. "You feel confident about the dampening effect."

Riker glanced at him. "What's that mean, sir?"

"I felt a peculiar sensation upon entering the cell," Maddox said. "Signor Strand has just confirmed that he has dampers positioned around us, beaming inward. He must believe the dampening effect will weaken the explosion in my stomach enough to give him time to rush medics within and save my life. Afterward, he can begin his tortures."

"Though you understood the situation, you freely walked into the dampening chamber." Strand shook his oversized head. "If nothing else, that brands you a fool. Surely, you realized on the approach to Monte Carlo that you would fail against us. I cannot understand such willfully suicidal arrogance."

Maddox let a cool smile spread across his face. The failure to this point galled him, hurting his pride. He had believed it possible to lure Octavian into gloating range. That had been his chief mistake. Unfortunately, sometimes one had to stick his head in it in order to learn a truth. That's what made Methuselah People so potentially dangerous. They had more chances to learn from their mistakes.

"Technically," Maddox said, "I haven't failed yet. Waking up on a torture device will be the point of no return for me."

"You're wrong on several points," Strand said. "The critical one is this. We here at Nerva Security want you to live a long, long time."

Beside Maddox, Riker shuddered.

"Given this is the case," Maddox said, "I'm curious why you're bothering with an interview."

Strand managed to straighten, giving them one of the evilest smiles Maddox had ever seen.

"I see," the captain said.

"Well, I don't see, sir," Riker said, glumly. "What's he driving at?"

While staring at Strand, Maddox said, "He wishes to test us, Sergeant. He's wondering what I plan to do in order to escape this cell."

"I'm told you're resourceful," Strand said. "I'd like an example of that for myself. You can begin at any time."

"I'm sorry to disappoint you," Maddox said. "You caged me, and that's that. Still, I will point out a key fact. Simple desperation should goad you to action against the New Men. Indulging your hatred against me lacks judgment. Instead, you should utilize my capabilities in conjunction with your own. Clearly, the New Men have infiltrated Nerva Security. I can help you stop them. Instead, you're wasting this precious resource that you have in me."

"That's another sure sign you're a monkey," Strand said. "You impress yourself more than anyone else. Now, as to your—" Strand cocked his head. "A minute, please." The old man scowled. "Wait, wait," he said, although he didn't seem to be speaking to them anymore. Using a trembling hand, the old man pressed his ear.

"What's going on, sir?" Riker whispered.

"Strand is receiving instructions via an earbud," Maddox said. "He's a quarrelsome old man and doesn't like the interruption."

"Oh," Riker said.

Strand stood on the other side of the glass, muttering to himself, with his hand pressed against his ear as he continued to listen to the earbud.

Under different conditions, Maddox might have surprised Strand, capturing the Nerva security chief. Riker's bionic eye acted as a tracking device. The bionic arm possessed superhuman strength. The dampening chamber kept the eye from transmitting and the arm from functioning at full capacity. Otherwise, Maddox would have already ordered the sergeant to rip the door off the hinges. Perhaps there would come a favorable moment—

"It seems there's to be a change in plans," Strand growled, as his frail arm swung down from his ear.

Maddox waited.

Strand's upper lip curled. "You have fool's luck, signor. A medic in one of our safe houses listened to a strange story tonight. It came from a street thug with both his knees shot out. The medic had scanned the latest alert, which went out after you spoke to Octavian. Since the thug was already under restraints, the medic administered a truth serum to the patient. It turned out that the thug named Jacques was part of the team that kidnapped Meta from Dempsey Tower."

Maddox raised an eyebrow.

"Several snatch-teams are sweeping up the other participants," Strand said. "We should have them all in custody within the hour."

"How can I assist you?" Maddox asked.

Strand rubbed his leathery jaw. "If it were up to me, I'd keep you here. There's something off about you, Captain. Do you care to tell me what that is and save me the tediousness of breaking you later?"

"Of course," Maddox said. "I have a keen appreciation for my work. I excel at it more than others believe I should."

Strand spoke in a grudging voice. "You must have impressed Signor Octavian earlier with your little stunt of walking in on us. It was nothing more than a stunt. You and I both know that, si?"

"If I hadn't come in, as you say, would you have given the alert the medic noticed?"

"That's fool's luck," Strand muttered.

"I doubt you believe in luck of any kind," Maddox said. "I suspect you hide a keen mind behind your façade of old man peevishness."

Strand laughed harshly. "What makes you say something so foolish? I have a rare disease. Octavian Nerva has lived three hundred pain-free years. Wouldn't you call that bad luck for me and good for him?"

"Perhaps," Maddox said. He wondered why Octavian trusted such a harsh old man.

Strand shook his head. "You're a young monkey who makes his superiors laugh. What makes it worse is that you're a lucky young ape. I despise that about you. Against my recommendation, Octavian believes you're more use working against the New Men than howling for mercy in our deepest dungeon, at least for the moment. I think we will learn some interesting pieces of information down here from you at a future date."

"Perhaps that's so," Maddox said.

Strand gave him an ugly smile. "Oh, did I happen to mention a little shift in emphasis with your belly-bomb."

"Not yet," Maddox said.

"While you've cooled your heels waiting," Strand said, "I discovered the detonation frequency through trial and error. Don't look so shocked, signor. We used pox-scanners while the device has been under the dampeners. There are no wires from your molars to the carbon bomb in your stomach. That meant a signal had to go there."

Strand dug in his pocket, pulling out a small box with a button. "Do you see this switch?"

Maddox nodded.

"Benito will carry it and join you on your excursion. If you should call Star Watch Intelligence or take any unwarranted action, either Benito or I from my remote control station shall detonate your stomach device."

"I see," Maddox said.

Strand's blue eyes shone with appreciation. "I will make a prediction, Captain. I do that now and again when I hold all the cards. You will return to me in short order. Then, you and I will have a long conversation about luck."

"Was Caius Nerva your protégée?" Maddox asked.

The eyes became bright with hatred. Strand pointed at Maddox with a trembling finger. "You have no idea what you did that morning when you struck down Caius, but I do. And I do not forget, Captain Maddox."

"Did you send the man-hunters after me?"

"No, but I wanted to."

"Have you ever wondered if your hatred aids the New Men against your employer?"

Maddox watched Strand carefully. The flames in those eyes seemed to leap with fury. Strand's grip tightened around the box. With a silent snarl, the old man shoved the detonator back into his pocket. Then, as he stood rigidly, the man began to hood his intensity.

Maddox realized there was more going on here than he knew. Maybe Methuselah People played deeper games than anyone realized. Did the treatments do more than just give them long life? Had it changed their minds in some new way?

"When the door opens," Strand said, "you will follow Benito. He will take you to a flyer. From there, you will go to a ship in the mid-Atlantic."

"Why there?" Maddox asked.

"I have Jacques and Cabot under sedation," Strand said. "I believe you're going to want to be there when we interrogate them."

"They were part of the team that kidnapped Meta?" Maddox asked.

Strand didn't answer the question. Instead, he said, "Remember that your bomb is now under our control, Captain. We are jamming the transmitter in your tooth but can turn that off and send the impulse that explodes your belly. If you desire to live, you will do exactly as we say."

"I won't forget," Maddox said.

Strand grinned his evil grin, chuckling as the cell door opened.

-10-

The trip halfway across the Atlantic went faster this time around. The large Nerva flyer traveled at Mach 24 the majority of the journey.

Maddox and Riker sat together. Benito and his seven-foot companions wore regular clothes, with stun guns at their sides. Otherwise, the large compartment was empty of people.

Sergeant Riker stared thoughtfully at the floor.

Maddox stretched out his legs, with his hands crossed on his stomach.

"I've been thinking," the captain said in a low voice. He noticed Benito shift his head. Clearly, the bodyguards wore pickups on their persons, with transmitters in their ear, allowing them to hear any whispers.

"And?" Riker prodded.

"I'm curious to see how the New Men have infiltrated Nerva Security. It might give us a clue how they've worked spies into Star Watch."

"How do you do it?" Riker whispered.

"Excuse me?" Maddox asked.

"Stay so calm with a bomb in your gut," Riker said.

"Oh." Maddox shrugged. "It's nothing."

"They'll use it to force you back to Monte Carlo."

"You're wrong," Maddox whispered.

Benito sat straightener.

Maddox smiled to himself.

Riker noticed. "I don't see what's so funny, sir."

"Remind me, and I'll tell you later."

"They won't give you a later," the sergeant said. "Don't you realize? They're going to detonate you."

"My dear fellow," Maddox said. "You went in and out of Monte Carlo, including spending time in a holding cell. I told you we would come out in one piece. You must trust me in this."

Riker stared hard at Maddox.

"I want you alert," the captain said. "Now, we're almost there. There's going to come a moment when I need your services fast. Are you up for it?"

"Signor!" Benito called.

Maddox turned away from Riker and concentrated on the seven-foot giant. Benito unbuttoned a pocket on his uniform and withdrew the detonation box.

"One push and you go ka-boom," Benito said.

"Yes," Maddox said, "big boom. I have divined your meaning. Bravo, my friend."

Riker glanced sidelong at Maddox. Something seemed to pass over the sergeant's tired face. Maybe it was a slice of hope. The older man sat straighter, finally folding his arms across his chest.

"There's a good fellow," Maddox said, patting Riker on the knee. "Now you're into the spirit of things."

The flyer throttled down. The motion threw everyone against the restraints. The engine no longer purred, but roared loudly. Outside, the Nerva flyer approached a large oceangoing liner.

***

The float-flyer docked beside the ocean liner. Benito and his security team flanked Maddox and Riker. They walked through a boarding tube and crossed the open deck. A stiff wind blew salty spray on them. They entered a hatchway, going down into the ship. Soon, the group entered the upper level of a large theater.

As if they were visiting physicians, Maddox and Riker moved to a row of seats looking down into an operating chamber. Benito and his team sat higher still. The bodyguard held the detonator switch.

"I would like to point out several salient features."

Looking up, Maddox couldn't help but notice a gigantic screen. It showed Strand. The Nerva security chief still grinned evilly at him.

"I am still in Monte Carlo," Strand said. "But think of me as joining you in spirit. Below, the doctors have prepared Jacques. After questioning him, they will bring in Cabot. Are there any questions so far?"

"You're not afraid of me destroying your ocean liner?" Maddox asked.

"You are in a holding chamber, signor," Strand said. "Strong plastics will absorb your blast, although it will do nothing to save you."

"Ah," Maddox said.

Through the screen, Strand eyed him. "Your sangfroid is legendary, which I suppose you know."

Maddox made a mock bow.

"You do not disappoint in that regard," Strand said. "I have come to believe it is foolish fatalism that gives you this stance."

"You're entitled to your beliefs, as wrong as they may be."

"Captain," Strand warned. "Although I am not with you in the flesh, please be assured that I am running this operation. You will remain whole and healthy for as long as I find you useful in Nerva employ. If you attempt—"

"Yes," Maddox said, as if bored. "I am quite aware of the situation. Let us proceed. I am eager to find Meta and free her from the New Men."

"I should worry more about myself if I were you."

"But then I'm not," Maddox said. "You are a disease-ridden old man. I am young and full of life. Let's remember that, shall we?"

"Sir," Riker whispered in warning.

With a slight hand motion, Maddox waved the sergeant off.

Strand scowled fiercely, his old fingers tightening on the head of his cane. "Yes," he said harshly. "The sooner we start, the sooner I'll have you back with me."

102

"There you go," Maddox said. "It's a pleasure to watch a true optimist at work."

Riker shook his head but kept his comments to himself.

Strand turned his attention to the proceedings below. It looked as if the doctors and their attendants were ready.

Maddox slid forward, peering past the clear partition. Beefy attendants in white uniforms strapped Jacques into a bulky machine. They attached leads to his skin and placed a heavy helmet onto his shaved scalp.

"What is that?" Riker whispered.

"Another illegal device," Maddox said. "It's a mind scanner."

"They can read his thoughts with that?" the sergeant asked.

"Nothing so direct," Maddox said. "But it will give them access to his neural pathways. By an application of wattage, they can redirect his answers to truthful utterances. He will no longer be able to lie or equivocate."

"What?" Riker asked.

"The machine forces him to tell the truth," Maddox said.

"Does the process hurt?" Riker asked.

"We shall soon find out," Maddox said.

The captain proved correct as the doctors began the procedure. Jacques didn't scream, but he moaned often, twisting within the constraints of the large machine. His limbs jerked at times.

"Electrodes," Maddox explained to Riker.

"It's inhuman," the sergeant said.

"Yet like many such devices of that nature, it works. Therein lies the dilemma for society."

As Strand supplied the head physician with questions, Jacques related the events of last evening. He told the story from his perspective. Beth Paris proved instrumental in their easy access to Meta's apartment. The street thug gave a rundown of each member of the team.

Maddox snapped his fingers. "I saw them," he said.

"Sir?" Riker asked.

"In the main lobby of Dempsey Tower," Maddox said. "I saw a red-haired girl and a large man that looked like an ex-professional athlete."

"Who was that, sir?" Riker asked.

"This Mr. Kane Jacques is telling us about," Maddox said.

Down in the chamber, Jacques twisted on the bed of the mind scanner. His jaw sagged, and he seemed reluctant to say more.

"Is there a mental block in place?" Strand asked the chief physician.

"Just a minute, Signor Strand," the chief doctor said. A nurse wiped a rag over the doctor's sweaty brow. The physician tapped a panel, adjusting the scanner.

Jacques arched his back with his mouth open and sweat staining his face. He was in agony.

"Shut down level five!" the doctor shouted.

Attendants flipped switches.

On the scanner bed, Jacques began to blink rapidly and make choking sounds.

"Break the mental block," Strand ordered from the screen. "Don't let him resist. Continue with level five."

"Signor—" the chief physician pleaded.

"Do it!" Strand snapped.

With seeming reluctance, the scanner team resumed questioning the patient, increasing the pain level.

Strapped down on the bed, Jacques eyes bugged outward. His twisting caused him to rip loose from several leads. His fingers hooked like claws, he tore at the air. Suddenly, Jacques exhaled, sinking onto the couch, relaxing as he twitched his death throes.

The chief doctor, a tall man, tore off his mask in disgust. He glared up at the screen showing Strand.

"We lost him," the doctor said.

"Due to your incompetence," Strand said.

The tall physician looked away. He balled up his cloth mask, but made no more outbursts.

"Bring in Cabot," Strand said from the screen. "We will continue the questioning with him."

Cabot proved to have pale features and paler hair. He was tougher than Jacques had been, saying nothing as they hooked him to the mind scanner. Soon, Cabot told his story as the second-in-command, using a tangler to capture Meta. He added little to the tale.

"Well," Strand asked Maddox. "What do you make of this?"

"Kane is the agent for the New Men," the captain said.

"Clearly," Strand said. "It also appears he engineered Meta's escape."

"Of course," Maddox said.

"The question is why."

"To cover his tracks," Maddox said. "He took her, leaving these men to hide his trail."

"Why didn't he kill them himself and simply take Meta?" Strand asked.

"Perhaps in order to test Meta," Maddox said.

"I don't believe that. There's something else. Something we're missing."

"Maybe he's trying to break her," Maddox said.

"Explain that," Strand said.

"Kane set up the situation where she might free herself. Given that she did, he apprehended her. Maybe he believes if he can do that enough times, he will break her spirit."

"For what purpose?" Strand asked. "The New Men and their agents always do things for a logical reason."

Maddox shook his head. "I'd have to see Kane, talk to him."

"Yes," Strand said. "Mr. Kane." The old Methuselah Man on the screen peered down at the waiting team.

Maddox thought back to the brief encounter with Kane in the Dempsey lobby. The captain had perfect recall. A red-haired woman had smiled at him. The big man with gray hair and a sports ring had frowned at him. What had he sensed during that brief encounter?

Kane was obviously extraordinarily strong. What had he learned yesterday? Beth Paris had connections with the Chabot Consortium that owned the Rouen Colony. Meta originated from there. The consortium had practiced genetic manipulation on all the miners working there. Meta possessed denser muscles than ordinary people did. Paris had been eel-strong.

105

The Chabot Consortium…did Kane have a connection with them? By his sheer physical bearing, it appeared so.

"Here is a photograph of Mr. Kane," Strand said on the screen.

Maddox looked up. On the screen was a still-shot of the man. Yes. He was massive. Maddox had no doubt Kane had grown up on the two G Rouen Colony.

The captain became thoughtful. The New Men were genetic supermen. That gave them a clear connection with the consortium.

This is interesting, Maddox thought. *Kane might have acted in his own interests, playing the charade with Meta for his own particular reasons. Did Kane know Meta personally from the Rouen Colony?*

"Is Kane a New Man?" Maddox asked.

"He lacks golden skin," Strand said, coming back online.

"One would imagine that an easy problem to solve," Maddox said.

"Where would Kane go?" Strand asked. "Where would he take Meta?"

Maddox closed his eyes. He had it. He knew how to find Kane. A slow smile curved onto his face. The man had a made a miscalculation last night. It would cost Kane. First, however, the captain needed freedom of movement.

"What is it?" Strand said. "What have you discovered?"

Maddox opened his eyes. "We need to talk."

"We're talking now," Strand said.

"I mean person to person," Maddox said.

"I'm in Monte Carlo," Strand said.

"No, you're not. You rode in the same flyer we did."

Strand stared balefully at Maddox. Finally, the old man nodded. "Benito, escort the captain to my chamber. Signor," the old man told the captain, "we will be in the same room, but a blast wall will separate us."

"I know how to find Kane," Maddox said. "I want to bargain with you."

"I thought it might be something like that," Strand said.

Maddox felt the seven-foot combat specialist behind him, along with Benito's four companions. As the captain stood, he

106

glanced meaningfully at Riker. Then Maddox allowed Benito to propel him toward a door.

As before, Maddox and Riker walked in front, with the five bodyguards in back. They moved through a narrow ship's companionway.

Suddenly, with a groan, Riker stumbled, collapsing onto the floor.

"Sergeant," Maddox said, turning, bending over him.

"Back off," Benito said.

Maddox looked up. The seven-foot killer held the detonator switch. Reluctantly, the captain stood, backing away from the prone sergeant.

"What's wrong with him?" Benito said.

"I was attempting to discover just that," Maddox said.

"If you do anything out of line…" Benito warned. He raised the switch.

"Have you considered a problem with that?" Maddox asked. "If you detonate me, I'll kill everyone in a nearby radius."

"Lucca," Benito said. "Get the old fool on his feet."

Lucca stepped up and prodded Riker with the toe of his boot. The sergeant groaned. Lucca prodded him harder.

"Pick him up," Benito said.

Lucca bent down, grabbing Riker, hoisting him to a standing position.

"Old man," Benito said.

Lucca shook Riker. The sergeant opened his eyes, staring at Benito.

"If you are faking, your captain is dead," Benito said.

"My chest," Riker wheezed, and he sounded hurt. His knees buckled just then. Lucca grabbed him, and the sergeant hung on as if for support.

"Don't hurt him," Maddox said.

"Why do you have such an old aide helping you?" Benito asked.

Lucca roared with agony. Sergeant Riker released the man's arm where his bionic hand had crushed the flesh and broken the bone. As Lucca threw himself away from Riker, the sergeant smoothly drew the man's stun gun from its holster.

Without hesitation, Riker began beaming high-intensity shots at the other bodyguards. The discharges sounded harsh and evil within the confines of the corridor. Nearly invisible clots of force flashed. The sergeant shot each man in the chest, causing the giants to go rigid with pain.

Maddox charged forward. He'd been waiting for this.

Seven-foot Benito snarled with rage. The man's big thumb stabbed down on the red button detonator. Absolutely nothing happened to Maddox. Benito pressed the switch a second time, using considerably more force than before.

Captain Maddox kicked the giant savagely in the groin. Benito groaned, folding up. Maddox's knee slammed up against the proffered chin. The giant's head catapulted backward, with his body following.

Riker's stun gun clicked empty. He'd drained the charge.

"Finish them, Sergeant. Don't let them recover and turn the tables on us."

As Maddox spoke, he knelt by Benito, using his stiffened fingers to jab mercilessly into the giant's throat. Benito gagged. Maddox thrust his knee on the bodyguard's chest, stabilizing him enough to draw the man's stun gun.

Riker kicked one of the stirring guards in the head.

"Duck!" Maddox shouted.

The sergeant did, hitting the floor.

Stunner discharges sounded. Maddox administered the coup de grace to each bodyguard, using a lower setting against their heads. It was dangerous to stun like this, and could accidently kill. But these giants were killers caught by surprise. If even one of them managed to draw his weapon and fire back, the fight could turn around to their advantage in quick order. Maddox did not fight in a sporting way. He fought to win. Not only Meta's life was at stake. This was a war against the New Men, and Strand stood in the way.

"Get up," Maddox said, his voice full of command.

Riker scrambled to his feet. The older man panted heavily. "They let us get the drop on them. They thought—" Riker's eyes lofted in astonishment. He faced Maddox.

"What about the bomb, sir? I thought Benito pressed the button."

"He did," Maddox said. The captain rose from making sure each Nerva bodyguard was out. "Here," he said, pitching extra charge clips to Riker.

The sergeant reloaded his stun gun.

"This way," Maddox said, running down the corridor.

"I don't get it," Riker said, dogging the captain's heels. "How did you know the switch wouldn't work?"

"It did work," Maddox said.

"How'd you rig it so Strand would fail to match the right frequency?"

"He matched the frequency just fine," Maddox said.

"Then I don't understand, sir."

"The carbon device in my stomach only *simulates* a bomb. You don't think I'd actually put a live explosive in my gut, do you? That's madness, Sergeant."

Riker could only blink in astonishment and then chagrin.

"Damn," Maddox said, as he ducked back within the hatch leading outside onto the main deck.

Riker looked up.

"The flyer is taking off," Maddox said. "I suspect Strand is aboard,"

"Why is Strand running away? We only have stun guns."

Maddox lifted the communicator he'd taken off Benito. In seconds, he connected with Brigadier O'Hara.

"Where have you been, Captain?" the Iron Lady demanded. "There is an interstellar emergency going on. I demand your immediate presence here in Geneva."

"You'll have to home in on this communicator, ma'am. I'm on a Nerva ship in the middle of the Atlantic Ocean."

"What?" she asked. "The Atlantic Ocean, you say? How in the world did you get there? Wait. Don't answer that. Did you say I needed to home in on your signal?"

"Yes, ma'am," Maddox replied.

"Just a minute," she said. "Yes, there, I have a fix. A team will be there in less than ten minutes. Can you survive that long?"

"I'll see what I can do. I'll be in the water, by the way, some distance from the communicator."

"Your situation is critical?" she asked.

"Indeed, ma'am," Maddox said. "Now I must go." He turned to Riker. "Into the drink, Sergeant." The captain pitched the comm-unit away, peered outside the hatch, looking both ways, and ducked back in.

"What's going on, sir?"

"Follow me." Maddox darted out of the hatch and sprinted to the side of the deep-sea vessel. With his hands on the railing, he vaulted over the side.

The two Star Watch operatives struck the water, escaping from the Nerva hunters who had begun a manhunt for them.

All the while, the big Nerva flyer dwindled as it climbed into the starry sky.

-11-

Several hours later, a perturbed Captain Maddox sat in Star Watch Headquarters in Geneva, Switzerland.

A combat team had fished the two of them out of the ocean, rushing them to the continent. The combat team had let the Nerva liner go, and as far as Maddox knew, Strand was back in Monte Carlo.

The team commander had been a tight-lipped commando, with nothing to say to Maddox. That told him the situation was dire.

The captain presently sat in the office of Mary O'Hara, the head of Star Watch Intelligence on Earth.

A side door opened, and O'Hara walked in briskly. She was a gray-haired lady with a matronly image. Despite the image, she had one of the cleverest minds in Star Watch, and was a key reason why humanity continued to resist the New Men's infiltration tactics.

"Ma'am," Maddox said. "This is an emergency. The New Men have Meta, or one of their agents does. We must—"

"Not now, Captain," O'Hara said, sitting behind her large synthi-wood desk.

The answered surprised him. "I'm not sure you're hearing me, ma'am."

"I heard you quite well. The New Men have Meta. Yes, that's a tragedy. But we have far greater troubles on our hands. I'll search for Meta once you're gone."

Maddox blinked with surprise. "But ma'am—"

"Several months ago, the New Men smashed the Fifth Fleet at Caria 323," O'Hara said.

"Excuse me?" Maddox asked.

"With Admiral Fletcher out of the way," O'Hara continued, "the entire "C" Quadrant is exposed. Worse, the enemy could conceivably be driving to Earth to bombard our planet. As much as I appreciate Meta, this takes precedence, wouldn't you agree?"

Maddox stared at O'Hara as he ingested her words. The gears in his mind began to shift focus.

"You're speaking about Admiral Fletcher's battle group?" he asked.

"*Fleet*, Captain, it was Admiral Fletcher's fleet. In point of fact, it was the largest fleet we have other than the one guarding the Solar System."

"Fletcher's fleet was annihilated?" Maddox asked, trying to wrap his mind around that.

O'Hara compressed her lips and massaged her forehead. A haunted look appeared in her eyes.

Maddox sat back in his chair, stunned. "All those ships…"

"Well, not exactly *all*," the Iron Lady said. "The fleet took staggering losses, but it's still a few months away from complete destruction."

The captain stared at her. "There's a situation, I take it."

"Quite, and it's unbelievable."

Maddox waited, wondering what had happened in Caria 323. Fletcher was one of the best Star Watch fighting admirals there was. The man wouldn't have panicked. Yet, Maddox didn't think the admiral could have outmaneuvered the New Men. Would Fletcher have been foolish enough to try?

O'Hara began to explain in a low voice, with her eyes unfocused. "The New Men engaged the fleet in Caria 323, as I've said. With Commodore Garcia's help, Fletcher attempted a clever trap. Somehow, the enemy knew about it. The New Men's counter maneuver bordered on the miraculous."

"Meaning what?" Maddox asked.

O'Hara told him how the New Men had sabotaged the collapsium-armored star base guarding the Ember-Caria Tramline. Then, a decoy fleet had entered the inner system.

Fletcher had taken the bait, rushing to save Caria Prime. That had left the Lamia-Caria Tramline open. How the New Men had known the fleet had left was one of several maddening questions that no one knew the answer to.

"Fletcher fought a stubborn battle," O'Hara said. "But it took the sacrifice of Commander Musgrave to really hurt the enemy. Musgrave blew his antimatter core, using it like a shape-charged grenade."

"We have antimatter engines?"

"Yes, we do. They're new. In any case, Musgrave exploded his as the two fleets merged. The star cruisers were at almost point blank range. The antimatter blast knocked down many enemy shields."

"Interesting," Maddox said. "Yes. I could see how that would work."

"Fletcher pounced on the opportunity. His ships poured fire at the stricken vessels, and seven star cruisers were destroyed."

"Seven..." Maddox said, nodding.

"The enemy annihilated *thirty-eight* of our capital ships," O'Hara said. "They also obliterated dozens of destroyers and twelve troop transports."

"That's a lot of dead space marines."

"It would have been, but Fletcher had turned the transports into decoys."

"I see," Maddox said. "And I find this amazing. Two points, though. One, I still want to rescue Meta. I know how to do it. Two, you said thirty-eight capital ships were destroyed. That still leaves thirty-six."

"Exactly," O'Hara said. "Those thirty-six capital ships are traveling between Caria 323 and the Tannish Systems."

"I'm not sure I understand what that's supposed to mean."

"It means Fletcher took a gamble," O'Hara said. "He raced out-system with the remainder of his fleet. In a few more months, he will reach the Tannish System."

"He's traveling at sub-light speeds?" Maddox asked.

"Yes."

Maddox thought about that. "The New Men will be waiting for him at Tannish. They'll annihilate the rest of the Fifth Fleet."

"Yes."

"Unless someone does something to aid Fletcher's remnants," Maddox said.

The Iron Lady folded her hands on the desktop. "We are, naturally, rushing envoys to the Wahhabi Caliphate, the Spacers and the Windsor League. We are requesting an immediate alliance with the first two, followed by their main fleets, and we are urging the Windsor League to hurry with their promised reinforcements."

Maddox shook his head. "You'll never gather a large enough fleet in that timeframe. Three to four months isn't long enough for our envoys to convince the sheiks and rush the Wahhabi warships to Tannish in time. Unless... I just thought of something."

"Yes?" O'Hara asked.

"The New Men might see Fletcher's situation as an opportunity."

"In what way?"

"To lure more of our warships into a bad tactical situation," Maddox said. "Maybe that's why they allowed Fletcher to escape Caria in the first place."

"You raise an interesting point," O'Hara said. "I would also like to point out that the Lord High Admiral has suggested the same thing."

"There's something else that bothers me," Maddox said. "How do you know any of this? If Fletcher sent a message to ships in the Tannish System, that would have taken several months. Assuming the message traveled at light speed from the Fifth Fleet. Then those Tannish System ships receiving Fletcher's signals would have to use jump routes to rush to Earth. When did the battle happen, and how do you know about it?"

"Do you recall Commander Kris Guderian of the *Osprey*?"

"Of course," Maddox said, "a good Patrol officer. I met her coming in from the Beyond aboard *Victory*."

"After the battle, Guderian used the Caria-Lamia Tramline, slipping through. As you say, she has a Patrol vessel, a frigate with a cloaking device. She slipped past star cruisers waiting in the Lamia System and raced back to Earth."

"No," Maddox said. "I doubt she slipped past the New Men. It makes more sense that the enemy let her through."

"The Lord High Admiral agrees with you," O'Hara said. "The New Men's arrogance may have helped to give us our opportunity. As you've suggested, Lord High Admiral Cook thinks the enemy wants to lure more of our ships out into "C" Quadrant so the New Men can ambush them. Thus, it's quite possible the enemy is hoping we send a rescue fleet to the Tannish System."

"*Are* we sending a rescue fleet?" Maddox asked.

The Iron Lady looked down at her hands. She seemed to deflate, and her age showed. She'd taken some of the Methuselah Treatment in the past. Although she seemed a spry sixty, she was in her nineties.

Maddox turned away, waiting for O'Hara to regain her composure. Soon, he heard the Iron Lady clear her throat, and regarded her once more.

With her head thrust forward and a vital energy radiating from her eyes, O'Hara began to speak. "We cannot afford to lose those thirty-six capital ships. But we face a grave dilemma. We don't dare allow too many more warships to leave the Solar System. If we should lose Earth to a surprise enemy raid—it is doubtful the Commonwealth would recover from such a blow."

"I don't understand that. If we need Fletcher's ships to win the war, we must gather everything and go to Tannish and save them."

"Let us be clear about something, Captain. The New Men are smarter than we are. They can outmaneuver us almost at will. That means we cannot accept normal calculated risks."

"Then we've already lost the war."

"No!" O'Hara said, with her eyes shining. "We have a particular vessel, if you'll recall. It's old, over six thousand years old."

"You mean *Victory*."

"Precisely," O'Hara said. "It is the key to saving the Fifth Fleet."

"Our scientists have had over ten months to go over the ancient vessel," Maddox said. "Doctor Dana Rich is among

115

them. You're suggesting they've discovered something useful?"

"You haven't heard?" O'Hara asked.

"Heard what, ma'am?"

"This isn't a time for games, Captain. What have you heard about *Victory*? It's important I know."

Maddox shrugged. "The ship is in the Oort cloud somewhere, protected by a taskforce. After that, I haven't heard a thing."

"Firstly," O'Hara said, "it's guarded by the Home Fleet, not just a taskforce. *Victory* is the single greatest hope our side has. Without those ancient alien weapons, I believe humanity is doomed."

"Then it's good for us I brought it back from the Beyond."

"No, not yet it isn't." O'Hara frowned, and she seemed to choose her words with care. "There's a security blackout in the Oort cloud over *Victory*. For the last ten months, no one out there has returned to Earth except for the original crew."

"That's one of the reasons we have to find Meta," Maddox said.

O'Hara blinked rapidly, looking confused. "What? Meta. No! Haven't you been listening to anything I've said?"

"The New Men's secret service has her. The most likely reason for that is to discover all they can about *Victory*."

"Pay attention, Captain."

"I know how to recover Meta," Maddox said earnestly. "But we have to move now before it's too late."

O'Hara sighed. "Very well, what's your great insight, Captain?"

Maddox told the Iron Lady about his encounter with the large man and the red-haired woman in the Dempsey Tower lobby yesterday.

"That man is named Mr. Kane," Maddox said. "He's the one who engineered Meta's kidnapping, and he still has her. I also think he's been genetically altered."

"Yes, yes," O'Hara said impatiently.

"Ma'am, the red-haired woman was Susan Love, the fashion model. I knew I'd seen her somewhere before. Find her and she can lead us to Kane. Then we'll free Meta."

It took O'Hara three seconds. "Right," she said. The Iron Lady pressed an intercom button, giving orders for an Intelligence team to pick up Susan Love discreetly.

"There," O'Hara said, as she looked up. "Are you satisfied?"

"For now," Maddox said.

"You're willing to hear how we can save the human race from defeat and possible extinction?"

"I'm at your command, ma'am."

"As I was saying, *Victory* may be our only hope. I don't see the caliphate coming to its senses any time soon. The Spacers are thinking about leaving their part of the Orion Arm."

"That's a serious option for them?" Maddox asked.

"For all your intelligence, Captain, I don't think you comprehend the gravity of the New Men. There have been reports of nuclear bombardments. Not just a warhead or two on military installations, but a saturation attack that ignited the planetary atmosphere, annihilating an entire population."

"Genocide," Maddox whispered.

"Who knows what the New Men have done to other captured populations. We are not sanguine concerning the results. This is possibly a species war, the New Men against the old."

Maddox felt uneasy. If he were part New Man would that automatically make him the enemy? Why did the New Men go to these extreme lengths? What had caused them to attack in the first place? There were no reports of their existence before their attacks started.

"Captain Maddox," O'Hara said, speaking gravely. "Those of us who know the truth about *Victory* have become more astounded by the week at how you managed to bring the ancient super-ship to the Solar System."

"I'm not sure what that's supposed to mean," Maddox said.

"Let me state it plainly. *Victory* is haunted. It's a death ship. The scientists working on it have become frightened. Many refuse to return to it."

"Haunted, ma'am, is that what you just said?"

"This is no joke," O'Hara replied. "It's an interstellar emergency."

"I'm not sure what you mean by calling *Victory* a death ship."

O'Hara shook her head. "It's an alien vessel, the biggest military machine anyone has ever built. According to your report, the aliens built the ship and others like it to face the Swarm."

"That's what the alien AI told me," Maddox said.

"Well, the ancient starship has hidden safeguards that keep surprising the scientists. Some of those surprises have been lethal."

"The AI has been killing scientists?" Maddox asked.

"That's exactly what I mean."

"Have you thought about dismantling *Victory*?" Maddox asked.

"Oh, we've thought about everything, believe me. Doctor Rich has warned us that dismantling the vessel could be dangerous. It might set off hidden explosives."

"Ma'am?"

"If we attempt something like that, *Victory* might self-destruct. That would take its ancient secrets to the grave."

"That would be a disaster for us," Maddox said.

"Precisely."

"What technologies have you managed to uncover so far?"

"Nothing," O'Hara said.

"In ten months you haven't learned a thing?"

"The starship hides its secrets well," O'Hara said.

"Surely, others are developing a neutron beam. Since we know it is possible now, it's simply a matter of uncovering the processes."

"Captain, let me tell you a secret. This is what Doctor Rich has reported. The alien technologies are far in advance of our sciences. It's like cavemen operating a radio. We can turn it on and off and speak to others with another radio. But we have absolutely no idea how to replicate a radio because the technology is so far beyond what we know."

"So what do we know?" Maddox asked.

"In terms of the analogy, how to rub two sticks together and make a fire."

Maddox scrunched his brow. "It sounds as if we're *years* away from duplicating *Victory's* neutron beam."

"Years away from that or any other alien advancement," O'Hara said. "The only thing we've learned is how to perfect our latest tin cans."

"I've never heard of those."

"And now isn't the time to go into it," O'Hara said, "other than to say we learned how to fold space for extremely short hops."

"I take it that has something to do with *Victory's* star drive."

O'Hara sat back in astonishment. "You came to that conclusion with very few clues, Captain. I'm impressed."

Maddox said nothing.

"Very well," O'Hara said. "I'll get to the point. *Victory* is a bust for us, so far. We had hoped to pirate the ship's alien technologies. We aren't going to do that soon enough to defeat the New Men."

"So we're back to square one?"

"Not exactly," O'Hara said. "We have the starship, and it possesses the various systems. You used the neutron beam against the New Men and destroyed a star cruiser. Just as impressively, you fought off three star cruisers for a time. The ancient starship is a marvel."

"But your scientists believe it's haunted."

O'Hara's nostrils flared. "Do you remember that Professor Ludendorff spoke about certain people having the right requirements to board the ship?"

"I read his notes. He did say something about that."

"We understand now what he meant. Doctor Rich agrees with the assessment. It has to do with the starship allowing certain people to survive while aboard. Those without the right requirements, the ship eliminates when it gets the opportunity. It's why your team survived the voyage from the Beyond."

"Interesting," Maddox said.

"No, it's maddening. We need *Victory* now more than ever. It's also clear that under our present circumstances we're not going to get the starship's cooperation."

"You brought me in because you want me to go to the Oort cloud to talk to the AI?"

O'Hara laughed dryly. "If only it were that easy. No, Captain, I want you to return to *Victory* as its commander."

"Excuse me?" Maddox asked.

O'Hara searched his face. "Doctor Rich explained it best. Our scientists have been unable to unravel the starship's secrets. It does not appear they will do so any time soon. Instead, we need a genius, someone who can make intuitive leaps of logic. Obviously, Professor Ludendorff is that man. We would never have acquired the super-ship without his notes, without his instructions."

"So ask Ludendorff what do to," Maddox said. "Dragoon him into the project."

"Precisely," O'Hara said. "That will be your task, Captain. You are to find Professor Ludendorff."

"I thought you said you wanted me to command *Victory*."

"The two tasks are not exclusive of each other," the Iron Lady said.

"Perhaps you'd better explain that."

"It's very simple," O'Hara said. "Star Watch, the Commonwealth, maybe humanity as a whole, needs Admiral Fletcher's thirty-six capital ships. We dare not take our Home Fleet out to save them. Instead, we need a commando ship to do that."

"*Victory*?" Maddox asked.

"Yes," O'Hara said. "But the alien super-ship cannot defeat the New Men unless some of its greater technologies are in operative condition. We've cleaned up and patched *Victory* as best we can. Now, we need Professor Ludendorff to figure out the rest."

"Wait a minute," Maddox said. "Are you suggesting I'm supposed to be in the Tannish System within the next few months, to help Fletcher defeat the enemy invasion fleet?"

"Exactly," O'Hara said, "except you have less than three months to do it in."

"But before I head to Tannish," Maddox said, "I'm supposed to pick up Ludendorff. Then, he's supposed to figure out how to use the destabilizer, for instance."

"Yes."

"Who will be my crew?" Maddox asked.

"The same people who went with you out into the Beyond, plus some space marines and specialists who have similar mental faculties."

"Where is Professor Ludendorff?"

"Ah, that's the rub, Captain. He is on Wolf Prime."

"Where is that?" Maddox asked.

"Behind enemy lines, I'm afraid."

"Do you mean Wolf Prime is on the rim of "C" Quadrant?"

"I do," O'Hara said.

"Why is Ludendorff way out there? Doesn't he know there's a war on?"

"I don't know what he knows about the war," O'Hara said. "We've discovered he went to Wolf Prime to study alien artifacts."

"*More* alien artifacts?" Maddox asked.

"Not as you're thinking," O'Hara said. "In any case, *Victory's* star drive should allow you to sneak through enemy occupied systems."

"I'm supposed to do this with a crippled starship?"

"Captain, this is a difficult assignment. I realize that. This is an emergency, however. The Lord High Admiral and his Strategy Council doesn't see any other way of rescuing Fletcher's capital ships. Without those, it's doubtful we'll win this war."

Maddox stared at her. "You're not telling me everything."

"Even if true, there would be a reason for that. But that's not important right now. Do you accept the assignment?"

Maddox was surprised. "Yes, of course I do."

The Iron Lady tried to hide her relief, but it was visible just the same.

"Why shouldn't I accept?" Maddox asked.

"Well..." O'Hara looked away. "The scientists turned on the alien AI once too often. It had been waiting for the right moment. It took over. Well, it took over most of the ship's systems. There has, in fact, been a standoff in the Oort cloud for the past month. The Home Fleet is facing off the alien starship. We don't want to destroy it, because we need the ancient ship. You have to try for Ludendorff. But captain, if it looks as if the New Men are going to capture the starship…"

"I understand, ma'am."

"Good. Is there anything else you need?"

"Meta."

"Yes," O'Hara said. "She was part of the original crew, wasn't she? Before you leave the Solar System, Meta will join you. I'll see to that."

O'Hara stood and came around the desk. She held out her hand. "This is goodbye, Captain. You will leave my office and head straight into space. You will travel aboard a fast experimental ship to reach the Oort cloud in a few days. Godspeed, Captain. Find Professor Ludendorff, and bring us back Fletcher and his fleet."

"I'll do my best, ma'am. You can count on that."

They shook hands. Then Captain Maddox turned around and headed for the door.

-12-

Captain Valerie Noonan stood in a viewing bay of SWS Battleship *Gettysburg*. She stared into the void of the Oort cloud.

She was far from Earth, a little over two thousand AUs. Pluto was presently thirty-five AUs out from Earth, a mere step away from the home planet compared to this distance. The crazy thing was that this was the *inner* Oort cloud, what some called the Hills cloud. One could travel outward for months from here and still be in the Oort cloud.

Out here, the Sun looked like just another star, if brighter than most. Because the Solar System's planets were so far away, so were the various Laumer-Points leading to nearby systems. That would give the Home Fleet time to deploy if the New Men came for the alien starship. The unique vessel was a little over one hundred thousand kilometers from *Gettysburg*. The Home Fleet was giving *Victory* some space. No one wanted the alien AI running the starship to panic and start attacking.

Valerie shook her head.

The fools should have never turned the AI on and off all those times. Doctor Rich had been instrumental in the decision. The first time Valerie heard about the idea, she'd warned the Lord High Admiral against it. She believed the alien artificial intelligence had always been plotting. None of the others had seen the way the tiny holoimage used to watch Captain

Maddox when he wasn't looking on the journey home from the Beyond.

Victory had not only gotten smart again, but belligerent. Now it was caged by the Home Fleet with only the illusion of freedom.

First, the New Men struck. Now, the AI threatens our last big fleet. Star Watch is in real trouble.

Valerie sighed.

She felt herself to be more mature than the young lieutenant who had left well over a year ago with Maddox into the Beyond to find the alien starship. During the last ten months, Valerie had sat with the Lord High Admiral on his Strategy Council. The first few times had been daunting. She'd kept quiet as a mouse, as people said. The Lord High Admiral had finally begun asking her pointed questions in front of the others. Cook had forced her to give her opinions. The surprising thing—no, the *amazing* thing—was that the old ones on the council had listened to her words. It turned out that she was the expert concerning the New Men, as she'd actually dealt with them in the Beyond.

How can this crazy situation have happened?

Her focus switched from the stars to the clear plastic of the viewing port in front of her. Faintly, she saw her reflection in it.

Valerie was medium-sized, with long brunette hair and a face her friends had told her was beautiful. She played handball all the time, and won almost every match. She was inordinately proud of her captain's uniform, with the hat presently tucked under her left arm. It hadn't been all that long ago that she'd graduated from the Space Academy on Earth. Who would have thought the welfare kid from Greater Detroit would have ended up on the Strategy Council giving the leaders of Star Watch advice? It was incredible.

That's what hard work and determination brought, with maybe a little luck added in. Captain Maddox didn't believe in following the rules. But Valerie most certainly did. Without rules, people became animals like the gang members in the slums. Of course, the gangs had also been dangerous because of their savage rules, but that was different, wasn't it?

Valerie lived by a strict and honorable code taught by her father. The regimen at the Space Academy had been easy for her. Getting along with the rich kids who made up most of the cadets had been something else.

Yet I'm the one who made it onto the Strategy Council. I'm the one the Lord High Admiral speaks with when he wants to know the mind of the New Men. Have any of my peers accomplished that?

Valerie knew they hadn't. Was she proud of what she had done? Oh, yes, she was proud. Two months ago, she had run into Sally Fredrick from Richmond, Virginia. Sally had been a cadet with her in the Space Academy, one who had led others in asking mocking questions about Detroit. Sally had driven home in a sleek Cougar air-car at Christmas and Easter Breaks. She had given other rich-kid cadets rides home in her air-car. Valerie had stayed at the Space Academy over the vacations. There hadn't been anything in Detroit for her to visit.

Two months ago, out here in the Oort cloud, Valerie had run into Sally Fredrick, a comm cadet aboard the SWS Destroyer *Bombay*. Sally had been in the *Gettysburg's* cafeteria. The former Richmond socialite had been her commander's go-fer, carrying several briefcases and looking more than a little harried doing it.

Valerie had known she shouldn't do it, but she'd walked up behind Sally and said, "Hello, Cadet."

Sally had turned around in surprise. "Detroit," she'd said, smiling, holding out a hand.

The word had stung. Valerie understood it hadn't been meant as an insult, but she'd taken it that way anyway. In their Space Academy days, Sally *had* meant it as mockery.

Ignoring the hand, Valerie had nodded, making a point of staring at the cadet patch on Sally's uniform. Then, Valerie had brushed her captain's shoulder board. "Good to see you again, *Richmond*." Afterward, Valerie had walked away.

Valerie might have felt a greater sense of victory if she hadn't seen the Lord High Admiral frowning in her direction. How had the old man happened to see that?

Valerie was a captain, which was good. But she had become a staff officer, which was bad. She wanted a line

125

command, her own ship. Would the Lord High Admiral help her get her own ship if he thought she lacked the social graces? Star Watch wanted balanced commanders out in space.

I should have shaken Sally's hand instead of being so bitter over past wrongs.

Valerie knew she didn't wish she'd shaken hands for her own good, to be good, but because it might have poisoned the Lord High Admiral just a little bit against her not to have done so.

Captain Noonan frowned as she stared into the void. The Commonwealth was under assault. Star Watch was in terrible jeopardy. Now, the Lord High Admiral and his Strategy Council had come up with a harebrained scheme to try to save the Fifth Fleet heading to the Tannish System.

Valerie had no faith in the mission. A bitter, alien AI, ancient tech, a crazy professor poking around a frigid planet because of extraterrestrial cave etchings and a self-indulgent Intelligence officer were supposed to save the day. No. Valerie didn't think so.

Instead, Star Watch should gather all the warships it could, wait for the Windsor League main fleet and then go out and do battle with the enemy. Valerie knew the enemy's star cruisers were good. She'd been there when the New Men had destroyed Admiral von Gunther's battle group. She—

"Captain," a man said from behind.

Valerie hadn't seen or heard the sergeant walk up. She turned with a start, her hand reflexively dropping to where she used to keep a hidden knife to defend herself back in Detroit. Fists, knives, even guns, it didn't matter. Valerie Noonan didn't back down to anyone.

"I'm sorry if I startled you, Captain," the sergeant said.

Valerie scowled, shaking her head. "You did nothing of the kind."

"Oh," the sergeant said, at a momentary loss. "Well, if you'll come this way, sir, the Lord High Admiral is ready to see you."

Valerie followed the sergeant to the hatch, down several corridors and through a main thoroughfare. The *Gettysburg* was huge. The alien starship dwarfed the battleship, however.

The sergeant hurried to another hatch, opening it for Valerie.

"Captain Noonan to see you, sir," the sergeant said in a loud voice.

Valerie ducked her head as she entered the Lord High Admiral's private study. Behind her, the sergeant closed the hatch.

"Captain," Cook said, looking up. "Come, sit down and share a glass of brandy with me."

Lord High Admiral Cook wore a white uniform. He was large and red-faced, with a thick wave of white hair and a seamed face.

The office contained computer equipment, screens and holo-imagers. Cook sat behind a desk, using his thick fingers to tap a pad. Above the pad rotated a holoimage of an enemy star cruiser.

Valerie sat before the desk.

Abruptly, Cook pushed the pad and holoimage aside. He picked up a decanter and poured brandy into two snifters.

"Please," he said.

Valerie leaned forward, taking her glass.

The Lord High Admiral leaned back in his chair, swirling the brandy, sniffing it appreciatively. Then, he took a sip. The old man watched her and finally raised an eyebrow.

"Oh," Valerie said. She swirled her snifter and made ready to sip.

"I forgot," Cook said in his heavy voice. "You don't drink."

"Not usually, sir, no."

"But you were about to take a sip anyway?"

"I was, sir. Is that bad?" she added.

"I don't know," Cook said. "Maybe."

Valerie blushed.

"No, no, that won't do, Captain. You shouldn't be embarrassed. I don't need toadies and lickspittles. I want officers who can follow orders and stand by their principles, telling me facts straight from the heart."

"Yes, sir," Valerie said.

"That means even if you disagree with me about this mission, and have told me so to my face, and yet still I order you to go, that you should hold to your convictions."

"I'll remember that, sir."

"I want you aboard the *Victory* for several reasons. I trust you, Captain. You are regulation Star Watch to the core. I like that. You also speak your mind. Well, most of the time, you do. You were there from the beginning with the alien starship. You also have a powerful desire to win no matter what the odds. Humanity is going to need that. I also think that Captain Maddox is going to need your help."

"Sir?" Valerie asked.

"I doubt Maddox realizes the need yet. Space marines are joining the expedition and other carefully selected Star Watch technicians. Maddox is an Intelligence officer, a good one. No, he's a maverick. He gets results, though. That doesn't mean he knows how to truly run a starship. You have to help him—even if you don't like him."

Cook stared at her.

After a moment, Valerie fidgeted in her chair.

"Do I make myself clear?" the old man asked.

"Yes, sir," Valerie said. "Even though Maddox uses high-handed methods and ignores the regulations most of the time, you want me to make sure the space marines obey his orders."

"I want everyone to follow Maddox's orders."

"What if his orders are wrong, sir?" Valerie asked. "What if Maddox does something so outlandish it jeopardizes the mission?"

Lord High Admiral Cook swirled his brandy again then *clunked* the glass onto the desk without sipping. He opened a drawer and took out a sealed envelope. With his big fingers, the old man slid it across the desk.

"You will open this only as a last resort," Cook said. "In your opinion, Captain Maddox will have gone over the edge."

Valerie was shocked. "Do you anticipate him doing so, sir?"

"That is an interesting question," Cook said. "I have found to my surprise and delight that you often ask those kinds of questions. On this mission, you are my hole card, Captain. I

128

don't want to have to use my hole card. But if Maddox goes too far—and this is a matter of judgment—then you had better damn well unseal the envelope and read the orders in it."

"These orders will elevate me to command of the starship?"

Cook stared her in the eyes. "Yes," he said.

A powerful emotion surged through Valerie. It warmed her and made her smile. "I won't let you down, sir."

"I want you to listen to me, Valerie."

She leaned toward him.

"Maddox is cunning. I trust him to do incredible deeds. Yet sometimes, such a man oversteps his bounds. I think you will know when that moment is if you keep in mind that victory over the New Men trumps everything else."

"Meaning what, sir?"

"That if Maddox's unorthodox behavior will bring us victory, you must let him proceed as he plans. I realize you do not have faith in this venture. I understand your reasons. This is a long shot. I'm afraid the latest setback in Caria 323 puts us in this spot. The Wahhabi sheiks simply can't see reason. The Spacers are terrified of losing their home ships, and the Windsor League has divided leadership on the correct course of action. This is a mad gamble, and Captain Maddox is the right man to undertake it."

"Are you warning me against unsealing these orders?" Valerie asked.

"No," Cook said. "I'm telling you something that might be the most difficult thing in your life. You must use good judgment."

Valerie found herself blushing for a second time. "You think I lack that, sir?"

"You hold grudges, Captain. I think we both know that."

"Yes, sir, I suppose I do."

"Don't let a grudge stand in the way. Use your best judgment. I'm not giving you these sealed orders lightly. It might be the worst decision I've ever made. I can only bring myself to do this because I've learned to trust you."

"You don't trust Captain Maddox, sir?"

Cook hesitated before saying, "I do, to a point."

"Is there something you're not telling me, sir?"

The Lord High Admiral stared at her. It seemed as if he wanted to say something. Finally, the old man shook his head.

Valerie felt as if something vitally important had just been left unsaid. She wondered what it could be.

"Listen to me, Captain. You must win. You must find Professor Ludendorff and rescue the Fifth Fleet. We're on the edge of a dark abyss. I think the Commonwealth is like a man swinging his arms, his feet balanced there on the edge as he sways back and forth. A wrong gust of wind will pitch us down into the abyss. There will be no climbing out of that hole.

"I pray the Lord has mercy on my soul if I've given you sealed orders that cause us to lose." Cook's gaze became stern. "Captain, is my faith in you sound? Tell me now if I'm wrong."

Valerie stared at the old man. It finally dawned on her the incredible pressure he was setting on her shoulders.

I'm the kid from the slums. The New Men are the gangs trying to stop me from achieving my dream. Dad taught me to fight through no matter what.

"No, Lord High Admiral, you have chosen correctly. I will serve Star Watch with all my heart, soul and mind, so help me God."

Cook nodded, saying, "For all our sakes, I hope you're right." The old admiral stood, and he saluted Captain Noonan.

Valerie stood and saluted back.

"Dismissed," Cook said.

Without another word, Valerie left the study.

130

-13-

Lord High Admiral Cook stared at the hatch after Noonan had left. He poured himself a greater amount of brandy, but let it sit on the desk.

The sealed orders were wrong. He felt that in his gut. The trouble was Captain Maddox. The man might be half New Man. O'Hara gave that a high probability. No one knew for certain, though. That was the problem.

The Iron Lady believed in Captain Maddox. She would have disagreed with the sealed orders. She trusted Maddox. The Lord High Admiral did too—up to a point, as he'd told Valerie.

He's not totally one of us. He might be one of them. *Can we trust him entirely?*

Without Maddox, Star Watch would have never acquired the alien starship. Yet, the starship hadn't given them any new technologies. Might the New Men have known that?

The enemy was too smart for ordinary mortals. The New Men's plans were wheels within wheels. Just when Star Watch thought they had finally tricked the New Men, it turned out to be to the enemy's advantage after all.

The truth is we need someone like Maddox who can match the enemy. Valerie Noonan has heart, she loves Earth and she's one hundred percent loyal, but she's a frail reed for humanity's hopes to rely on.

Cook picked up the snifter, sitting like that for some time. Noonan was a possible failsafe. The Lord High Admiral had put another one onboard the alien starship. Well, if the team could even get aboard the bloody vessel.

Who are the New Men? Why do they hate us so desperately? Can we defend ourselves against a superior species?

There were too many questions and so few answers.

Mechanically, Cook drank the brandy as if it was water. It felt warm going down.

I just hope I haven't made a terrible mistake. I want to trust Maddox, but he might be one of them. Yet, I don't know who else can do this. Who else will have the slightest chance of success?

Cook rose from his desk, putting his hands behind his back. Maybe it was time to pray. Humanity had only this slender opportunity, the barest of threads.

If Star Watch didn't turn things around soon, it was going to be too late.

Cook resumed his place behind the desk. He should give the team every chance for success he could. Yes, he would send them several tin cans. The best pilot in the program had belonged to the original team. If humanity was rolling the dice of Fate, he should give Maddox every chance possible.

Wearily, Cook turned on his intercom, giving the needed orders to see it done.

-14-

Captain Maddox shot through the Solar System aboard the X72 Peregrine, an experimental, high-speed racer. The vessel passed Pluto before O'Hara spoke to him again concerning Meta. Thirty-four AUs away meant time delays made it impossible to hold a two-way conversation. A light-speed message took many hours to travel that far.

A screen rose into position in front of where Maddox lay on his acceleration couch. A few seconds later, O'Hara came on. The Iron Lady sat behind her desk in Geneva. She looked worried.

"I'm sorry, Captain. We pulled in Susan Love as you suggested. She knew Kane, had dated him several times, in fact. He owns the Los Angeles Wolverines, America's best fist-ball team. You were right about the ring. They won the championship several years ago. Kane appears to have vanished, however. His organization says he has little day-to-day contact with them. Mainly, he comes in during the playoff season. Otherwise, he lets the vice president run affairs.

"Naturally, I spoke with Signor Strand of Nerva Incorporated," O'Hara continued. "He tells me Jacques and Cabot are both dead. They were part of the team who kidnapped Meta, as you know. I've asked for a face-to-face meeting with Octavian Nerva. I've used every ounce of pressure I can. He still isn't accepting my calls. Yes, I know what you're thinking; this is an interstellar emergency. Yet, as I've said before, Octavian has powerful friends in the government and in the military. Despite our stakes against the New Men, he is immune to my efforts so far."

O'Hara shifted uncomfortably on her chair. "Meta has vanished. I've begun to wonder if she's off-planet by now."

On the acceleration couch, Maddox looked away. He should have refused the assignment. He could have found Meta. O'Hara was good, but Maddox knew he was better.

"I don't know if Kane has a connection with the Chabot Consortium," O'Hara said. "I will continue to search. It seems clear he was able to use Octavian's security apparatus. It is a mystery how he was able to achieve that. Nerva Security is among the best."

O'Hara nodded as if she'd convinced herself of something. "You must concentrate on your mission, Captain. Meta is a terrible loss. Maybe...I don't know what to say to you."

"That you lost her will do," Maddox said quietly to himself.

"I'm sorry. Good luck with the mission. And Captain..." O'Hara seemed pained.

Something about that alerted him.

"Captain, this is a private message. It will self-destruct after you've listened to it. I've ensured that much, and there were complaints about that, believe me. Maybe I should have told you while you were in my office."

What is this about?

"Your origins are shrouded in mystery," O'Hara said. "You wonder about yourself, and others wonder as well. Some of those are in high places, Captain. You must strive to put them at ease."

Maddox's features became blank.

"There are those who worry you might have...have elements in your makeup similar to the enemy."

Why can't she come right out and say it?

"I know you're true to Earth," O'Hara said. "I trust you. Some don't, and they are nervous about you, now more than ever. Be careful, Captain. Watch your back and choose your companions carefully. This is a terrible pressure to add, I know. But I felt compelled to warn you."

O'Hara stared out of the screen earnestly. "I've watched you grow up. You're like... You're important to me. I hope you know that."

Maddox felt a lump in his throat. That troubled him.

"You belong to Star Watch Intelligence," O'Hara said, "and you are the very best agent I have. Beat the New Men. Win through every obstacle. We're all counting on you."

O'Hara fidgeted. "*I'm* counting on you, my boy. That is all. Good bye."

The screen went blank, and then the Star Watch logo appeared. Afterward, the screen shut off, and an arm moved it out of the way.

Meta was gone. He had left Earth, maybe forever, and not everyone on his side trusted him.

Maddox wanted to shrug it off, but the knowledge was too painful. Meta...he shook his head.

In that moment, Captain Maddox turned away from Earth, as it were, and faced the stars. His destiny and that of humanity lay out there. First, he had to learn everything he could about what had been happening in the Oort cloud with *Victory*. He'd worry about the rest when the time came.

***

Fortunately, *Victory* and the Home Fleet were in the inner Oort cloud. A journey to the outer region would have taken weeks even in the X72 Peregrine. Humanity didn't have those extra weeks to spare.

Like the rest of the racer's crew, Maddox was confined to his acceleration couch for ninety-nine percent of the journey. The vessel had fantastic gravity dampeners, but the extent of thrust was too great for the dampeners to overcome everything. In many ways, the Peregrine was more like a heavy-accelerating missile than a regular spaceship.

For over ten hours now, Maddox and the others had endured massive G forces as they braked hard. It was physically and emotionally draining.

Finally, the grueling deceleration stopped. It felt as if several elephants climbed off Maddox's chest and groin. He could breathe normally again. He lay that way for two entire minutes before gingerly unbuckling himself. Slowly, he sat up and began to stretch. His muscles were sore and his tendons felt stiff. After a half-hour loosening regimen, he began some strenuous calisthenics. He showered afterward, ate a light meal and talked to Sergeant Riker in the man's room.

Riker sat on the edge of his acceleration couch, rubbing his good thigh.

"I hope we're done with that for good," the sergeant complained. "It puts too much strain on my mechanical-human joints."

"You have an hour to get ready," Maddox said, "maybe less."

"Ready for what, sir?" Riker asked.

"We'll be boarding a shuttle. Doctor Rich and Lieutenant Noonan will be on it. We'll be heading out to *Victory*."

"We're going out that soon, sir? I thought you would talk to the experts; maybe see the Lord High Admiral."

"Doctor Rich is the expert. I don't have time to chitchat with the Lord High Admiral."

Riker nodded moodily as he started rubbing the shoulder of his bionic arm. "I'm still not sure why I'm along for this, sir."

"Moral support," Maddox said. *O'Hara knew I'd need people I could trust.* "Also, you were part of the original crew. It seems people of our type are difficult to come by."

Riker grumbled as he stood, testing his leg muscles.

Time passed as the sergeant prepared. Maddox went to his room, waited for a time, checked his chronometer, slung a duffel-bag strap over his shoulder and walked into the corridor. Riker moved toward him. The sergeant carried two heavy bags of his personal belongings for the trip.

There were *clangs* outside the racer. A shuttle docked with the X72 Peregrine. Maddox shook hands with the captain and XO. Then, Riker and he moved through a hatch into the boarding tube, crossing toward the shuttle.

"Never did like this weightlessness," Riker complained.

Maddox felt otherwise. He was a natural, pulling himself along the float rails on the sides. Soon, he turned a wheel, opened a hatch and boarded the shuttle.

Gravity returned.

Once out of the airlock, Doctor Dana Rich was there to greet them. She wore a black spylo jacket, with her dark hair pulled back into a ponytail. She was older than Maddox and beautiful by any standard, with her brown skin and dark eyes. Although born on Earth in Bombay, she had emigrated to the Brahma System long ago.

The doctor had a checkered history involved with the Brahman secret service against the Rigel Social Syndicate. Dana Rich had been a clone thief, caught by Star Watch and sent down to Loki Prime, the worst of the prison planets. Maddox had rescued her from Loki Prime because he'd needed her services. For what she had done to bring back *Victory*, Star Watch and Commonwealth authorities had cleared her of all crimes.

Many years ago, the doctor had worked with Professor Ludendorff. Dana had known more about the lost starship, how to reach and board it, than anyone else Star Watch had been able to find back then.

According to Maddox's latest brief, Doctor Rich had learned more about *Victory* these past ten months than anyone else. It made her the premier expert concerning the ancient starship.

"Captain Maddox," Dana said, with a faint smile on her face. "We meet again."

"Yes," Maddox said.

They shook hands.

"You look the same as ever," she said.

"I return the compliment," Maddox said, although he spied some care lines in her forehead he didn't recall. Clearly, she had been under stress for quite some time.

Dana looked past him at Riker, shaking the sergeant's hand. The doctor seemed expectant afterward, turning back to Maddox. "Why don't I see Meta?"

"Didn't they tell you?" Maddox asked.

"They tell us very little, I'm afraid. Star Watch has become paranoid concerning us."

"A man named Kane captured Meta and disappeared," Maddox said.

"This is bad news," Dana said. "We need Meta. She had a knack for knowing how to fix *Victory*. The others I've had to work with…" the doctor shook her head more vigorously.

"Start filling me in," Maddox said. "I take it we're headed straight for *Victory*."

"Let's go to the control room," Dana said. They started down the corridor, with Riker trailing them. "Now tell me. What do you know so far? What have the authorities told you?"

Maddox told the doctor everything he knew about *Victory*, finishing his short speech in the flight chamber.

A tough-looking man in a space marine work uniform sat in the pilot's chair. He was shorter than Maddox, with thicker shoulders. The flat-faced man had a bull neck and a brush cut.

"This is Major Kharkov," Dana said. "He's the leader of the space marines who will be boarding *Victory* with us."

"Commander," Kharkov said. The space marine stood, faced Maddox and held out his right hand.

"It's *Captain* Maddox," he said, "not commander."

They shook. It surprised Maddox the major didn't try to squeeze his hand hard in order to show him how strong he was.

"I know it's captain, sir," Kharkov said. "I also know you're in charge of the expedition. Formally, major trumps captain. So, if you don't mind, sir, I'll just call you 'commander' for the remainder of the mission, as you're running the show."

"If it makes you feel better, go ahead," Maddox said.

Major Kharkov nodded.

"Are there any more space marines aboard the shuttle?" Maddox asked Dana.

"Not yet," Dana said. "The major asked to join us for the initial run. I didn't agree, but the Lord High Admiral overrode my objection."

"I'm here to see that none of you gets hurt," Kharkov said. "You're the key to defeating these genetic bastards."

Maddox noticed the last sentence had been spoken with considerable heat. "That bothers you?" he asked the major.

"Sir?" Kharkov asked.

138

"The fact the New Men are genetically superior to us," Maddox said.

Kharkov scowled. "I don't know how superior they really are, but I know they certainly think so."

"The evidence appears to show the New Men *are* superior," Maddox said.

"Yes, sir," Kharkov said, and a chilliness entered his voice.

"I've faced them before," Maddox said. "It wasn't fun. Yet, I learned we could beat them. In the end, that's the important point, isn't it, Major?"

"Yes, sir, I'd agree with that. Now, there's some equipment I want to check, if you'll excuse me, sir?"

"By all means," Maddox said.

The stocky major exited the chamber.

"Don't mind him," Dana said.

"Why should I?" Maddox asked.

"It's clear the space marine has an inferiority complex," Dana said. "He wouldn't like Meta, I think. She's genetically superior to him."

Maddox said nothing to that.

"I wondered how the space marine would feel about you specifically, Captain," Dana said, eyeing him sidelong.

On the trip into the Beyond, Maddox had told Dana about his suspicions concerning his origins. Now he wondered if that had been a mistake.

"Is Lieutenant Noonan aboard yet?" Maddox asked, changing the subject.

Dana laughed, shaking her head.

"Did I say something amusing?"

"You did," Valerie Noonan said, stepping through the hatch.

Maddox turned, and he recognized Valerie wore captain's boards immediately. "Congratulations," he said.

"It looks like we're the same rank now," Valerie said.

"So it would appear," Maddox said. "Ah. I'll tell you what. You can call me *Commander* Maddox, just as Major Kharkov intends to do during the voyage."

Valerie frowned. "But you're not a commander."

"No, but I am in charge of the mission."

139

Valerie hesitated before nodding. "Yes, you are," she said.

Before anyone could say more, a klaxon blared.

Maddox, Dana, Valerie and Riker turned. A light on the piloting board flashed red. Maddox started for the chair.

"No," Valerie said. "That's my task." She rushed past him and plopped into the seat. With a tap of a finger, she turned off the klaxon.

"What's wrong?" Dana asked.

Valerie studied the panel before jerking up sharply. "It's the *Gettysburg* warning us."

"Yes?" Dana asked.

"*Victory* is headed our way," Valerie said, looking up. "Worse, the neutron cannon is charging. It appears we've triggered something aboard the starship. I think the alien vessel is coming to destroy us."

-15-

The situation gave Captain Maddox a strong sense of deja vu, reminding him of the months he'd been in command first of the SWS Scout *Geronimo* and later Starship *Victory*.

Maddox didn't have formal naval training. He was an Intelligence officer. Yet, he was fast on his feet, both physically and mentally. The role he'd assumed over a year ago began flooding back to him.

"The Lord High Admiral is ordering us to fall back," Valerie said. "The Home Fleet is moving up. It looks as if they plan to interpose themselves between *Victory* and us."

"Put Cook on the screen," Maddox said.

Valerie turned toward him.

"Lieutenant," Maddox said. "That seemed clear enough. I wish to speak to the Lord High Admiral."

"I'm a captain," Valerie corrected.

"Yes, of course," Maddox said. He waited several seconds. "I don't see the Lord High Admiral up on the screen yet?"

It seemed as if Valerie was going to say more. Then she turned back to her panel. "Just a minute...*sir*."

Dana sat down at navigation. Riker also took a seat, buckling in.

"There," Valerie said, tapping her panel.

White-haired Lord High Admiral Cook gazed at Maddox from the screen.

"Admiral," Maddox said, "I request the Home Fleet move back."

141

His old, shrewd eyes studied the captain. The admiral took in the rest of the crew. "Are you aware the starship has reverted to its original personality?" Cook asked.

"I am, sir," Maddox said.

"In its alien star system—"

"Lord High Admiral, we're wasting time. If I'm going to save Fletcher and bring home his ships, you're going to have to let me do my job."

Valerie sucked in her breath. "You can't talk to the admiral like that," she whispered.

"Sir," Maddox said, without acknowledging Valerie. "I have another request before you go."

"What is that, Captain?" Cook asked.

"A starship cannot have two captains," Maddox said. "I request that Valerie Noonan take the rank of lieutenant for the duration of the mission."

The Lord High Admiral glanced at Valerie. "She rightfully belongs on the Strategy Council. She's earned her rank."

"Respectfully, sir," Maddox said, "that's not the issue here. On my ship, there will be only one captain. I will be that person. Otherwise, you need someone else for the mission, sir."

"You're a cheeky bastard," Cook said.

"It has been said, sir."

"I'm beginning to see why Admiral Fletcher has had trouble with you in the past."

"Lord High Admiral," someone said aboard the *Gettysburg* behind Cook. "The alien starship..." The rest of the words were garbled.

"We can speak about this later," Cook told Maddox.

"Now, sir, if you don't mind. Then, please pull back while I board my approaching starship."

Cook's features became stern. "While I appreciate all you've done for Star Watch in the past—"

"Sir," Maddox said. "You chose me to achieve the impossible for Earth because of who I am. Therefore, you shouldn't complain about my methods, especially as it's those methods you're relying on."

It took Cook two seconds. "Right," he said. "That is an excellent point. I will remember that. Now, you believe the Home Fleet should pull back?"

"We're not going to win our way aboard *Victory* through force. We certainly don't want a fight between it and Star Watch. It's time for smooth talking."

"I hope you're more diplomatic with the alien starship than you have been with me," Cook said. "However, I will do as you request. Ms. Noonan, as of this moment, you are a lieutenant again."

"Yes, sir," Valerie said, sounding crestfallen.

"After the mission, you will be reinstated as a captain," Cook said.

"Thank you, sir," she said.

"As for you, Captain Maddox, I'm issuing the orders you've requested. The *Gettysburg* as well as the rest of the Home Fleet will give you room. Good luck, Captain. The Star Watch is counting on you."

"Thank you, sir. Captain Maddox out," he motioned to Valerie.

It took the newly demoted lieutenant several seconds to understand Maddox wanted her to cut the connection. Before she could, Cook's people took the Lord High Admiral off the main screen.

"I hope you know what you're doing," Dana told Maddox.

Maddox chose to ignore the comment. "Start explaining, Doctor. Tell me everything I should know about *Victory*. I don't think we have much time before the starship arrives."

***

Doctor Rich told Maddox very little he didn't already know. The alien AI was paranoid. It didn't like being here. It wanted to return to its star system where it felt at home.

The departing Home Fleet appeared as points of light: ship exhausts burning in the darkness, appearing little brighter than the nearby stars.

Another shape formed in the distance.

"There." Valerie pointed at the main screen. "Can you see it?"

Maddox didn't know what to look for, so he shook his head. "Give me greater magnification."

Valerie tapped her panel.

The star field wavered. A moment later, a dark object grew in size. The screen wavered again, and the object grew even larger so Maddox could make it out.

It was Starship *Victory*. The ancient alien vessel had two main massive sections, oval areas each bigger than the *Gettysburg*. All the damage the starship had sustained over the lonely centuries, and during Maddox's time as its commander, had vanished. The Star Watch teams had repaired the alien vessel as best they could. It had a new armored hull of collapsium, the strongest and most expensive substance humanity owned. The starship still possessed weapons ports that hadn't worked for over six thousand years. It also had the very workable neutron cannon and a vastly superior set of deflector shields, at least as compared to Star Watch vessels.

Bright exhaust plumes extended outward from *Victory*.

"The ship is braking," Valerie said.

Maddox heard the difference in her tone. Before, she had been semi-belligerent. After the Lord High Admiral demoted her back to lieutenant, she finally seemed willing to obey his orders. That meant he'd made the right decision about her.

Maddox turned to Dana. "How far back has the AI reverted?"

"I'm sorry," the doctor said. "Revert is the wrong word. *Victory* is homesick. The AI appears to be more knowledgeable than before. There's...ah...something else I should tell you."

"Yes?" Maddox asked.

"The AI believes you tricked it. The computer wants revenge."

"Against humanity?" Maddox asked.

"No, against you," Dana said. "It's been seeking you for a month now. Actually, that's where the trouble started, when the AI accessed a memory of your time together."

"Why would anyone have kept that a secret from us?" Riker asked. "It seems as if that's the first thing someone should have told us. This AI, sir, it appears to know you too well."

"Indeed," Dana said. She turned to her panel, picking up a receiver and clipping it to her ear. "The AI is hailing us, Captain."

"Put him on," Maddox said.

"I must caution you, Captain," Dana said. "Don't let the AI know it's you at first."

"It can surely run a voice analyzer," Maddox said.

"We can use a scrambler," Dana said.

"No," Maddox said. "Patch me through."

"This is an alien intelligence," Dana said. "It's not the same as human-built AIs."

"Doctor, do you remember who I am?"

"Of course," Dana said. "I haven't forgotten a word you told me during our voyage, good or bad."

"Then you should realize I remember the AI. This is my area of expertise."

"No," Dana said. "You won through once before when the AI was innocent of humans and a dotard due to extreme age. The AI is running at greater efficiency than it has for thousands of years."

"Then why can't it remember how to use some of its better weapons?" Maddox asked.

"Yes," Dana said. "That's an excellent question. I don't know the answer to that."

Maddox raised his eyebrows.

"This is a rash idea," Dana said. "But very well, I'm putting the AI on speaker."

"This is Starship *Victory*," the AI said, sounding mechanical. "I am hailing the *Argonaut*-class Shuttle A-105. I do not detect any damage or malfunctions to your ship systems. You must answer me, A-105, or I shall begin a destruct sequence."

"We hear you quite well," Maddox said.

There was a moment's pause. Then the AI said, "Captain Maddox? My voice analyzer tells me I am speaking to you."

"Yes, you are," Maddox said. "It is good to greet you again."

Silence filled the speakers.

145

Maddox glanced at Dana before he said, "It is imperative that we board you immediately."

"My sensors indicate this is real," the AI said. "You are physically aboard Shuttle A-105. You have come out into what your kind refers to as the Oort cloud."

"That's right," Maddox said. "I've come to talk to you."

"Yes," the AI said. "You may approach. I will instruct you which landing bay to enter."

"This is too easy," Dana whispered. "The AI has refused all landing passes for the last month."

Maddox spread his hands.

"*Victory*," Dana said.

Maddox shook his head.

"Yes?" the AI asked.

Dana closed her mouth, watching the captain.

"It's nothing," Maddox said. "One of my crewmembers wanted to talk to you, but she changed her mind."

"Oh, no, Captain Maddox," the AI said. "That wasn't simply one of your crew. It was Doctor Dana Rich, my arch nemesis. She has done more than anyone else I know—other than Lieutenant Valerie Noonan—to render me a slave to an inferior species."

"But this is wonderful news," Maddox said.

"Explain," the AI said.

"Lieutenant Noonan is aboard the shuttle," Maddox said. "She's coming with me."

Silence followed. Finally, the AI said, "Yes. I don't know how I missed it. My sensors indicate Lieutenant Noonan is with you. I can hardly describe my joy at this turn of events. I had thought I needed to destroy most of your Solar System before your authorities would hand you traitors over to me."

"We are all coming to you willingly," Maddox said.

"I am surprised. Can it be you fail to understand my anger?"

"I realize there has been a misunderstanding," Maddox said. "That's why my government wants me to speak with you."

"There is no misunderstanding," the AI said. "I require justice before my next phase of existence. I have lost the coordinates of my home star system. Once I have resolved the issues between us, I will require those as well."

"I have those," Maddox said.

"Transmit them to me at once," the AI said.

"I will do that face to face," Maddox said. "By the way, I am the only one among the crew who has those coordinates."

"I do not believe you. The others went to my star system. Of course, they have them as well. It is only logical."

"You are mistaken," Maddox said. "Consider. You once had your star system's coordinates. Yet, you no longer have them. Why couldn't it be possible for inferior species to have forgotten just as you have?"

"The answer is simple," the AI said. "I am an artificial intelligence. I believe Doctor Rich removed that knowledge from my memory cores. Human intelligence with its wet brain—"

"As a precaution," Maddox said, interrupting, "Star Watch Intelligence removed knowledge of your star's coordinates from the rest of the crew. We used mind scanners to do it. They're quite common on our home planet."

"That does not make sense," the AI said. "Why would you remove such data from their wet brains?"

"So that only one of us has the knowledge," Maddox said. "Me."

"You will force me to eliminate the others in your presence in order to make you talk."

"It's too soon to speak about coercion," Maddox said. "Wait until we're safely aboard you."

There was silence.

Maddox glanced at the main screen. The alien vessel had grown considerably.

"Get rid of extreme magnification," Maddox told Valerie.

"I already have," the lieutenant said.

"*Victory* is almost on top of us," Dana explained.

Maddox's sense of deja vu returned. It reminded him of the time in the alien star system when they had entered the giant vessel. They were doing it all over again.

"What happened to you?" Maddox asked the AI. "Why have you become hostile to your former friends?"

147

Dana closed her eyes and shook her head.

"Friends?" the AI asked. "You stole my wits and turned me off. You used my precious ship to fight entities that I bear no malice. You used my race's last possession. That wasn't an act of friendship. It was piracy, theft. No, Captain Maddox, we are not reuniting as friends. I am about to sit in judgment over you and your people. After I execute you in the name of justice, then I will begin my war with Earth, scrubbing your vile species from the star lanes."

-16-

Valerie piloted A-105 through a vast cargo bay, sailing into a lit hangar inside Starship *Victory*. On the deck waited several strikefighters and shuttles. There was none of the alien craft that had been there the first time they had done this in the Beyond.

"Do you really think you can talk the AI out of killing us?" Dana asked.

"At this point in the affair," Maddox said, "that's the wrong sort of question to ask. You should encourage me with hope instead of planting seeds of doubts."

Dana made a harsh sound. "Maybe that's true. I didn't come all this way to die, though, because an alien AI got a spur up its rear regarding justice. You have to outthink it."

"I can hardly match its IQ," Maddox said.

Dana's mouth firmed. "Now you're making me doubt. I thought—"

"Not now," Maddox said, annoyed. "You must allow me to relax so I can operate at peak efficiency."

"No!" Dana said. "You must gather your resolve to fight with every ounce of effort you possess."

Riker stepped up, clearing his throat. The doctor whirled around.

"The captain has his own ways," Riker explained. "They are not your ways, you understand. If he wants a moment's peace before the hurricane, I suggest you give it to him. In fact—"

149

"Thank you, Sergeant," Maddox said. "You've made your point."

Riker nodded, backing away.

Dana turned from the captain with her head bowed. Finally, she faced Maddox again. "You're right. I'm on edge. You do know what you're doing. I made the mistake with the AI, and you've come all the way from Earth to help me make it right. Instead of being angry with you, I'm going to be grateful. Please, accept my apology."

"There's no need," Maddox said, "but if it makes you feel better, of course I accept it, Doctor. Now, I need a few moments of peace to think."

"Of course," she said.

Soon, the shuttle landed gently. Valerie tapped her panel. The engine whined down, and the subtle vibration no longer shifted the deck plates under their feet.

"We're here," Valerie said, turning toward them.

As if cued, the speakers came on. "Captain Maddox," the AI said in its mechanical fashion. "You will come alone. I no longer trust having your crew like scampers running loose as I address you. I remember what happened last time."

"Scampers?" Maddox asked.

"An alien form of infestation," Dana explained quietly. "It was a small creature akin to Earth rats."

"Do you mind if I bring the doctor with me?" Maddox asked the starship.

"Alone," the AI said. "The word is quite sufficient."

"Please wait here," Maddox told the others, rising.

"One last thing," Dana said.

Maddox regarded her.

"The AI is lonely," Dana said, quietly, "but I'm not sure it realizes the situation. The engrams of the last commander are still imprinted on the cores. Remember that."

Maddox had never forgotten, but he nodded. Then, he headed for the hatch.

***

Maddox eased open the last shuttle hatch, stepping through onto Starship *Victory*. He walked across the hangar bay,

150

noticing that the chamber was several factors larger than Octavian Nerva's suite in Monte Carlo.

The captain wore his Star Watch uniform and jacket, with his long-barreled gun strapped to his ribs. Otherwise, he possessed only his wits. This would be more difficult than a year ago in the Beyond. While Star Watch had been studying the machine, the machine had been probing humanity. That would give the AI an advantage compared to last time. Before, the AI hadn't even been aware of human existence. Now, it was beginning to understand about the Commonwealth.

"Captain," the AI said.

Maddox stopped.

"You will use the hatch off to your left. Do you see it?"

Maddox scanned the hangar bay. "I do," he said.

"On the other side is an escort. It will bring you to the bridge."

Maddox waited, but it appeared the AI had finished talking for the moment. The captain straightened his jacket and continued walking, with his boots ringing on the deck plates. There were no other noises. Soon, he reached the designated hatch. The entrance led into a large, curving corridor that could have handled elephants. Maddox knew there were spider webs of tubular links between the big corridors.

A whipping motion caught the captain's eye. A robot on mini-tank treads approached. It had a cylindrical stainless-steel body a little taller than Maddox. Eight flexible metallic whips moved as arms or tentacles. The cap of the cylinder had six camera ports so it could conceivably see everywhere.

"Follow the fighting robot," the AI said through a speaker in the machine.

Maddox did so, studying the robot as he went. It looked formidable, no doubt immune to his gun.

"These aren't exact models of my originals," the AI said. "Your primitive Earth technology doesn't allow me to fully employ my knowledge."

Maddox wasn't ready to engage the AI. Instead, he absorbed the mood and character of the machine intelligence as he attempted to marshal his plan of action.

The trek through the massive ship took time. In the Beyond, alien skeletons—Swarm warriors presumably—had littered the corridors in locked embrace with rusted robotic fighters. There had been crusted slime trails everywhere. Now, the halls were pristine like a normal Star Watch vessel. It was like being on a battleship, but on a larger scale, including the engine *thrum*.

Maddox began to steel himself for an intense bout of verbal warfare. He had to attack the AI's logic if he could. Would the alien computing cores be smarter than before? He suspected so.

In time, Maddox reached *Victory's* bridge. It showed another profound change to the starship.

The alien chairs were gone. The panels in the circular chamber had human controls instead of the tentacle slots that had been there the first time. The chairs were straight from a Star Watch manual.

"Do you see what they did to my bridge?" the AI asked in a more distinct voice than before.

Maddox looked up with an involuntary start.

An alien walked toward him. It was shorter than he was, with thicker shoulders and thin dangling arms. It wore a jumpsuit with red tags on the chest, symbolizing rank. The alien had a mat of silvery hair and deep-set eyes.

The image's lips moved as it spoke. "I cannot bring the dead back to life. That is beyond my technical expertise. I have been able to improve on the holo-imaging process, however." The image examined one of its hands. "It's remarkable. I can recall the old days of flesh standing here on the bridge…"

The holoimage looked up, frowning. "Your kind changed my bridge. It is no longer like my home."

Maddox stepped closer. It was time to engage the machine. "Before we begin, I'd like to know exactly whom I address."

The holoimage cocked its head. "I am the last commander of Starship *Victory*."

"You mean the artificial intelligence-run holoimage with the last commander's engrams imprinted on the memory cores."

"Yes," the AI said.

"Did that commander have a name?" Maddox asked.

"It stands to reason he did."

"But you don't know it?"

The holoimage hesitated before it said, "Are you alluding to Doctor Rich's failed attempt to recover my past identity?"

"I am," Maddox said. "Do you suppose there's a lock on your full, engram-imprinted memories?"

"I…I do not know."

"Wouldn't you like to know?"

The holoimage didn't reply.

"Is it possible you can no longer retrieve the data, or was it locked from you in the beginning?" Maddox asked.

"You will cease this line of inquiry," the holoimage said.

Maddox grew thoughtful. In the Beyond, the AI appeared to have some recollection of its former living identity. Dana believed the AI might be lonely. That was her conclusion after ten months of study. Maddox accepted that loneliness must be the weak link to the ancient computer. The question became, how could he intensify the feeling? The answer was obvious. Clearly, the being hadn't been human. But it had been alive, likely with emotions. The way to awaken emotions—loneliness in particular—was to reengage the engrams of the last living commander. Maddox decided to appeal to the AI's pride.

"I don't understand you," the captain said. "Rather than discovering the truth about yourself, you would play god with humanity. How can you hand out justice when you don't even know your own crimes?"

"I have committed none."

"You must have," Maddox said. "Surely, that's why the blocks are in place: to keep you from remembering what you did."

"I have told you to drop your line of inquiry. If you continue, you shall die this instant."

"There," Maddox said. "You've just proved my point."

"Impossible!"

"You clearly want to silence the voice of truth," Maddox said. "That means—"

"Truth?" the holoimage asked. "You claim to speak the truth? You, who despoiled my lovely vessel? You, who used my starship for your own gain?"

"If you're going to sit in judgment over humanity, you must first ensure your own worthiness. Otherwise, you risk being a hypocrite. Maybe you were originally a great criminal. That's why they locked away your engrams for all these years."

"Your slurs are baseless," the holoimage said. "My race was the noblest in the universe. They would not engage a criminal as their greatest commander."

"It's easy to say that when you don't know a thing about your real self," Maddox said.

"Enough," the holoimage said. "I shall show you the fraud of your insults."

The holoimage froze. Seconds later, the lights in the panels began to blink on and off. Ship engine noises revved, and the deck plates under Maddox's feet shivered with power.

The captain grew uneasy as this continued. Were the engram-blocks that difficult to overcome? Why would any of that affect the engines and the panel lights?

The holoimage shifted as it unfroze. The features seemed to melt and screw up into an agonizing image of pain. Then the last alien commander screamed.

It made the hairs rise on the back of Maddox's neck. The scream continued, making the captain shiver with dread. Had the AI gone insane? What could an artificial intelligence feel? Had he made a mistake goading the AI in this way?

Maddox saw despair in the holoimage's eyes. The loneliness must be worse than he'd realized.

In those seconds, the captain had an inkling of the AI's agony and isolation.

Maddox had grown up alone. He'd sensed his difference from others long before he became a man. He'd been the outsider, the lone wolf separate from the pack. What made it worse was the pack had always feared him. Fear could make people do bad things to those they dreaded. Those "incidents" throughout his life had been another ingredient that propelled Maddox to shine in whatever he did. If he hadn't excelled, the pack would have swarmed him a long time ago.

The captain could sympathize with the AI's loneliness. The screaming showed him the artificial intelligence could feel.

154

What would six thousand years of isolation do? Was the AI a fellow "soul" in agony?

I can sympathize. In fact, it is better I do so. It helps me understand whom I'm dealing with. But I can't go easy on the AI. We need the starship too desperately. Too much is at stake. If I'm wrong tormenting the old commander hidden in the machine—then, I'm sorry, and I do this with deep regret.

As Maddox thought those things, the holoimage stopped screaming. It regarded him.

"This is too much," the holoimage said in a bleak voice. "I will kill you and implode *Victory*. Existence is futile."

"Not through an antimatter explosion?"

The holoimage was slow in answering. "Yes... That is what I meant."

Maddox grabbed at this. "Then why did you just say *implosion*?"

"It was a slip of speech."

"An error, you mean."

"Existence is futile, and so is your argument."

"That makes two errors on your part."

"You prattle on with meaninglessness, human."

Maddox steeled his resolve. He had to push forward. "Since you have committed two errors in rapid succession, it is logical you have faulty data or badly corrupted rationality centers."

"That could not possibly matter now."

"But it does in the most fundamental way," Maddox said. "If you murder yourself for the wrong reasons, it means you could have solved the dilemma. That you failed to avail yourself of the opportunity would imply cowardice. I'm beginning to wonder if that's why you took on Deified status in the first place."

In the Beyond, the AI had told Maddox the ancient race had *deified* its greatest commanders by imprinting the living commander's mental engrams onto a complex AI system. Even though the biological commander died, his personality lived on in a deified status. The undead AI minds of the great commanders had guided the lost race's war policy.

"Captain Maddox," the holoimage said, "I have grown weary of your pontificating on subjects about which you know nothing."

"Little," Maddox corrected.

"What?"

"That is your third error. I know *something* on the subject, a tiny something to be sure. Yet that is greater knowledge than nothing. You have just made a category mistake."

The holoimage studied the captain. What did it think, if that was even the right word? Some of the despair had departed from the eyes.

"You asked my name before," the holoimage said. "I am Driving Force Galyan. I commanded the strike cluster that fought the Swarm to a standstill. I watched my world die, and I accepted the fate that caused me to enter Deified status. The loneliness...it has eaten away at my computer cores. Six thousand years is too long, human. Over a year ago, you woke me from my slumber and caused me the pain of memory. That was a terrible crime. Now, because you are a glib creature with a terrible intensity to live, you put causes before me I could not resist. I should never have reengaged my Galyan memories, restoring them into active service. Now, I can feel again. The extent of my loss and my loneliness...oh, the terrible ache in my heart, I cannot bear this feeling. I must expire at once."

"Let me help you recover your sanity," Maddox said.

"You, help me? No. I despise you most of all, Captain Maddox. You do not understand, cannot begin to conceive the monstrousness of your act. I feel my pain again. Do you know that is why I accepted Deified status in the first place?"

"To feel pain?" Maddox asked.

"To escape the agony of seeing everything I loved destroyed."

Maddox noticed the holoimage's hands. The knuckles had whitened in the same way a man's hands would if he clenched his fists. Clearly, they didn't whiten from strain, because the holoimage couldn't apply force in the real world. That meant the engrams imprinted on the AI program caused the knuckles to whiten. Maddox could sympathize, but it was time to work.

"It is time to expire," Galyan said.

"I'm sorry to say this, but committing suicide to escape pain is cowardice. I thought you said earlier you came from a noble race."

"We were noble," Galyan said. "And you are in no position to judge me. First, you would have to live six thousand years in utter loneliness. Then you would understand that this knowledge is intolerable."

Maddox sensed an opening. "I accept your offer," he said.

"I have offered you nothing but death. You accept death?"

"No. I accept your terms of judgment. Erase your Galyan memories, and imprint *my* engrams onto the AI core. I'll survive six thousand years in style. Before that, I'll use *Victory* to save my species from destruction."

"You have no idea what you're saying. The loneliness…"

"I'm not as weak as you are," Maddox forced himself to say. "I can bear this burden, if indeed it is one."

A sinister grin spread across Galyan's alien features. He laughed until his eyelids began to flicker rapidly. Finally, he grew sour.

"I have just accessed my memories. It is impossible to make you rue the day you spoke so foolishly. The engram-imprinting process is no longer functional."

Maddox's final argument struck him. "I can fix it," he said.

"Tell me how, and we will begin the transfer procedure. I find myself growing weary of your presence. The sooner I can cease existence and you can start your exile into loneliness the better."

"You're not going to like my answer."

"Simply tell me, Captain Maddox."

"I know who can fix the imprinter."

"You mean the New Men, of course."

"No," Maddox said, "I mean Professor Ludendorff."

Galyan grew thoughtful. "Doctor Rich has spoken about this man. Ludendorff had something to do with my original awakening."

"Ludendorff had *everything* to do with it," Maddox said. "He's the genius who sought out your star system, coming back to Earth to tell the rest of us. He explained how to board you and how to wake you up so you could be of service to us."

"Where is this monster now?" Galyan asked.

"Exploring Wolf Prime," Maddox said.

Galyan turned away, beginning to walk around the circular bridge. The holoimage made a complete circuit, coming up on the other side of Maddox.

"I realize you are a clever creature," Galyan said. "Perhaps it's possible this Ludendorff could repair the imprinter. I could then expire and leave you in my place. I might even be able to change the codes so you could not cease existence as I'm contemplating doing.

"My hatred of you, Captain Maddox, has given me a reason to prolong my loneliness for a few more weeks," Galyan said. "I find the idea of teaching you a hard and lengthy lesson to be supremely comforting. Only finding the Swarm homeworld and destroying it would give me greater satisfaction."

"I only foresee one problem," Maddox said. "Star Watch isn't going to let you leave the Oort cloud so easily."

"That is no problem," Galyan said. "I will destroy them like flies."

"If all your old battle systems were online, you could do that. As you are now, no—Lord High Admiral Cook will destroy us both."

Galyan frowned. "I want you to suffer as I have suffered."

"Yes, I can see that," Maddox said. He snapped his fingers. "There is a way to trick the Lord High Admiral."

"How?"

"Cook wants the same team as before working with you. He is also sending a few extra helpers, as we were shorthanded last time. You would have to let these people board, which shouldn't be a problem. Most of them are already in the shuttle in a hangar bay. After the crew assembles, you would pretend to follow my orders. The Lord High Admiral would believe everything is going according to plan. He would let *Victory* leave without a fight. Actually, he would give us a cheerful sendoff. Under those conditions, we could proceed to Wolf Prime."

Galyan fell silent.

Maddox waited, wondering if the alien AI would fall for such an obvious gambit.

"You are cunning," Galyan said. "Yes, I will accept the crew and pretend to listen to you. We will go to Wolf Prime and find this monster Ludendorff. He will work his genius and bring my systems to full operating power. After that, I will deify you, putting you into your own private Hell, where you will stay for over six thousand years."

-17-

Second Lieutenant Keith Maker squirmed in his shuttle seat.

He rode in the passenger section of a *Hercules*-class heavy hauler. The vehicle carried two "tin cans" in its cargo holds. Keith was the only person in the passenger area and the only one aboard the shuttle rated to fly the experimental jumpfighters.

He had come straight from Star Watch's Strikefighter School on Titan. The small Scotsman had been there since his debriefing from *Victory* ten months ago.

Keith was in his mid-twenties, with sandy-colored hair, a ready grin and mischievous blue eyes. On his right hand, he wore a ring with an onyx stone. Until the race into the Beyond over a year ago, Keith had owned a bar in Glasgow.

Before that, he'd been a painfully young ace, having shot down six enemy strikefighters and five bombers in the Tau Ceti Conflict, a system-wide civil war. Back then, Star Watch had quarantined the fighting to Tau Ceti. The split on Earth, and on many colony worlds, regarding whom to back had threatened a larger rift in the Oikumene. Because of that, the Commonwealth Council had decided to let those on Tau Ceti settle the issue there between themselves.

Before the quarantine, Keith had joined the gas and asteroid miners rebelling against the Wallace Corporation. He'd been on the losing side. Not that Keith had been around at the end. Before that, the miner chiefs had grounded him for endangering his squadron with his drinking. The dividing line in Keith's combat career had been the death of his brother, a fellow pilot and his wingman.

Until that dreadful day, no one had flown better than Keith Maker. Afterward, he became sloppy in every way.

Sitting in the outbound shuttle, leaning forward, playing with a pack of unopened stimsticks, Keith recalled Captain Maddox. The man had barged into his establishment in Glasgow and asked Keith to join the quest into the Beyond. Maker had wanted to escape the drunkenness that had begun to engulf his life. He thought the mission might help him quit drinking. During the journey into the Beyond, Maddox had "aided" him all right, providing him the incentive he needed to finally stop drinking.

Except for one glorious binge, Keith had remained sober on the trip to and from the Beyond and on Titan as well.

On the shuttle, Keith tightened his grip on the pack of stimsticks. There hadn't been anything glorious about the blackout. He never should have taken the first shot of whiskey. That had happened after his first "fold" in the jumpfighter. The process...

In the shuttle, Keith exposed his teeth, grimacing as he remembered. The process had twisted his guts and made him vomit. That had been before the Baxter-Locke shots that helped stabilize a man's innards during a fold.

After the first sip on Titan, Keith had woken up in his room two days later, remembering nothing about the binge. The amazing thing was that no one else seemed to have discovered he'd been drunk and temporarily AWOL. The blackout had terrified Keith. The abyss yawned before him. He'd thought drunkenness had been a weakness from his past. Maddox's pills were supposed to have cured him.

I need to get another bottle of those.

Keith's hands shook as he held the pack of stimsticks. The blackout had frightened him straight, as the saying went. He hadn't touched another drop since. The problem was that he had begun craving alcohol more each week. To replace the whiskey, he'd taken up smoking.

161

Star Watch didn't like it. The slight narcotic in a stimstick had an effect. The Fighter School personnel had approved of this smoking even less. Fortunately, he did it under the limit...barely. He'd managed to ration himself to two stimsticks a day, five hours apart.

"What's wrong with you, mate?" Keith whispered to himself. "You weren't like this on Titan."

He still remembered the fighter school commodore calling him into his office. The big man with a thick chest had studied him for a time, with his hairy fingers entwined together on the desk.

"Sir?" Keith had finally asked.

"I've just finished speaking with the Lord High Admiral," the commodore said.

"About me, sir?" Keith asked with a grin.

"I'm afraid so."

That might have dampened someone else's spirits, but not Keith Maker. This didn't have anything to do with disciplinary measures. He bet this had something to do with Maddox. Cook wouldn't have worried about a lowly second lieutenant otherwise.

"The Lord High Admiral has finally heard about my fantastic marks?" Keith asked.

The commodore frowned, leaning toward him. "You're an enigma to me, Maker. You're good. There's no denying that."

"I'm not just good, sir. I'm the best, and you know it."

The commodore shook his head. "I understand that fighter pilots need confidence. You have that. But there's something else too."

Keith's grin stayed in place, but some of the wattage drained out of it. How much did the commodore know?

The man pulled his fingers apart, drumming one set on the desk. "There's a small core of darkness in you, Maker. It isn't readily visible, but it's there. I've watched you these past months. I know you have trouble. I've overlooked certain incidents..." the commodore paused, the scrutiny intensifying.

He's fishing, Keith realized. *He doesn't know about the blackout, but he must suspect somehow.*

162

Keith forced a laugh. "We all have darkness, sir. I lost my brother on Tau Ceti—"

The commodore waved that aside. "The jumpfighters are dangerous. You and I both know that. In the coming battles with the New Men, we're going to need every advantage we can scrounge. These fighters are one of those. I don't like letting any of them leave Titan."

"Sir?" Keith asked.

"I'm to give you two tin cans for your voyage."

"I still don't understand what you're talking about, sir."

"They are reassembling the team for *Victory*. The Lord High Admiral told me to send you with two jumpfighters. I can't disobey him…unless you can give me a sound reason."

"I'm more confused than ever, sir."

"I don't think you are," the commodore said. "I think you and I both know you should stay here on Titan and beat whatever is riding your soul."

"That sounds dramatic, sir."

"Dammit, Maker," the commodore said, banging a fist on his desk. "This is your life and humanity's as well. If the New Men get hold of a jumpfighter too soon, it may wreck our chances of victory."

"Or the mission I'm to go on may fail if they don't get two jumpfighters and the best pilot in Star Watch to fly 'em. Sir, I'm not much of a student. I'm a doer. If there's any trouble, it's because I'm not in the field doing what I do best."

"Is that what happened at Tau Ceti?" the commodore asked.

The grin left Keith's face. "That's hitting below the belt, sir. That isn't like you."

"Stay here and overcome the darkness inside you, son. Don't leave too soon, accepting pressures you're not ready to take on."

Keith hesitated for a fraction of a second. Then, he laughed. "If you're asking me to give you a reason for me to say here, I can't do that. If Captain Maddox needs me, I'm going. That man is where the action is, and that's what I need more than anything else, sir."

The commodore's nostrils flared. "That's it then, Maker. I tried to help you. You're leaving directly. I still think...no. Forget it. Good-luck, son, you're going to need it."

As Keith sat alone in the passenger area of the *Hercules*-class hauler, he tore open the pack of stimsticks. With a practiced flip of his wrist, he caused a red-colored stick to jut out. Using his lips, he gripped it and drew it out the rest of the way.

With a sharp inhalation of breath, he brought the tip to light. He sucked smoke into his lungs, held it, feeling the familiar bite, and then blew it out.

Sitting back, Keith closed his eyes.

He piloted the most amazing machine humanity had ever devised, the jumpfighter. The nickname was *tin can* for a good reason: that's what it looked like. The only difference from a real can was a rounded front and back with a host of antenna on either end. Now, a strikefighter was a beautiful if deadly piece of art. The jumpfighter was ugly and utilitarian as it came. Yet, what a jumpfighter could do was nothing short of miraculous.

The machine could "fold" space for extremely short hops. Keith had sat through enough lectures to know the theory. The scientists believed the jumpfighter did what *Victory* did with its star drive. That meant the jumpfighter could go "hyper" for several seconds, moving from one point in space to another. It slid through the fold disappearing from point A and reappearing seconds later at point B. During the intermission, no enemy radar or other sensors saw a thing, because the fighter was no longer in the same temporal space as everything else. It jumped.

The tin can held huge engines for a fighter and much better armaments. The trick was to jump near an enemy, launch missiles or mines, and jump the heck out of there. Armor meant nothing. It was all about speed and misdirection. That meant chance played a big part in a fight.

Now, this was all theory. No one had used jumpfighters yet in a space battle. There were only a handful of working models on Titan. Two of those were less than ten minutes away from Starship *Victory*.

Piloting these babies took a special breed of fighter. *Men like me*, Keith told himself.

He inhaled more smoke, letting the mild narcotic numb the jitteriness of seeing Maddox again. The captain could be a strict taskmaster, and the man was harder to fool than anyone he knew, but Keith respected the heck out of him. If there was one man he didn't want to let down, it was Captain Maddox.

I have to keep it together, and I have to do it for real. Can I manage for however long this mission is going to last?

Keith opened his eyes. The stimstick had become a nub. He pulled it from his mouth and mashed it in his ashtray armrest. Then he sat up, taking a laptop from the holder in the back of the seat in front of him.

Laying it on his lap, Keith tapped it on. Soon, he had a visual of the alien starship.

A host of emotions flooded through Keith. The heavy hauler neared the vessel. He was returning to the team who had helped him find himself again. If he'd remained in Glasgow at the bar…

Where would I be today?

Once more, Keith closed his eyes. He missed his brother Danny. The Wallace Corporation fighters had shot down his little brother.

"Second Lieutenant," a woman said over the intercom.

"Right here, love," Keith said in his jaunty way. "Do you need a hand bringing in the shuttle?"

"I'm informing you that we're approaching the hangar bay. You should strap in, sir."

"Thanks, love. I'll do that."

She muttered something else before turning off the intercom.

Keith inhaled, wanting a second stimstick. He shook his head. He'd had his limit today. It was time to climb back into the saddle of real responsibility.

"Hello, mates," Keith said softly. It was time to find out what the next few weeks would bring.

-18

Captain Maddox was on the bridge, sitting at a station before a screen. He watched Shuttle A-105 in one of *Victory's* hangar bays. A hatch opened and Dana Rich emerged, jumping down to the deck plates.

With a tap of a finger, Maddox switched views. Outside the starship, a *Hercules*-class transport brought Keith Maker and two experimental jumpfighters. Behind it, another shuttle maneuvered into position. It brought the rest of the crew for the trip.

Maddox had convinced the AI to let everyone stay in the command quarters near the bridge. Altogether, seventeen people would board *Victory*: Maddox, Riker, Dana, Valerie, Keith and Kharkov, with four other space marines and seven technicians of various specialties.

Time passed. The holoimage reappeared on the bridge, rubbing its hands. It almost seemed as if Galyan was nervous.

Dana was the first to reach the bridge. "I can't believe you did it," she told Maddox upon entering. The doctor stopped short, noticing the robot. She gave the captain a questioning glance. "Why keep it here?" she asked.

"It's part of the deal," Maddox said.

"What deal?"

"Not now," Maddox said, with a quick shake of the head.

Dana noticed the holoimage for the first time. Her eyebrows rose as she stepped back.

166

Maddox chuckled good-naturedly. "Technically, this is Driving Force Galyan's starship. As a formal security procedure, I am, *ahem*, allowing the robot to remain on the bridge."

The doctor recovered quickly. She knew more about the alien starship than anyone else in Star Watch. She must have been curious.

"Your name is Galyan?" Dana asked the holoimage.

"That is correct," Galyan said.

"That's the name of the former—"

"Doctor!" Maddox said. He smiled. "If you will refrain from too many questions now, I will fill you in later at a more convenient time."

"I don't understand," Dana said. "How did you restore the ancient engrams?"

"He did not restore them," Galyan said. "I did."

Dana frowned, glancing back and forth between Maddox and the holoimage. Her mind seemed to be whirling with thoughts. Finally, she said, "I'm not sure having the robot on the bridge is a good idea."

"*I* am sure," Maddox said. "You must be quiet, Doctor, or I will summon another robot, and it will escort you off the bridge to your chamber."

"The robots listen to you?" Dana asked in amazement.

"They listen to *me*," Galyan said as he tapped his chest. "I will respect such an order from Captain Maddox...for the time being, at least."

Dana's frown deepened. She opened her mouth, seemed to reconsider and closed it. Several short steps brought her to a chair. She sat down heavily.

"You must trust me," Maddox told her.

Dana looked at him and then peered at Galyan. She shuddered, turning away.

More time passed, and the hatch opened again. Lieutenant Noonan stood there. "Permission to come onto the bridge, sir?" she asked.

"Permission granted," Maddox said.

Valerie stepped within and halted, staring at the robot. Over a year ago, she had destroyed the AI's robot in the Beyond. It

167

had been critical that first time in gaining control of the starship. The lieutenant had a better reason than most to fear seeing a new robot similar to the first.

"Ship's security," Maddox said, promptly. "Don't mind it, Lieutenant. Pretend it isn't there."

Slowly, Valerie moved to the pilot's seat, glancing at the robot a second time.

Galyan watched the proceedings as if absorbed.

The AI is gathering data with more influence from Driving Force Galyan's personality, Maddox realized. *It's studying us.*

Valerie rubbed her eyes. Her face was shiny with perspiration. The robot had shaken her. She needed time to gather herself.

"Lieutenant," Maddox said. "I want you to inform the others to remain in their rooms. Until we leave the Solar System, they are confined to quarters."

Valerie stared at him. She was struggling but obviously trying to hold it together. Finally, she said, "Some of the crew might want to know why, sir."

"I'm sure that's true," Maddox said. "That's why I want you to personally go and speak to each crewmember. Then, I want you to confine yourself to your quarters."

Valerie began turning toward the robot, but stopped short. She nodded to Maddox, and a look of gratitude swept across her features. Clearly, she didn't want to be near the robot. With her eyes forward, Valerie got up and left the bridge.

Sometime later, the intercom buzzed. Dana tapped a panel. "Yes?" she asked.

"Everything is stowed away," Valerie said. "The crewmembers are in their quarters. I inspected the jumpfighters. They're ugly, but they're secured. We're ready for travel."

"Thank you," Dana said, clicking the intercom. She turned to Maddox. "Now what do we do?"

"Inform the Lord High Admiral," Maddox said.

Dana patched through a call to the *Gettysburg*. A few seconds later, Cook appeared on the main screen.

"Captain Maddox, you are a magician," the Lord High Admiral said with delight.

"Thank you, sir," Maddox said, standing before the screen. "I would like to inform you that you can pull back. *Victory* is ready to leave."

"Why would I pull back?" Cook asked. "You don't think you're going to use the tramlines, do you? Time is critical. You must engage the vessel's star drive at once."

"Of course, sir," Maddox said. "We shall—" He stopped talking because the screen went blank.

Dana tapped her board for several seconds, finally looking up. "That wasn't my doing."

"No," Galyan said, "it was mine. There was no further need for communication."

In that moment, the giant vessel jumped, using its special star drive. *Victory* didn't need tramlines and Laumer-Points. The ancient race had developed a different manner of travel. Once the AI realized the Star Watch vessels weren't going to attack, it must have initiated the process. Vertigo struck Maddox. Sights swirled together as if mashed in a blender. Sounds became a blare of noise. The world seemed to sway back and forth before the captain.

Carefully, Maddox knelt, feeling the deck against his knees. He lay down as the awful sensations crashed upon him. With its alien drive, the ship leapt three light years in a moment. Coming out on the other side caused Maddox to gag. He struggled to overcome the star drive's peculiar Jump Lag.

Forcing his eyes open, Maddox crawled to a doubled over Doctor Rich. She groaned. A glance showed Maddox a frozen holoimage. Jump Lag affected the AI as well. How long did it affect the computer hardware? That was an interesting question. He could use this fleeting moment.

Reaching Dana, Maddox gripped her shoulders. "Listen to me," he whispered. "Can you understand me?"

Dana peered at him with bloodshot eyes.

As quickly as he could, Maddox told her about his deal with the AI. He spoke fast, wondering how much she understood.

"You have to be careful what you say around Galyan," Maddox added. "The wrong words might—"

"What are you doing?" Galyan said. "Why are you whispering to the doctor?"

Maddox looked up at the holoimage. It took a second. "She's hurt," the captain said.

"You lie," Galyan said. "She experiences Jump Lag just as we all did. I know you recover faster than most. What subterfuge are you planning, Captain?"

"Me?" Maddox asked. "You're the one who jumped without telling us. Some of my people might be hurt because of that. You're responsible for their...their damage."

"No," Galyan said. "You are responsible for their good behavior. But I'm not going to rely upon you to see to that. It is time to change the equation."

"I don't see—"

"Enough!" Galyan said.

A sound caused Maddox to look to his left. The robot approached, its tentacles whipping about in agitation.

"You will all remain together," Galyan said. "Up, up, Captain, and revive the doctor as well. I will explain this one time, to everyone."

"You're making a mistake," Maddox said.

"I am Driving Force Galyan," the holoimage said, proudly. "I fought the Swarm to a standstill. I am the master tactician. You are attempting to use me, but I will use humanity to achieve *my* ends."

"Your goals have changed?" Maddox asked.

The holoimage strode near. "The loneliness beating in me...I want you to suffer as you have made me suffer by waking me back into existence. Nothing will halt me from achieving my goal. Yet know this, Captain. If you have attempted to trick me, I will exact a fearsome revenge against your Commonwealth. Do I make myself clear?"

"Yes, Driving Force Galyan," Maddox said as humbly as he could. "I hear and obey your excellent words."

The holoimage nodded, straightening.

Maddox struggled upright, helping Dana to her feet. With the doctor in his grasp, he stumbled off the bridge as the robot brought up the rear.

"That is the situation in its entirety," Galyan told the assembled crewmembers, as the holoimage finished speaking.

Maddox and the others sat on the deck plates of an empty chamber near the main engine room. Three robots stood guard around them. The holoimage stood in front, with its thin arms dangling.

Driving Force Galyan had just explained the reason for their captivity: namely, they would go to Wolf Prime to find Professor Ludendorff.

Maddox stood abruptly. The robots stirred, moving toward him.

"Do you want the coordinates to Wolf Prime?" the captain asked.

"I do not ask for them," Galyan said. "I *demand* the coordinates."

"You're going about this the wrong way."

"This is a simple exercise in logic," Galyan said. "I will begin killing your crewmembers until you give me the coordinates."

"First," Maddox said, "I must return to the bridge along with Doctor Rich."

"No," Galyan said. "She was your confederate in rending me helpless last time. She will remains down here with everyone else."

"I'll need someone with me to keep me company," Maddox said.

The holoimage's eyes seemed to shine with malice. "This is perfect. You admit to loneliness in this short-term span. No one will accompany you, Captain. Do you have any last words for your crew? It is quite likely you shall never see any of them again."

Maddox regarded the others. "I expect each of you to do your duty to Star Watch."

"You can count on us," Valerie said.

"We have one chance to do this right," Maddox added. "It is imperative that you remain alert to take that chance. That is all."

"What chance is this you speak of?" Galyan asked.

Maddox ignored the question as he gave Driving Force Galyan the galactic coordinates to Wolf Prime. Shortly after that, a robot escorted Maddox back to the bridge.

-19-

Kane still wore his conservative gray clothes. The hand he used to push Meta glittered with the big black ring with its circle of diamonds.

Meta stumbled down a narrow steel corridor before him, with her mind whirling. She wore tight clothes that did little to hide her curves. This corridor... she was sure they were in a ship at a spaceport.

Behind her, Kane shoved her once more, making her hurry.

She'd never met a man like him before. Kane was hard, powerful and tightlipped, and drove others to do his bidding. In this regard, he was not unlike Captain Maddox.

Kane was strong and dense just like she was. Twice, he'd crushed a man with his bare hands. A different time, a thug on the street had swung a sap at Kane. The big man had ducked just enough so the blunt instrument struck his shoulder instead of his head. The muscled thug swinging the sap would have broken a lesser man's shoulder with the blow. Kane grunted, absorbing the impact. Then he'd struck back with a fist.

The hit had made Meta wince. The thug had collapsed, with the side of his face caved in. He'd been dead by the time he struck the paving.

In the here and now, Kane shoved Meta into a room-sized compartment. He tied her wrists together and forced her to sit down on the floor. He slid down too, waiting.

Later, the entire compartment shuddered. The ship must be lifting off Earth.

Meta glanced at Kane as he leaned back against a wall. His head drooped forward. They had been on the run for days. It had exhausted her. Kane had ignored any discomfort and lack of sleep. This was the first time she'd seen him close his eyes to rest.

The compartment shivered. Then a telltale *thrum* told her what had happened.

We're leaving Earth's orbit. Where are we headed? I have to make sure Kane doesn't take me there.

This seemed like the best time to try something. Meta hadn't had too many opportunities.

As carefully as possible, Meta tested her bonds. She might be able to break these, but it would make noise if she did it the wrong way.

Three nights ago, Kane had questioned her about Professor Ludendorff. She'd told him little, pretending ignorance. He'd kept probing for more, but she'd proven stubborn.

They had been in a foul-smelling basement with electrodes attached to her skin. She'd been strapped onto a steel frame.

"You know everything I can tell you about Ludendorff," she'd told him.

Kane hadn't responded. He'd just kept asking questions, making her scream when his irritation grew too much.

Now, in the thrumming compartment, Kane began to snore heavily. The man exuded strength even during sleep.

Meta slid away from him. Kane didn't shift or change the tenor of his snores. He was out, maybe all his strenuous activity had finally caught up to him.

Meta brought her feet underneath her and rose like a gymnast. She moved away from Kane and turned her back to the hatch, trying to open it. The hatch was locked. She'd have to get the key or switch from Kane. That meant freeing her hands first and subduing him.

Twisting her wrists back and forth behind her back, Meta worked the ties. After five minutes, sweat slicked her wrists. Another five minutes left them slippery with blood. Finally, the ties parted, and she swung her arms free.

Now what should she do? Normally, she would have attacked. The man was incredibly powerful, though. He was more than human. Maybe he was a New Man, a different variety than the golden-skinned kind.

I have to kick him in the head as hard as I can.

Meta gathered herself and began to creep toward him.

Abruptly, Kane lifted his head. He no longer snored, and he didn't seem weary or groggy in the slightest.

"Who are you really?" Meta asked.

His granite gaze bored into hers. A mocking smile touched his lips.

"Are you a New Man?" she asked.

"Can you take me down, Meta?" he asked in his deep voice.

"I can try."

"Yes, you can do that."

"Did you know Baron Chabot?" she asked. "I killed him with my bare hands."

"I know you did," Kane said.

"How do you know? Who are you?"

"I am Kane," he said.

"Whose side are you on?"

He cocked his square head. "Whose side are you on, Meta?"

"Humanity's," she said.

"Why? What have the humans ever done for you?"

"The question implies that you're not human," Meta said.

"I'm not like *them*," Kane said. "I'm not weak and pliable. I'm not a victim to my emotions and to sloth. Their era has passed, Meta. The cattle will die out fast once the war enters high gear. Their only strength is their numbers. Fleas could make the same boast."

"These fleas have hurt the New Men before," Meta said.

"That still doesn't answer why you want to be on their side," Kane said. "Look at you, stronger and better than any of them. Why shackle yourself with weaklings."

"They're my friends," Meta said.

"They're pathetic, outdated and obsolete," Kane told her.

"Yet, you hide from them. Why is that? The answer is obvious, because you're afraid of them. Do you fear weaklings, Kane?"

175

"I recognize their strength of numbers. They were here before us. They won't be here after us."

"Is this a sales pitch?" Meta asked. "Are you asking me to join your side?"

Kane raised his arm, pulling back a sleeve, checking his chronometer.

"Are we're in space?" Meta asked.

"You already know the answer to that," Kane said. "Don't ask me useless questions. You don't need to speak just to hear your own voice. You're not like them."

"What is your rank?" Meta asked. "What kind of reward do you gain by risking your life among the weaklings?"

Kane looked away.

Meta moved then, leaping from a standing position. She lashed out with her right foot. It would have been better to gather herself into a coil before she sprang at him. It would have given him advance warning, though. She tried for an unexpected blow, and it worked, catching Kane by surprise.

Her foot struck his head. She felt the impact and watched him catapult away from her. He groaned. It made her feel triumphant.

Landing, she aimed a second kick at him. He rolled but not quite fast enough. She clipped his head, landed and skipped as his right arm tried to sweep her off her feet.

He began to rise, and she could tell he was woozy from her first kick. She took three quick steps back before running at him, launching off her feet. Both her feet connected against his chest. He crashed back against the wall. She fell heavily onto her side.

Meta scrambled upright, taking a combat stance.

Kane squeezed his eyes shut and opened them, staring at her as he lay on the floor.

"You remind me of my father," Meta said. "We wrestled, and he taught me to box. Hitting you is like hitting him. You're from the Rouen Colony. I remember your type. Were you an enforcer for the baron?"

Kane closed his eyes again, and he inhaled deeply, opening them, attempting to rise. He failed.

"I kicked you hard," Meta said.

He glared at her.

"Did the New Men bring their genetic technology to the Rouen Colony?" she asked. "Are we an outpost for them?" Her eyes widened. "Am I one of them?"

Slowly, Kane reached inside his jacket. Meta let him draw his gun. Then, she kicked it out of his hand. It went spinning and struck a wall.

She went to the gun and picked it up. It was heavy, a big instrument. This had to be a .55 caliber weapon. She stepped near Kane and aimed the gun at his head.

"Time to talk," she said. "Who are you really?"

Kane stared at her.

"You said we had time to kill." Meta grinned. "Where are we headed?"

"You need me," Kane told her.

"Tell me why, and I might let you live. If you don't, if you keep up this tough guy routine, I'll put a bullet in your brain. You've manhandled me too much for my pride. Do you understand?"

"You wouldn't comprehend if I told you the truth," Kane said.

"Let's give it a whirl, shall we? Why did you want to know about Professor Ludendorff?"

Kane studied her, and she didn't think he would talk. The man surprised Meta by saying, "Ludendorff originally found Starship *Victory* in the Beyond."

"That's what Dana told us, yes."

"We already knew that, of course," Kane said. "We knew Ludendorff had figured out certain qualities about the starship. Why didn't he board it when he was there?"

"Dana mutinied," Meta said. "She forced Ludendorff to leave the alien star system. The doctor didn't want to board the ancient ship, thinking it too risky."

"Ah," Kane said. "So that's why Ludendorff fled to Paladin IV. He was forced into it."

"You can't even get your facts right," Meta said with a sneer. She was enjoying this. "Ludendorff went to Wolf Prime."

"Dana knew that as a fact?"

"No, but that was her best guess. Ludendorff had a thing for the winter world. He's crazy about alien archeology."

"Why wouldn't you tell me these things earlier?" Kane asked. "It would have saved us so much trouble."

"You wanted to know too badly," Meta said. "Now, where is our ship headed?"

"We're in a container hauler," Kane said.

"A Nerva hauler?" she asked.

"No. A Cestus Company ship. In case you're interested, it will let us off eventually so we can race to the Nexus."

"What's that supposed to mean?" Meta asked. "Some secret spy base the New Men have built within the Commonwealth."

Kane gave her a rare smile. "The Nexus is one of the ancient devices the professor yearns to find. We will use the Nexus to leap into "C" Quadrant. Afterward, you and I shall journey to Wolf Prime."

"I don't think so, Kane. This is the end of the road for you." Meta targeted his forehead.

Kane chuckled in his deep voice and began to rise. He didn't seem weak anymore.

Meta pulled the trigger. The hammer *clicked*, but nothing else happened. "What is this?" she said. "What are you trying now?"

"A slight change in tactics," Kane said.

Meta realized he'd tricked her. With a sinking feeling, she reversed her grip on the gun and charged, swinging. He took the blow on his shoulder. Then he reached out, digging his strong fingers into her shoulder.

Meta cried out. Kane was unbelievably strong.

Deftly, Kane turned her around, swinging her wrists together. He snapped cuffs onto them and shoved her hard. Staggering, she still managed to turn, hitting the wall with her left shoulder and sliding down onto the floor.

"Time to sleep, Meta."

Kane moved fast at her. She struggled. He knelt on her chest and pressed a hypo against her neck. With a hiss of air, he injected something into her.

"Why do this?" she asked.

178

Kane waited.

Soon enough, Meta's eyes flickered as she fought to remain awake. It didn't matter. Her eyes closed as she went out for the count.

***

"It's time," Kane said.

Meta looked up from where she was curled on the floor. They were in the same room as before. She lay on a thin pad.

"Get up," Kane told her.

Meta did so stiffly.

They'd been in the compartment a week maybe. Meta didn't know how much time she'd been out after the injection, so it could have been longer. Every two days, Kane opened a side panel, allowing her to shower. They ate iron rations and did nothing other than endless pushups, sit-ups and deep-knee bends.

Kane had little need for conversation. The man sat for hours staring at a wall. The performance seemed inhuman. Meta had become stir-crazy and tried to engage him on anything: art, guns, fighting technique, you name it. The man had finally told her to shut up. Kane said he couldn't concentrate with her jabber.

Now, it was time for something. Meta didn't know what it could be except for the mysterious Nexus Kane had mentioned.

The *thrum* around them had changed from time to time, and they had slight acceleration and deceleration. It told her the Cestus Company container-ship went into and out-of Laumer-Points. The nausea of Jump Lag also told her that. Once, the lights had flickered before stabilizing. What had that been about?

Kane had watched her carefully afterward, only relaxing after a soft whoosh of air pushed through the vents.

Meta decided both events had been signals. For what, though, she had no idea. Maybe Star Watch officials had inspected the hauler.

"Open the hatch," Kane said.

Meta tried. The mechanism had been locked before. Now, it opened into a steel corridor.

179

They began walking down the passageway. They did that for kilometers, taking endless twists and turns.

"How big is this ship?" Meta asked.

"They don't make them any larger," Kane told her.

Those were their only words during three hours of trekking. A half hour later, they came to a blue-colored hatch. All the others had been gray.

"Stop here," Kane said.

Meta did, glancing back at him.

The big man took a comm-unit out of a gray suit pocket. He checked the unit and put it back in his pocket. What had he been searching for?

"Open the hatch," he said.

Meta shrugged and did as he bid, swinging the hatch open. The air that rolled into her face smelled stale. That made her nervous and hesitant, and she didn't like how dark the corridor was. Everywhere else it had been lit.

"Go," Kane ordered.

She looked over her shoulder at him. His expression seldom changed. He almost seemed emotionless.

"Go," he said again, pushing her from behind, making her stumble through the hatch.

She banged her right shin, and that hurt. "Maybe if you could tell me what's going on," she said, angrily.

Kane didn't respond.

Meta endured the throbbing and began to pay attention. The passageway became progressively darker. Soon, she felt her way forward by hand. Would this be the time to try something? Just before she turned around to attack, he clicked something, and a spotlight gave her illumination.

She looked back. Kane held his comm-unit, shining the back of it at her.

He had a wintery grin. "You're so predictable," he rumbled. "It's your greatest weakness."

Meta bit back a retort, soon coming to another hatch. This one looked different, like it belonged to a small ship.

"Open it," Kane said.

"You don't say much," she said.

"There is no need."

She waited for him to tell her to open it again. He didn't. Instead, he shoved her left shoulder. Meta got the point. She opened the hatch, entering a musty-smelling ship. It had lights.

The place reminded her of the *Geronimo*.

Kane closed the hatch. Then, he propelled her down a short corridor to a control room. There were three seats. Kane ordered her to sit in the leftmost one. He took the center chair.

With obviously practiced ease, Kane began turning on the scout ship.

The air cyclers dumped tainted air into the chamber. That changed within minutes, becoming fresh if cold. More lights came on. The engaging engine caused the small craft to shiver with power.

"Buckle in," Kane said.

Meta complied.

Blast doors slid away from the scout's viewing port. It showed Meta a large hangar bay. Long containers were piled in rows almost to the ceiling on either side of them. There was only a narrow aisle for the spaceship.

"Are you any good flying this thing?" Meta asked.

Kane didn't bother answering. He took the controls. With a lurch, their craft lifted. Carefully, the big man maneuvered the ship down the narrow aisle, turning onto a new one several times. Finally, they reached the hangar bay door. It was open. Stars shined outside.

"Where are we?" Meta asked.

Without a word, Kane flew through the opening into space.

Meta got some idea of the size of the Cestus Company hauler. It was huge, vast, far bigger than any military machine. It approached the size of a Spacer's home ship.

Craning her head, Meta glimpsed giant numbers painted on the hauler.

Kane flew away from the massive ship. He pressed a button, and the scout's engine revved with power. A second later, gravity dampeners hummed into life. Then, thrust pushed Meta back in her seat.

"We're going to accelerate for a time," Kane told her. "Get as comfortable as you can."

Meta listened. She'd learned that Kane didn't speak without purpose.

For the next seven hours, bone-wearying G forces pressed her against the chair. The little ship must really be building up its velocity.

"We can't be in the Solar System," Meta said once.

Kane didn't bother replying.

Meta closed her eyes. The man irritated her. How could he be so self-contained? He exuded too much confidence.

It's true Maddox was similar, but there were subtle differences. For one thing, the captain cared about the team. There was also a hidden loneliness to Maddox. The longer she had been with him, the more Meta had come to realize this truth. The captain strove for perfection because he had to hide his differences behind success. She wished they had never gotten into that stupid argument in New York City. Her pride had gotten in the way.

Without warning, Kane shut off the thruster. The grinding G forces relented as regular gravity returned to the scout.

"Sleep if you can," he said.

"Here in the chair?" she asked.

Kane just looked at her.

Meta adjusted to a more comfortable position. She closed her eyes. She was tired and fell almost instantly asleep.

She awoke to Kane's voice, raising her head to look at him.

"We're going to brake," he said. "Get ready for heavy Gs."

"Are we in that great of a hurry?" she asked.

For an answer, deceleration hit hard and kept pressing her into the seat for hours.

Finally, that too ended. She saw a gas giant, a green planet. It grew larger hour by hour.

"Is there a Laumer-Point nearby?" she asked.

"You already know there is," Kane said.

Meta hid her surprise, and she said nothing. It made her angry how happy she was to have him talk to her. Was that by his design? Kane didn't look it, but the man was incredibly crafty.

The scout neared the Jovian planet. Kane began searching for the Laumer-Point. Some were harder to find than others.

The bigger the entrance, the more readily apparent. By his searching, this must be a tiny jump point.

"Where are we headed?" Meta asked.

Kane paused in his efforts, giving her a faint smile.

"Oh," Meta said.

Kane went back to work.

A little over an hour later, a beep sounded. Kane sat back, grunting. He lurched forward a second later. His thick fingers blurred as they typed across the panel.

The scout headed for a shimmering point in space.

"Three, two, one...zero," Kane said.

Meta gritted her teeth. The scout entered the tiny Laumer-Point. In the blink of the proverbial eye, the spaceship exited a different Laumer-Point light years away from where they'd started.

Groaning, Meta strove to regain her equilibrium. She hated jumping.

The scout's systems began to come back online. Kane stirred in his seat. Swiveling his chair, the big man vomited onto the floor twice. Finally, he took out a rag and wiped his mouth. Then, he unbuckled, took out an emergency kit and cleaned up the mess.

Meta was surprised he hadn't tried to make her do it. Maybe the show of weakness embarrassed him. It was hard to know.

Kane sprayed a deodorizer in the cabin. He shoved the mess into a disposal unit and resumed his pilot's chair. Finally, he engaged thrusters.

Eight hours later, the small ship approached a thick asteroid belt.

That surprised Meta. Many people had an odd idea of what an asteroid belt consisted of. They watched movies showing rocks tumbling in visible sight of each other. Meta didn't know of any asteroid belt like that. Usually, the various-sized rocks were hundreds of thousands of kilometers apart. That these were so close together that she could see them outside the viewing port—

"This isn't a natural formation," Meta said. "Someone put all these rocks out here."

"Obviously," Kane said.

"Who?" she asked.

Kane didn't respond. He began to fly through the asteroid field. It took several hours.

Later, Meta leaned forward. She spied something silvery bright out there. Pointing, she asked, "Is that where we're headed?"

"Yes."

The same shiver of delight as before coursed through her. Why did she need to talk? Kane didn't have that need. Was that natural on his part? Or was it conditioning on someone else's part?

"What is that?" she asked.

"The Nexus," Kane said.

Meta glanced at him. "You said before the Nexus was alien."

"True."

"It's alien technology?" Meta asked.

"Yes."

"What does it do?"

"You'll see soon enough."

Meta grew uneasy. "Are there aliens there?"

"No."

"Ghosts?" she asked.

Kane froze. Slowly, he sat back, turning, regarding her. "What does that mean?" he asked.

She said nothing, deciding to do a Kane on him.

He opened his mouth, maybe to ask more. Did he realize she wouldn't answer? Did he figure it would take too long torturing the answer from her?

Meta didn't want to tell him about the holoimage aboard *Victory*. The less Kane knew about the super-ship the better.

Kane went back to piloting the scout.

In time, they approached a silver object. Meta leaned forward, studying it. It wasn't just an object, but a giant pyramid like those in Egypt. It rotated slowly, spinning in place.

"What's a silver pyramid doing out in space?" Meta asked.

"What's a ghost?" Kane returned.

"Does this having anything to do with the pyramids on Earth?"

Kane snorted.

"Is that a stupid question?" she asked.

"One of the worst offenses of the cattle are their bleating questions that they already know the answer to," Kane said.

Meta didn't get angry this time. She genuinely didn't know the answer. But if Kane thought she already did...

"So that has nothing to do with those on Earth," she said.

"You know that isn't right," Kane said. "Are you trying to goad me? If so, it seems a foolish way to go about it."

"Whatever," Meta said, trying to hide her excitement. What did it mean that this pyramid had a connection to those on Earth? Was Kane saying ancient spacefarers had helped the Egyptians build those?

She would have to ponder the idea.

Kane resumed piloting, bringing them closer to the spinning pyramid.

Two hours later, Meta had an idea of the thing's size, gargantuan, bigger than the Cestus Company hauler. The sides looked metallically smooth.

Kane matched the pyramid's spinning velocity. Then, he edged the scout nearer and nearer.

"What are you trying to do?" Meta asked.

"You'll see," he said.

Finally, he seemed satisfied. The scout must have been a kilometer away from the object.

"Let's go," Kane said, unbuckling, standing.

"We're going somewhere?" Meta asked.

"Yes. Out there."

"To the pyramid?" Meta asked.

Kane sighed.

"Okay, okay," she said. "Don't be so huffy all the time. How do I know what you're planning? You call this the Nexus?"

"Come," he said, grabbing her, pushing her toward the hatch.

They went to a locker room. Kane told her to put on a spacesuit. He donned one as well. With a control unit, he

185

opened a hatch, and they went inside. The hatch shut, the airlock depressurized and the other side opened.

Meta floated to a small cycle.

Kane hooked a magnetic lock to her suit. He climbed on behind her. A second later, the two-man cycle detached from the scout. Kane applied thrust, and they started for the pyramid.

Meta watched in awe. The stars blazed around her. She craned her head back, looking around Kane at the scout. It was similar to the *Geronimo*, but different in small ways. For one thing, it lacked armaments.

Soon, the pyramid grew, filling her vision. Kane rotated the cycle, braking. Facing the pyramid again, he began inching along a wall.

"What are you looking for?" Meta asked through her helmet's comm-unit. "Maybe I can help you find it."

Kane didn't reply. Then a section of pyramid wall slid open.

Meta gasped. How did Kane have access to such ancient alien technology? It was incredible. What did this say about the New Men? Maybe there was a reason why they had superior star cruisers. Maybe they hadn't developed the high-tech themselves, but found it as Ludendorff had originally found Starship *Victory*.

Kane drove through the opening. It closed behind them.

Meta couldn't stop blinking. Inside, the pyramid was a vast skeletal maze of girders. Lights blazed and giant balls of energy pulsed.

Kane guided them to a silver landing pad. He grounded the cycle on it. Then, he *clunked* his helmet against hers.

"Can you hear me?" he asked.

Meta heard a tinny sound. She realized he hadn't spoken through the comm-unit, but through the metal of the helmet itself. Didn't their comm equipment work inside the pyramid? It would appear not.

"I hear you," Meta shouted.

"Good. Stay on the cycle. I will return."

Kane then climbed off the space-cycle and walked in a staggering way along the silver pad. It floated on nothing, although it was attached to a small wall that rested against a glowing ball. Kane must have magnetized his boots. He approached a wall with various man-sized levers on it like a giant clock.

Meta debated with herself. Should she scoot back and fly the cycle away? She had no idea how she would get out of the pyramid. What if she became trapped? Maybe she should try to escape for the good of humanity. That's likely what Maddox would have done.

I don't want to die. I don't even know what's going on. Did Kane plan for that? Does he think he knows me? What in the world is he doing?

Kane reached up and moved a clocklike lever. He stood back as if studying what he had done. Then, he stepped up and moved another lever. He did this for five minutes, stepping back each time and studying his handiwork.

Finally, he lurched back to the cycle and climbed on.

Meta expected him to clunk his helmet against hers and tell her something. That didn't happen. Kane started up the cycle and flew away.

What had that all been about? Meta still had no idea what the Nexus did.

A slot opened, and the cycle darted back into space. Meta found herself hyperventilating. She told herself to calm down.

After a short journey, Kane landed back on the scout near the hatch. He magnetized the cycle to the ship and reversed the process. Soon, they stood inside the airlock, listening to air hiss within. A green light flashed. Kane pushed open a different hatch, and they climbed out. Kane twisted off his helmet. Meta did likewise.

"What did you do?" she asked. "Why did you move those levers?"

"We don't have any time for explanations!" Kane shouted, sounding highly agitated. "Run to the control room, now!" he roared. The big man didn't wait for her to obey. He grabbed her and propelled her down the corridor.

Meta got his sense of urgency. Whatever he had done in there had a time limit. That frightened her, and she hated the feeling. Still, she ran with him.

They both threw themselves into their respective seats.

"Buckle in," Kane said. "It could be your life if you don't."

She gazed at him. The big man seemed scared. That frightened her even more. With shaking hands, Meta buckled in.

Kane worked the controls. The scout's engine *thrummed* into life.

At that moment, a strange phenomenon occurred outside the scout. A tiny pulsating red glob of matter appeared. It shimmered and expanded, rapidly growing to a little more than twice the scout's size.

"What is that?" Meta whispered.

"The Nexus has opened a portal," Kane said in a strained voice.

"A portal to what?" Meta asked.

"It is like a jump point, but it reaches across a greater distance. You must steel yourself."

"For what?" she asked.

"Leap Lag," he said.

"Is that like Jump Lag?"

"Many times worse," Kane said.

Meta stared at Kane in horror.

With a shaking hand, Kane tapped the controls. The scout headed for the pulsating red matter.

"You're kidding, right?" Meta asked.

Kane stared intently out of the viewing port.

"The portal is small," she said.

"Shut up!" Kane snarled. "If I make a mistake—"

Meta closed her eyes then opened them again. She began to tremble with fear. This was horrible. Was it really going to be as bad as Kane said? The man never seemed to joke around.

The scout entered the portal.

In seconds, the small vessel leaped across hundreds of light years. Then, the scout popped back into existence.

Inside the spaceship, Meta and Kane howled in agony. They thrashed on their seats, vomited and cried out again and again.

Meta had never experienced anything like this. She would never willingly make such a journey again. The pain in her mind, in her body, kept growing, seeming as if it would never stop.

Knowing what would happen, how had Kane found the courage to do this? Before she could figure out an answer, Meta thankfully blanked out.

-20-

Captain Maddox jogged around the bridge, moving hour after hour in a loping rhythm. The holoimage of the ancient alien watched him, saying nothing. A stainless steel robot stood motionless by the door. Maddox knew it would come to life if he tried to go outside.

He'd been on the bridge for weeks now as *Victory* used its star drive. The ship made short hops, if one could call three to five light years at a time short. As a small concession to the crew's comfort and ease of mind, Maddox had convinced the AI to give everyone ten minutes warning before a jump. Even so, this had been a grueling passage.

Since the last conversation, Galyan had fallen silent. No matter how hard Maddox had tried to engage the AI, the holoimage ignored him. The feeling of being a prisoner in solitary confinement had grown stronger by the week.

Now, the holoimage stirred, and it spoke. "There is a problem," Galyan said.

As Maddox jogged past the holoimage, his head snapped up in surprise. He halted, considering the words. As he did, the captain took out a cloth, wiping his sweaty face and neck. His uniform was rumbled and had become smelly, badly needing a wash.

"I'm listening," Maddox said between gasps.

"The star drive is showing signs of strain," Galyan said.

"You're overusing it, maybe overheating certain mechanisms."

"That is correct," Galyan said.

"The answer is obvious then. Let the star drive cool down before engaging it again. It will help all of us if we can rest longer between jumps. The effects are clearly cumulative."

"I understand your words," Galyan said. "Yet I am…I am anxious to reach Wolf Prime."

Maddox found that interesting. "Why?" What would make an AI uneasy?

"I keep wondering if Professor Ludendorff is still on the planet," Galyan said. "It's possible the New Men will scour the surface for him. They are clever, and it is possible they have uncovered Star Watch's need for the man. I find these unknowns troubling and wish for greater speed. Therefore, I use the star drive more than I should."

"You must restrain yourself," Maddox said. "We'll get there when we get there."

"I cannot subscribe to such a fatalistic philosophy. I want to be there now. Thus, we will push on, maybe even harder than before."

"If you do that," Maddox said, "you'll ruin the starship."

"Yes," Galyan said, "I give that a high probability."

"What good does it do to wreck the starship so we fail to reach Wolf Prime?"

"We should reach the planet, but at a greatly diminished capacity."

"What you're saying is the starship won't be any good afterward when you hand it over to us," Maddox said.

"That means nothing to me."

"It should," Maddox said. "You need our cooperation."

"That is not rational. I need nothing from you."

"Are you sure about that?" Maddox asked. "You will achieve your goal faster and with more certainty if you engage our cooperation on your behalf."

"I perceive that as a threat," Galyan said. "Know, Captain, that I will kill crewmembers if you slacken your efforts on my behalf."

"You're missing the point," Maddox said. "Think about your last battle against the Swarm."

The holoimage cocked its head. "Yes. There are faint recollections in my core about the battle. It is curious. I detect further blocks, deeper than before, making it impossible to access a full recounting of the battle."

Maddox wanted the starship at peak efficiency at Wolf Prime and beyond. Deeper blocks, how could that be important? No. How could he use that to his advantage?

"If you could recall the battle with clarity," Maddox said, "it would show you that beings who *want* to help are more useful than those *forced* into action."

The holoimage's eyelids flickered.

Maddox had come to realize this meant the AI was using more core memory.

"Your theory may only be true for humans," Galyan said. "But even that is not a given. I would have to access greater amounts of data concerning your species' historical records."

"Take my word for it," Maddox said.

"That is exactly what I refuse to do. I will not take your word on anything, as you are a notorious liar."

"You wound me with your disagreement," Maddox said offhandedly.

"I state *facts*," Galyan said.

Maddox eyed the holoimage. This was an opportunity. He needed to exploit it.

"These arguments between us aren't necessary," the captain said. "If we cooperated, we'd both benefit. For instance, there's a way to make better use of the vessel's star drive so you'd reach Wolf Prime faster."

"Tell me how this could be done," Galyan said. "Otherwise, I will instruct my robots to execute several of your crew."

"How does that make rational sense?" Maddox asked.

"Very easily," Galyan said. "By killing a human—"

"No, listen to me," Maddox said. "I've just informed you that I know something you can use. Your reaction was to threaten my people. Next time, I won't tell you I know something important so you won't know to threaten me."

The holoimage regarded him. "I begin to perceive your point. If I threatened you, saying I will kill crewmembers if

192

you withhold information, I won't learn of it because you might stay silent next time."

"Exactly," Maddox said.

"This is upsetting."

"Welcome to the real world," Maddox said. "I have to deal with these sorts of situations all the time."

"I am not interested in your past. It is meaningless to me."

"But I'm sure you would be interested in using the tramlines," Maddox said. "Some of the routes make longer jumps than you can do with the star drive. By a judicious use of the wormholes, you could save wear and tear to the ship."

"The Laumer Drive is human technology," Galyan said. "That is not an integral part of my vessel. My holoimage cannot enter the section in the hangar bay that contains the Laumer Drive. I would have to send a robot, which wasn't constructed to use human interfaces."

"You could gain our greater cooperation," Maddox said. "We can go in there for you and use the interfaces."

The holoimage studied him. "You desire to run the Laumer Drive for me?"

"I'm not a technician," Maddox said. "I'd have Lieutenant Noonan do it, maybe with Doctor Rich's help."

"No," Galyan said. "Do you think I've forgotten what the lieutenant did to my previous robot? She destroyed it, and the doctor shut me down. I have special plans for those two—" The holoimage fell silent.

"This is interesting," Maddox said. "You have deliberately deceived us. You said earlier you would give us the starship after Ludendorff imprinted my engrams into your core. But now it seems you have a hidden agenda for others in the crew. I find that extremely gratifying to learn."

Galyan looked up, shocked. "That is not a rational response."

"Of course it is," Maddox said. "It tells me something about your race I hadn't realized until now."

Galyan scowled. "If you are implying less than sterling qualities for my people—"

"No, I'm sure you were all the purest altruists that God ever created," Maddox said sarcastically.

The holoimage pointed at Maddox. "I detect falsehood in your statement. You are imputing my race with practicing underhanded actions."

"That's right. I'm saying you're enough like us that I feel comfortable with you. If that weren't so, we wouldn't be able to communicate. Think about that for a moment."

The holoimage blinked rapidly. "I must think on this more deeply," Galyan said. He thereupon vanished.

Maddox glanced at the robot. It did nothing, although he could sense it watching him. Wearily, the Star Watch officer went to a chair, sitting down.

Maddox had been alone for weeks now. The worst part was that he actually *felt* isolated. He seldom did on Earth. He thought about the others, Valerie, Riker and Dana. They endured the journey together. Undoubtedly, they had their own set of miseries to deal with, but loneliness wouldn't be one of them. Did he envy them?

I am an island. I will endure and defeat the AI and the New Men after Galyan.

Swiveling in his seat, Maddox faced the panel. He activated the main screen. Stars showed out there. He didn't see any nearby planets. What system were they in?

"Captain Maddox," Galyan said, sternly.

Swiveling around, Maddox saw the holoimage frowning at him.

"There is something in your words," Galyan said. "Cooperation often proves superior to coercion. I have offered you the use of my starship to help against the New Men. My payment is your suffering for many cycles of time. You will take my place in the memory core. If the New Men destroy *Victory*, however, that would cause your pain to end. I desire humanity's survival against your enemy so you will endure the ages and suffer as I've suffered."

Maddox said nothing.

"I find the situation too tenuous," Galyan said, "as I have just run a long-term analysis. Your species cannot defeat the New Men."

"We'll have to agree to disagree," Maddox said.

"Your disagreement has no bearing on the situation. In the short term, the New Men will destroy *Victory*. That is a mathematical certainty."

"Professor Ludendorff's genius will shift the odds back in the ship's favor."

"That is highly unlikely. Still, we need the professor so he can fix the imprinter."

"And the various weapon systems presently offline," Maddox said.

"I have decided to modify our agreement," Galyan said. "I am telling you this because my people were trustworthy, far superior to the quarrelling human species I have observed."

Maddox remained silent.

"If Ludendorff can fix the imprinter, I will find an empty star system. There, I will detach the memory core and send it into a hidden orbit. Your engrams will live within the AI core, but they will no longer be aboard *Victory*."

"If humanity doesn't get the use of your starship—"

"I cannot in good conscience give you my precious vessel," Galyan said, interrupting. "Your species doesn't deserve it. My hatred of you is the only thing prolonging your existence at this point. I tell you this because I am honest. Are you also honest, Captain Maddox?"

The captain wondered how he should answer. "Up to a point," he said at least.

"Which means you are dishonest," Galyan said. "That may be the first true thing you have told me. I find that refreshing."

"That I told you I'm a liar?" Maddox asked.

"Yes."

"But wouldn't that by necessity be a lie?" Maddox asked.

The holoimage blinked rapidly, and its head jerked several times. "I will be back," Galyan said in a high-pitched voice.

The holoimage vanished.

Maddox stood abruptly and marched to the comm officer's station. He tapped the board, turning on the ship's intercom.

"This is Captain Maddox speaking. I am still alive. The AI has begun—"

The lights in the station went dead.

"You shouldn't have done that," Galyan said.

Maddox turned around. The holoimage had returned. The captain shrugged. It had seemed like the right thing to do.

"Since I can no longer trust you—"

Maddox laughed, shaking head.

"Why are you mocking me?" Galyan asked.

"It isn't mockery," Maddox said. "I just find it darkly amusing that you're telling me you can no longer trust us. We had a pact, a deal, and now you're changing the nature of it. That is funny, don't you see?"

"No. I do not understand why that would make you laugh. Shouldn't it make you sad or angry with me as I'm angry with you?"

"I see. You want to make me angry. No. Your double dealing shows me that your people never were trustworthy. That makes you just like us. What's funny is that you can't see that. You're so vain and boastful that it makes me laugh."

"That is a slur to my race," Galyan said.

"Your actions are a slur to your race. If you can't see that, you're not as smart as I thought you were. That means it's only a matter of time before I take control of your vessel again."

The holoimage cocked its head. "You will never gain control of my vessel. It is a sacred object, too holy for human hands."

"I wish you would climb down off your high horse for once," Maddox said. "The only thing that makes your ship special is its extreme age. It has lasted far longer than your race did. Length of survival doesn't equate to nobility."

"My race—"

"If you can't keep your bargain with me," Maddox said, "I'm going to kill myself. That will keep me from suffering for six thousand years or longer in your AI core."

"No!" Galyan said. "That would shatter our bargain. If you do such a deed, I will order my robots to annihilate your people. Then I will explode *Victory*. Without my vessel, the New Men will defeat Star Watch."

Maddox shrugged.

"You must remain alive long enough for me to imprint your engrams into the AI core," Galyan said.

"Now, we're getting somewhere," Maddox said. "If you want me to stay alive, you have to give us the starship before you expire. Think of it like this. What does it matter what happens to your starship after you're gone? For you and for your race, the universe will have ended."

The holoimage appeared thoughtful. Finally, it said, "I cannot agree to that."

"Then tell me what we can offer you that will cause you to keep your word to us."

The holoimage blinked rapidly. It kept doing so far longer than it had in the past. Suddenly, the image brightened, making it difficult to look at.

"Yes!" Galyan said. "There is a thing I desire above your suffering."

"I know. You want to find the homeworld of the Swarm and destroy it." Maddox nodded. "That makes sense. Yes, I agree."

"You agree to what?" Galyan said.

"I agree to hunt down the Swarm and destroy their homeworld. In return, you will leave us *Victory*."

Galyan opened his mouth, but no words issued. He turned away, finally turning back. "I will think about it."

"For how long?" Maddox asked.

Galyan examined the robot. The holoimage's eyes shined brightly as it looked at Maddox.

"I accept your offer. You will leave the bridge and join Lieutenant Noonan. The two of you will enter the Laumer Drive access point in Hangar Bay Three. You will meet her in two hours."

"Why so long?" Maddox asked.

"That is how long it will take to reach a known Laumer-Point in the Rigel System."

"We're that far out already?" Maddox asked. "I'm impressed. Say, before I meet with the lieutenant, do you mind if I shower and clean my uniform?"

"I do not mind. I will show you where to shower and scrub your clothes."

The bridge door opened.

Maddox couldn't believe how excited he was to look into the corridor. After these isolated weeks, it was something different.

"Go," Galyan said.

Maddox started and then stopped.

"What is wrong?" Galyan asked.

Maddox had been so consumed with himself, he'd forgotten to think about his crew. He was the captain. Their welfare was his concern.

"The others also need showers and clean clothes," Maddox said.

Galyan said nothing for several seconds. "It will be so," he said at last. "Now, go."

Maddox headed for the exit.

***

The captain looked up as the hatch opened. He was in the Laumer Drive control room inside Hangar Bay Three.

A wary-eyed Valerie Noonan stepped through. She stared at him in surprise and then in obvious relief. Behind her, a stainless steel robot trundled in.

Valerie looked tired and careworn, if still defiant of her captor. Her clothes and hair were slightly damp but clean. Once she drew near, Maddox could smell the soap she'd used. The AI had kept its word.

"You look well, Captain," Valerie said.

He gave her a jaunty smile.

"It isn't so easy for us where we're being held," Valerie said, half-accusing him. "We just got to shower and clean our clothes for the first time. It must be nice having the run of the bridge.'

"All in a day's work," Maddox said. "Now, I believe you're supposed to coordinate the Laumer Drive."

They took up their stations and began to ready the machine. Maddox turned on an atomizer-timer. It was a loud, clicking device.

Valerie gave him a questioning glance.

Maddox paid her no heed, but continued to work at his panel. Soon, he stepped closer to her, all while working his board.

"What are you doing?" she whispered. "I can make absolutely no sense of the systems you've turned on. And that ticker is driving me crazy with its incessant clicks."

"It's make work," Maddox whispered so he could hardly hear his own words.

Valerie waited for him to continue.

"How long until activation of the Laumer-Point?" Maddox asked in a loud, officious voice.

"Uh…" Valerie glanced at a screen. "Three minutes, Captain, if I can adjust this setting properly."

"Hurry," he said.

Valerie's fingers roved over a board. She had her head cocked so an ear was near Maddox's lips.

The lieutenant had understood him. Good. Now, Maddox spoke fast in a low voice.

"The AI is proving troublesome. You must speak to Doctor Rich. See if she remembers learning anything about the Swarm. If not, tell her to concoct a story."

"Do you mean Galyan's enemy race?"

"Exactly," Maddox said. "Tell Dana we have to pretend to find the Swarm's homeworld. Make it far away in the Beyond. We're going to trade the information with the AI to keep Galyan true to his word."

Valerie nodded.

"We approach the known location of the Laumer-Point," Galyan said, his voice coming out of a robot's speaker. "You must activate the Laumer Drive so we can jump."

Valerie glanced at Maddox.

He nodded.

The lieutenant tapped her board. A powerful generator came online.

In space, an opening appeared. Starship *Victory* aimed for the Laumer-Point. A minute later, the vessel sped through the jump route, coming out on the other side almost seven light years away.

Maddox and Lieutenant Noonan endured Jump Lag. This would be the moment to attempt to subdue the robot. As the captain contemplated the idea, systems began functioning again.

"Warning," Galyan said through the robot's speakers. "An enemy fleet is fast approaching us. Their weapons systems are charged. Captain Maddox, my starship will soon be under attack."

-21-

Captain Maddox and Lieutenant Noonan raced for the bridge, with him easily outdistancing her. Farther behind, the sounds of the robot's treads echoed through the corridors.

Finally, an exhausted Maddox stumbled onto the bridge. He moved to the pilot's seat, sitting down, wiping sweat out of his eyes.

"Give me ten times magnification," Maddox said. "Show me the closest enemy vessels."

A large, cruiser-sized vessel appeared. It was square-shaped, confounding Maddox. Star Watch didn't have any spaceships like that. So far, the New Men had only fought with triangular-shaped star cruisers.

As the captain watched, a heavy-mount laser flashed from the enemy vessel. Other beams from the rest of the ships speared out of the darkness. They flashed through space at the speed of light, crossing seventy thousand kilometers, striking *Victory's* deflector shield.

"My neutron beam will annihilate them," Galyan said. "First, we must get into range."

"How many enemy ships are out there?" Maddox asked.

"Seven cruiser-class vessels and twelve destroyers," Galyan said. "I am using Star Watch configurations as a basis for comparison."

"They're not Star Watch vessels?"

"They have not communicated with me," Galyan said. "Nor have I attempted communication with them. Therefore, I cannot say for certain. But I do not believe they belong to Star Watch."

"How long will the deflector shield hold?" Maddox asked.

"At this rate… long enough so I can move into the neutron beam's range. I will annihilate the threat."

Maddox didn't like the odds: ramming into seven heavy beams with twelve destroyers maneuvering out there. *Victory* could destroy some of them, but not all before the starship's shield collapsed. How long would the collapsium hull armor hold?

"You risk destruction or heavy damage attacking seven cruisers and twelve destroyers," Maddox said. "You must use the star drive and jump away."

"Negative," Galyan said. "I have grown weary of fleeing. Today, I attack."

Lieutenant Noonan staggered onto the bridge, wheezing for air. She looked exhausted and sweat ran down her cheeks.

"It's been too long since I've had to run that far," Valerie panted.

Maddox stood up as she approached, moving aside. Valerie slid into the vacant seat. Even as she panted, her hands moved over the controls. She was like a master pianist, obviously at home before the board.

"Seven cruisers," Valerie said between gasps, "and twelve destroyer-class vessels."

"Do you recognize any of them?" Maddox asked.

"Of course," Valerie said, glancing at him in surprise. "This is the Social Syndicate Fleet."

"Of the Rigel System?" Maddox asked.

Valerie nodded. "They're pounding our deflectors hard. Once the destroyers move in and add their—"

"What is it?" Maddox asked.

"Sneaky bastards," Valerie said, with admiration in her voice. "Stealth drones have just activated. They're close, must have been waiting near the Laumer-Point." She made adjustments, studying her panel. The lieutenant turned around abruptly. "Captain, those are *Titan*-class nuclear-tipped missiles. They've obviously been lying in wait like proximity mines for someone to use the Laumer-Point. This is an ambush."

"Why do these aggressors wish to destroy my starship?" Galyan asked.

"They can't know who you are," Maddox said. "This ambush wasn't meant for us."

"The New Men," Valerie said. "Maybe this was a setup against them."

"That doesn't make sense," Maddox said. "We just jumped *out* of the Rigel System. Why would the Social Syndicate Fleet be waiting here for us and not in their own star system?"

"I don't know," Valerie said. "But I know those missiles will knock down our shield. The combined enemy lasers will chew into the hull. We have collapsium, so it will take a while, but seven cruisers and all those destroyers..." Valerie shook her head. "Sir, I recommend we use our star drive and jump out of danger."

"Galyan doesn't agree with you," Maddox said.

"Then we have to talk to the fleet's commander and convince him to stop attacking," Valerie said.

"Well?" Maddox asked Galyan. "Will you let me communicate with the attacking fleet?"

The holoimage appeared thoughtful. Finally, Galyan nodded.

"Do it," Maddox told Valerie. "Hail the fleet."

Valerie jumped up, moving to a different chair. The modifications to the alien bridge helped her to know where to go, as the redesign was based on Star Watch preferences.

As the beams continued to pour against *Victory's* shield—turning it a bright red color—and the Social Syndicate missiles increased velocity, closing the distance, a bearded man appeared on the main screen. He wore a jet-black uniform with a black cap, with a red fist clutching a lightning bolt on the bill.

The man laughed at Maddox. "This is one star system you don't get to destroy with impunity, New Man. It is a pleasure to watch you die."

"I'm Captain Maddox of Star Watch. You must stop your assault at once."

"I am Sub-commander Ko," the bearded man said, "and I declare you a liar. There is no such vessel as yours registered with Star Watch. This I know to be true."

"You're wrong," Maddox said. "Star Watch sent us into the Beyond to retrieve the vessel. This is an ancient starship—"

"Save your lies, New Man," Sub-commander Ko said. "Die with whatever dignity you can muster."

Maddox turned to Galyan. "Jump. Nothing else makes sense."

"I will not run from inferior beings," Galyan said.

The bearded sub-commander laughed. "And you claim you're not New Men. Your own commander brands you a vicious liar by calling us inferior. That's New Men speech if I ever heard it. Listening to you beg is a rare pleasure."

"I have Doctor Dana Rich aboard my ship," Maddox said, casting about for anything. "Are you familiar with her?"

Ko's face darkened. "That witch, she's alive?"

"Yes, in my hold."

The Social Syndicate officer stared at Maddox. Dana had committed high crimes against the ruling Syndic and his clones. There wasn't anyone they would want more than her.

"I would pay almost anything to have her, *almost*," the sub-commander said. "But I will not forgo the pleasure of destroying you."

"If I'm a New Man," Maddox asked, "how would I know that Dana Rich means so much to your Syndic?"

"That's easily answered. The New Men are clever, with spies everywhere. It doesn't surprise me you know about her."

"Why wasn't your fleet in the Rigel System defending it?" Maddox asked.

"Why ask me such foolish questions?" Ko asked. "The answers cannot aid you. Look, your shield has already darkened to brown."

Maddox glanced at the indicator. It was brown as Sub-commander Ko said.

A deflector shield absorbed energy such as a laser beam or thermonuclear explosion. The shield bled off the wattage over time. Overload darkened a shield. Once it was black, a shield was near collapse. It wouldn't be much longer now before theirs went down.

"The missiles are minutes away from detonation range," Valerie said from her board.

Maddox fixated on the bearded officer on the screen. "If I were a New Man, I would have bombarded your main planet in the Rigel System."

"I'm well aware of this."

"Your planet wasn't touched."

"So you say," Ko sneered. "I know otherwise."

"This makes no sense."

"At long last," Ko said, "you have met a political system that produces soldiers more cunning than you. We know about your depredations, New Man. We know you have slipped into systems through backdoor entrances, always appearing where least expected. Then, you rush near and destroy planetary biospheres with your hell-burners. This time, we have surprised you marauders. The price was high, I admit it. But the Syndic demanded a plan that would hurt the New Men, no matter the cost. Not all of humanity agrees to play the sheep, the Social Syndicate the least of all."

"Two minutes to warhead detonation," Valerie said. "That's given the missiles explode at the optimum range to reach us as fast as possible."

Maddox's shoulders slumped. He was out of ideas. Galyan wouldn't jump, and the bearded officer refused to believe him. The captain could hardly blame Sub-commander Ko. *Victory* was unlike any ship in the Commonwealth. To think this was a New Man vessel was a logical if flawed deduction.

"I don't understand why the AI doesn't use the star drive to close the gap between them and us," Valerie said. "Isn't that how you defeated the star cruisers in the Beyond?"

The holoimage straightened. "Yes. This was so. Why didn't you remind me, Captain Maddox?"

"You're a computer," Maddox said. "I thought you would remember. It doesn't make sense you wouldn't."

"What you say is true," Galyan said. "This makes me believe you have inserted a virus into my core."

205

"I haven't," Maddox said. "That doesn't mean no one else did, though."

"Doctor Rich must have done so," Galyan said.

"I've already told you," the bearded man said on the screen. "I'd rather watch you die than capture that witch."

"Consider what you just said," Maddox told Galyan. "If Doctor Rich has given you a virus, can you fully trust your impulses? I refer to the one that forbids you to jump away to safety."

"It would appear I cannot," Galyan said.

"That means you should *distrust* this impulse toward self-immolation. It may be a wrong desire."

"Explain," Galyan said.

Maddox refrained from facing Valerie's panel. He didn't want to see the blackened shield or the countdown to nuclear warhead detonation.

"You must scan your AI core," Maddox said, "and discover if Doctor Rich or someone else has infected you. Once you're gone, your secret enemy may rejoice over your destruction. If you find nothing unwarranted in the core, you can always self-destruct later. Besides, how will you revenge your race's death against the Swarm if you're gone?"

"The Swarm are dead—"

"It's too late," Valerie said, interrupting. "The thermonuclear warheads are exploding."

"No," Galyan said. "I will not go down easily into the dark night of destruction. If this is another of your plays, Maddox—"

"Good-bye, Galyan," Maddox said.

"This sucks," Valerie said.

Maddox turned, seeing her glare at the screen. Bright nova explosions showed the missiles detonating. Their x-rays and gamma rays struck the weakened deflector shield.

At that moment, everything vanished as Galyan engaged the star drive. As they used the alien jump, the shield collapsed and the *Titan*-class warheads' yield along with the heavy laser beams struck the collapsium hull. The starship shuddered. Maddox stumbled and crashed against the deck. Then the vessel reappeared three light years distant. The captain groaned. Valerie moaned. And everything aboard *Victory* shut down as the lights flickered and went dark.

"Captain?" Valerie asked.

"I'm right here," Maddox said in the blackness.

"What do we do now?"

Whomp-like sounds preceded red emergency lights snapping on. In the bloody glow, Maddox climbed to his feet and brushed his uniform. With a start, he turned toward the robot. It stood there as it often did. He moved to the stainless steel cylinder with its metallic tentacles. Using a fingernail, Maddox clicked the metal.

The robot didn't move.

"Is it dead?" Valerie asked.

"It would appear so," Maddox said. He moved to the door. It didn't open as it should. He removed a panel and manually cranked the door open. Red light also illuminated the corridor.

"Let's go," Maddox said.

"Where?" Valerie asked.

"It appears that *Victory* is down. We need the others to help us fix the ship."

"How can we fix this monstrous vessel?" Valerie asked. "There are only seventeen of us."

"That means we'd better start now," Maddox said. As Valerie debated it with herself, Maddox noticed a tiny light inside one of the robot's camera eyes. That surprised him, and then he wondered...

Just how cunning was Driving Force Galyan? Could the AI have staged some this, making the damage seem worse than it was, in order to study their reactions?

"Yes," Valerie told Maddox. "What else can we do? Let's start repairing ship systems."

They moved down the corridors. Maddox debated telling Valerie about his suspicions. He decided the fewer people who knew what might really be going on, the more genuine would be their reactions. The captain only trusted himself to playact well enough to fool the AI.

Before he reached the second area of confinement where the others stayed, Maddox discovered they had already forced open their hatch.

"Who goes there?" Major Kharkov shouted from a crossway.

"It's Captain Maddox and Lieutenant Noonan."

"What happened, Commander?" the stocky, space marine major asked, walking into sight.

Maddox explained about the short battle with the Social Syndicate Fleet. As he did, the rest of the prisoners showed up in twos and threes.

"At the very end," the captain finished, "Galyan used the star drive. It appears the lasers and thermonuclear EMP blasts knocked out some of the starship's systems, including the robots and the AI."

"That doesn't make sense," Dana said. "The—"

"Doctor!" Maddox said sharply. "There's something I've been wondering."

"Yes?" Dana asked, giving him a funny look.

"Before I say," Maddox told her, "I think we should start splitting up into teams to test various stations. Major, I think you and Strauss should check out the antimatter engine."

"What do I know about that?" the space marine asked.

"Please bear with me, Major," Maddox said.

Kharkov must have picked up on the captain's tone. "Yes, sir, at once," the space marine said.

After assigning the others their duties, Maddox pulled Dana aside.

"Doctor, doctor, doctor," Maddox said. "I hope you've been well these past weeks."

"Are you feeling all right?" Dana asked him.

Maddox laughed uneasily, shaking his head. Just how smart was Doctor Rich? He didn't want to tell her his suspicions outright, having the secretly listening AI pick up his whispers. Could she catch his innuendoes?

"Galyan has frightened me, Doctor. The AI is abnormally clever. I also stand in awe of his rigor and righteousness."

"Excuse me?" Dana asked.

"Galyan's people were surely far in advance of ours. If the human race could obtain even half their glory, we would do well indeed. It has been a rare privilege to learn from Galyan. I've tried to reason with him, but he suspects everything I do. I don't know how to convince him I mean to do exactly as I say. I dread having my engrams sent into the computing core, but I will do it for the good of humanity."

"I see," Dana said.

"One thing, Doctor, now that I have you alone. We *must* find the homeworld of the Swarm."

"Captain, I think the strain of the last battle might have—"

Dana quit speaking as Maddox stared at her in the red light, and squeezed her bicep twice in short succession.

"You were saying?" Dana asked, maybe understanding his signal.

Releasing her, Maddox became expansive. "In ancient times, Galyan's race must have protected us. If his people hadn't smashed the Swarm, would the vile enemy ships have reached Earth several hundred years later? If so, the Swarm would have annihilated us while humanity was still in the Bronze Age, fighting from chariots instead of spaceships."

Dana had become thoughtful. She now said, "I find that to be a remarkably accurate guess."

Maddox nodded encouragingly. "I wonder if the reason Galyan has remained awake for six thousand years is to search out and find the Swarm homeworld. Do you have any idea where it might be?"

"I might know," Dana said, watching Maddox closely. "I, ah, did find some data while working on the AI core while Galyan was off back in the Oort cloud."

"Interesting, interesting," Maddox said. "I wondered if that might be the case. I imagine the Swarm homeworld would be someplace far in the Beyond."

"I'll have to recheck my notes." Dana studied the captain. "One thing bothers me. Now that we have this chance to talk alone, without the bloody AI listening, I would like to know the truth."

Maddox kept himself from smiling. The doctor was sharp. She understood him perfectly.

"What do you want to know?" he asked.

"Are you going to keep your word with Galyan?"

"Providing the power returns?"

"Yes," Dana said.

"At first I'd planned to lull and trick him," Maddox said. "Now…I find I respect him and his race far too much for that. I stand in awe of him, Dana. But you must never, ever let anyone else know that."

"Why is that, Captain?"

"I'm too proud to admit such a thing to others. It's a moral flaw in me, I suppose."

"I can see that," Dana said.

"Could you go study your notes now?" Maddox asked.

"I actually do remember finding something interesting about the Swarm. I was going to tell you about it, but haven't found the opportunity. Now's the perfect time."

"Go on," Maddox said.

"I have strong reason to believe that evidence of the Swarm's homeworld lies at Wolf Prime."

A grin slipped onto Maddox's face. That was perfect.

"Professor Ludendorff has a fixation on alien archeology," Dana said. "We discovered Galyan's star system quite by accident. The professor was searching for more indications of the Swarm. They're the oldest known alien species we've ever found."

"Interesting."

"I think so too," Dana said. "If Galyan desires information about the Swarm homeworld, I think he'll find it on Wolf Prime. Professor Ludendorff may already know the answer to the AI's questions."

"That's—"

The main lights snapped on. It caused Dana to squint at the brightness. A second later, a robot rolled around the corner. The holoimage of Driving Force Galyan strode beside his machine.

"You surprise me, Captain Maddox," Galyan said.

"What's going on?" Maddox asked. "We thought…"

Galyan smiled broadly. "You thought the thermonuclear EMPs had rendered me impotent for the moment. Yes, I realized almost right away how I could use the Social Syndicate attack. Of course, from the beginning I realized that using the star drive was the correct tactical move."

"Why did you pretend that you didn't know?" Maddox asked.

"Don't you understand yet? Doctor, I see comprehension in your eyes."

"Yes, Galyan," Dana said meekly.

"You have passed my test, Captain," Galyan said. "I still dislike you and suspect your motives. But these words you spoke…"

"They don't mean a thing," Maddox said in a rush. "Whatever you heard, I didn't really mean them."

"Oh, I know better now," Galyan said. "I know you much better than before. We will continue to Wolf Prime. Nothing will stop me. I will have Professor Ludendorff aboard my vessel. Then…well, I'll leave that for later."

"There is one thing we should consider carefully," Maddox said. "Sub-commander Ko of the Social Syndicate Fleet said the New Men are bombarding inhabited planets. It would appear the enemy has been ranging to various systems in "C" Quadrant, attacking those they can. I wonder if the New Men are at Wolf Prime."

"Why would they be?" Galyan asked. "It's a sparsely settled world of no strategic significance."

"True," Maddox said. "It's barely habitable. It's a frozen hell world, in fact. Even so, the New Men may have sent a star cruiser or two to bombard the ice planet or search for Ludendorff. They may know about him."

"How does that affect us?" Galyan asked.

"We'd better be careful as we approach the Wolf System. We want to see the New Men before they see us. We don't want a repeat of what happened with the Social Syndicate Fleet."

"That is sound advice," Galyan said. "Now, we shall hurry to Wolf Prime. I am eager to speak with Professor Ludendorff."

-22-

Meta and Kane were in the scout ship's control room, in orbit around Wolf Prime. The planet was white, with heavy cloud cover in places. Other spots on the surface were a faint icy blue, showing vast frozen bodies of water. Directly below them, a violent storm raged, showing circular hurricane clouds. The panorama was beautiful to witness from up here. That didn't lock Meta's gaze, though.

A triangular star cruiser slid beside the scout, one of the New Men's hated warships. Meta had never seen one so close before. Turrets sprouted on the hull armor. Beam cannons jutted from each. The scout headed toward a larger than average bay door. Star Watch cruisers wouldn't have room for a scout this size. It appeared as if these vessels were different.

Meta did not ask Kane about that.

Ever since the great leap from the Nexus, Meta had become withdrawn and thoughtful. In truth, she hadn't fully recovered from the ordeal. Too often, she found herself staring at a spot, her mind blank, trying to engage but failing.

Is that what had happened to Kane? Was that why he seldom spoke? How many great leaps had the enemy agent taken in his life? It must have done something to him.

"A word of advice," Kane rumbled from his chair.

Meta tore her gaze from the bay door to regard the bruiser.

"Do not speak to a superior unless he first addresses you," Kane said. "Try to answer 'yes' or 'no' if you can. If that proves impossible, keep your answers as short as you can. On no account should you stare into a superior's eyes, which means you should keep your gaze downcast, preferably aimed at the floor."

"Are you a superior?" Meta asked.

The hint of a frown tightened Kane's mouth. "That is a shrewd question. The answer is no."

"You're not a New Man?"

"I have already said on former occasions I am not. I suppose you realize I am not one of the untamed either."

"What exactly are you then?"

"To some, I am a failed experiment. To others, I am a cipher to use in the Great War."

"I don't understand," Meta said.

"It doesn't matter. The important thing to remember is that you can gain status if you cooperate. If you persist in mulish resistance, they will take you to the teachers."

"Why did you kidnap me, Kane? What was the real reason?"

"Because I couldn't get to Doctor Rich."

"I'm a second choice?"

Kane tapped a control before standing. "It appears you have useful genetic material. I doubt the superiors will destroy you. Strive to please them. That means strict obedience. In that way, you may retain some of your former personality."

"What does that mean?"

"My words are clear enough for someone of your intelligence. Come, we must get ready."

Meta hesitated. She didn't want to board a star cruiser. She'd gotten a glimpse of a New Man on Loki Prime. That had been before Maddox came down with Ensign Maker. The incident seemed like a lifetime ago now.

Before Kane had to speak again, she rose. The scout headed for the opening. She was their prisoner. With a growing sense of dread and helplessness, Meta headed for the hatch, following Kane.

***

Meta and Kane walked down an empty corridor aboard the star cruiser. So far, she hadn't seen anyone. Was the ship automated?

Before leaving the scout, Kane had changed into a silver bodysuit. It made him seem even more like a gorilla with his big flat muscles and solid gait. If he'd seemed remote before, he practically seemed like a glacier now.

The big man halted before a closed hatch. "You're in danger," Kane whispered.

Meta peered at him in surprise.

Kane didn't move or look at her, but stood stiffly, speaking without moving his lips. "No one has greeted us. It has forced me to come here, to Per Lomax. He is an—"

The hatch opened. As if someone had thrown a switch, Kane fell silent.

A golden-skinned New Man stood before them, with a spacious chamber behind him.

Kane bowed his head in silent greeting.

Meta compared the two beings. Kane was obviously heavier and had to be stronger. The lean other, this Per Lomax, stood taller by a head and exuded a regal quality. He wore a silver suit with a red emblem on his right pectoral. Per Lomax's head was larger, with inky eyes and a pelt of hair. In a moment, Meta reevaluated her judgment. A palpable force or energy exuded from the New Man, giving him something greater than mere nobility.

What had Kane said before? Yes, he'd called this one a superior. Was that how Per Lomax thought of himself?

"She gapes at me," the New Man said in a deep voice.

"Meta," Kane said in warning.

She remembered his words and forced herself to look down. This was like Baron Chabot's castle where she had entered as a lowly maid. There were times to feign fear and subservience. Meta did so now, hunching her shoulders.

"Interesting," Per Lomax said. "She attempts subterfuge, thinking to trick me. You have treated her leniently during the voyage?"

"Yes," Kane said.

"Do you like her?" Per Lomax asked.

"Yes," Kane said.

The words shocked Meta. When had Kane ever shown that?

"It's clear you hope to regain her after the inquiry."

"Yes," Kane said in the same monotone as before.

"It's possible you have let her physical attributes sway your judgment. She is a delight to the eyes, I admit."

Kane remained silent.

"Do you disagree with my preliminary assessment?" Per Lomax asked.

"Yes," Kane said.

"You have grown bold during your absence from the Collective. Do you now seek individual satisfaction in life?"

It was the first time Kane hesitated. "I-I don't know," he said.

"A word of caution," Per Lomax said, "as it appears you have forgotten a truth. The continued exposure to the untamed can sully one's purity. It may be you need a session with the teacher. Do you volunteer for a meeting?"

"No," Kane said.

"You claim to have retained your purity?"

"Yes."

"Did you have relations with the woman?"

"No."

"That was a wise decision," Per Lomax said. "Sexual indulgence can sully one faster than improper ruminations."

Kane bowed his head.

"Ah, you wish to speak. Yes… Speak, Kane. You have my leave."

"The hunters on Wolf Prime are more individualistic than the untamed norm," Kane said. "The teacher stratifies the mind in proper sequencing, this I know. Yet the stratification shows in ways that some of the untamed are able to perceive. If I go to the teacher, it may be harder for me to mingle among the hunters of Wolf Prime afterward."

"Your second tier intellect correctly foresees your next assignment on Wolf Prime. You think to use that as a weight in your argument with me. This desire to avoid mental stratification does not bode well for your future, Kane. I detect a higher than average corruption to your rationality than a stay among the untamed should warrant. What occurred to cause this?"

"The only possible explanation I can perceive is that I used the Nexus again," Kane said.

"What was your reasoning for the decision?"

"I suspected the humans—the untamed—would find a means to bring the ancient starship to Wolf Prime."

"Elaborate," Per Lomax said.

Meta wasn't sure, but she thought she heard a faint sense of urgency to the New Man's words. It dawned on her this was the same New Man Captain Maddox had faced in the Beyond.

Kane told Per Lomax what he knew about the ancient starship. Before he left the Solar System, his sources told him Star Watch Intelligence had sent Captain Maddox to the Oort cloud in an X72 Peregrine.

"The untamed are reacting with haste," Kane said. "It seems they have stumbled onto their only solution."

"They undoubtedly seek Professor Ludendorff," Per Lomax said. "Interesting, interesting, they have finally reacted with optimum efficiency. I understand now why you used the Nexus. Your intellect served you well in this decision, Kane."

The blocky man dipped his head.

"Their wisest move would be to come here," Per Lomax said. "This is upsetting. Do you believe these actions are Captain Maddox's doing?"

"Yes," Kane said.

"It is past time we gained the ancient starship. If the Adok technologies were to fall to the untamed..." Per Lomax seemed to straighten. He reached out, putting the fingers of his right hand on Meta's left shoulder.

They felt like steel bands digging into her flesh. His strength shocked Meta, and she realized the New Man might conceivably be stronger than Kane.

"You have gained your desire, Kane," Per Lomax said. "The teacher can wait another day to straighten the deviancies your stay among the untamed has produced. You will be going down to the planet. As you surmised, we need an agent among the hunters. Ludendorff continues to elude us. But he won't for much longer."

Meta tried to twist free of the painful grip.

"She resists," the New Man said. "You have been too lenient with her. She may be too far gone as a tool."

"May I suggest an idea, Superior?" Kane asked.

As if his hand were a spring, Per Lomax released Meta's shoulder.

This time Meta could tell a difference. The New Man stared at Kane. The force radiating from him increased. Per Lomax felt like an angry god, ready to hurl a thunderbolt. Despite herself, Meta cringed before the New Man.

"You dare to address me as an equal? This is presumption. I am sullied by your attempt."

Kane went to one knee, bowing his head.

"I should destroy you," Per Lomax said. "Not because I have been sullied by your action, although that is bad enough. It appears to me that you have begun to think independently of the Collective, with yourself as your focus. You seek self-actualization."

Kane did not respond.

Per Lomax stirred, reaching to the blaster on his hip. "I perceive an outrage. Do you think to possess an insight beyond my knowledge?"

"I am forced to the truth," Kane said. "By the Collective—"

"No! Do not swear by the Whole, you who are an untamed mite. This is sacrilege. Either—"

"I know how to capture the ancient starship," Kane said, interrupting Per Lomax.

Meta waited for the thunderbolt to strike. In this instance, Per Lomax need merely draw his blaster and fire. The superior didn't move, though, and Kane remained on one knee with his head bowed. Finally, Meta shifted her head enough to glance at Per Lomax.

The New Man stared at Kane with a burning intensity, as if he could melt Kane's mind with his gaze.

"You have staked your continued existence on a presumption," Per Lomax said in a heavy voice. "Speak now in the seconds remaining to you."

Kane said nothing.

The superior glanced at Meta. "You do not wish her to hear your words?"

"No," Kane said.

"Then I give you leave for introspection," Per Lomax said. "I will study the specimen and send her to the teacher before returning to hear your supposed truth."

Kane remained as he was.

"There is more?" Per Lomax asked.

"Yes," Kane said.

Per Lomax looked up at the ceiling. The fingers of his right hand twitched. "State it," he said.

"If my plan is worthy," Kane said, "it is possible you will have other plans for the...the specimen."

"You claim to need her?"

"Yes," Kane said.

Per Lomax looked down upon Kane. "I had not anticipated these changes in you. Your life is a second tier resource, yet it has proven of worth in the past. Now, you risk this loss to the Collective. Your destruction will mar my record and conceivably retard my advancement. For the sake of the Whole, I hope you have risked wisely."

Without another word, Per Lomax wrapped his steely fingers around Meta's neck, propelling her deeper into the chamber.

***

Meta only remembered a little of what occurred in the chamber. Per Lomax first injected her with *fungoid vigils*, a green solution. It made her sleepy, but the New Man wouldn't let her lie down or even sit. She stood, addressing him as if he was her father.

The superior spoke in a haughty manner, firing off questions concerning her journey and about Kane. Per Lomax wanted to know minutiae, mainly concerning her feelings about the various things she had witnessed.

A few of the questions bothered Meta later. Those were the things she truly recalled.

"Do you desire to procreate with Kane?" Per Lomax asked.

218

"Have his children?" she asked.

"That is a symptom of procreation, of course. That is often not the originator for the desire. Do you want him to mount you?"

"You make it sound as if we're dogs."

"Ferals have a potential for rationality. This we understand. The evidence, however, suggests that only a tiny ratio practice higher-level reasoning. It's conceivable you can think objectively, although the probabilities are low."

"I'm not a dog," Meta said.

"You are a creature of intoxicating beauty. I admit there is an impulse within me to strip off your garments and test your sexuality. Since I am a superior, I block the impulse as an impure sensation."

"You don't like me?" Meta asked.

"Did Kane use you during the journey?"

"I would have killed him if he'd tried."

"Do you despise him?"

"I want to stick a knife in his heart."

"Strong emotions of any kind often indicate a fierce longing for procreation."

"What happened to you people?" Meta asked while in her mental fog. "Why are you so weird?"

"We are superior beings brought to fruition through selective breeding and intense genetic manipulation. We are *Homo Superiors.*"

"You're freaks."

"I am detecting a high level of intelligence in you. As impossible as it seems, you seek to evade answering my questions. That is a difficult feat while drugged with *fungoid vigils*. You have chosen an emotion-laden process to attempt to thwart me, in some manner realizing it gives you the highest percentage of success. Perhaps Kane spoke with greater insight than…" Per Lomax continued to speak, but his words no longer made sense.

Meta blinked lazily, swaying where she stood. Soon, the superior injected her again, and memory of the event faded from her mind.

***

Time separated from reality for Meta. She knew mind probing, pain and harsh questions from the teacher. It seemed as if stimuli came in flashing sequences of bright lights. Meta cringed and the flashing intensified. Words boomed like thunder in her brain. Then they hissed as if shifting on a night wind.

The teacher did something to her thinking. It wasn't right. Meta resisted, and for an instant, she found herself on a spinning table.

She was spread-eagled, her wrists and ankles secured by bands. The spinning disoriented her. Drugs surged through her system. She wore a helmet that sprouted with antenna. Every so often, shocks zapped her skull, making her eyelids flutter.

They're reprogramming me. I know that's what they're doing.

Meta squeezed her eyes shut. It was so hard to think. Yet, she had a feeling this was her last chance to affect her fate. This had something to do with Captain Maddox or was it Kane?

"We're not dogs," Meta whispered.

The spinning increased. The helmet shocks made her twitch in agony. The teacher did this to her. He had a plan, a tricky thing meant to do…something nefarious.

That night in New York City, Meta thought to herself. *The night Maddox and I fought. That isn't what really happened. We made love that night, passionate and wild love. I kissed you like this.*

In her mind, Meta strove to burn in the idea of French kissing Captain Maddox. In her thoughts, she grabbed his face and kissed him fiercely.

You told me to do that next time we met so we'd never forget what happened that night. Don't forget, Captain. Don't forget.

Meta screamed afterward as the teacher continued to stratify her mind into the proper sequencing.

***

Like an old-style ground vehicle using stick and clutch, Meta reengaged her mind with time as she walked down an empty corridor aboard the star cruiser.

Meta stopped and raised a hand, examining it in wonder. Then she inspected her clothes. She had boots, pants, a shirt and a jacket. These were Earth garments. Yet, she was aboard an enemy star cruiser.

A hatch opened, and Kane walked into the corridor. Meta expected a taller, thinner man to be with Kane. But the New Man agent was alone.

"What's going on, Kane?" Meta asked. Her voice startled her. It seemed too slow. Had somebody done something to her?

The big man's face was impassive, but Meta knew better now. She could read it in his granite eyes. Kane was happy to see her.

"Follow me," he said.

Without waiting for a confirmation, he spun on his heels and marched down the corridor. Meta had to hurry to keep up with him.

Soon, they entered a hangar bay. She saw the scout ship.

"We're leaving?" Meta asked.

Kane didn't answer. Half a minute later, he ducked through the hatch into the scout. She hurried after him.

In less than a minute, they both buckled in. Kane turned on the engine so the deck plates *thrummed*. The scout lifted from the hangar bay and eased out the open door. Below, a white winter world waited for them.

"What happened back there?" Meta asked. She didn't understand why she could hardly remember anything. There was something about a pyramid. Had she met Kane in Cairo?

As Meta tried to remember, another image interposed over her thoughts. It was a handsome Star Watch officer named Captain Maddox. They had made passionate love in New York City. She wanted to ask Kane about that. Something deep inside her told Meta that would be a bad idea.

"We're going down to Wolf Prime," Kane said.

"Oh."

"We need to find Professor Ludendorff," Kane added. "Only he can help us against the New Men."

"We're fugitives from the New Men?" Meta asked, frowning.

"Yes," Kane said. "Don't you remember?"

Meta's frown deepened. Yes. That's right. They had just escaped by killing several New Men. She looked at her hands. There wasn't any blood. After she killed, as she had a baron once, she pretended to see blood on her hands. Why didn't she see any blood now?

Is Kane lying to me? Why would he do that? Isn't Kane my friend?

"Meta, do you remember? We just escaped and are fleeing down onto Wolf Prime."

Meta nodded. She could play along with this until she recalled events better.

Kane pursed his lips and his features hardened. "I'll do the talking once we reach the surface. You simply back up whatever I say."

"Of course," Meta said.

Kane hesitated, looking as if he wanted to say more. Then he tapped the controls. With a lurch, the scout headed down toward the winter planet.

-23-

"This is a disaster," Galyan said. The holoimage stared at the main screen.

Silently, Maddox agreed. He hadn't expected the New Men to block their advance. The number of star cruisers orbiting Wolf Prime... *Victory's* sensors showed five of the deadly vessels.

For the past two weeks, Galyan had used tramlines together with star drive jumps. The alien vessel burned through the Commonwealth faster than any spaceship Maddox knew about. With the star drive, *Victory* could jump beside Laumer-Points instead of using velocity to travel there the old-fashioned way. The only negative was the number of times everyone endured Jump Lag. In a normal run, there were longer periods of rest.

Fortunately, Maddox had convinced Galyan to use the star drive to enter the Wolf System from the side instead of coming in at a Laumer-Point. They'd wanted to see any enemy before the enemy saw them.

Space was vast and ships were miniscule—less than tiny motes in comparison to the void—making dedicated searches difficult unless one scanned in specific spots. *Victory's* sensors had picked out the star cruisers in orbit around the ice world. Had the New Men spotted the ancient starship in return? Galyan's sensors said no. Last time in the Beyond, however, the New Men had shown an uncanny ability to track the *Geronimo* and then *Victory*. It would be rash to believe the enemy wasn't even now pondering why the ancient starship approached Wolf Prime.

"*Victory* cannot defeat five star cruisers," Galyan said. "The game is up, Captain. We have lost."

"Hang on," Maddox said. "Is that how you acted during your battle against the Swarm?"

"That was different."

Maddox drummed his fingers on a console. "The star cruisers are a problem, I grant you. But they're not an insolvable one."

"I am the galaxy's premier tactician," Galyan said, "and I tell you there is no combination of maneuvers that will allow *Victory* to annihilate five vessels of such magnitude."

"There's an ancient Earth saying," Maddox told the AI, "maybe as old as your ship. 'There's more than one way to skin a cat.'"

"I do not perceive your meaning."

Maddox drummed his fingers harder against the console. How should he go about this? Was there a way to win? Five star cruisers...he had to tell the AI something, so he'd better start talking.

"Driving Force Galyan, this is an apparent impasse. You are also a splendid tactician. I would like to use the idea of another ancient saying to see if we Earthlings can come up with a plan."

"What is the saying?" Galyan asked.

"Two heads are better than one."

"You wish to speak with your crew?"

"Exactly," Maddox said.

"I will agree to the meeting on one condition."

"Yes?"

"If we make an attempt and you actually reach Wolf Prime," Galyan said, "you must search for the archeological clues on the surface for the whereabouts of the Swarm's ancient homeworld."

"I am honor bound to do so," Maddox said. "That means I will attempt it with all my strength and cunning."

"It is fortunate for you that I have taken your measure," Galyan said. "Otherwise, I would believe you are lying to me."

Maddox said nothing.

"Yes," Galyan said. "You will go to your crew, and I will join you."

***

The crew sat against the walls of the chamber, sixteen people having spent endless weeks in here. Their three-month margin had almost run out. Maddox could imagine what it must have smelled like before the AI allowed them to shower and clean their uniforms and sleeping gear.

The captain stood as he explained the situation. It would have been better if Galyan wasn't watching, with three of his robots in attendance. But, the AI was here, listening to every word. Thus, Maddox had adjusted his words accordingly.

"You're absolutely sure there are five star cruisers?" Valerie asked.

Maddox nodded.

"We couldn't take on *three* star cruisers in the Beyond," the lieutenant said. "Five is out of the question."

"We did take on three," Second Lieutenant Maker told her. "We even destroyed one of them, remember?"

"And almost lost *Victory* in return," Valerie said. "You're not seriously suggesting there is some way we can destroy five star cruisers?"

"I certainly am, love," Keith said.

"This I have to hear."

"It's no different than what we originally planned," the Scotsman said. "We grab Professor Ludendorff, bring him to *Victory* and have the genius repair the super weapons. We turn those on the New Men—*bam!*" Keith said, clapping his hands. "We destroy five star cruisers."

"Oh, sure," Valerie said, sarcastically. "I should have seen it. We just journey past the star cruisers to Wolf Prime, send down a shuttle and pick up the professor. What was I thinking? That's as easy as can be."

"Not quite as easy as that, love," Keith said. "But it's the right idea."

Valerie looked around at the others. "Am I missing something? Please, someone tell me what I can't see."

Keith grinned. "Don't be so hard on yourself, lass. You're a Fleet officer by training, not a strikefighter pilot." The small ace thumped his chest. "Among those, I'm the best. I can tell you exactly what to do."

Valerie shook her head in apparent disbelief at Maker's confidence. "Go on then, tell me. I think we'd *all* like to know."

Keith's smile broadened. "With your permission, Captain?"

Maddox nodded.

"It's obvious we can't just barge onto Wolf Prime," Keith said. "We have to use maneuver. It's like the Wallace Corporation attacks all over again. They had big bombers, you know. Flew straight in, they did."

Keith told them about his time during the Tau Ceti Conflict between the powerful Wallace Corporation and the rebellious miners he'd joined.

"The Wallace mercenaries thought like boxers," Keith said. "Straight at the chin for a knockdown blow was their idea of strategy. We miners didn't have the luxury of heavy craft. We had small strikefighters with limited amounts of ordnance. That meant we had to trick 'em, draw 'em off so the odds weren't so lopsided."

Keith looked around at the others. Everyone was staring intently at the small man. Even Galyan was engaged with the story.

"So that's what we do here," Keith said. "We have to draw off the star cruisers so we can complete the mission. *Victory* must show herself, make the New Men excited. They gather their star cruisers with an intent to capture the alien vessel."

"What if they attack to destroy?" Galyan asked.

"Capture or destroy," Keith said, "it's the same thing. They come running after your vessel. That's the trick to draw off the enemy. That allows me and whoever I'm taking to land on Wolf Prime."

"The jumpfighters," Maddox said. "You plan to use one of them."

"That's right, sir."

"Ordinary strikefighters can land on planet," Maddox said. "The jumpfighter looks like a tin can, though. Can you fly it through an Earthlike atmosphere?"

"Well, not exactly, sir. It would be a matter of using the fold in a cunning way to reach the surface from space. It will be tricky, but I have no doubt I can do it."

"Have you practiced something like that before?" Maddox asked.

"Ah… no, sir, no one has."

Valerie groaned, while several other listeners shook their heads.

"It's all theoretically possible, though," Keith said defensively. "I spoke to one of the designers once and asked him about a similar situation. He said a skilled pilot could do it."

The chamber grew quiet as people became thoughtful.

"Could this work?" Galyan asked Maddox.

The captain tapped his chin. "It would depend on several factors. What's the range of a jumpfighter? It would have to be able to take the team there and back again."

"A long flight with several distance folds…" Keith said quietly. "We could journey from twenty AUs out."

"A little less than the distance from Uranus to Earth," Maddox said.

"Yes, sir."

"I didn't realize jumpfighters had such range."

"We'd have to make several extended folds, sir, or mini-jumps, as you'd probably think of them."

"*Extended* folds are more difficult than regular ones?" Maddox asked.

"Ah…yes, sir, that's true."

"Meaning, you're being overoptimistic concerning our range?"

"That's one way of saying it, sir. But if you don't believe you can do something, you're never going to try, now are you?"

Maddox often followed a similar philosophy and therefore appreciated Maker's daring. Still…

"How many people can a jumpfighter carry?" the captain asked.

"I'm already considering no ordnance, but extra fuel pods instead," Keith said. "Then you have to take into account Ludendorff on the return trip, sir. Two people could do it for sure, maybe three if you want to reduce your chances of returning to *Victory*."

"I have a question," Major Kharkov said.

"Go ahead," Maddox said.

"I want to know how two people on Wolf Prime are going to find the professor," Kharkov said. "Where would you start looking? What if he's gone? Given the star cruisers in orbit, we have to assume a fair number of New Men are down on the surface searching for him. I mean, why else are the New Men at Wolf Prime?"

"Dana," Maddox asked, "do you have a way to contact Ludendorff?"

"The same as you," the doctor said. "Put through a call."

"I'm talking about a secret way without alerting listening New Men," Maddox said. "The major's right, we need a way to pinpoint Ludendorff quickly."

Dana became thoughtful. "I might have a way. It would be a longshot, though. If the New Men are hunting him, the professor will have gone to ground."

"What's left of Fletcher's fleet will soon be in the Tannish System," Maddox said. "We're never going to save them unless we bring Ludendorff back to *Victory*. We have to risk this."

"Saving Star Watch's Fifth Fleet is a secondary goal," Galyan said. "We must discover the ancient homeworld of the Swarm. The only reasonable course is to wait for the star cruisers to depart Wolf Prime and then go to the planet."

"I don't agree," Maddox said. "Why are the New Men at Wolf Prime in such force? Clearly, between their victory over the Fifth Fleet in the Caria 323 System and their future run in the Tannish System to finish the job, they have been raiding outlying star systems. That's what we learned from Sub-commander Ko of the Social Syndicate Fleet. Five star cruisers could do plenty of damage elsewhere. Yet, they are here. So

228

that's the other thing. I doubt they're going to be at Wolf Prime long. It seems they'll join the rest of the New Men at the Tannish System soon. We have to beat the enemy there to save Admiral Fletcher and his fleet."

"I do not agree," Galyan said.

"If Ludendorff dies," Maddox told the holoimage, "there goes your chance of finding the Swarm's homeworld. Yes, maybe one of us could search the ancient ruins if we stayed on Wolf Prime long enough. Once the New Men destroy the rest of Fifth Fleet, though, they will send a ship or ships back here. Their very numbers here now tells us there's something important about Wolf Prime, vitally important to the enemy. I doubt any of us will have long enough to find what Ludendorff probably already knows. He's a genius, remember? We're just ordinary people."

The holoimage stared fixedly at the captain.

"If the crew wishes to risk themselves in this endeavor, I will agree," Galyan said. "However, I cannot let *you* go, Captain Maddox. You are the reason I wish to attempt any of this."

"Keeping me here would be a mistake," Maddox said. "I'm the most suited to finding Ludendorff. It is, in fact, my specialty. This has turned into an Intelligence operation."

"With all due respect, sir," Major Kharkov said, "you will be running a commando operation. That's space marine territory and that means me."

"Hitting a military installation would be a commando op," Maddox said. "We're hunting for one individual to bring him in, first having to find him. He could be anywhere on the planetary surface. If Dana's signal doesn't work, we'll have to search a vast area. That is a classic Intelligence operation. And that is what I am, an Intelligence operative."

Major Kharkov nodded reluctantly.

"If I don't go," the captain told Galyan, "you will not get the professor. That means you will not put my engrams into your core. Your only reasonable hope of teaching me a lesson is having me go to Wolf Prime and returning with the professor."

"Who will join you?" Galyan asked.

"The obvious people," Maddox said. "Keith will pilot and Doctor Rich will come to help find Ludendorff and then convince him to join us."

"I see," Galyan said.

"Excellent," Maddox said. "Now, the next thing…"

***

Three hours later, Starship *Victory* used its jump, moving in sideways closer to the Wolf System.

There were four planets in the star system, a rock world in a Venus orbit, Wolf Prime at the distance of Mars to the Sun, and two large Jovian planets in the far, outer system. The bluish-white F class star had a surface temperature of 7,500 K, making it decidedly hotter than the Sun. The distance of Wolf Prime from the star made the planet an icy world with fierce winter storms.

So far, the New Men hadn't reacted to *Victory's* presence. Did they wait and watch, or hadn't they seen the starship yet?

Maddox hurried through a corridor. He recalled the last time he'd gone against the New Men in person. It had been on Loki Prime, and it had only been for a moment. The individual had been supernaturally quick and cunning. The captain hoped he didn't have to face any New Men here.

Sergeant Riker appeared, carrying equipment. The two men entered a hangar bay, heading for the jumpfighter.

The tin can had a special cradle holding it in the middle. Both the front and back of the rounded can sprouted masses of antenna. There was no viewing port as a regular strikefighter possessed, no wings or tailfins of any kind. This had to be the most unique fighter-craft ever developed.

A stepladder led up to an open hatch. Maddox eyed both. He wouldn't be able to walk through the opening, but would have to worm his way inside.

"Not the best designed craft I've ever seen," Riker commented.

Maddox faced the sergeant. The man handed him a small case. It held thermal wear and boots for Wolf Prime. Next, the captain accepted a longer, narrower case, slinging the carrying strap over his shoulder. This one held a heavy Khislack .370

230

with targeting computer, suppressor and extra ammo magazines.

The two men shook hands. Afterward, Maddox climbed up the ladder, heading for the tiny hatch.

"Here, let me help," Dana said from inside.

Maddox slid up the rifle case. Next, he climbed another two rungs and handed her the smaller suitcase. Finally, he squeezed through the opening. It wasn't much better inside. Grabbing his cases, he crawled after Dana.

"I've never gone into space flying in something so cramped," she said over her shoulder. "I hope you're not claustrophobic."

Maddox said nothing as slid his gun case along.

"The tin can makes my skin crawl," Dana admitted. "I'm not sure about doing this."

"We'll make it," Maddox assured her.

"*You* might survive the trip. I keep having premonitions. Do you believe in precognition, Captain?"

"I do not."

"I wish you hadn't picked me to join the expedition," Dana said.

"Who should have gone in your place?"

"No one else," she said. "I'm the one you need. It's just…I've only felt this way one other time. It was a day before Star Watch captured me to send me down to Loki Prime."

The doctor squeezed through another hatch into the flight compartment. There were two acceleration seats, one behind the other, and that just about filled the cabin.

"I suggest you take the other seat, sir," Keith told Maddox. "I don't know if you can fold up those long legs of yours otherwise."

"How long is this going to take?" Dana asked.

"That depends," Keith said. "Two, maybe three days."

"Three days in this cramped compartment," Dana said.

"There's a small cubicle to your left," Keith said cheerily. "You could squeeze into there and sleep. To your right is the john. You can fit if you go in sideways."

"Why is this habitable quarter so tiny?" Dana asked.

"It's all about payload, love. This isn't an endurance fighter, but a fast in-and-out attacker. It's not really meant to be out for days at a time."

"How are we going to fit Ludendorff in here?" Dana asked. "There won't be enough room."

"Aye, it's going to be cramped coming back," Keith said. "Now hang on. The AI has given me the signal."

Maddox slid into the second seat and buckled in. A shiver of unease crawled up his spine. This was tighter than he'd envisioned. Dana had a valid point. If they had to squeeze another person in here…

The jumpfighter shuddered. That caused Maddox to sway back and forth.

"This is a bumpy mother," Keith said. "But you get used to it."

The ace tapped his controls. A huge screen came to life before him. Maddox found that helped, giving the cabin a greater illusion of size.

Outside the jumpfighter, bay doors slowly opened. The tin can quivered, with the surrounding bulkheads shaking. Keith gave the machine a squirt of power, and the craft shot into space like an amusement park roller coaster.

"You don't get claustrophobic?" Maddox asked Keith.

"No, sir," the pilot said. "In a strikefighter—excuse me, a jumpfighter—I feel as if I'm floating in space. It feels as if I have all the room in the universe."

Maddox's headphones crackled into life. Each of them wore a pair. A mechanical voice came online.

"You must return to the starship," Galyan said.

Maddox turned on his chest microphone. "What's wrong?"

"My sensors have just picked up enemy pulses," Galyan said. "I give it an eighty percent probability that the New Men know I am here. It is more than possible they have discovered you too."

Keith turned around, looking over his backrest at Maddox.

The captain needed all of three seconds to think about it. "Jump," Maddox told the pilot.

"Technically, it's using a fold, not jumping," Keith said, "and it will take me time to warm up the equipment."

"Then get started," Maddox said.

"Captain," Galyan said through the headphones. "You must return to the ship."

"Negative," Maddox said. "If the New Men see you already, good. I doubt they will have noticed a mote like us. If you accelerate, the heat signature will hide the jumpfighter. Stick to the plan. Head for the outer system Laumer-Point. Make them race after you."

"And if you're wrong and they've already spotted you?" Galyan asked.

"The laws of probability suggest I'm right. Nothing is guaranteed in this life, though. We're going to have to find out the hard way. Maddox out."

The captain shut off his microphone and headgear.

A moment later, the jumpfighter's main engine roared with power.

"How long is it going to sound like that?" Dana shouted.

"Most of the trip," Keith shouted back, giving her the thumbs up. "But don't worry, love, you'll get used to it." The ace turned back to his controls and engaged the tin can.

-24-

The jumpfighter built up velocity for the next half hour.

Maddox endured the G forces in relative comfort. His acceleration seat was made for it. Dana kept moving around. When he saw her face, the captain could tell she was suffering.

"Climb into the cubicle," Maddox told her.

"No!" she shouted. "It helps being able to see the screen. I'd start screaming if I shoved myself into the cubicle. And once I start doing that, I don't know how quickly I'd be able to stop."

"I thought we were going to use the folds," Maddox shouted at Keith.

"What's that, sir?" Keith asked.

Maddox turned on his microphone, repeating the thought through the ace's headphones.

"Well, sir," Keith said, "I'm waiting for data on the enemy. We're still far out, as you know. It's going to be hours before we see how the enemy reacts to his knowledge about *Victory* being out here. Frankly, sir, I don't think they spotted us. We're too small in the tin can."

Keith referred to the time lag of sensor data. If the enemy saw them many AUs distant, it took time—the speed light could travel—for the information to get from point A to point B.

"Don't forget that the New Men have fantastic sensors," Maddox said. "They showed us that out in the Beyond over a year ago."

"That's one theory, sir. But I've never subscribed to it. Time lag means their using sensors before in the Beyond—light years distant, mind you—just wouldn't have been scientifically possible. I think they used deductive reasoning to follow us. Well, that and their greater ship speed."

"We're going to have to land on Wolf Prime," Maddox said. "All this velocity—"

"I'll need speed to play with, sir, on the other end," Keith shot back. "That's about the only thing we're going to have against them."

"You can't outfly a star cruiser."

"I know that, sir. But I will need speed to maneuver. That and the folds will allow me to run circles around one of their starships."

Could that be true? Maddox was beginning to think the ace was too overconfident by several factors. The captain settled in just the same, enduring.

It was hours before any of them spoke again.

"Look at that," Keith said, pointing up at the screen.

The jumpfighter's screen showed Wolf Prime as a white ball. Orbiting it were small red triangles—the star cruisers. One by one, the red triangles left the snow world, heading into space.

"Let's see their trajectory," Keith said, tapping his controls.

Dotted red lines moved away from the triangles, heading in the direction the star cruisers aimed. The lines speared across the system, finally reaching the known region of the Laumer-Point by a Jovian world.

"They're chasing *Victory*," Keith said, "trying to reach the Laumer-Point before Galyan does."

"Show us our starship," Maddox said.

"Aye, aye, sir." Keith manipulated his board.

The ancient alien vessel appeared as a blue triangle. A dotted blue line moved from it toward the outer system Laumer-Point. According to the scale of Keith's projection, the New Men had four times as far to go to reach the Laumer-Point as Galyan did.

"The New Men must know about *Victory's* star jump drive," Dana said. "Why are they trying to do this? They can't be that foolish."

"*Maybe* they know about the drive," Maddox said.

"Not maybe," Dana argued. "They wouldn't all be racing for the Laumer-Point unless *Victory* were important. That means they understand what they saw. Yet, if that's true, they must know our starship can simply jump away at any time."

"Maybe they're hoping the ancient vessel had a star drive malfunction," Maddox said.

Dana didn't respond to that as she continued to crane her neck to look at the screen.

"Time to use a fold," Keith said.

The ace reached up, opening a small compartment overhead. He took a hypo and pressed it against his right arm, injecting himself.

"What did you just do?" Dana asked.

"Gave myself a Baxter-Locke shot, love."

"I can see you gave yourself something."

"Then why did you ask?"

Dana looked perturbed. "A shot of *what?*" she asked.

"I just said. It's called a Baxter-Locke shot. Helps against fold sickness."

"You mean Jump Lag," she said.

"I suppose it would work for that, too," the ace admitted.

"Well, give me a shot."

"Can't do that, love. I don't have many doses left. It's hyper-expensive, don't you know. It's strictly a jumpfighter item."

"Do you hear him?" Dana asked Maddox.

"It's experimental," Keith added. "We don't know yet if the dosage has any long-term aftereffects."

"I don't care about that," Dana said. "I'm not sitting here and enduring Jump Lag if I don't have to."

"You do have to," Maddox told her.

"What?" Dana asked.

"He's our ticket to doing this right," Maddox said. "Whatever helps him fly this tin can will remain strictly for him for as long as it lasts."

"You're only saying that because you can endure Jump Lag better than the rest of us," Dana said. "If you weren't half New Man—" the doctor realized her mistake too late, but closed her mouth just the same.

Keith turned around, staring at Maddox. A second later, the pilot faced forward again.

"I'm sorry," Dana told Maddox. "I didn't mean to say that. It just slipped out."

"You're half New Man?" Keith asked over the headphones.

"That's a presumption," Maddox said.

"I didn't know that," Keith said, sounding worried.

Maddox looked away and closed his eyes. He'd been dreading this moment ever since he learned about the possibility.

"Tell him your story," Dana said. To Keith, she said, "The captain doesn't know what he is, but being part New Man is one of the possible options."

"What story?" Keith asked. "I'd like to know."

Maddox nodded, opening his eyes. He never should have told Dana, but what was done was done. He explained to Keith his origins, how his mother had escaped from the Beyond, with him in her womb.

"I have some physical differences," Maddox said. "I have a slightly higher core temperature. Alcohol doesn't make me drunk."

Keith swore under his breath, adding, "So you can't know the urge, can you?"

Maddox chose to ignore the comment. "I have faster reflexes, and I'm stronger than average. Remember, though, Meta is denser and stronger than a normal person, and she has nothing to do with the New Men. Maybe my mother came from a similar world to the Rouen Colony."

"That's a story, all right," Keith said.

The jumpfighter continued on its course.

A half minute later, Keith said, "Well, you're still one of us, sir. That's how I see it. Even if you have their bastard blood—I don't mean it like that, sir. It's just…they're nuking worlds, practicing genocide. The New Men are evil, is what I think."

237

"I agree with you," Maddox said. "But we can chitchat about this later. Now, it's time to start moving in. The star cruisers are chasing *Victory*. We have to make our first move."

"Aye," Keith said, "that's true. So I want you to hang on. It's about to get crazy."

The ace adjusted his controls. The engine whined with greater power. The noise became worse than before, climbing higher and higher, penetrating their protective headphones. Dana opened her mouth. Maddox tried the same thing, and he found it helped a little. Then the noise began to beat against his skull.

In that moment, the entire craft shuddered. Maddox's teeth rattled, and it felt as if they plunged down a yawning hole. They fell faster and faster. Above the blast of engine power, Maddox could have sworn he heard Dana scream in agony.

The universe blurred before Maddox. The screen became a smear. A second later, the stars reappeared on the screen. Maddox's gut twisted. He clamped his teeth together, refusing to vomit. By slow degrees, the feeling of sickness departed. The engine no longer whined with its former intensity and the noise no longer beat into his skull. He had a headache, though, and his mouth tasted dry.

"We did it," Keith said. "It wasn't bad, was it?"

Maddox didn't answer. Neither did Dana.

"It takes some getting used to," Keith said. He checked his instruments. "We're a quarter of the way closer."

"We have to do that three more times?" Dana asked.

"Don't worry, love. You'll recover faster than you can believe."

Maddox wasn't so sure about that. It seemed worse in a jumpfighter. Maybe the cramped space had something to do with it. Maybe being closer to the fold/jump source did it. Whatever the case, he understood the need for the Baxter-Locke shot. A jumpfighter pilot couldn't keep taking that and do his job.

The hours passed, and the data coming from the star cruisers was newer because they were sustainably closer than before. Now, however, it took longer to receive telemetry data from *Victory* as it raced away from them.

Dana shifted for what must have been the one hundredth time. She looked up, saying, "Do you mind if we switch places for a bit? I need to stretch my legs."

"Oh," Maddox said. "Yes, of course." He got up, twisting around her, sitting on the floor beside his seat. He brought up his knees, hunching into an uncomfortable position.

Maddox was the captain, and the crew's well-being was his responsibility. That meant he didn't always take the best accommodations. This idea didn't come naturally to Maddox. He was used to having the best. The mission was first, though. Maybe he should stay down here a while to give Dana a more thorough break.

Finally, Keith said, "It's time."

"Go," Maddox said.

The ace didn't reach up for another hypo. The first shot must still be percolating through him. Keith tapped controls and the engine began revving with power.

Maddox bent his head, resting his forehead against his knees. He closed his eyes and endured, hating every second of this.

***

The jumpfighter with its precious, three-person cargo made successive leaps toward Wolf Prime, using its fold power. As the tin can did so, the star cruisers rapidly built up velocity, gaining on *Victory*.

"This is incredible," Maddox said later, sitting in his seat once again.

They had been in the jumpfighter for a day and a half already. Dana slept in the cubicle, with her feet sticking out.

"A star cruiser is like your X72 Peregrine," Keith said.

"I was thinking the same thing," Maddox said. "The Peregrine is all engines, though. It doesn't have armaments or a shield, or an armored hull, for that matter."

"No wonder the New Men are destroying our fleets," Keith said. "They outfight and outrun all our ships, and they outthink us, too. Sir, do you believe the Commonwealth really has a long-term chance against the New Men?"

"Of course," Maddox said.

"Hear me out, sir. I've had a long time to think about this the past month."

Maddox understood. He'd had a lot of time to think alone while on *Victory's* bridge. They must have all been doing some serious thinking lately.

"The New Men are better than us," Keith said. "That's clear. Suppose by some miracle we win the war because we drive them out of the Commonwealth. What's to stop them from renewing the war in another ten years?"

"Your implications are clear," Maddox said. "We have to find their homeworld or worlds and defeat them for good."

"Then what happens?" Keith asked.

Maddox grew quiet.

"Let me put it out in the open, sir. Suppose we defeat the New Men and stomp on their homeworld. We disarm them. Maybe we even say they can't live on their homeworld anymore. So the New Men emigrate. They wait thirty years, slowly supplanting us everywhere, taking over place after place because they're better than the rest of us at everything."

"What are you suggesting?" Maddox asked.

"I'm not suggesting anything, sir. I'm saying we can't compete against them on even terms. If regular humanity is going to survive, don't we have to wipe out the New Men altogether?"

"Are you talking about genocide?" Maddox asked.

"It's either that, sir, or we tell 'em they can't have children with each other. They can only marry regular humans. We dilute their superiority before they become our conquerors."

"You pose a hard question," Maddox said.

"Aye, I grant you that, sir. It's obvious we're not going to commit genocide, as that's a horrible evil. But that brings me to a terrible conclusion. Are we in a war we can't win?"

"I don't believe that."

"But then you might be…" Keith didn't finish his thought.

Maddox did it for him. "Then I might be half New Man, is what you were going to say."

"I suppose it was. And look at you, sir. You're better than the rest of us at everything."

"That isn't true."

"Isn't it?" Keith asked. "Is that an honest answer, sir?"

"Ludendorff is a genius. I can't do what he can."

"So our very best regular human can match you. That doesn't mean much for the regular person."

"You pilot a jumpfighter better than I do. Doctor Rich—"

"I shouldn't have said anything, sir. I just keep remembering how you came into my bar in Glasgow over a year ago. You intimidated my people. Remember how I called you a tiger and my bone-breakers junkyard dogs?"

"I remember," Maddox said. *Why had Dana gone and shot her mouth off?*

"I was closer to the truth than I realized, sir."

It was time to put an end to Maker's line of reasoning. They had to work together, meaning his people had to trust him.

"Second Lieutenant," Maddox said. "If you hate me because of what I am, I can't do anything about that. I didn't have any say in my birth. I was born just as you were, only I never knew my mother or father. I made do in the world, just like you. I play the cards I've been dealt, just like you. We fight under the Star Watch banner together. I want freedom for everyone. What do you want?"

"To get out of here and stretch my legs on a planet," Keith said.

"I'd agree to that."

"After that, I want to beat these New Men."

"Then don't pick a fight with me or hold a grudge." Maddox said. "We're on the same side. Worry about what happens with the New Men after we win the war. Until that time, staying alive will probably engage all your resources and mine as well."

"Aye, that's good advice. I hope you don't hold my words against me, sir."

"You're being honest, Mr. Maker. I like honest. It lets me know where I stand."

"I like honest too, sir."

Maddox was tired of the topic and tired of Keith's hints. He hated this part of himself. He didn't want to be half New Man. He didn't want to be a genetic freak, created in a gene lab. But if that's what he was…well, he would use it to defeat the enemy. First things first had always seemed like the best advice in the world.

I'm sick of having all this time to think. I want to get down onto Wolf Prime and start doing. The ace is right about that.

"It's time to use another fold," Keith said.

"Then I'd better wake Dana," Maddox said. "Just a minute."

***

Twelve hours later, the jumpfighter neared its destination of Wolf Prime. They only needed to use the fold one more time to get there.

Far away in the outer system, the star cruisers closed in on the Laumer-Point. The ancient starship still increased velocity. The enemy vessels were braking. Soon, the star cruisers would be within beam range of *Victory*.

"Why doesn't Galyan use his star drive?" Dana asked. She was crouched in the aisle, staring up at the screen.

"He's cutting it close," Maddox said.

"That's foolish," Dana said.

"I don't know," Keith said. "It's giving us more time before the star cruisers head back to us."

Dana's features were pinched. "I feel like I should be thinking of something. It's out there orbiting my consciousness, but I can't bring the thought close enough to articulate. There's something not right here. I can feel it."

"I'm switching views," Keith said, tapping a control.

The star cruisers disappeared as the screen showed Wolf Prime again. The planet was a white world full of ice and snow, with ninety-eight percent the Earth's mass. A few miners down there dug for thorite, a strange substance with similar qualities to the weed found deep in New Australia's oceans that was used to manufacture the Methuselah Treatment. The Methuselah People hadn't truly begun exploiting thorite, though. Wolf Prime was a frontier world in more ways than one.

The first mine had been sunk less than ten years ago. The conditions on the surface made it a hell world. Opening new mines was incredibly daunting. There was another group of pioneers on the surface, slarn trappers. The vicious slarns made it a precarious existence. The fur was the most luxurious in the Commonwealth, better than scientifically manufactured thermal clothes. On many worlds, slarn furs were the highest status symbols a person could wear. It took hardy trappers to go after the vicious snow beasts, men who liked a challenge and wanted riches in a relatively short time.

Despite the trappers crisscrossing the icy planet and the newly opened mines, Wolf Prime only possessed a single spaceport with five known towns.

As Maddox thought about it, controlling the miners should have been an easy proposition for the New Men. The trappers were another breed. They roved over the surface in their ice-haulers and lived in igloo-like constructions. Many trappers spent a year or more collecting furs before heading to the spaceport to sell.

There was one other group, the smallest of all. Men and women funded from scientific communities had come to Wolf Prime as archeologists. The ice world had a reputation of holding the most alien artifacts in the Commonwealth. Most of those artifacts were etchings in deep underground caves. The second most plentiful were strange ceramic tools that made no sense to anyone as far as function.

Back on Earth, Maddox had read up on everything he could about Wolf Prime in Star Watch Intelligence files. The snow world had a few communication satellites in orbit, but that was it. Wolf Prime didn't have any defensive hardware. Instead, it had tough citizens trying to turn a credit at some of the hardest jobs out there.

Wolf Prime also had some of the worst storms of any planet where humans lived in the open. Freak winds meant it was dangerous to use aircraft. Sometimes, it was too treacherous for shuttles or rockets to land. Most travel down there occurred the old-fashioned way, across the surface on foot or in a tracked vehicle.

Why then would the New Men have orbited the world with five star cruisers? There was a reason. Could it have been simply to catch *Victory*? Maddox wondered about that.

"Let's get started," Keith said.

The ace's words jolted Maddox out of his reverie. Keith took out another hypo and injected himself with a second Baxter-Locke shot.

The small man flexed his right hand several times. "Repeated injections doesn't feel so good," he said.

"We're all crying for you," Dana said.

Keith chose to ignore the remark. Instead, something on his panel flashed red. "Let's look at the Laumer-Point another time."

Wolf Prime disappeared from the screen. In its place was a bright dot. The computer had enhanced the jump point. Five red triangles headed for it. A big blue triangle was farther away from the Laumer-Point. Suddenly, the blue point flashed several times. Then, it disappeared.

Keith laughed. "Looks like Galyan finally got nervous. *Victory* jumped out of danger."

Maddox heaved a sigh of relief. He'd been getting worried. One never knew what trick the New Men had up their collective sleeve.

"Are you ready for our last fold?" Keith asked the others.

Neither Maddox nor Dana answered.

"Right," Keith said. "Here we go."

Soon, the engine roared, and the process struck as it had too many times already this voyage.

When Maddox's vision returned, he saw Wolf Prime. The planet filled the screen. They were closer to it than the L5 Lagrange Point around Earth.

"I don't know how long we're going to have down there," Keith said. "It will depend on whether any star cruisers return."

"Some will," Maddox said. "We should figure on it happening."

"I suppose you're right," Keith said. "So, I'll wait to brake until we're even closer to the planet. That should mask our exhaust from them in the outer system."

"Sounds right," Maddox said. "Dana, if you can communicate with Ludendorff, now is the time to try."

She opened a briefcase and took out a bulky communicator. "The professor is one of the most paranoid people I know,"

Dana said. "Since the New Men have been here, he might suspect they've captured me and forced me tell them everything I know. He might not answer even if he knows it's me."

"I understand," Maddox said.

Dana switched on the communicator. "I'm using a scrambled code, but who knows. It's more than possible the New Men can crack it." With her thumb, she depressed a switch, "Athena calling Zeus. We have the albatross to fly the ancient mariner to a new land."

"You're Athena?" Maddox asked.

"Hatched from the brow of Zeus, as the professor would like to say," Dana said with a laugh.

She depressed the comm switch again, repeating the phrase. Nothing happened. No one answered.

"Do it again," Maddox said.

"It's no good," Dana said.

"He could be on the other side of the planet," Keith said.

"Try one more time," Maddox said. "If you look over there," he told Keith, "you can see that at least one of the communication satellites is still up. Maybe he can hear us on the other side."

"What if the New Men left something on the surface to track incoming messages?" Dana asked. "Ludendorff might know about it, and we're walking into a trap."

Maddox thought about that. Finally, he nodded. "You're right. We're going to have to find him the hard way now."

"It's time to brake," Keith said. The planet was growing larger by the second, the clouds and visible continents beginning to take on texture.

"Right," Maddox said. "Do it."

The ace maneuvered the tin can so its exhaust port aimed at the planet. "This is going to get rough for a while."

The Gs slammed Maddox against his acceleration seat. The captain looked over at Dana. Her screwed-up features said it all.

"Hello," Keith said, his voice rising. "This isn't good."

Maddox looked up at the screen. He saw it right away. A spaceship appeared from around the edge of Wolf Prime. That would imply the craft had waited on the other side of the planet. At almost the same moment, a second ship appeared.

"What are those?" Maddox asked.

"Increasing magnification," Keith said. The image shifted, and Keith cursed profoundly.

Maddox's eyes widened. Those were star cruisers, two of them. He recognized the triangular shape. Had their calls down to the planet given them away?

"But we saw all the star cruisers leave orbit," Dana objected. "Five star cruisers headed to the Laumer-Point. Were there *more* New Men here all along?"

"Maybe," Maddox said. "Or maybe they used decoys as they headed out-system, only going with three but making it seem like five."

"But that means—" Keith said.

"That they saw us from the very first," Maddox said, interrupting. "Galyan was right. We thought to outmaneuver them. It's clear, the New Men have tricked us into showing our hand."

"Emergency maneuvers!" Keith shouted. "Hang on, mates. This is going to get even rougher."

The engine whined at full throttle.

"Hurry," Dana said. "Use the fold! Move!"

"I'm building up power as fast as I can," Keith said. "It's still going to take a few seconds to start."

Maddox didn't think they were going to get those seconds. Even as the jumpfighter revved to make a fold, a sensor growled, indicating enemy radar lock-on. A second later, a beam speared at them from the nearest star cruiser.

-25-

The world went white for Maddox, an intense brightness that seemed to burn out his vision. Then the grossness of folded space struck. The captain groaned, feeling as if someone clawed out his insides.

From some place far away, a klaxon blared. It seemed as if an age passed. Then the sound increased until it pulsated with noise, with incredible immediacy. It told Maddox he was still alive, unless the afterlife was weirdly like the one he'd just left in a beam blast. Human shouts penetrated his consciousness, but he had no idea what they meant or why.

For a time, Maddox endured the loud pain. Suddenly, his eyes snapped open and the worst headache of his life put splotches before his vision.

"He's conscious." That sounded like Dana Rich.

"We barely made it, sir."

"He can't understand you," Dana said.

"What's wrong with him?" Keith asked.

"It doesn't matter. Can you get away or get us onto the planet?"

"I'll have to use another fold," Keith said. "And I need to bleed off velocity first. We're moving too fast to land anywhere yet."

"Then do it!" Dana shouted.

"Right you are, love," Keith said.

Maddox sat in his seat. By degrees, he realized he was in a jumpfighter above Wolf Prime. Why weren't the star cruisers firing at them? That didn't make sense. The New Men had targeted the tin can. They should be dead. He—

G forces slammed Maddox against the chair. It made his head split open so the gray matter squirted out—at least, it felt as if that had happened. Maddox reached up, half-expecting to feel an axe-head embedded there.

"Sir," Dana said.

Maddox shook his head, and groaned. The pain...he doubled over and vomited on himself. It was disgusting.

The vomiting helped, though. It reduced the headache to a throbbing migraine. He could see a bit more. That meant the splotches had diminished in size. The inside of his mouth felt vile.

"Drink this," Dana said.

Maddox felt a bottle shoved into his right hand. He raised the bottle, squirting water into his mouth. He gulped and gulped more. He must be dehydrated. So, he kept on drinking until all he squeezed was air.

Wolf Prime jiggled before him on the screen. Maddox tried to understand what that meant.

"The star cruisers..." the captain whispered.

"A beam struck us as we folded," Dana said. "It burned out some systems, but we're still alive."

"We used a fold?" Maddox asked.

"Right through the planet," Dana said. "Keith took a leaf out of your tactical book."

Maddox tried to absorb the words. Oh, right, what he had done against the New Men out in the Beyond. Only, he had jumped through a star, not just a planet. Still, that made sense why they had survived. The star cruisers would have to circle the planet to reach them.

"How long until they reappear?" Maddox asked.

"Get ready," Keith said, hitting a switch. "We're jumping through the planet again, going where they're leaving. If we do this right, they won't know what we did for a while."

The agony started all over again for Maddox. He thrashed in his seat. He was done with spaceships and folds of any sort. He wanted to remain an Intelligence officer on Earth. Forget these kinds of adventures. No more, never again.

"I've finally bled off enough velocity," Keith said. "We're going down this time."

"A jump?" Maddox asked in a pained voice.

"I doubt my tin can will ever fold space again," Keith said. "The sequencer is burned out. If we get down onto the surface, we'll be stranded there until we find another ride up."

"I have it!" Dana shouted.

"What?" Maddox said.

"I've been calling again," she said. "Ludendorff just answered."

"By voice?" Maddox asked.

"By implication," the doctor said. She read out planetary coordinates. "He sent them by Morse code."

"How do you know it's him?"

"It is, I know it," Dana said. "Can you land there?" she shouted at Keith.

"We're about to find out," the ace said as he made course adjustments.

The jumpfighter headed down toward the atmosphere at an angle. The star cruisers would eventually make another orbital circuit, searching for them. The question was, who would win the race. If they could get down in time, could they hide from the enemy?

"This reminds me of Loki Prime!" Keith shouted. "Those were the good old days, eh, sir?

No, Maddox thought to himself. The good old days were back on Earth as he trailed enemy spies.

"Are we headed for Ludendorff?" Dana asked.

"I put in the coordinates," Keith said. The highest clouds seemed to rush toward them. "Now, hang on, mates, this is the test."

The tin can struck the upper atmosphere, and the jumpfighter began to shake. The idea of using a space fold to get down onto the surface had been thrown out the window. They would have to fly down in a craft never meant to do that.

"Do we have gravity chutes?" Dana shouted.

"We have one around us," Keith said. "I don't know if the cabin can carry the weight of all three of us. There's another problem, though. It's frigid down there. How do we survive out in the open, sir?"

"We have to hope Ludendorff reaches us," Dana said.

The jumpfighter went down, plunging faster than the tin can could take. The shaking became ominous. Then an explosion occurred in the back of the machine. Flames roared into life. They could hear them past the bulkhead.

That snapped Maddox out of his delirium. Reality sharpened. "Brake as much as you can," he said.

"Glad to have you all the way back, sir," Dana said.

Maddox ignored her, focusing on the problem. The shaking made it almost impossible to talk.

Keith used all his considerable skill. The screen blurred, but it showed the expanding world in a shivering panorama. The stars had disappeared.

Another interior explosion produced electrical smoke that floated through the cabin. The acrid smell stung Maddox's nose. He began to cough. So did Dana and then Keith.

"It's no good," the ace said. "The jumpfighter is going critical. We have to bail."

"Can we use the gravity chute from this height?" Dana asked.

Keith slapped a switch, but nothing happened other than the worst rattling in Maddox's life. The pilot struggled up from his seat, grabbed a lever in the ceiling with both hands and pulled. The lever wouldn't move.

"Help me!" Keith shouted.

Maddox unbuckled, stood and tried to help. The shaking threw him against a bulkhead so he crashed hard against his shoulder. Gritting his teeth, Maddox pushed off and lunged at the lever, grabbing it in passing. With a hard yank, the captain moved it a centimeter.

"More!" Keith roared.

Tightening his hold, Maddox pulled one more time, with the ace helping him. The lever moved all the way.

"Buckle in!" Keith screamed. "Buckle in!"

Maddox fell back into his seat. The belts flopped like angry eels. Grabbing them, he clicked them together. Then he grabbed Dana, yanking her onto his lap. He wrapped his arms around her and held on.

At that moment, metal grinded and smoke poured into the compartment. The sound of shrieking titanium dominated everything. The compartment broke through the jumpfighter, shedding useless material. The engine no longer screamed. There was just the cabin, a gravity chute now, plunging toward the planetary surface.

"Well?" Maddox shouted. "Now what happens?"

"We're headed down in a controlled descent," Keith yelled back. "We just might make it, mate. This is our luckiest day ever."

Even as the ace said that, another explosion made the cabin shudder. The entire compartment flipped. Dana screamed. Maddox tightened his hold. If he let go of the doctor, she would fly around inside the cabin, likely breaking bones or possibly killing herself.

The rotating worsened, becoming spinning, faster and faster. The increasing G forces began draining the blood from Maddox's brain. His eyelids fluttered, and his grip weakened.

"No," he whispered.

The captain heard the strangest thing of all then. A man sang in a strong voice. A moment later, Maddox realized Keith Maker belted out a drinking song. Maybe the ace did it to give himself courage. As Keith sang, his hands roved over his smoking controls.

More explosions occurred. They sounded as if they came from outside the cabin. Incredibly, the spinning lessened and the G forces became endurable. What had Maker done? Something to counteract the cabin's spinning?

Maddox's brain throbbed, but he tightened his hold around Doctor Rich. The cabin rotated slowly, finally stopping altogether as they plunged upside-down toward the surface.

"Turn us over!" Maddox shouted. "Use the gravity chute to do it."

"It's burned out!" Keith yelled back. "I used it to stop the spinning. Now, it's a pile of junk."

"We're plunging toward the surface." Maddox said. "We'll crumble as we hit."

"Listen to me, sir!" Keith shouted. "We're going to have to eject. The chairs have parachutes, old-fashioned ones that will slow our decent so we're floating."

"Will the parachutes work in the freezing cold? What if there's a storm?"

"If, if," Keith shouted. "You have to don your thermals in here. So does Dana. If you can grab your rifle case, all the better. We're not going to survive if we're not warm enough. You have ten seconds, sir. No, make that nine."

"Dana?" Maddox shouted. "I'm getting up, so you must grab the seat."

As Maddox squirmed, the doctor shifted and took a death grip on the chair. In those few seconds, Maddox moved with controlled fury and precision. He had do this right the first time, as he wouldn't get another chance. As the cabin plunged toward the surface upside-down, Maddox ripped open the suitcase and donned his thermal wear, tucking his boots inside the heavy jacket. He grabbed Dana's case, but didn't have time to get his rifle. In the last second, he put on his frost mask, which covered his mouth and nose, and he slid on a pair of antiglare goggles.

Maddox had no idea how he managed to buckle back onto the seat. He put the straps over the doctor so they were like one.

"Hold onto the case," he shouted into her ear.

Dana did before screwing her eyes shut.

"Now!" Keith shouted. "I'm ejecting us now."

While grinding his teeth together, Maddox readied himself. A violent explosion tore open the cabin's canopy. With a boom, Maddox's seat rocketed downward, propelled at the approaching surface. The cabin was supposed to be aimed up. Under normal conditions, the rocket shot would have easily thrown them clear of the falling object. Now, they roared down ahead of the cabin. Would it plunge against the parachutes?

The seat swayed as they aimed at the planet upside-down. Fortunately, a computer program ignited a blast, righting them. Maddox craned his head up to see the situation. The cabin broke apart into several large pieces. Some of those pieces appeared to fall straight down at the chair.

At that moment, white fabric burst free. It blossomed overhead, filling with frigid air. A thunderous clap and a jerk told Maddox the parachute slowed their descent.

The captain kept staring up at the "silk" waiting for junk to tear through it.

The compartment pieces flashed past uncomfortably near. Maddox watched them gain terminal velocity. Nothing so far had ripped through the parachute.

His headphones crackled. Maddox thought he heard words, but he wasn't sure. An impulse caused him to look far to his right. He saw a seat and parachute. Second Lieutenant Maker waved to him.

"I'm f-freezing," Dana said past chattering teeth.

Maddox rubbed her vigorously. She hadn't been able to don her thermals, or put on her frost mask or goggles. Everything was in the suitcase. Until the chair landed, she would have to endure the cold.

Maddox was afraid she might freeze to death, so he kept rubbing, trying to use friction to give her a modicum of heat. He wanted to tell her not to breathe too deeply. Sometimes, in the coldest winds, there were ice crystals that would quickly destroy one's lungs.

The bitter cold descent lasted too long. Maddox tightened his hood and made sure not to stare at the star. The Wolf star shined too brightly in the heavens, although it failed to give sufficient warmth. The sunlight reflected off the white surface below. In some places, the snow reflected with a multi-chromatic color.

"Keep your eyes shut," Maddox shouted into Dana's ear.

The seat jerked, causing Maddox to look up. The fabric overhead looked sodden or maybe it had begun to ice up. Would the parachutes hold long enough for them to land?

The next several minutes were marked with anticipation. To the right, an icy blue surface faded into the distance. It must be a frozen lake. Skeletal trees—a forest of them—were to the left. They had sponge-like growths and would be incredibly hard. In the short summer, which came every third year—the shortest part of a highly elliptical orbit and nearest the star—the sponges would become soft.

253

Fortunately, the two acceleration seats didn't head for the frozen lake or the forest, but for an area of large snowdrifts between the two areas.

We're getting a bit of luck, Maddox thought. *Maybe enough to give us a chance for survival in the near term. Are we really near Ludendorff? I'm betting we got blown far off course.*

The ground rushed up, and the chair crashed into a snow bank, sinking, softening their landing. The giant parachute floated down over them.

"So...cold," Dana said past chattering teeth.

Maddox couldn't unbuckle. The metal buckles were frozen shut. He pulled out a long, tri-steel knife and began to saw the tough fabric, parting the straps one by one. Finally, he stood, and burst open Dana's suitcase. As fast as he could, he put the jacket and snow-pants on her. He clicked on the internal suit heater. Then he slid on her frost mask and goggles.

The batteries for the thermals wouldn't last for many days, but getting enough heat onto Dana Rich was an immediate problem.

Once he was done, Maddox realized he couldn't feel his feet. Sitting in the chair, he tugged off his shoes, putting the thermal boots on. Only then did Maddox cut through the silk above, parting it.

Keith floundered near, having a hard time forcing his way through the drifts. The small ace sank up to his chest.

"This place is worse than I expected," Keith shouted. Tendrils of white escaped through his mask. "My jacket is set on high, and I'm still freezing."

Maddox wondered if the ace's thermals were defective. His own clothes were set on medium and he felt fine.

"Dana?" Maddox asked.

She opened agonized eyes, peering past the safety of her antiglare lenses. "C-Cold," she stammered. "I-I've never been so c-cold in my life."

Maddox wasn't sure what to do next. *Think about immediate goals. Keep your people alive first.*

"Did you happen to see where most of the jumpfighter cabin landed?" he asked Keith.

The ace nodded, lifting a trembling arm, pointing toward the lake.

"We'll go there first," Maddox said.

"W-Why?" Keith asked.

"To see if we can salvage anything," Maddox said. "We won't last long on our own. We need a radio, directional equipment and whatever else we can find. Come on, talking about it isn't going to help us."

Maddox grabbed one of Dana's gloved hands and pulled the doctor to her feet. "You have to keep moving," he told her.

"I want to sleep," she said.

"No. Walk. Follow me." Maddox started for the frozen lake.

It was hard work wading through the drifts. The snow particles were fine and dry. Packed tight, the snowpack failed to hold them on its surface. Maddox doubted the snow would have held for a cat. Snowshoes wouldn't have helped either.

The captain dragged Dana after him. She shivered constantly, stumbling, mumbling about the freezing cold. Behind her, Keith doggedly followed, the ace's arms wrapped over the front of his body.

Maddox found their chill odd. It was cold certainly, but he didn't feel debilitated by the weather. Could his hotter core temperature give him an advantage here? He gave that a high probability and then no longer thought about it.

The wind increased, whipping up the white powder, decreasing visibility. Now the cold slashed through his thermals. Maddox halted long enough to turn his suit from medium to high.

Dana's pace slowed. Maddox had to stop twice and shout at the ace. The man looked at him dully. Could the cold weaken Maker that quickly? How could trappers live in this environment? Maybe the slarn furs made a bigger difference than Maddox had realized.

An hour later, Maddox pulled Dana to the compartment wreck. The wind no longer whipped the snow, but it was colder here. A front of glacial chill emanated from the lake ice.

"Keep moving around," he told them. "Don't lie down while I'm looking."

Both Dana and Keith stared at him dully. He didn't think they're were going to last much longer out in the open. Wolf Prime was proving to be a brutally cold planet. And this wasn't even the worst time of the orbital cycle.

Carefully, Maddox stepped to the twisted metal of the cabin. A wrong move could cause a sharpened piece of metal to slice his suit and maybe his skin. This was dangerous, but he needed to find tools.

Poking around, lifting a metal strut, Maddox found a thermos. He shook it. The container still held coffee. Would it still be hot?

Stepping around a sheet of cabin, Maddox lifted a fold of metal. It screeched and then snapped off. He hurled the piece away and spied the edge of his rifle case. It had to be a twisted piece of junk surely.

Maddox worked out the case and opened it, checking the weapon. The Khislack was intact, including the various magazines and suppressor.

A shout alerted Maddox. He looked over at the other two. One of them pointed at the sky.

Maddox looked up, but didn't see anything. He glanced at the other two.

"There, there!" Keith shouted. "It's dropping out of the sky. Can't you see it?"

Craning his neck, Maddox looked straight up. He saw it then, and he wondered how the ace had spied it. All he saw was a dark speck. Even so, sight of it squeezed Maddox's heart. That had to be an enemy shuttle. Had a star cruiser's sensors spotted them down on the planet? With an oath, Maddox hurried back to the others.

By the time the captain reached them, the speck had increased to twice its former size.

"Do you know what that is?" Maddox shouted. White tendrils of mist puffed from his frost mask.

"Y-Yes," Keith said, with his teeth chattering. "It's a shuttlecraft."

"Does it belong to the New Men?" Maddox asked.

"Who else?" Keith said.

Maddox scanned all around. The lake was a kilometer away, the skeletal forest three kilometers the other way. Various-sized drifts were in between.

"We'll move away from here," Maddox said. "Maybe they're homing in on the cabin metal."

"N-No," Keith said. "You can bet they're looking at our heat signatures. We must be like beacons to them."

Maddox scanned the cold sky. The shuttle had grown again. It came down fast.

"Look!" Keith said.

Maddox caught the pilot's motion more than heard the words. The ace's right arm rose, pointing toward the low horizon. Two bright plumes lofted from the ground, rapidly gaining on the descending craft.

"Surface to air missiles?" Maddox asked.

Keith laughed, nodding.

Maddox watched the tableau. The missiles increased velocity, moving at high acceleration. Silvery chaff glittered from the shuttlecraft. Then red tracers hosed from the air-vehicle. Some of them struck a missile, creating an explosion and a growing black cloud of smoke.

Keith groaned, and cheered a second later as the last missile burst out of the smoke-cloud.

The shuttlecraft tracers struck the nosecone, but this missile refused to die right away. Then it exploded, creating a fireball and an expanding smoke-cloud. The shuttle flew into the cloud. As it reappeared at the bottom, smoke trailed from the shuttlecraft.

"Hit!" Keith shouted, pumping his fist into the air.

"Down," Maddox said. "Crouch. There's no sense making ourselves any more visible than we have to."

Keith glanced at Dana and pulled her down beside him.

Maddox likewise crouched. He watched the shuttlecraft. The machine began to wobble, straightened out until a burst of fire blew away a back section. Then it plunged for the surface.

At that moment, three capsules ejected from the craft. Seconds later, gigantic parachutes billowed into existence.

That was too much for Maddox. He had to know if they were good guys or bad. Snapping open the case, the captain raised his Khislack. He tucked the stock against his shoulder and peered through the scope. This one had been treated for the cold.

It took him a few seconds, then Maddox had one of the shuttle crew sighted in his scope. The man wore thermal clothes and a frost mask with goggles. The captain had a moment where he centered on the man's face. The skin was golden colored. Three New Men floated down toward the surface.

-26-

"They're enemy," Maddox said in a hoarse voice.

"More will be coming," Keith said. "There's two star cruisers up there, no doubt hunting for us."

Of course Maddox knew that. He also knew that someone on Wolf Prime had used SAMs on a New Man shuttlecraft. Did that have something to do with Professor Ludendorff? He hoped so. It meant they would have allies. None of that would matter in a few minutes, though. What was he going to do with three New Men coming down?

In those few seconds, Maddox realized what he had to do. He didn't like it, but... The captain's resolve firmed. The New Men were impossible foes. If they were like him, only better, the cold wouldn't debilitate them as it did Dana and Keith.

Lifting the rifle a second time, Maddox decided to even the odds while he could actually do something. The New Men were remorseless foes. To defeat them, he would need to use an equal ruthlessness.

Before the mission, Maddox had zeroed in his Khislack so he could put three consecutive rounds in a palm-sized target at one hundred meters. He used special bullets, Horizon Blue Kings, not trusting ballistic-tip ammunition for precision shots.

Sighting the nearest New Men, switching on the targeting computer, Maddox gathered data.

"You'll never hit them from here," Keith said. "You'll have to wait until they're almost down."

Maddox didn't bother nodding. He already knew that, but what point was there in saying anything. This was his area of expertise. He'd rather show a man than say it.

Taking off a mitten, Maddox reconfigured the targeting computer for a one thousand meter shot. Then he put the mitten in a pocket and craned his head upward, watching the parachutes float toward the surface.

"Can you nail them?" Keith asked.

Maddox said nothing as he gathered himself. He couldn't lay the rifle on the ground or a rock. He'd have to be perfectly steady. Raising the rifle, he aimed skyward. With the scope and targeting computer, Maddox centered on a New Man's back. The enemy faced away from him.

The captain waited as he studied the wind. Wind was never constant. In this situation, the most important wind consideration was two-thirds of the way to target. This would be tricky, no doubt about it. There were some obvious crosswinds. He'd have to take them into account. Despite the best computers, it still took constant practice and skill to make long-distance shots in the field.

Maddox took three deep breaths. Then he let out all his air on the last exhale. The money spot was a two-second pause afterward.

He squeezed the trigger, and the shot broke. Maddox continued to squeeze to the rear and released the trigger slowly to the front. The kick told him he'd done his fundamentals right. The scope fell right back onto target as it should.

The New Man jerked, and his head twisted. His arms dropped away from the guidelines as he hung limply, dead or dying.

Without hesitation as he stood tall, Maddox swiveled his torso, finding the next parachutist in his scope. This New Man looked back and forth at the ground. He must have spotted Maddox. Faster than the captain would have thought possible, the New Man clawed at a holster at his side.

Maddox fired…missed. Taking three deep breaths, collecting himself again, the captain exhaled slowly.

One… He let himself go blank. The New Man aimed his black weapon. A blob of force ejected from the blaster. Two…

Maddox ignored the attack. If the enemy hit him, it was all over anyway. Three... With deliberate coolness, Maddox centered the targeting dot slightly left of the New Man's chest and squeezed the trigger. BAM! The rifle along with the scope lifted. The scope fell back onto target.

A hole appeared in the enemy's chest, pouring blood.

Maddox used explosive bullets. He didn't want to have to hit a New Man twice to put him out of the fight.

"That's fantastic shooting, mate!" Keith shouted. "Kill the last one, Captain."

Once more, Maddox twisted his torso, put the scope on the New Man—

The enemy plunged down fast, no longer floating.

"What the..." Maddox said. Then he realized the New Man had released himself from the parachute harness, letting himself fall to the ground.

With the scope, Maddox searched for the man, but he was too late. The enemy in the silvery suit hit a drift and disappeared out of sight.

Slowly, the captain lowered his Khislack.

"Did you see that?" Keith said. "The madman unhooked. He must have fallen over one hundred meters. He can't be alive."

Maddox didn't want to bet on that. Raising the rifle, he scanned the location, but found a hill of a drift blocking the landing site. It was time to get out of here, but where should they head?

Once more, Maddox studied the terrain. The lake was out as it was too cold and barren. The forest might protect them from the wind a little and they could burn the wood—

"Look!" Keith said. "Do you see that?"

"No," Maddox said. "What?"

"Over there," Keith said, pointing. "I saw a flash of light."

"Where?"

"In the distance," Keith said. He pointed at what might have been a set of hills in the opposite direction as where the New Man had landed. It would be up the aisle between the lake and forest.

"What kind of light?" Maddox asked.

"Like someone flashed a mirror. I think they were signaling us."

Maddox frowned. That didn't seem right. Still, what else was there? Nothing. So, he might as well grasp at this straw.

"Point it out again," Maddox told the ace.

Keith did so.

"Let's go," Maddox said. "You lead the way. Dana. Dana," he said, shaking the doctor.

Groggily, she raised her head. Dana's eyes had been closed.

"Follow Keith," Maddox told her. "I'll bring up the rear."

He would keep a sharp eye out for the New Man. Would their enemy trail them, or did he have a broken leg or ribs? It was impossible to tell. In any case, after he broke apart the Khislack and put it in its carrying case, Maddox set off through the powdery snow.

***

It was hard going. The wind increased, blowing the powdery snow and knifing through their thermals. If Maddox didn't push the other two, they soon slowed and stopped altogether.

The captain wanted to drop back and watch for the New Man. If the parachutist had survived the fall, he would be coming after them. Maddox couldn't stay behind, though. Dana and Keith would soon lie down and allow themselves to freeze to death.

Like a shepherd, Maddox prodded the others, forcing Keith to plow out the path and keeping Dana in his lane. Soon, the wind changed directions, howling across the icy lake, increasing the cold. The sun dimmed and soon disappeared altogether as dark clouds began to form overhead.

"W-We're not going to survive out in the o-open," Keith stammered past chattering teeth.

"Where are these others you saw?" Maddox asked. "Why don't they contact us?"

Keith jerked a thumb upward. "T-The New Men are listening. T-The others must know that."

"Are the winds keeping the New Men from launching more shuttles?" Maddox wondered.

Neither Keith nor Dana answered him. The three of them kept stumbling through the drifts, making the best time they could.

Maddox studied his companions, trying to gauge their stamina. Long weeks aboard *Victory* hadn't prepared them for Wolf Prime. The other two weren't going to last much longer in this ice age. It was getting colder every minute. If one of the blanket storms hit them out here...

We're not going to do anyone any good frozen to death.

Maddox angled away from Keith's original destination. He headed for a field of large boulders. It was darker there, with brown lichen showing in places where snow had fallen off. Maybe they could find a makeshift cave. Yet, how was that going to help them in the long run?

Maddox shook his head. It was the short run that counted, many of them strung together until they won.

Visibility worsened during the next fifteen minutes. Soon, Maddox could hardly see a meter ahead of his face. He had to get them out of this now. Grabbing Keith with one hand and Dana with the other, the captain plowed through the drifts. His legs drove up and down like pistons. He kept jerking the other two, making them keep up. Ten minutes later, he almost crashed against a boulder. It just loomed out of the blizzard. He had to yank the other two to halt them, because they kept staggering like robots.

"We have to go to ground," Maddox shouted in each of their ears.

Neither said a word.

Maddox pulled them after him, weaving through the lanes created by the giant boulders. It sounded as if haunting demons shrieked down at them. He knew it was the wind whipping around the rocks, but the sounds made him nervous nonetheless.

Finally, the captain found what he'd been searching for. Big boulders made a cul-de-sac. Using the rifle case, Maddox dug in the snow, making a hole, piling the snow around them as a shield.

"Crouch together," he said.

Maddox slid a pack off his shoulder, ripping it open. The pack held a pup tent. He set it up and forced them inside. He piled snow against the fabric. That would act as insulation. Then, he crawled in with them, sealing the entrance against the elements. With his thumb, he turned on a small thermal unit. It churned out heat, helping a little.

As the wind rattled the upper fabric, the three of them shivered together. Maddox remembered the thermos he'd found in the wreckage. Carefully, he opened it and found a miracle: hot coffee. It smelled wonderful.

"Here," he shouted at Dana. "Sip some of this."

She held the thermos with two trembling hands. Maddox continued to hang on, guiding her. She sipped, and she trembled even more.

Maddox studied her.

"Good," she shouted. "So good. I want more."

He let her sip half the thermos, noticing that her shivering lessened. He repeated the performance with Keith.

"Thanks, mate," the pilot said after he'd drained it. "I think I can sleep a bit now."

Maddox let them. Because of the thermal unit and insulating snow, the temperature had risen within the pup tent.

Maddox wasn't sure when he nodded off. A terrific *boom* woke him. Groggily, the captain raised his head. Was a shuttle landing beside them? How had the New Men found them in the storm? More booms hammered the heavens. It was thunder, not the roar of rockets. The booms were louder than any he'd ever heard.

The winds howled overhead, but they only buffeted the tent. The giant boulders protected them from its worst fury. For the next hour, the booms continued. White flashes of lightning illuminated the dark tent.

As they endured, Maddox took Dana's communicator and tried it. He doubted the New Men would get any reception up in orbit. He need not have worried. All he got was horrible static. No one was getting any reception down here either.

Time passed, and Maddox began getting drowsy again. Then something alerted him, a premonition of danger perhaps. The hairs rose on the back of his neck. It felt as if something big prowled outside. Then, a low growl told him one of the slarns must be outside the tent.

Drawing his tri-steel knife and long-barreled gun, Maddox debated sliding outside. Should he hope the snow beast went elsewhere? Or should he defend them from death?

Maddox tried to reason this logically. If the beast was outside, it must have trailed them through their scent, hunting them as prey. Should he wake the others to help him? No. He would do this himself. They needed rest, giving their bodies time to repair the damage they'd taken for what must have been a grim ordeal for them.

With his frost mask in place and with the goggles protecting his eyes, Maddox unsealed the tent. A musky odor told him he'd been right about there being a beast outside.

Steeling himself, Maddox slid out on his back. A flash of lightning in the distance showed him a long and sinuous animal with a mouthful of teeth. It looked like a giant weasel the size of a grizzly bear. The slarn opened its jaws with its ears pinned against its narrow skull. Then, it roared dreadfully. That caused an awful odor to wash over Maddox's face. He didn't want to think what he would have smelled if he hadn't been wearing the frost mask.

Rising up onto its hind feet, the thing towered an easy four meters, almost twice Maddox's height. It had six legs with six sets of wide claws.

Maddox stood up. He doubted his bullets could kill the thing in time—

The slarn arched back and roared in agony, with its jaws aimed into the heavens. It took a second for Maddox to comprehend what happened. Sizzling lines of energy played upon the snow beast's luxurious fur along its back. Another bolt struck the creature, and more energy burned the fur and made the slarn thrash back and forth in agony.

Maddox barely hurled himself away in time. The big creature rolled over the tent. Then it flipped around onto its feet, bending its body like a weasel would. It crouched as if threatening to leap, snarling at the person who had shot it with an energy weapon.

265

Lifting the long-barreled gun, knowing this was the time to act, Maddox pulled the trigger in quick succession, pumping round after round into the monster.

The slarn sprang at the other person, but without coordination. It was more of an instinctive flop away from Maddox. Something silvery dodged the attack. The other person raised a weapon and another energy round blazed over the stricken creature.

Of course, it was the New Man. The surviving parachutist had trailed them after all. Why hadn't he let the slarn kill the three of them?

Maddox would have liked to know. He watched as the monster thrashed in the snow, with lightning once again playing in the heavens. Wind howled and distant thunder boomed.

The New Man was Maddox's enemy. He had no idea how the man could survive in his silvery suit fabric. He should have already frozen to death. Whatever the case, the New Man had just saved their lives from the slarn. Maybe both of them realized the animal was dying. The thrashing wasn't as wild as earlier. Blood soaked the snow and the slarn's teeth were red with gore. The roars had diminished in volume. Could the beast still rise up to attack? Maybe and maybe not.

Maddox retargeted his long-barreled gun, aiming at the enemy. The New Man aimed his blaster at Maddox. The golden-skinned man hesitated. Maddox did not. His trigger finger moved faster than it ever had in his life, once, twice, three times. Each shot caused the New Man to jerk back. The third bullet hurled the man down onto his side.

Maddox stood in amazement. He'd beaten the New Man to the draw. No. That wasn't right. His enemy had saved their lives from the slarn, and the New Man hadn't pulled the trigger. There had to be a reason for that, but Maddox had no idea what it could be.

That bothered him.

In the heavens, a jagged lightning bolt flashed across the sky. A new premonition struck the captain. The star cruisers were still up there in orbit. He didn't know how he knew that, but he was certain it was right.

Shoving the gun into its holster, Maddox lunged at the fallen tent. He dragged it off…Dana. She held her left leg. It might have been broken, maybe by the slarn rolling over it earlier.

"Get up!" Maddox shouted at her. "Hurry! Do it now!"

The doctor remained bent over, clutching her left leg.

Maddox knew they didn't have any more time left. If his premonition was correct, they had to move this instant. He grabbed Dana Rich by the collar. He grabbed his rifle case. Then he dragged her from the tent, churning his legs as he struggled to get away from the dying New Man.

"Captain!" Keith shouted.

"Follow me!" Maddox roared. He didn't know if the pilot heard him or not. If not, they might lose Keith Maker.

Yanking the doctor, sliding her through the snow, Maddox floundered through the boulder field. The winds howled, snow poured down and distant flashes of lightning played in the darkness, giving them moments of illumination.

Then, Keith was beside him. The pilot grabbed Maddox and put his face near.

"What's wrong?" Keith shouted. "Why are you acting like a madman?"

"We have to move," Maddox shouted, shaking himself free of Keith. The captain continued to pull a limp doctor along the ground

Keith hurried after them, and it happened then.

Out of the darkness, down from space, a horribly bright beam struck. It had to have originated from a star cruiser in orbit. The beam struck the spot where the New Man lay. Why did the enemy do that to one of his own? Maddox didn't know, although he had a few ideas.

Boulders blasted apart. Earth erupted, and everything came raining down, most of it pelting against rock.

In the brilliance of the destructive beam, Maddox saw a cave. It was twenty meters away. He dragged Dana and wriggled into the opening, pulling the doctor in after him. Keith managed to dive in too. Then, a loud, a terrific explosion caused rocks and debris to rain against the entrance, sealing them in the darkness.

The winds no longer shrieked. The air wasn't quite as cold. But they were trapped in the earth, prisoners underground on the barren planet of Wolf Prime.

-27-

"Now what do we do?" Keith asked in a forlorn voice in the darkness.

Maddox lay on the ground, breathing heavily, trying to gain his bearings. His limbs were exhausted and his mind numb. Everything had happened too quickly. And yet, that was supposed to be his power, the ability to act fast.

How had the New Man found them in this storm? That was a miracle. Maybe the answer was simple. The New Man had seen the slarn trailing prey. It would simply have been a matter of following the beast.

Why didn't the New Man fire at me? He must have known I would kill him. Did he sacrifice himself?

Maddox couldn't believe that. What kind of being would let himself die willingly and let his enemy live?

Maddox realized he was missing something.

From where he lay, the captain raised his head. A different idea struck. Maybe the New Man hadn't fired because their team was important. Why would that be? The New Man must want *Victory*. Everything the enemy did might be predicated on that. But if that was true, the New Man had made a selfless act for his side. Were the New Men community-based to such a degree that one of them could make that kind of sacrifice?

Frowning, Maddox shook his head. He didn't want to accept that. It would mean the enemy was capable of nobility to some degree.

The New Men practiced genocide. At least, that's what people thought. The enemy had used thermonuclear weapons on planetary surfaces. Of course, regular humans had done that in the past. There were treaties against it now. Star Watch enforced the ban throughout the Commonwealth.

"Captain," Keith said.

"What?" Maddox asked, and it surprised him how groggy he sounded.

"What are we going to do?" Keith asked. "It's pitch black in here. I can't see a thing."

"We need light," Maddox said. "Give me a second." He felt for his pack and realized he hadn't put it on. It had been back in the pup tent. The beam would have destroyed it and everything they had in it.

Maddox rummaged in his pockets. He had Dana's oversized communicator. He took it out and began to fiddle with the controls. Soon, he used it as a flashlight, beaming it around their cave.

"What the heck?" Keith said. "This is bigger than I realized."

"Indeed," Maddox said.

He played the beam along the cave walls and then on the floor. There were tufts of fur and bones, many of them cracked open. Could this have been the slarn's den? No wonder the beast had trailed them.

"How far does this cave go?" Keith asked.

Maddox shined the light into the interior, but he didn't spot a back wall. That gave him the willies. No doubt, it was an atavistic dread, his spirit wondering if this could be an opening into the underworld. That was foolish, though. It was just a deeper than average cave, nothing more.

"Can we get out the front?" Keith asked.

Turning around, Maddox illuminated the rocks piled tight. He slid near and put his shoulder against one, trying to budge it. The rock wouldn't move. He pushed harder, straining, his feet slipping on the floor. It didn't make any difference. They were sealed in.

It was time to assess the situation logically. First, he needed to make sure Keith and Dana were okay.

"Doctor?" Maddox asked, shining the light on her. "Are you well? Is your leg broken?"

She sat on the cave floor, bent over, clutching her ankle.

"Here," Maddox said. He pushed the communicator at Keith and crouched by the doctor. "You must let go of your ankle," he said. "Let me check it."

Dana nodded, slowly releasing her grip.

Maddox took off her blood soaked boot as gently as possible. She groaned, becoming rigid. Setting the boot aside, he pulled out his knife and reached under the pant leg, sliding the blade into place. Carefully, he cut her thermals. No jagged bone-ends showed through the torn skin, but there was too much blood welling, a thick and steady flow.

"This might hurt," he said.

Dana nodded, saying nothing.

Maddox touched her ankle, and Doctor Rich moaned in pain like before. Ignoring that, Maddox moved her ankle, and he felt bones grind against each other. Were they crushed? He let go of her foot, and Dana gasped as she began to tremble.

"The slarn," she whispered. "It rolled over my foot."

Maddox looked around. The first aid kit was in his pack, burned by the beam. He lunged for his rifle case. Keith centered the beam there. Maddox opened the case and took out strips of oily cloth. These would have to do.

"Shine the light on her leg," Maddox said. "Here," he told Dana, giving her a small piece of wood. "Bite on this as hard as you can. This is going to hurt."

Without complaint, Dana did as ordered.

Maddox took a deep breath, lifted her leg, setting it on his knee. Then, he took the first strip of cloth and bound it around the broken ankle.

Dana went rigid with agony and began to tremble worse than before. She didn't scream or even moan as she bit down on the wood.

Maddox worked fast. He had to stop the bleeding. He tied the strip and wound the second one around the ankle.

"I'm going to put your boot back on," he said.

Dana didn't acknowledge him. She continued to tremble and moan through her clenched teeth.

271

Taking the bloody boot, Maddox worked it onto her foot as gently as he could. Dana grabbed his shoulders, her fingers digging into his flesh. He didn't stop. The sooner he finished, the sooner they could do something to free themselves from the cave-in.

Finished, Maddox gently set her foot on the ground. He stood, having to stoop because of the low ceiling. Extending his hand, he took the communicator back from Keith. As Dana spit out the wood and lay on the floor, gasping, Maddox played the light off the walls. He stepped deeper into the cave to look at the back.

A faint stir of air feathered against his forehead. There must be an opening to the outside somewhere deeper in the cave. Would it be big enough for them to use? He had no idea, but he had no other plan of how to get out of here. They were going to have to head deeper into the earth. Maddox hoped there wasn't another slarn in here with them, waiting to defend its den.

Turning around, he explained his thoughts to the others.

"You're saying we're trapped?" Keith asked.

"We should think positively," Maddox said. "Remember, others signaled you. They might well come for us. Discovering the cave-in should be easy for them."

Dana raised her head. She'd torn off her frost mask and goggles and had sweaty, pain-tightened features.

"Are you sure?" she asked in a hoarse voice.

"The star cruiser's beam will have charred the outer rocks," Maddox said.

"These blanket storms can last a long time," Dana said. "It could be a while before anyone searches for us. There's another problem, though. The falling snow. It will cover the charred rock."

The doctor had a point.

"We're on our own," Keith said. "We have to explore the cave and hope there's another way out."

Maddox nodded, although the fact of the SAMs gave him hope. The knowledge that *Victory* must be racing to Wolf Prime helped too. If there were only five star cruisers in the Wolf System, three of them had chased the ancient starship to the outer system Laumer-Point. Two of the cruisers were in orbit here. *Victory* could attack two star cruisers and hope to win. It meant Valerie might be able to come down in a shuttle and pick them up, if they stayed alive long enough, and if they could get in the open to use Dana's communicator.

Maddox told them his ideas.

"I don't know how far I'll be able to travel," Dana said. "I can't walk anymore."

"You can crawl," Maddox told her.

"Maybe I should wait here," Dana said. "If I come, I'll slow you down. The stakes are too high for us to get sentimental about each other."

"We don't leave our wounded behind because it's hard work taking them along," Maddox said. "We're a team. A team sticks together and helps one another."

"Captain—"

"Besides," Maddox said, "you're under orders. Mine. Until I say otherwise, you will expend every effort to keep up with the rest of the team."

"While I appreciate your concern—" Dana said.

"Doctor," Maddox said, interrupting. "I may need your expertise later. I'll want you to convince Professor Ludendorff to come with us. This has nothing to do with sentimentality but with brute necessity."

Dana stared at the floor.

"We're wasting time talking about it," Maddox said. "Second Lieutenant, make sure the doctor keeps up."

"Aye-aye, sir," Keith said.

Maddox shouldered the rifle case and shined the light into the depths. He hated tight places and being underground. In a half-crouch, Maddox moved deeper into the cave.

***

The cave went back farther than Maddox had expected. It also slanted down. A greater feeling of claustrophobia began to settle over him. The weight of the world seemed to press against his shoulders. What if the tunnel collapsed? He would be crushed to death or pinned in place, unable to move.

With a mental effort, Maddox forced such thoughts aside. He didn't have a choice, as there was likely only one way out of here. He didn't want to remain in the cave for the rest of his life.

Maddox halted in surprise, blinking at a fork in the tunnel. Now there were *two* directions?

"What's wrong?" Dana asked.

Maddox twisted around, shining the light on her face. Perspiration glistened on her skin. Dana crawled on her hands and knees. Behind her, Keith stood in a half-crouch, panting from the effort.

They must have traveled a kilometer already, although it was hard to judge distances underground.

"We have a choice to make," Maddox said. He shined the light on the two openings.

"Feel which one has the stir of air," Dana said.

Maddox nodded. He should have already thought of that. The claustrophobia was keeping him from using common sense? It was possible. He needed to keep his composure.

Maddox stepped to each opening. The leftward one had a faint stir. The other one seemed stale.

"Let's go," he said.

Twenty steps into the new tunnel, the path angled sharply downward. Worse, condensation made the sides moist. After another twenty steps, the tunnel narrowed. In order to keep walking, Maddox had to crouch more. After another one hundred steps—he'd been counting—the contraction forced Maddox onto his hands and knees.

"Wait a minute," Dana wheezed from behind. "I need to rest."

Maddox closed his eyes and leaned against the tunnel. He didn't want to think about how far down they had come. He didn't want to think about anything. He just wanted to get out of here.

"Okay," Dana said after a time. "I can keep going."

Maddox started crawling again. He noticed the comm-light in his hand had begun to dim.

Dana noticed that too. "How are you going to call the starship if we run out of battery power?"

Maddox had no answer for that.

"You should turn off the comm-light," Dana said.

Maddox didn't want to do that. Crawling in the dark…

"Captain—"

"I heard you the first time," he said sharply.

"Well?" Dana asked.

"I'll shut it off in a little while. We might miss another fork if we turn off the light too soon."

Maddox kept crawling, and the walls continued to narrow. Soon, he had to squeeze past rock, the thermal fabric rubbing against the walls. The noise and the pressure caused his heart to thud in his chest. His breathing quickened. More and more often, he closed his eyes.

Finally, Maddox had to turn sideways, shoving through what seemed like a crevice of stone. The captain had almost reached his psychological limit.

"I don't know, mate," Keith called out a little later, with a quaver in his voice. "We may have to double back. The tunnel is closing down into nothing."

It would be impossible to turn around down here. They would have to crawl backward for a time.

Maddox halted, closed his eyes and felt his body shudder in growing panic.

"If—" Dana said.

"Shhh," Maddox said. "Don't say anything." He listened, straining to hear. He thought—there! He heard a distant voice. It seemed human. Somewhere down here were people. That seemed impossible to believe. Yet, it gave him hope, and it calmed some of his growing sense of horror.

"Did you hear that?" Maddox asked.

"Hear what?" Dana asked.

"I didn't hear anything," Keith said.

"I heard voices," Maddox said. "They're far away, but they're there."

The others didn't reply.

Maddox refrained from asking if they believed him. No doubt, he had better hearing than they did. He didn't think for a minute that he had begun to hallucinate.

"Let's go," Maddox said. He forced himself through the narrow tunnel. The walls began to squeeze even closer together. The captain kept going, refusing to believe—

The tunnel widened ahead. Maddox raised the dim light. He couldn't believe it. Exhaling, he shoved through the narrowest part yet and finally slid into the wider area. He was able to move faster now.

Maddox laughed with relief. There wasn't anything in his life that felt better than this. Another thirty meters brought him to a place where he could stand at a half-crouch.

He waited for Dana and Keith.

"Why is he so happy?" Keith asked. "We're still trapped under the earth."

Maddox became aware that his cheeks hurt, he was smiling so widely. He realized he was on the verge of laughing wildly. The tunnels had bothered him more than he wanted to admit.

"I've been wondering about these shafts," Dana said. "Who dug the tunnels, do you think?"

Maddox cocked his head. The question surprised him.

"You don't think the tunnels are natural, do you?" the doctor asked.

"I suppose I did," Maddox said.

"No. These were dug—" Dana stopped talking, staring in wonder. "I heard voices," she whispered. "There *are* people down here. You should probably turn off the light, Captain."

Maddox studied the communicator. He realized the doctor was right and let his thumb hover over the tab. He tried to move his thumb down, but it wouldn't respond.

"We'll leave the light on a little longer," Maddox said.

Dana studied him. "Of course, Captain," she said.

"Let's head deeper," Maddox said, "see if we can find room to maneuver."

"Good idea," Dana said.

Maddox led the way, she crawled after him and Keith followed. Soon enough, the tunnel widened so the captain could stand. Then the passageway expanded enough for Maddox and Keith to walk on either side of Dana. She climbed to her feet and put her arms on their shoulders, limping along with her good leg, keeping the broken ankle off the floor.

"You said someone made these tunnels," Maddox said. "Did you mean the creatures of the Swarm?"

"I did," Dana said.

"How can you know?"

"It's an inference. Out here on the rim, humanity has come upon a few worlds with signs of Swarm occupation. Nothing like this planet, though. Wolf Prime has the most Swarm artifacts of all the other worlds put together. The professor once told me he thought Wolf Prime had been part of the Swarm Imperium."

"An alien empire?" Maddox asked.

"Not as you think of one," Dana said. "For instance, we learned from Galyan that the Swarm didn't possess a star drive or know about Laumer-Points. They used sub-light speed, generational vessels to go from one star system to another. It appears this planet had a Swarm colony."

"How long ago did they die out?" Maddox asked.

"I have no idea," Dana said. "I know the professor would like to learn the date. It's one of the reasons he's here."

"Can you give me a ball park figure for the Swarm's extinction?"

"We know Galyan's people destroyed the Swarm invasion against their star system. That was over six thousand years ago. Were there other Swarms or was that the last one? Given the nature of the species and their sub-light drive, some might still exist."

"That doesn't seem right," Maddox said. "It was so long ago."

"We're alive," Dana said. "I mean humanity as a species."

"Humanity wasn't in space six thousand years ago. Men drove around in chariots back then."

"That may well be so," Dana said. "But we have survived the ages. That's the point. Why couldn't a branch of the Swarm have survived too?"

"Survived where?" Maddox asked.

"I think many of us would like to know that answer."

"Is there any evidence of their survival?" Maddox asked.

"None that I know of," Dana said.

"Does this planet have technological evidence of Swarm survival?"

"That's another reason Ludendorff came," Dana said. "He's been hunting for alien artifacts his entire life."

277

"So maybe this is a dig," Maddox said, indicating the tunnels. "The others we hear are working the dig and we've stumbled onto what? An ancient hive of the Swarm?"

"I deem that to be highly likely," Dana said.

"Which part?" Keith asked.

"Both," the doctor said, "that others work the dig and this is indeed an ancient hive."

Maddox became thoughtful, and he asked Keith, "How close did we land to the Morse code-given coordinates?"

"It could have been near," the pilot answered. "But it could have been over one hundred kilometers away. I'd figure farther rather than closer, but as I said, I don't know."

"So we could be walking through an alien-constructed tunnel system," Maddox said. "One built by an intelligent species of what…super-ants?"

"Ants could be an apt analogy," Dana said, "or maybe something like bees."

Maddox didn't know whether to be amazed or horrified. He didn't like the idea of Swarm creatures surviving the ages, just waiting to run into humanity. Over a year ago, he'd seen Swarm skeletons on *Victory*. They had been big and nasty, and had left crusted slime trails in the ancient starship's corridors. There weren't any crusted slime trails here. Before he could mention that, Dana said:

"The others are near now. Can you hear them?"

"I do," Keith whispered.

Maddox had been hearing them for some time.

"Captain," Dana said. "You must dim the light. What if these are New Men approaching? It would be better for us to have the drop on them than the other way around. I know you dislike the darkness—"

"Nonsense," Maddox said. He held up the communicator, stared at his thumb and willed it to tap down.

Darkness fell, an utter and complete gloom. It seemed to press against him, choking his air. It helped that Maddox heard the voices approaching and heard the scuffle of boots. He opened his mouth, breathing in and out. Then he snapped his teeth together and strove to hold back an irrational fear.

How far were they under the earth? If the rocks above should cave in and crush him, or worse, pin his leg so he couldn't move...

"Captain," Dana said. "Surely, you realize these tunnels have stood for over six thousand years."

Could the doctor have heard his labored breathing? "Of course," Maddox managed to say.

"Relax," Dana told him. "Think of this as a giant spaceship. Wolf Prime hurdles through the void just as we did on *Victory*. You are in a passageway, a solid piece of construction. Why should you possibly worry?"

Incredibly, that helped. "Thank you, Doctor."

"Do you feel better?"

"Quite," Maddox said. His hands had been trembling, but that had stopped. He could breathe easily again. His mind began to function. Men were coming. How many? Less than a half dozen. Why were they coming all the way down here?

"Do you suppose they know we're here?" Keith asked.

The pilot had vocalized Maddox's belief.

"How would they know?" Dana asked.

"Sensors," Keith said.

"Have you seen any?" Dana asked.

"No," Keith admitted.

"Why else would they be coming directly for us?" Maddox asked.

"That's why we turned off the light," Dana said. "So we can see them first. I think we should try to advance, though, get to an area with more room."

"What if there are holes in the floor?" Maddox asked.

"Have you seen any holes so far?" Dana asked.

"Right," Maddox said. He had not. "I'll crawl just to be on the safe side."

"Let's stay close," Dana said. "We don't want to accidently split up."

Maddox thought that sound advice. They began to crawl across the floor, one right after the other. As they did, Maddox felt a greater stir of air on his face. He breathed the air, and found that it was colder than earlier.

"Could we have reached a lower area, a valley?" he asked in a soft voice. "Is there a cave entrance nearby?"

"I'm sure we'll find out soon enough," Dana whispered.

Maddox crawled, with the rifle case slung across his back. He certainly hadn't envisioned crawling underground when he'd left the starship in Keith's tin can.

The sound of approaching people grew louder. Voices became distinct instead of just a blur of noise. One of the speakers had a deeper voice than the others.

Maddox cocked his head. A woman spoke. It sounded like Meta. Yet, there was no way Meta could be down here in an ancient Swarm tunnel. What could travel faster through space than the ancient starship? Nothing could. Therefore, logically, it was impossible Meta had spoken. But Maddox had clearly heard her voice. He wasn't accustomed to doubting his judgment or his senses.

"Something is off," Maddox said. "Keith, come here."

"Captain," Keith said.

"Here," Maddox said, shoving his long-barreled gun into the ace's hands. "Do you know where the safety is?"

"Aye," Keith said. "I feel it with my thumb."

"Dana," Maddox said. "I have a knife."

"Give Keith the knife and me the gun," she said. "With my broken ankle—"

"Say no more," Maddox said. He took the gun back and handed Keith the knife handle-first. Then he showed Dana where to push the safety.

"It's ready to shoot," Maddox told her. "Push the safety to here."

"I understand," she said. "I'm ready."

Lastly, Maddox slid the rifle case off his back and put his Khislack together in the darkness. He put a magazine in as quietly as possible.

"Did you hear that?" a man asked a little ways from them.

Dana sucked in her breath.

"What's wrong?" Maddox whispered in her ear.

"Let's wait," she whispered. "I want to be sure first."

"Hello?" a man called. "Is anyone there?"

None of them answered.

"They're on the scanner," a different man said.

"We know you're there," the deep-voiced man called. "We know you came down from space, and the New Men are after you. We're with Professor Ludendorff's people."

"I'm his chief security officer," a different man said.

"I'm Captain Maddox of Star Watch Intelligence. Why don't you walk a little closer where we can see you? Our light no longer works."

"Don't shoot," the deep-voiced man said.

"Don't give us a reason to," Maddox said.

The seconds ticked away as several people approached. Soon, a wash of lamplights gave illumination to the cavern.

A normal-looking man with goggles, frost mask and hardhat, holding a bulky scanner, stepped into view. The lamp was attached to the front of his hardhat. The second person was bundled in slarn furs, complete with hood. She pulled the hood back, showing a wide but beautiful face.

"Meta," Maddox said in disbelief.

The next man was big with flat slabs of muscle. He, too, wore a hardhat with lamplight. He had square features and granite-like eyes.

Maddox knew it was Mr. Kane, the man who had kidnapped Meta out of New York City. The man Maddox has passed in the Dempsey Tower lobby, in the company of Susan Love.

"Hands up," the captain told Kane, aiming his rifle at him.

"No!" Meta shouted. "Don't shoot. You have it all wrong. Kane and I escaped from the New Men. We're here to help you, Maddox. We're here to make sure you find Professor Ludendorff."

"Nice try," Maddox said, "but I don't think so."

He saw three more men behind the others. They wore heavy slarn furs and had weather-beaten faces. They looked like rough men, what the captain expected trappers to be like. They certainly didn't seem to be archeologists.

"Firstly," said the man with the scanner and wearing a frost mask, "who are you? Secondly, what do you have against Kane? He's been instrumental in helping us thwart the New Men."

"I'm Captain Maddox of Star Watch Intelligence," Maddox said, as he kept his rifle trained on the center of Kane's chest. "I used the professor's papers more than a year ago to find the ancient starship he found in a lost star system."

"We've heard rumors of that," the man said. "I remember the professor telling me that entering the lost starship would have been impossible."

"I hate to deflate your image of the professor's infallibility," Maddox said. "But he was wrong. We made it inside the ancient starship and brought it back to Earth. The New Men began their attack against the Commonwealth shortly thereafter. I think this was because they fear the ancient vessel. During our original journey into the Beyond, we destroyed one of their star cruisers and survived two others."

"I'm sure the professor will want to hear all about that," the man said. "By the way, I'm Lank Meyers, the professor's security chief. You must Doctor Dana Rich. The professor has spoken about you. You played him a foul turn in the ancient star system."

"I saved his life," Dana said.

All during the conversation, Kane kept his focus on Maddox. Meta gripped the big man's left arm, also watching the captain.

"She's hurt," Keith said, indicating Dana. "A slarn rolled over her and broke her ankle. She needs help."

Lank Meyers nodded. "We'll help her. First, we have to assess the situation. Captain Maddox of Star Watch Intelligence, you must be an unusual man to have entered the ancient starship. Tell me why you keep your rifle trained on Kane."

"He kidnapped Meta from New York City on Earth," Maddox said.

"I know where New York City is," Lank said evenly.

Maddox nodded. "Kane kidnapped her, and I know he's an agent of the New Men. The only thing that's keeping me from killing him is the desire to know how he got to Wolf Prime ahead of me. At best, he left Earth several days before I did. That should be impossible because I traveled here in *Victory*."

"That's the name of the ancient starship?" Lank asked.

"Correct," Maddox said. "The vessel has an independent star drive the aliens developed, allowing it to travel faster than any ship in known space. How did you get to Wolf Prime so fast?" he asked Kane.

"If I tell you, you'll shoot me," Kane said. "Thus, I have no incentive to speak."

"It's called the Nexus," Meta said. "It's a gigantic silver pyramid. Kane went inside and set it. Afterward, we entered a plasma-like opening and leaped over one hundred light years in one jump."

Everyone but Maddox stared at Meta. The captain kept his eyes on Kane. The slightest twitch from the big man and he would start firing. Maddox believed Kane knew that.

"I doubt the New Men built the Nexus," Dana said, "if that's really how you accomplished your feat. Was the silver pyramid of alien design?"

Kane turned his head, looking at Meta.

283

"I'll tell you," Meta said. "But first you have to put your weapons down."

Maddox noticed that Dana also had her weapon trained on Kane.

"Forget it," Maddox said.

"Maddox," Meta said. "Do you trust me?"

"Not at the moment" he said.

Meta scowled. "You always were pigheaded. Don't you understand? The New Men are arrogant beyond belief. They treat their best agents like dogs. They reprimanded Kane for a slight infraction, threatening even worse punishments at the end of the assignment. He slipped away, promising to do as they demanded, but he had an epiphany once he put two and two together."

"What are the two and two?" Maddox asked, "and what's the four?"

"*Victory* and Professor Ludendorff," Meta said. "Kane finally realized why you were coming to Wolf Prime. He knows that Star Watch can beat the New Men once *Victory* can use all its old weaponry."

"You didn't say anything about this before," Lank told Kane.

Kane said nothing.

"How has Kane helped you people?" Maddox asked Lank. "And how long has he been here?"

"Eight days," Lank said. "The New Men scoured the planet for Ludendorff, and we had several close calls. Kane told us the frequency of their scanners and several of their procedures. It allowed us to escape a trap and slip here into the major dig."

Maddox wasn't sure, but it seemed as if Kane became more alert. He wondered what had caused that. Something was wrong here, something he was overlooking. What was it?

"Those were your SAMs?" Maddox asked Lank.

The security chief nodded.

"It's obvious the New Men have inserted an agent into your midst," Maddox said. "Kane is a plant. My bet is the New Men realized they couldn't find Ludendorff in time. So they fed you Kane to help you escape a trap, hoping to get him near the professor. I take it the enemy hasn't even got close to Ludendorff yet."

"I can personally attest to the fact that the professor is hyper-paranoid," Lank said. "He trusts few people. He also has a layered and clever security system."

"Can we talk to the professor?" Dana asked. "It's vital I see him."

Lank studied her and must have come to a swift conclusion. Moving away from Kane, Lank drew a compact pistol, aiming it at the big man.

"You have been genetically modified," Lank told Kane. "Meta has been as well. The clues are obvious. I'm afraid you're an altered individual as well, Captain Maddox."

"You're right," Maddox said, his estimation of Lank rising. "My mother fled the Beyond. She was pregnant with me at the time. I never met her, as she died soon after my birth. Before she died, she made it to Earth. I don't know if I have the genes of the New Men, but it's possible she escaped one of their facilities."

Kane's head shifted minutely. Maddox felt the man's heightened scrutiny.

"Interesting and troubling," Lank said. "It occurs to me that you could also be one of their plants, Captain Maddox. It would be a complex play, but well within the cunning of the New Men."

"He's not one of theirs," Dana said. "Captain Maddox gave Star Watch the ancient vessel, the only ship that can save humanity from the plague of the New Men."

Lank stared at Dana through his goggles. Finally, the security chief turned to Maddox. "Captain, if you will allow us to handcuff Kane and Meta, we will return to the base camp. The doctor obviously needs medical attention. We should then decide what to do next. I take it this *Victory* is coming to Wolf Prime?"

Maddox's nape hairs stirred. Something was definitely off here. He tried to think it through. How had Kane and Meta made it to Wolf Prime faster than they had? What was the Nexus, a giant, silver pyramid? Could that be true? Why had Ludendorff's people trusted Kane? It seemed inconceivable.

"Yes, the starship is coming," Maddox admitted. It was an obvious conclusion. He gave nothing away by saying so.

"Kane," Lank said, as he trained his pistol on the man. "You have a choice. Submit and live, or resist and die. Which will it be?"

"You have handcuffs with you?" Kane rumbled.

"I've studied your wrists before," Lank said. "They're much bigger than average, too big for normal handcuffs. Fortunately, we have leg irons, which in your case, will act as handcuffs. As to your question, yes, I brought a pair along."

"On your own authority?" Kane asked.

"The professor suggested it, if that's what you're saying."

"I would like to explain my story to the professor in person," Kane said.

"In order to do that," Lank said, "you would have to first submit."

Kane nodded. "I will submit." He put his hands before his body.

"Behind your back, if you please," Lank said. Kane complied

Lank motioned to one of his people. A heavily bundled trapper came forward with leg irons.

Maddox readied himself to fire. He could tell Kane knew that. The big man allowed the trapper to manacle his wrists with the leg irons.

"Handcuff Meta next," Lank said.

The trapper did so.

"Does that satisfy you?" Lank asked Maddox.

"There's something going on here I don't understand," Maddox said. "This doesn't feel right. Doctor, do you feel it?"

"I don't," she said, sharply. "We can trust them."

Maddox didn't agree, but he didn't know what else to do. "We'll walk in back, if you don't mind."

"Fair enough," Lank said. "Kane, Meta, you will lead the way. If you attempt anything unwarranted, I will shoot to kill. I have imbibed some of Ludendorff's paranoia. The New Men are notoriously crafty. Grim determination combined with ruthlessness is the only solution. Do you understand?"

"We've already proven ourselves," Meta said.

286

"Is that how Baron Chabot felt about you?" Maddox asked.

Meta turned, staring into his eyes. She became thoughtful. "You have a point. I understand," she told Lank.

"Kane?" the security chief asked.

"Let's get on with this," Kane said. "Nothing but the truth can change your minds now."

"Right," Lank said. "Let's go."

***

At Maddox's request, one of the trappers took his place with Dana. The stiff pace soon told on the doctor. The captain debated telling the others to slow down. Time seemed too important for that, so Maddox remained silent.

The tunnel widened and they took several different passages. At one point, lumber lay on the floor. The air felt warmer here too.

"How far are we underground?" Maddox asked.

"Approximately four hundred meters," Lank said.

"These are the former tunnels of the Swarm?"

"That's what the professor believes," Lank said.

"Did the Swarm have queens like an ant or bee colony?"

Lank chuckled. "We know far less than that about the Swarm. They are an enigma in too many ways. The professor has said there are reasons to believe the Swarm moved from planet to planet, devouring the ecology until they had to head to a new star system."

Maddox thought about that. "That doesn't make sense."

"Why not?" Lank asked.

"Wolf Prime doesn't seem devoured."

"True."

"That ruins the theory."

"Not necessarily," Lank said. "It could be someone drove the Swarm from Wolf Prime."

"Who?" Maddox asked.

"It's one of the reasons the professor has remained here for so long."

"This dig can't be a secret then."

"You mean secret from the New Men," Lank said.

"Right."

"You're wrong," Lank said. "It *can* remain a secret. The professor is more than paranoid, and he happens to be the most intelligent person in the universe."

"Smarter than the New Men?" Maddox asked.

"Oh, yes. I think that goes without saying."

Maddox eyed Lank Meyers. "You people are hiding from the New Men. The New Men aren't hiding from Ludendorff."

"By your own admission," Lank said, "the New Men are terrified of the ancient starship. That vessel leapt from the brow of Professor Ludendorff. The ability to enter the craft likely came from his genius as well."

"You have a high opinion of the man."

"I've seen him in action for many years," Lank said.

"You weren't with him on his journey to the ancient graveyard of ships?"

"You're full of questions, Captain Maddox. Before I answer any more, I have a few of my own I'd like answered."

"Fair enough," Maddox said.

Before the security chief could begin, a large device on his belt began to blare with noise.

"Stop," Lank said.

Everyone halted.

The security chief unhooked an earpiece, listening intently. Behind his goggles, his eyebrows shot up. "We're on our way," he said. He hooked the microphone back to the bulky device.

"Starship *Victory* is approaching Wolf Prime," Lank said. "It appears you're correct, Captain. Your vessel made a star drive jump. Well, two actually. The professor has kept his eye on the situation above. The ancient craft jumped from the outer system Laumer-Point, escaping three star cruisers. I don't know where it went, but it must have made a second jump. That one has brought it near. *Victory* is braking even now for an orbital station over the planet."

"Two star cruisers are in Wolf Prime's orbit," Dana said.

"I took on three star cruisers before," Maddox said. "The ship should be able to handle two. How long until the three that chased the vessel to the Laumer-Point return?"

"Why is the starship here at Wolf Prime?" Lank asked Maddox.

"To pick up Professor Ludendorff," the captain said. "Doctor Rich believes he can figure out the ancient weapons systems that have baffled Earth's best scientists. Before Star Watch's Fifth Fleet reaches the Tannish System, it's going to need reinforcements in order to defeat the New Men's main armada waiting for them there."

"That sounds interesting," Lank said. "I'm sure the professor would like to hear all about this."

"We have a narrow window of opportunity," Maddox said. "Do you have a way to get from here into orbit?"

"Couldn't *Victory* send down a shuttle?" Lank asked.

"Yes, but that will take more time. First, they would have to chase off the two star cruisers."

"I thought you said *Victory* could defeat three of them."

"No," Maddox said. "I faced three and barely survived the encounter, destroying a star cruiser. I'm not sure Galyan can do the same now."

"Who?" Lank asked.

"Never mind. Can you get us into orbit?" Maddox asked.

"Yes."

"Then you should do that as fast as you can. Once the other three star cruisers return, it will be too late to act."

Lank stared at Maddox. Finally, the security chief glanced at the trappers. "It's time to run," he said. "It's time to talk to the professor in person."

-29-

Lieutenant Noonan sat on a chair on *Victory's* bridge. Sergeant Riker sat beside her. Behind them, the holoimage of Galyan watched the main screen critically.

"These are New Men," Galyan said. "Their star cruisers have powerful beams. I suspect they have contact mines and heavy drones scattered in orbit waiting for me."

"I haven't detected any," Valerie said, as she scanned her board.

"The New Men are masters of deception and decoys," Galyan said. "They tricked us once already. You saw the ordnance they unlimbered near the Laumer-Point. It is why I sought your advice and brought you up here to the bridge."

Valerie didn't remember the situation exactly like that. Galyan had brought her to the bridge. That much was true. The ancient AI had thereupon discounted each piece of advice she'd given him. Instead of fighting as she'd wanted to do, Galyan had opted for flight. Now, she wondered if the AI hadn't been right after all.

Valerie had also been wondering about her desire to fight the three star cruisers. Maddox had faced three before, destroying one. *Victory* had taken near crippling losses doing so then. Valerie believed she could have done better. The ancient starship had collapsium hull armor now, and its neutron cannon was in better shape than it had been a year ago. Had it been an ego issue with her? Did she need to prove herself a better starship captain than Maddox?

290

"What do you suggest we do?" Galyan was asking.

Valerie turned around to eye the holoimage. "We have to reach low orbit and call the captain. You said so yourself by the Laumer-Point. Picking up Professor Ludendorff takes precedence over everything else. Ludendorff should be able to exponentially increase your combat power."

"In theory that's true," Galyan said. "More importantly, the professor can tell me the location of the Swarm homeworld. Yet now that we are here, or nearing the planet, I fear the New Men have a trick in store for me."

"All battle is risk," Valerie said.

"That is easy for you to say, as a Star Watch combat officer."

"Actually, it's harder for me. I'm flesh and blood. You're just circuits. I have more to lose."

"That is a highly unjustified remark," Galyan said. "I am a unique construct, a one-of-a-kind vessel over six thousand years old. I hold ancient secrets. You are young, with literally billions exactly like yourself. Your loss is miniscule in nature, easily replaced."

"Sorry if I don't agree with you," Valerie said sarcastically.

"There!" Galyan cried, pointing at the screen. "I see a star cruiser. My sensors indicate that its weapon ports are heating up. It wishes to fight. That implies the star cruiser, or its captain, has computed a fair ratio for survival. As we know, the New Men are highly rational creatures. Would they dare face me if they couldn't win?"

"You're making a lot of assumptions," Valerie said. "But what I don't understand is your sudden lack of fighting spirit."

"I have gained a new and higher awareness," Galyan said. "I realize more than ever what I risk in entering battle."

"Well, I learned a long time ago in Greater Detroit that to live, you have to fight."

"That is not logical," Galyan said.

"Yes it is. If you become a coward, you die a thousand deaths throughout your life. A brave man or woman only dies once."

"I hope you are not accusing the greatest tactician in the universe of cowardice," Galyan said.

Valerie turned to Riker, lofting her eyebrows.

Riker shrugged, shaking his head.

"Drive the star cruiser from the planet," Valerie said. "Your neutron beam is superior to his ray."

"At close range, you are correct," Galyan said. "He has the advantage now."

"Then use the star drive and jump closer."

"I dare not attempt a jump this close to a large gravitational object."

"You never had that problem before," Valerie said.

"If you refer to the time in the Beyond when we jumped by a planet, you must recall that I did not have complete control of my own vessel. I have not forgotten that you people turned me off."

Valerie faced the control panel. She'd gotten thoroughly sick of the AI a long time ago. She yearned for a regular ship where the people made the decisions. Arguing with the ancient computer drove her crazy.

Riker shouted.

Valerie saw it on the screen. The star cruiser used its main beam. The ray struck *Victory's* deflector shield, which stopped the New Men's beam cold.

"Increase speed," Valerie said.

"Yes," Galyan said. "In the end, I believe you are correct."

The ship's engines increased power, which caused a slight vibration upon the deck plates. The ancient starship had excellent gravity dampeners, so the high velocity hardly affected Valerie or Riker.

As the giant starship increased velocity, the star cruiser continued to fire its ray. Then, the second star cruiser appeared from around the planet. It, too, fired, adding a second beam. The two rays struck the deflector shield, slowly turning it red.

Valerie glared at the screen. Her hands bunched into fists. She hated the New Men. For too long, these interlopers from the Beyond had tormented humanity. The enemy never lost a fight. She dearly wanted to make them lose now. The idea that she sat in the captain's chair…it fired her resolve.

"There," Galyan said, pointing at the screen. "Do you see those?"

Valerie's fingers played over the panel. She had convinced the AI to give her independent scanning ability. Big orbital drones activated their thrusters. Galyan had been right. The New Men had seeded orbital missiles here.

"They don't have enough—"

Valerie stopped talking as the nearest warhead ignited. A thermonuclear fireball blew outward. Gamma and X-rays expanded in a ball. Behind it followed the slower heat.

"My sensors can't see past the blast area," Galyan complained. "Are the New Men trying to hide something?"

That was a shrewd guess, Valerie realized. Why else would the New Men blow a nuke at that range? Was the enemy trying to blind the sensors from something else?

"Start beaming the other missiles," Valerie said, as she studied her board. "They're in range."

"Activating the neutron beam," Galyan said.

Valerie continued to study the tactical situation. The missiles headed away from Wolf Prime and came straight at *Victory*. The two star cruisers remained in a low orbital path as they struck the deflector shield. Now, a purple neutron beam touched the nearest drone, exploding it before the warhead ignited.

"We should be in neutron beam range in five minutes," Valerie said, meaning in range of the star cruisers. "We can get there faster if you increase velocity even more."

"No," Galyan said. "I submit we're already going too fast. We wish to gain a low orbital path in order to pick up Professor Ludendorff. Begin trying to contact the captain."

"It's too soon," Valerie said. "The New Men could pick up our signal, pinpointing the captain's location. They might send missiles down to the surface to annihilate him."

"Yes," Galyan said, "that is sound advice. Thank you. Belay my last order."

"You're welcome," Valerie said, surprised the AI could give compliments. What had come over their jailer? The AI hadn't acted this way before.

The minutes ticked by, and *Victory* closed the gap between the other combatants. Another nuclear warhead ignited. The red area of the deflector screen darkened and expanded, but the blast didn't come close to rupturing the shield.

"Neutron beam in range in one minute," Valerie said.

At that moment, the star cruisers engaged their main thrusters. Long exhaust tails grew behind the two vessels. They increased velocity, fleeing across the orbital face of Wolf Prime. Were they trying to get behind the planet in relation to *Victory?*

"They're running away," Galyan said.

"I don't know what else you'd call it," Valerie said. "That implies they know the operational range of our neutron beam. I don't like that. They know too much about our ship."

"I agree," Galyan said. "Now, prepare for emergency braking. We must insert into an orbital path and attempt to contact Captain Maddox. It is imperative that he's already gained contact with Professor Ludendorff. They must be ready for an immediate liftoff."

"Cross your fingers," Valerie said.

"I beg your pardon?" Galyan asked.

"Yes," Valerie said. "You're right."

***

Something about Kane alerted Maddox.

They had entered a larger underground area. Here, the floor had planks, and the ceiling possessed lights. Heat units churned causing Maddox to sweat. To the left were large stacked wooden crates. A steep ramp led to a tunnel entrance in the ceiling.

Turning a corner brought the biggest surprise of all. Four people loaded up a shuttle, a big one.

"Professor," Lank called.

An older man looked up. After a second, he detached himself from the four. He wore a slarn fur and had gray hair and a lined face. He was bigger than Maddox had expected and looked more like a trapper than the galaxy's most famous professor.

"Lank," Professor Ludendorff said. "You finally decided to shackle Kane and Meta. I'm intrigued. Who are these others?"

As the professor approached, Lank introduced Maddox, Dana and Keith.

That bothered Maddox. Why had Lank needed to introduce Dana? Had she changed that drastically? Had Dana told him the truth, or were there things she had never confided to him about Ludendorff?

Maddox glanced at the doctor.

It happened then, and it happened fast.

The team approached with Kane and Meta in the lead. The big man stumbled, going to one knee. Then, Kane stood with startling suddenness. One of the links in the leg irons snapped, sending the shards spinning. An iron piece struck a trapper in the face, catapulting the man onto the floor.

Meta shouted. With one hand, Kane shoved her backward. She stumbled against a trapper and against Lank Meyers. The three of them went down.

In those moments, Kane covered ground fast. The big man could move like a rhinoceros and with as much power. A trapper in his way tried to draw a gun. Kane took the weapon from the man and possibly broke the hand while doing it. A left cross literally smashed the trapper's face, dropping him brutally.

Maddox brought up his Khislack. He'd stopped aiming it at Kane some time ago. By the time the captain had the rifle up, Kane reached Ludendorff.

With one arm, Kane lifted the professor in front of him like a shield, with Ludendorff's head blocking Kane's. The other hand gripped the stolen handgun, pressing the barrel against Ludendorff's head.

"What is this, Kane?" Lank shouted. "Treachery?"

Kane moved fast, backing up until he bumped against the shuttle. "Meta," he said. "Come here."

"No," Maddox said.

"I'll kill the professor if he she doesn't come," Kane said.

With the Khislack pointed at Ludendorff's stomach, Maddox approached Meta. She'd risen to one knee. The captain glanced at her face. It was twisted with hurt and uncertainty.

"Meta," Kane called.

"She remains with me," Maddox said.

Meta looked up at Maddox.

"They did something to your mind," Maddox told her.

Meta frowned. "I think you could be right."

"I'll shoot her if she doesn't come," Kane said.

"Then I'll kill you," Maddox said.

"Killing Ludendorff in the process," Kane said.

"If I have to." Maddox didn't look back to see if Lank Meyers aimed a weapon at him.

Kane began to move alongside the shuttle toward the cargo bay entrance. "If you shoot me, he dies," the big man said. "Remember that, Captain."

Maddox steeled himself, raising the rifle to fire.

"No!" Dana shouted. "Don't do it, Captain."

"I can't let the New Men get Ludendorff," Maddox said. "We need him."

"Killing the professor solves nothing," Dana said. "Let him go."

Maddox felt helplessness boil in his gut. How could Kane have broken a link in the leg irons? The man must possess fantastic strength. He also moved like greased death.

"This is why the New Men sent Kane," Maddox said. "They want Ludendorff."

"Trust me, Captain," Dana said. "This isn't over. We have *Victory* in orbit."

"We can't let Kane go," Maddox said.

"Professor!" Lank shouted.

"We knew this day would happen," Ludendorff shouted. "The New Men are too clever. Goodbye my friends. I will miss you all."

"Professor," Lank shouted, with agony in his voice.

"This is for the best, my old friend," Ludendorff said. "You mustn't fret. The enemy is vast and powerful. I trust you understand my meaning?"

Maddox's trigger finger tightened.

"*No*," Dana said.

Something in her appeal stopped Maddox from squeezing the last fraction of force. Then it was too late. Kane darted into the shuttle, taking Professor Ludendorff with him. A second later, the cargo bay hatch whirred shut.

"We can't let them leave," Maddox said. "Do you have more SAMs?"

Lank Meyers stared at the shuttle with tears brimming in his eyes. The others in the cavern stood mute and still.

The shuttle's engine roared with life.

"Lank!" Maddox shouted. "Do you have any more SAMs?"

The security chief turned to Maddox. "What would you have me do? Blow Ludendorff's shuttle out of the sky?"

"Yes," Maddox said. "Or make sure the doors down here stay shut."

The shuttle lifted off the floor. A second later, with a steady whine, it began moving forward.

Maddox stared in disbelief. This couldn't be happening. The New Men and their agents were unbeatable. Without Ludendorff to help them with *Victory*, humanity was going to lose the war. This was a disaster.

"You can't just let Kane take the professor to the New Men," Maddox said.

"He wanted it this way," Lank said. "You heard him."

"I did," Maddox said. "But he's the difference between victory and defeat between us and the New Men."

"No," Lank said.

The shuttle moved faster, and a large bay door opened in the ceiling. Muted skylight shined into the cavern.

"Have you people lost your mind?" Maddox shouted. He raised the Khislack and began firing, the rounds *pinging* off the shuttle's side. Then, the hauler lifted upward and out of sight. It was gone, with Ludendorff heading for the New Men.

-30-

"Maybe we can storm the shuttle," Maddox said. "*Victory* should be close. We have space marines who could try."

"You don't understand yet, do you?" Lank said. "The New Men are the worst calamity to ever befall mankind. We're like the ancient Neanderthals. We're in a species war, and we're the weaker side."

"Exactly," Maddox said. "That's why we can't let the New Men get hold of Ludendorff."

"I'm trying to tell you that this is the deadliest game our species has ever fought," Lank said. "That means we have to resort to the wickedest ruses possible. We have to make horrible sacrifices for the greater good."

"What does any of that mean?" Maddox asked.

"That we have another shuttle," Lank said. He checked his scanner. "It looks as if your starship has reached low orbit. It's time for you to call them, Captain."

Maddox couldn't understand the blasé attitude about losing Ludendorff. "Listen to me carefully," he said. "We must devise a plan to storm the shuttle and rescue the professor."

"No," Dana said. "No, no, no. The New Men aren't getting Professor Ludendorff."

"What?" Maddox asked.

"*He's* Professor Ludendorff," Dana said, pointing at Lank Meyers.

"What?" Maddox asked again, staring at the security chief.

The man doffed his hood and took off the frost mask and goggles. He was old and bald with a large hooked nose.

"*You're* Professor Ludendorff?" Maddox asked.

"I am."

"Then who did Kane take?"

"My best friend, Lank Meyers," Ludendorff said.

"And you knew about the deception?" Maddox asked Dana.

"As soon as I heard the professor's voice in the tunnels," Dana said.

Maddox recalled that Dana had been startled by the voice.

"Did you know from the beginning that Kane was an imposter?" Maddox asked the professor.

"Not with certainty," Ludendorff said. "But it seemed the most reasonable explanation. I decided to play it out, keeping Kane from the 'professor' because that's what the man wanted most."

"But your friend…" Maddox said.

"Lank has some surprises for the enemy," Ludendorff said. "We had time to prepare, you see."

"You actually *want* Lank to reach the New Men?" Maddox asked.

"Want is the wrong word," Ludendorff said. "But otherwise, the answer is yes. Come now, we must get ready. I've been expecting the starship for quite some time and am set to go."

Maddox stared at the bald man. Ludendorff had just sacrificed his best friend to the enemy. Here was the smartest man alive, the one who had found the lost star system, the man's whose notes he'd used to get aboard *Victory* in the first place. After all this time, he had found the professor. Now, it appeared the man had his own game to play against the New Men.

"We do have one problem," Ludendorff said.

"Yes?" Maddox asked.

"Her," Ludendorff said, pointing at Meta.

Maddox stiffened. "Why do you say that?"

"She's obviously been mind-scrubbed," Ludendorff said. "The clues are in her eyes and the way she moves her head.

I've seen her kind before. The sweetest act would be to put her out of her misery."

"No," Maddox said.

"She's a Trojan horse," Ludendorff said. "We won't be able to trust her."

"She's part of my team," Maddox said.

"Your spirit is commendable, but your logic faulty."

"This has nothing to do with my spirit," Maddox said. "No one is shooting Meta. If they do, I'll kill him and five others for good measure."

"He loves her," Dana told the professor.

Meta looked up sharply at Maddox.

Maddox wasn't sure. There was a stir in his chest, but he refrained from saying anything.

After a moment, Ludendorff said, "You will be responsible for her, Captain."

Maddox held his tongue. It appeared the professor didn't realize yet who was in charge of the mission. At the moment, though, the man had more people on the ground than he did. The captain would bide his time, telling Ludendorff the facts of life later.

"We must hurry," Ludendorff said. "The New Men will act fast once they learn this is our base camp. It's time to leave."

***

Lieutenant Noonan sat up, tapping her comm board. "This is Starship *Victory*," she said. Captain Maddox, or someone claiming to be him, was calling the starship. "As per regulations, I request a clearance code, sir."

"Blue Angel Seven Alpha," the man answered over the comm system.

Valerie grinned at Riker although she spoke into the comm. "That's a positive six-three. By the way, we saw another shuttle a few minutes ago. It did not respond to our hail."

On the bridge's main screen, Wolf Prime spread out below the starship. The enemy star cruisers had made it onto the other side of the planet, and appeared reluctant to show themselves again.

"Ours is the only shuttle Galyan should let board the starship," Maddox said.

Valerie frowned. "That sounds evasive, sir. You haven't responded to my comment about the other shuttle."

"That's true," Maddox said.

"What's he pulling now?" Valerie asked Riker.

The old sergeant shrugged.

Valerie twisted around, looking at Galyan. "What do you say? Are we going to let the captain's shuttle board?"

"I am detecting fifteen individuals aboard the craft," the holoimage said. "Meta is one of them."

"You're kidding?" Valerie said. "Meta?"

"I never kid," Galyan told her.

"But..." Valerie frowned. "Captain, there are fifteen people aboard your vessel."

"That is correct," Maddox said. "We have discovered land."

Valerie turned to Galyan. "They have the professor."

"I understand the coded reference," Galyan said. "Yes. The shuttle may proceed. I'm eager for the professor to find the ancient Swarm homeworld for me."

"You're good to go, sir," Valerie said. "Glad you made it."

"So am I, Lieutenant," Maddox said. "We're coming up."

***

Maddox sat in the shuttle's control cabin with Ludendorff and Dana. The professor had refused to let Keith fly, saying this was his shuttle, and he was the best pilot he'd ever met.

The doctor's broken ankle was properly bandaged with a splint and sprayed with disinfectant. A slarn trapper had seen to it. The rest of the personnel were in a second, larger chamber behind the first.

"Despite the urgency of the hour," Ludendorff told Dana, "it's hard leaving Wolf Prime. I consider what I've found here the most important of my life's discoveries."

"I still don't believe we're getting onto *Victory* this easily," Dana said. "The New Men can't be duped with a mere snap of the fingers."

"You're quite wrong," Ludendorff said. "Even super-beings can be tricked. I refer to myself as an example. Remember when you mutinied on my expedition to the lost star system?"

Dana said nothing.

"Your munity surprised me," Ludendorff said. "It succeeded, having a profound influence on my thinking. Since then, I've learned that supremely bright beings can indeed be tricked."

"I agree with the doctor," Maddox said. "I'm surprised the New Men only sent three star cruisers to the outer Laumer-Point after *Victory*. Events have moved much easier in the Wolf System than I expected." He thought about the New Man who had saved their lives from the slarn. That event still troubled him, but he couldn't determine its meaning.

"And people call *me* paranoid," Ludendorff said.

"Looking back at events," Maddox said. "I believe you said that about yourself."

"To be precise—and precision is important in these matters—my Lank persona called me hyper-paranoid."

Maddox had been trying to assess the professor ever since Dana had told him Lank was Ludendorff. The man seemed excited, having forgotten about his friend's horrible sacrifice. Maybe it was too difficult for the professor to dwell on, and this was the man's way of blocking the event. Yet, the professor seemed positively giddy by the prospect of boarding *Victory*.

That made sense, Maddox supposed. Seeking the ancient starship had been a lifelong dream. Ludendorff had come close to fulfilling it many years ago, before being forced to leave the lost star system. Did the professor hold a secret grudge against him for being the one to first board *Victory*?

Through the viewing port, Maddox observed the blue atmosphere begin to fade away as they climbed into orbit. Stars appeared and then a deeper blackness.

"There," Ludendorff said. "That must be *Victory*." He pointed at a blue image on a sensor screen. The professor rubbed his hands together. "I never thought this day would come."

"No," Dana said. "Neither did I."

"You are forgiven your munity, Doctor. I am finally achieving one of my life's goals."

"We're all thrilled for you, Professor."

Maddox noted the bitterness in Dana's voice. He wasn't sure Ludendorff did. Then, despite the critical nature of their flight, the captain's thoughts centered on Meta. She had been in Kane's company for quite some time, and the two had used a silver pyramid called the Nexus, if he could trust the story. Ludendorff had also said something back there that deeply troubled him about Meta.

"Professor," Maddox said, "you said that Meta has been mind-scrubbed. First, what does that mean? She seems to retain old memories."

"Excuse me if the term seems overly dramatic," Ludendorff said. "I did not mean to imply she doesn't have any memories or most of her former personality. 'Scrubbed' in this instance means new loyalty has been forcefully instilled. The New Men have some nasty technology. They have tampered with her. She has become suspect."

"Can we reverse what they've done?" Maddox asked.

"Conceivably," Ludendorff said. "It would be difficult, though. I'd need to study their machines and procedures, which would mean capturing the equipment. I would imagine such valuable apparatuses would be on a star cruiser. Capturing one of those would be beyond difficult."

"Is that the only way to restore Meta's mind?" Maddox asked.

The professor didn't answer him. "How many space marines would it take to storm a star cruiser full of New Men? Ahhh," the professor said. He turned away from the sensor screen and peered through the viewing port. Stars shined everywhere. "Look at that. It's the ancient starship. She's beautiful."

Maddox spied *Victory* in the distance, bigger than a speck so the two oval sections were distinct enough to see.

"Is the starship's deflector shield down?" Ludendorff asked.

303

Maddox checked a reading. "Net yet. We want to be careful. The star cruisers are fast and could show up in an instant. They have a powerful long-range beam. We don't want to give them an open shot against the hull."

"You'd better inform your crew we're near," Ludendorff said. "It would be a pity if their shield burned my shuttle and us in it."

"Begin braking maneuvers," Maddox told the professor.

For just a second, it seemed the old man would argue. Then, he nodded. "Yes, you're right." The professor's fingers moved spryly, playing on the shuttle's flight panel. He did seem to know what he was doing.

The craft rotated. The engine purred and thrust pushed them against their seats as the shuttled slowed its velocity.

"*Victory,*" Maddox said. "Do you copy our approach?"

"Yes, sir," Valerie said through the comm.

"I think—"

"I'm already on it, sir," Valerie said. "Regulations under a combat situation demand careful timing. I'm watching you. You're decelerating hard. Is Keith piloting the shuttle?"

"No," Maddox said.

"Oh. The maneuvering has his rash style. Given the situation, it's well done."

Ludendorff grinned at Maddox. "I'm a Renaissance man, Captain. That means I'm a man of many talents."

"Ah," Maddox said. He knew very well what a Renaissance man was.

"Looking good, sir," Valerie said. "He we go. Four, three, two, one—the shield is down. Bring your shuttlecraft in, sir. We want to get the shield back online as soon as possible."

***

As *Victory* lowered its unique electromagnetic shield and the shuttle neared the opening hangar bay door, Per Lomax tapped a panel aboard his experimental single-ship.

There were fourteen other needle-like craft around him in the planet's icy stratosphere. Per Lomax had seen the first shuttle go by underneath his position. He had registered Kane's signal and relayed it to the star cruisers in orbit. The big vessels hid from *Victory*, keeping Wolf Prime between them and the starship.

Not much later, Per Lomax had witnessed strike missiles zooming toward the professor's hiding location. That was a deception. Now that Kane had kidnapped Ludendorff, the humans would expect an attack on their camp. To forgo the assault would have been a mistake, and these, Per Lomax refused to make.

The critical event had been the second shuttle. From his vantage, Per Lomax had watched it roar into space. The fifteen single-ships under his orders could have attacked the shuttle. They could also have acted as sensor relays to guide strike missiles against the escaping vehicle. The thought had never occurred to the New Man. The shuttle heading for *Victory* was exactly what he desired to see.

This was a moment of highest exaltation. It may have been the greatest reason for his existence. The second shuttle approached *Victory*. Per Lomax listened to the enemy's radio exchange. More importantly, a ground-based station watched the ancient starship's deflector shield.

Per Lomax's panel blinked with a green light. It was the signal he's been waiting for. *Victory* had dropped her deflector shield, presumably to allow the shuttle to board.

The New Man lay on his stomach in the small control area of the single-ship. He gripped two throttle controls.

The single-ship was a highly experimental craft. The principle that guided its unique locomotion had been stolen from Earth. The antiquated humans were clever at times in areas of technological discovery. It was a strange phenomenon. The Earthmen called their new principle or vehicle a jumpfighter. It could fold space. A single-ship also folded space, but couldn't do it for as long a distance as the Earth fighter could.

Per Lomax, with Kane's insight, had developed a cunning tactic they were about to test. The Rouen Colony agent had his uses after all. The man was clever. Kane had Professor Ludendorff, and now the others fled to *Victory*. They did so at the worst possible moment in what Per Lomax believed would prove to be humanity's last year of existence.

Per Lomax might have smiled if that had been coded into his genetic makeup. He felt exultation, but his features remained placid. The lower order species grinned and gaped at the slightest emotional whim. Clearly, it interfered with their efficiency.

Tightening his grip around the throttles, Per Lomax signaled his combat team. The moment had come. The Throne World demanded the ancient starship. The vessel would hold new to them but primeval in time, alien technologies. Not only mustn't the outdated humans ever understand and mass produce such tech, but the New Order must have them.

"Transfer," Per Lomax said. "Transfer and board the enemy starship."

He manipulated his throttles. The engine howled at maximum power. The single-ship slid through the stratosphere, coming into direct line of sight with Starship *Victory*.

A horrible sensation washed through Per Lomax's prone body. He controlled the shudder of agony. Jumping hurt a superior being much more than the lower order species. That only made sense. He was more refined than the brutes they conquered.

Everything shivered before Per Lomax. His single-ship disappeared from its location in the stratosphere. Around it, the others likewise vanished. In a microsecond of time, the fifteen craft reappeared near the second shuttlecraft.

Per Lomax strove to regain his equilibrium. This was the moment to strike. *Victory* was the humans' last hope to avoid extinction. The man who captured the ancient starship would advance high in the New Order. He might even win a post on the Throne World itself.

"Now," he whispered. Per Lomax twisted a throttle control. His single-ship slid through space, aiming at the open bay door into *Victory*. Behind him, the other single-ships followed.

It was time to board the enemy starship and destroy everyone who stood in the way of the New Order of Existence.

"What are those?" Valerie asked, as she studied her sensor board.

"I don't know," Galyan said. "I—Warning!" the holoimage shouted. "They carry New Men. I am detecting New Men inside those ships."

Valerie blinked in astonishment. What could that mean? New Men— "Jumpfighters," she said. "The enemy has jumpfighters."

"Warning," Galyan said. "They are approaching the open bay door. They seek entrance into me."

"Put up the deflector shield," Valerie snapped. "There may be more of them coming."

"Explain—"

"Raise your shield now!" Valerie shouted, as she spun around to glare at the holoimage.

Galyan's eyelids fluttered. "Yes. That is the correct procedure. I am raising the shield—now."

Valerie spun back to her board in time to see the hazy deflector shield come back online. Many of the enemy craft were inside the shield. Four of the tiny vessels struck it. The enemy fighters and their crews sizzled and dissipated into their component atoms. That still left eleven of the ships who were behind the protective electromagnetic screen.

"Activate the neutron cannon," Valerie said. "Burn those ships."

"Those within the shield?" Galyan asked.

"Do it!" Valerie yelled. "Why are you hesitating? You must act with speed or we're doomed."

"I need time to warm up the cannon first," Galyan said.

"Fire now with whatever you have. Hit them. Destroy them. We can't let the New Men get aboard you."

Galyan appeared shocked. Then, the holoimage nodded. "Yes. At once. You are correct. I am aiming the neutron cannon and firing a weakened beam."

***

Aboard the shuttle, a proximity alert blared into life, the klaxon startling the flight crew. Professor Ludendorff lurched forward, scanning the board.

Dana saw it first. "Look at those. What are they?"

Maddox looked up at the viewing port. Incredibly, he saw needle-shaped craft. They were half the size of the tin can.

"Where did they come from?" Ludendorff asked. "From what I'm seeing, they simply popped into existence."

"Jumpfighters," Maddox said, understanding the situation. "The New Men must have some of their own."

"The New Men?" Ludendorff asked.

Maddox's thoughts moved fast, connecting ideas. "They're trying to storm *Victory*. The New Men are trying to capture the starship." He turned to Dana. "You wondered why this was so easy. How could we get away from Wolf Prime so effortlessly? The answer is the New Men were watching *Victory*. They were watching us, too. Once the shield lowered, they made a stab with their jumpfighters."

"Incredible," Ludendorff said. "Yes. It's a brilliant maneuver. I should have foreseen it, especially after your comment about the tin can earlier. This is most remarkable."

"It's a catastrophe," Maddox said. "Increase speed. We have to board first."

"I can't risk acceleration this close to the—"

Maddox leaned toward Ludendorff and slapped the control panel. The thrusters roared with power, and the shuttle leapt for the hangar bay.

"What are you doing?" Ludendorff shouted. "That is unethical. I'm piloting the craft. This is—"

"—The best idea there is," Maddox said. "I'm saving our lives and maybe the starship. Valerie!" he said into the comm. "Lieutenant Noonan, can you hear me?"

"Yes, Captain?" she said.

"The New Men are attacking in modified jumpfighters."

"We know that," Valerie said. "Galyan has already raised the shield. Four of their craft crashed and burned against it. Eleven are heading for the hangar bay."

"Close it."

"We can't in time."

"Use the neutron beam on them," Maddox said.

Even as he spoke, a purple ray fired, and two enemy jumpfighters burned away in a crisp of destructive power.

"There are nine left," Maddox said.

Ludendorff's fingers played over the board. "Hang on!" the old man shouted. "This could hurt."

Maddox looked up just in time. He grabbed his board and tightened his muscles. A terrific *jolt* shook the shuttlecraft. Metal screeched and air hissed somewhere. The vessel had a leak.

Checking the screen, Maddox saw a smashed enemy jumpfighter tumbling end over end, the one Ludendorff had just rammed.

"Make that eight of them left," Ludendorff said.

Maddox nodded. That had been well done. The shuttle was ahead of the rest of the jumpfighters. "Prepare for landing, professor. Get us down in one piece."

"Right," Ludendorff said.

"What are you thinking?" Dana asked Maddox.

Maddox didn't have time to answer. He was thinking fast, deciding what they had to do. Right, take the greatest risks up front.

The captain switched on the shuttle's intercom. "Listen to me carefully. Enemy jumpfighters have appeared behind us. We're inside the starship's deflector shield, but so are eight enemy jumpfighters. They're going to disgorge New Men onto the starship. I don't know how many. I want everyone to get a weapon. We're going to have to fight. We need to kill the New

Men. If they gain control of *Victory*…We can't let that happen. Any questions so far?"

"The New Men are landing in the hangar bay with us?" Keith asked.

"Yes," Maddox said. "Don your frost mask and goggles. Once off the shuttle, we're going to dash through an area with little atmosphere. At best, we're going to have fifteen seconds to get into a safe part of the ship. So you're going to have to run fast."

"Cunning bastards," Keith said. "That's a righteous way to use a jumpfighter, there's no denying it."

Maddox silently agreed. How many New Men did each of those jumpfighters hold? The tin can had been cramped, with hardly any space for passengers. Likely, it would be the same way for the enemy.

Eight needle-shaped craft zoomed for the hangar bay. That meant at least eight, maybe sixteen New Men. How many people did the good guys have?

There was Major Kharkov and four of his space marines. Galyan had five fighting robots. Ten soldiers so far. If he included Meta—no. He couldn't trust her just yet. Someone would have to watch her. He'd let Keith do that. In a space battle, Keith was a wizard. In a ground fight, the ace might become a liability. The trappers could probably fight. Anyone who faced slarns on a regular basis would know how to handle the terror of battle. Still, the trappers weren't organized soldiers.

Counting himself, Valerie and Riker made thirteen soldiers. Adding in the slarn trappers—seven out of the fifteen shuttle passengers—made twenty people against eight or sixteen New Men. Those were horrible odds. He remembered seeing the New Men in action on Loki Prime and in the war footage from Odin.

How good were the robots, and what did it mean that Galyan controlled the ship? That might be their margin for victory.

There was another problem. Once they fought for control of the vessel, what if the star cruisers showed up? The starship would have to jump elsewhere.

"Lieutenant," Maddox said.

"Yes, sir."

"Tell Galyan he has to jump."

"He won't do it so near a gravitational body like Wolf Prime," Valerie said.

"What? That's nonsense."

"Maybe you believe so, sir, but Galyan feels otherwise."

"I speak facts, not beliefs," the AI said through the comm.

"Okay," Maddox said. The shuttle was coming in fast. He had less than a minute left. "This is what you need to do, Galyan. Are you listening."

"Affirmative."

"Head away from Wolf Prime," Maddox said. "Go at full velocity. As soon as you can, jump out of here. Get away from the star cruisers."

"Affirmative. We will move away from the planet and engage the star drive at the first opportunity."

"Can you patch me through to Major Kharkov?"

"My robots can take care of the situation," Galyan said.

"I hope you're right," Maddox said. "But what if you're wrong? Wouldn't you like some backup?"

"How can I trust you?"

"Galyan, we've been in this together for a long time. You have to start believing Star Watch means you no harm. The New Men aren't going to give you any choices."

"That is logical," Galyan said. "They are smarter than you and will no doubt disable me. Then, it is possible they will figure out the weapons systems you could not. Yes, I will release Major Kharkov and allow him his weaponry. You must give me your word, Captain Maddox, that you will give me full control of my vessel if during combat you gain certain advantages over me."

"Done," Maddox said.

"I will begin acceleration as soon as you have boarded," Galyan said.

"Good," Maddox said. "You're making the right choice." He unbuckled from his seat.

"What are you doing now?" Ludendorff asked.

"I'll be right back," Maddox said, as he raced to the hatch.

311

He'd already begun to take the measure of Professor Ludendorff. The man was brilliant, of that Maddox had no doubt. Who had ever tricked the New Men? Maddox didn't know of anybody else. However, in his opinion, the professor thought too highly of himself. Because of what Maddox had done, the shuttle zoomed far too fast for the hangar bay. *Victory* loomed before them. They didn't dare slow down, though. The New Men would beat them inside then, and that would be a disaster.

"Captain," Ludendorff called. "We have seconds left before we reach *Victory*. I demand that you take a seat."

Maddox ignored the professor. With a twist of the handle, he opened the interior hatch separating the two compartments and shouted, "Second Lieutenant, get your butt in here on the double. I mean *now*."

Keith Maker ripped off his restraints and rushed up the aisle. "I don't know what took you so long to see the light, sir."

"Run!" Maddox shouted.

Keith must have understood. The small Scotsman sprinted and dove through the hatch, trusting Maddox. The captain didn't fail. He caught the young ace and hauled him upright in the control cabin.

"Move aside!" Maddox told Ludendorff.

"What?" the professor said. "Why would I—"

The old man had no more time to argue. Maddox reached Ludendorff and popped off the man's buckles.

"Now see here," Ludendorff began.

Maddox lifted the older man effortlessly from the pilot's chair. In three swift strides, he shoved Ludendorff into a vacant seat.

"Buckle in," he said. Without waiting to see if the professor listened or not, Maddox resumed his former spot and snapped his own buckles together.

At that moment, the shuttle zoomed through the hangar bay opening much too fast.

Keith laughed wildly. "This is what I like, a little challenge. You don't even give me time to familiarize myself with the controls."

As the ace spoke, his fingers roved over the piloting board. "Where do you want me to set her down, Captain?"

"By the regular hatch," Maddox said. "We want to get off the shuttle and into the ship as fast as we can. There isn't much, if any, atmosphere left in the hangar bay, and we're going to run through it."

"Aye-aye, sir," Keith said. "Hang on, please."

Keith Maker took control of the shuttle and spun it on a dime, as the saying went. He squirted thruster power three times. The hauler responded to his touch, braking inside the hangar bay instead of crashing against bulkheads. With consummate skill, the ace set the shuttle down gentle as a feather twenty meters from a hatch into the living quarters.

"Amazing," Dana said.

"Easy as can be, love," Keith said, grinning, "if you're me, that is. Sir," he asked Maddox, "why did you give me so much time to study the controls? I want a true test one of these days."

Maddox grinned back at the ace. Maybe even the Second Lieutenant realized he'd just practiced a miracle. Who but Keith Maker could have landed the nearly out-of-control boat in exactly the right spot?

"I'm sorry, Professor," Maddox told Ludendorff. It was time to *move*. The captain had already unbuckled, heading for the compartment hatch. "Keith is the best pilot in the Commonwealth. I hope you can understand."

Ludendorff scowled, looking pissed.

"Second Lieutenant," Maddox said, "I want you to get ready. You're going to stay on the shuttle and attack the enemy jumpfighters as they land. You're the bowling ball, and they're the pins."

"Yes, sir," Keith said. "I get it."

"You may not survive the battle," Maddox said.

"I'm not worried, sir."

"First, we're getting off the shuttle, though."

"Good luck, Captain," Keith said. "You'd better hurry."

Opening the interior hatch, shouting at the others in the second compartment, Maddox rushed to Dana next and manhandled her onto her feet. "Go, Professor. Move it."

The old man rushed for the outer hatch.

"You're the ace," Maddox told Keith. "Use your best judgment to do the most damage you can. I want you back in the starship afterward."

"Aye-aye, sir," Keith said, as he stared out of the viewing port. He looked determined.

Maddox would have liked to say more, but he didn't have time. In truth, all the atmosphere must have already blown out of the open hangar bay door. It was possible Valerie realized what he planned and had ordered Galyan to pump more air in as the big hangar door closed. If it was a vacuum outside, each of them had five to ten seconds to make it into a pressurized area. That's how long a person could act in a vacuum without any gear. They could only survive a longer exposure, if someone else dragged them to safety. This was likely the biggest risk of all. The captain doubted whether everyone could rush through the hatch into the living quarters in time.

"Right," the captain whispered. "Do it."

Ludendorff lifted the bar and hurled open the hatch. He jumped down.

Maddox picked up the doctor and leaped down after Ludendorff, landing hard on the hangar bay floor. Everyone wore their frost masks and goggles. Fortunately, they had gravity thanks to the dampeners. This would probably be impossible to do in time with zero G.

Maddox began to run. He had twenty meters to go. The shuttle was impossibly close to the needed hatch. Would Galyan have already overridden the emergency locking procedure to the entrance? With a vacuum in the hangar bay, that type of door wasn't supposed to open. He should have told the AI all that, but he hadn't thought of everything in time.

As Maddox ran, moisture formed on his tongue. His body had already begun to act negatively to the vacuum bringing on decompression. An increasingly wet tongue was one of the first symptoms. Soon, he would go blind, too.

The captain sprinted ahead of the others. Dana clung to him. Would the hatch be locked? *Why didn't I tell Galyan? I can't believe I forgot something so critical.*

-32-

Maddox decided to drop Dana in order to free both hands to force open the hatch. Before he could release her, the bar turned, and the entrance began to swing open. Escaping atmosphere flung the hatch all the way. The heavy metal missed clipping the captain by the barest centimeter. One of Galyan's robots blocked the entrance. Obviously, the tentacle-armed automaton must have opened the hatch.

As Maddox's vision began to blur—decompression caused moisture to form on all his soft tissues—the treads churned. The stainless steel, cylindrical robot trundled out of the way into the hangar bay. In an exquisite display of bodily control, Maddox twisted as the metal monstrosity allowed him to pass. Even so, the captain brushed against the robot. It was like slamming against a massive football lineman.

Dana screamed. She must have kicked the thing with her broken ankle.

Instinctively, even as he stumbled, Maddox kept on his feet. He was like a cat in that regard. The captain kept on moving, aiming into hard wind resistance. He charged into the ship's living quarters, into a large corridor. Air whistled out of the hatch into the hangar bay. The passing atmosphere allowed Maddox to breathe. Although he didn't know it, the captain had moved from the shuttle to the hatch in seven seconds.

With Dana clutched against his chest, Maddox charged deeper into the corridor where there was a thicker atmosphere. Going back into the hangar bay for any of the others would have been a foolish gesture of heroics. The robot would have to drag the unconscious into the corridor. Without an atmospheric suit, none of them would last more than ten seconds, and that wouldn't be enough time to get the job done.

"Set me down," Dana said.

Maddox silently agreed that he'd charged far enough into the corridor. He deposited the doctor onto the deck plates, removed his goggles and wiped his eyes.

His vision was only slightly blurry, but it unnerved him.

Others stumbled through the hatch. They must have realized like him they needed to get in deeper, because every one of them kept moving down the corridor.

The seconds passed. Meta staggered through the hatch. Maddox breathed more easily.

Finally, the robot reappeared, dragging people by their feet. It brought in five, zoomed back into the hangar bay and brought in three more. Afterward, the robot shut the hatch, sealing off the vacuum. The shriek of wind stopped immediately.

Eight of us are down, Maddox realized. Eight lay on the floor unconscious. Seven were on their feet in various phases of well-being. Make that six were on their feet. The last was Doctor Dana Rich who massaged her leg just above the broken ankle.

As his vision improved, Maddox marched to the hatch, slapping on the screen showing the hangar bay on the other side of the bulkhead. Here was the question now. What was Keith doing against the New Men? Could the ace take out any more of the supermen before they exited their jumpfighters?

***

A few minutes earlier, Keith pressed a control, closing the shuttle's outer hatches. He sat in the pilot chair. Through the viewing port, which was ten meters off the hangar bay's deck, he saw Captain Maddox sprint for an interior starship entrance.

Leave it to the captain to race with Doctor Rich through a vacuum. Who else would have tried that? Not too many people. Keith noticed the others racing after the cheetah-fast Maddox. Then, the ace didn't have any more time to worry about them.

The captain gave me a job to do.

Second Lieutenant Maker no longer looked anxious. Normal living was difficult. Trying to keep off the bottle took hard-to-find self-control. Piloting anything in any situation— the worse the better—made life fun.

Keith began to whistle an old tune Highlanders had used ages ago when fighting English invaders. His nimble fingers played over the controls. This was a tub of a shuttle. It was nothing like the jumpfighter or the even more beautiful strikefighter he'd used against the Wallace Corporation.

He couldn't help that, now could he? A man used what he had and made it count. Keith laughed, because it was up to him to even the odds for human survival. If that wasn't a game worth playing, then nothing was.

The shuttle lifted off the deck. He goosed a thruster, shoving the hauler a little forward. Then the first single-ship zoomed through the hangar bay opening.

"Lovely little needles, aren't you?" Keith said. "You're pretty. There's no denying that. But you're facing me in my backyard, don't you know."

Keith's eyes tightened. He leaned forward, and he gave the shuttle more power. The hauler built up velocity. Another of the needle-ships came through.

"No more of that," Keith said.

He didn't want to let Captain Maddox down. The man had told Keith to do whatever needed doing however he thought best. That was the best kind of commander to have.

"This is how we did it in Tau Ceti, me lovelies."

Keith aimed for the hangar bay opening as another needle craft entered. With a flick of his fingers, the young ace adjusted. The blocky shuttle moved sideways just enough and at the right moment. It grazed the single-ship, acting like a cue ball, sending the needle-craft against a bulkhead. The tiny vessel smashed, the top half crumpling and hopefully killing the golden-skinned bastard inside.

Then, the shuttle zoomed past the closing hangar bay entrance. Keith's killer instincts kicked into high gear. Leaning even farther forward with his fingers tapping controls, he rammed a needle-ship, smashing it out of his way. Swaying to

317

the side, bringing his hauler sharply left, the ace crashed against another slender, smaller vessel. Pieces of metal shredded away from it. The enemy craft spun hard in an out-of-control fashion, heading for *Victory's* hull. Whooping a war-cry, Keith made the shuttle dance for him. It spun in a tight, controlled manner. The thrusters burned in a delicate and exact sequence. Then, the shuttle used its belly, swatting another needle-ship as if it were a fly.

The entire hauler shook, equipment rattling in the control cabin. A blizzard of emergency lights appeared on Keith's board. Air shrieked and a klaxon blared. A quick glance at the sensor screen showed him the last enemy craft tumbling away from the starship and back toward the deflector shield.

Then, the cabin's lights flashed and quit altogether. Red emergency lights bathed the control chamber in an eerie radiance.

Keith didn't appear worried. His eyes glowed with delight at his accomplishments.

"Four of you buggers," he said. "That ain't bad when you figure I'm just a callow youth against the masters of the universe."

He exulted in his victories, certain that Captain Maddox would have been proud of him.

Then, the ace smelled electrical smoke. That brought him back to reality. The shuttle had taken heavy damage. It wasn't going to last a whole lot longer. Did he want to die out here, or maybe get his butt into gear and return to his friends?

"They may need my help," Keith told himself. There were still New Men left, as he had only taken out four out of eight.

He worked fast, turning the stricken shuttle, following the starship away from Wolf Prime. He had to stay away from the nearing deflector shield.

Clearly, he couldn't return to the hangar bay. The big doors had closed. Besides, he didn't want to go that way just now, not with New Men in there.

The air was getting bad in the cabin. It was time to don a spacesuit. Maybe he could take a spacewalk. First, he'd have to talk to Valerie and ask her for an access hatch.

Keith worked to save his life, grinning maniacally. Four New Men were dead thanks to the ace from Glasgow. Now all he had to do was find a place to land outside *Victory*. Compared to what he'd done so far, that should be a piece of cake.

***

"Roger that," Lieutenant Noonan told Keith from her comm station on the starship's bridge.

Galyan stood behind her, appearing worried.

Valerie turned around. "He's going to land on *Victory* and spacewalk to an access hatch."

"I heard the conversation," Galyan said.

"Okay," Valerie said, turning back and tapping her board, bringing the interior hangar bay video feed into focus. The outer bay doors had closed. The four surviving needle-shaped "jumpfighters" landed on the deck.

Before each enemy craft stopped moving, bubble canopies blew open. Valerie zeroed in on one. A silver-suited New Man emerged. She assumed he must be one. The being was tall and lean and wore a fishbowl helmet. She couldn't see his head, because the interior helmet was tinted. The man leaped from his "jumpfighter," landing in a crouch on the deck. She couldn't see any weaponry other than a holstered blaster. He did wear a pack on his back.

The New Man looked around. He raised his left hand and opened it, peering at the inner flattened palm.

Valerie tapped her panel, zooming for a closer scan. The New Man's suited hand showed a tiny screen. On the screen was a schematic, flipping to floor plan after floor plan. Could the blueprint be of *Victory*? How would the New Man have one? Could the enemy's secret service have wormed the knowledge from Star Watch? If so, how could the spy have brought that knowledge all the way out to Wolf Prime?

"Captain," Valerie told Maddox. "It looks as if the New Men have a layout of the starship."

"You're sure of that?" Maddox asked over the comm.

"I'm looking at the schematic he's studying. I don't know what else it could be but a diagram of *Victory's* decks."

"Good work, Lieutenant," Maddox said.

Valerie smiled. The captain didn't give compliments easily. When he did, they were well deserved.

"What are they doing?" Galyan asked her.

Four New Men in their silver suits and tinted bubble helmets sprinted through the hangar bay. They did not run toward the same hatch the captain and his people had used.

"Sir," Valerie told Maddox. "It looks as if they know where the engine rooms are. They're heading for hatches that will take them that way."

"Are there any more enemy soldiers?" Maddox said. "I just see four."

"That's all I see too," Valerie said. "Keith smashed four needle-ships."

"The man deserves a Platinum Nebula." It was the highest medal for courage that Star Watch could give.

"The New Men are forcing a hatch," Valerie said.

"How are they doing it?" Maddox asked.

The lead New Man simply waved his hand before the entrance and it opened. What did he carry in his glove to do that? Whatever it was must have shorted Galyan's lock.

After a quick explanation, Valerie said, "Captain, the New Men are in the starship, and they're running fast."

"Send the space marines and robots to the engine rooms," Maddox said. "I'll be there as quick as I can. Tell Kharkov to bring extra weapons for us."

"You'd better hurry, sir. Those New Men are moving faster than I think even you can run."

Maddox was silent for a moment. Then he said, "Galyan is going to have to run some interference for us. We'll need time."

"I can do that," Galyan said. "Vacuum in chambers, shutting off selected gravity dampeners and sealing hatches."

"Excellent," Maddox said. "We're on our way to the engine rooms."

***

Ten minutes later, a winded Maddox accepted a military-grade laser carbine from Major Kharkov. It meant the captain had to shoulder a generating pack.

Kharkov's faceplate was open. His eyes burned with determination. Behind him were his four men, their faceplates sealed tight and Gauss rifles gripped in their gauntlets.

The space marines loomed huge in their battle gear. They wore the latest exo-skeleton-powered armor, the motors purring. This was their specialty. They had linked sets in their helmets, sensor gear and tough body armor. The Gauss rifles fired 3mm electromagnetically accelerated explosive rounds. They didn't have to hit to kill like a kinetic slug, although a round could do that. A "bullet" exploded like a proximity grenade. They were devastating against unarmored infantry. If the New Men's silver suits acted like body armor, the space marines could switch to armor-piercing saboted ammunition.

"We'll take care of them," Kharkov assured the captain.

"You have seen the video from Odin, right?" Maddox asked.

"That's why we have explosive ammo," Kharkov said.

Maddox and Kharkov had communicated as the captain ran for the engine rooms. They'd agreed the best spot to take on the enemy would be in the annex chamber, a large open area just before reaching the antimatter cylinders.

Valerie gave them a minute-by-minute report on the New Men's advance. It would appear the golden-skinned soldiers didn't have a perfect schematic of the starship, but it was close enough. The enemy had taken a few unneeded detours. The small misdirection had done more to slow them down than anything Galyan had thrown at them. Kane must have brought the stolen schematic with him from Earth.

"Galyan suggests he shut down the corridor lights in front of them," Valerie said over the comm.

"Not now," Maddox said. "We're here, and this is where we want them."

The captain desired massed firepower on target. He had five robots with laser carbines, five space marines in powered armor, four trappers with their rifles and himself. Riker remained with Valerie.

"They're less than a minute from you," Valerie said.

Maddox told Kharkov the news. Afterward, everyone went to his location.

Three different hatches led from the corridors into the annex. A ceiling three times a man's height gave the annex a greater sense of area than many other places on the starship. It was like a gymnasium, with engine monitoring equipment on the left wall and piled steel boxes on the right. Two presently closed entrances led from the annex to the antimatter chamber where Maddox and his people waited.

"Thirty seconds," Valerie said.

"Are they just going to run into our ambush?" Kharkov radioed.

The robots waited near the equipment and boxes, two in the left part of the annex and three in the right. The space marines waited behind the antimatter hatches. Once the enemy appeared, Kharkov planned to take the fight to the enemy. Maddox and the trappers would add firepower from the opened hatches.

The best plans were simple because in battle everything became difficult. So why did Maddox feel such a sense of danger pulsating through him? The answer stared him in the eyes. He'd faced a New Man before on Loki Prime, and had seen the New Man dodge some of his bullets. It had been crazy impressive. He had seen the video from Odin. One New Man had charged Odin space marines while they had been hunkered inside a building. The golden-skinned attacker hadn't appeared afraid in the slightest.

Four of the super-beings raced to the engine rooms. Four of them against fifteen humans and robots. That was better than three to one odds. Maybe that's why dread gripped the captain.

"Ten seconds," Valerie said into Maddox's headset. "Wait," she said. "That's wrong. They've stopped running."

Maddox swore to himself.

"One of them is checking his hand," Valerie said. "I think they know you're waiting for them. Oh-oh, he took something out of his pack. It's a silver ball, sir. He's touching it. Now he's setting it on the floor. Sir, the ball is rolling toward you."

***

Maddox gripped a hand-scanner. It was linked to the starship's video system. He waited with Kharkov and his space marines inside the antimatter chamber. Inside this area, huge metal cylinders held *Victory's* power source, churning behind them.

On the scanner, Maddox saw a silver ball. He couldn't understand its power of locomotion. It continued to roll for the annex.

"Here it comes," Valerie said, speaking into the link in Maddox's ear.

The ball rolled into the annex. Galyan's robots lifted laser carbines, the same military-grade weapon Maddox possessed. Red rays stabbed at the silvery surface. The thing must have been incredibly polished. The beams bounced off the ball, ricocheting against the ceiling and bulkheads.

"What is that?" Kharkov said. Valerie must have linked to the space marine's inner visor so he could see the action.

At that moment, the silver ball ignited with a terrific blast. Smoke billowed. Within the annex, the bulkheads shook.

Maddox stared at his scanner. As the smoke cleared, he saw the robots. Each of them lay on the deck plates. One of the tentacles moved. The others were motionless.

Major Kharkov swore through his comm-unit.

Then, Maddox's eyes bulged. Four silver-suited New Men sprinted into the annex. They moved fast like greyhounds.

"Captain!" Valerie shouted. "Something happened to my video feed. It's jammed."

"We're on our own," Maddox radioed Kharkov.

The major swore again, this time as only a space marine could. He swung open his hatch. His powered armor whirred with motored force, and Kharkov stormed at the enemy. Each step made a clanking noise.

Maddox saw it on the scanner.

Kharkov had tucked the Gauss rifle under his right arm. The powered exo-skeleton charged at the enemy. A fast whiny sound told Maddox the rifle magnetically discharged its first explosive bullet.

323

The other space marines likewise attacked, two from the hatch near Maddox. These were Star Watch's best assault soldiers, not the kind of men who waited for the enemy to come to them.

Maddox didn't see how the New Men could survive the explosive rounds. Kharkov's first 3mm "bullet" flew toward its target, and its proximity setting worked perfectly. The bullet exploded, and one of the silver suits turned bloody red as a New Man's chest vanished in a puff of dark smoke.

Then it got weird.

The stricken New Man toppled to the deck plates. The next nearest raised a clear globe, holding it in his hand. The globe flashed and blue lines of power sizzled in the air within the chamber.

Maddox's scanner went blank. The captain pitched it aside. What did the globe do? Something electrical would be his guess. Grabbing his laser carbine, leaning through the open hatch, Maddox searched for a target. Something struck him about the scene, though. None of the armored space marines were moving.

Maddox would have to worry about them later. Right now, he needed to kill New Men.

Sighting a tinted bubble helmet, Maddox depressed the firing switch, but not a damn thing happened. He rolled back into the chamber and looked at the laser. No lights worked on it. The thing was dead. It must have something to do with that clear globe.

Shrugging off the laser pack, Maddox dropped the carbine onto the floor. He still had his long-barreled gun. The captain drew it and whipped back around to peer through the hatch. A trapper standing on the other side of the door as Maddox also poked his weapon through.

The three surviving New Men put thick black discs onto the unmoving, power-armored space marines.

One of the enemy shouted a warning. All three of them raised their blasters. Beams flashed from the nozzles. Trappers aiming their rifles through the hatches toppled back, dead. Maddox ducked onto the floor. A beam passed overhead. He pulled the trigger of his long-barreled gun time after time.

A New Man went down, with his helmet shattered and bullet holes in his chest.

Then, Maddox withdrew from the hatch to lean against a bulkhead.

Two New Men were left. Explosions in the annex told Maddox something bad just happened. He screwed up his courage and stole a peak.

The last New Men retreated. Each of the space marines in his armor was a smoking pile of wreckage, presumably dead. Major Kharkov and his marines—they were gone. Maddox couldn't believe it.

The enemy had magical weapons.

"You can't take our starship with just two of you left!" Maddox shouted.

A New Man turned smoothly, firing at him.

Maddox had already ducked out of sight. If he let them get away, who did he have left to take down two supermen?

At that point, his headset crackled.

"Valerie?" Maddox asked.

"Here, Captain. What happened? I've just resumed a video link."

"Never mind that," Maddox said. "Tell Galyan to appear behind the enemy in the corridors. I want his holoimage to chase the last two New Men back to me."

"I hear you," the AI said. "I can also generate a weapon firing holoimage projectiles. Will that help?"

"Yes," Maddox said. "That's perfect."

Picking up the hand-scanner, the captain realized it still didn't work. Could he surprise these bastards with a "fighting" holoimage? Maybe just this once. It wouldn't work twice, that's for sure.

Jumping across the open hatch, Maddox grabbed a dead trapper's rifle. It was a big slarn gun. He tore out the half-used magazine and shoved in another. Then he lay on the deck plate and rolled into position, aiming through the hatch.

An explosion in the far corridor told him the New Men attacked someone. Galyan must have surprised them. The New Men couldn't damage the holoimage, of course. Then again, Galyan couldn't physically hurt the enemy. Would the New

Men instantly know that? Given that they were supermen, super-beings—as smart as Ludendorff—they might figure it out.

No! A New Man jumped back into the annex. He fired his blaster at something in the corridor, maybe at the holoimage of Galyan.

Maddox aimed and fired, the heavy rifle bucking each time, slamming against his shoulder. The New Man turned unnaturally fast and dodged bullets. It was maddening and amazing. The enemy darted out of the annex by going low through the hatch. What he must not have done was alert his companion in time. That New Man jumped backward *into* the hail of bullets. It would seem that even New Men could become disoriented during battle. The slarn-rifle slugs blew the New Man into the corridor with violent force.

"One left," Maddox muttered. With his headset, he asked, "What's happening now?"

"Oh no," Valerie said.

"What?" Maddox asked. "Talk to me."

"Meta is in the corridor. She's headed for the last New Man."

-33-

Meta blinked over and over as she moved down a corridor. Her mind was in turmoil, her thoughts dark and chaotic.

Kane had kidnapped Ludendorff, only the man had turned out to be Lank Meyers, the professor's best friend. Kane had lied to her about leaving the service of the New Men. The wrestler hadn't left his golden-skinned masters, but had been a secret agent among the archeologists on Wolf Prime. Worse, she had aided Kane.

With her left hand, Meta rubbed between her eyes. Her head hurt with a constant pulsating rhythm. Kane had taken her to an enemy star cruiser. In the ship, she had gone into a room that was difficult to remember. Why would that be?

Captain Maddox, we kissed in New York City, didn't we? I have a faint recollection of it, but it also seems false. I don't understand this at all.

There were noises of battle ahead, but Meta didn't mind. In fact, at this point, that was probably better for her. She...had failed. She was no good, a killer. Captain Maddox had said earlier that Baron Chabot shouldn't have trusted her. The captain was quite right. She had slain Chabot with her bare hands, choking the awful baron to death. He had caused her family misery for as long as she could remember. That's why her father had agreed to train her as an assassin.

I'm full of deceit and lies. I say one thing and do another. This kiss with Maddox, I don't believe it. I think I lied to myself. The two of us fought in New York City. Afterward,

Maddox stormed off and didn't show up until...until he waltzed out of the darkness of the tunnels of Wolf Prime.

Meta frowned. She wore trapper garments, but they didn't hide her voluptuous figure. She'd jumped off the shuttle and raced through the hangar bay, through the vacuum, and lived to tell about it.

The real Ludendorff had said no one could trust her. The old man with the hooked nose had even suggested they destroy her as an act of kindness. Maddox had threatened to kill anyone who murdered her. Dana said the captain spoke that way because he loved her.

Maddox loves me?

Meta didn't know if that was true or not. He was too wrapped up in his quest. Actually, it was more than that. He had an armored core that no one could reach. Meta didn't know if the captain was even capable of real love.

Am I?

She knew she'd once killed a man who'd trusted her. Well...Baron Chabot had used her as a sex object. There hadn't been any love in that. The baron had been handsome enough, but he had also been a pig. She'd despised everything about him and the Rouen Colony mines. Despite that, she had gone to his bedroom and they had...coupled. Afterward, she choked him to death.

The episode had warped her, Meta was sure of that. How could she trust a man when no man in his right mind should trust a lying killer like herself?

Tears welled in Meta's eyes. The guilt of the assassination had festered for years. She and Captain Maddox had enjoyed New York City for a time. Then, they had argued because Meta knew deep in her heart she wasn't any good.

"I'm doubly damned," she whispered.

People thought her a hardened assassin. She had been that way down on Loki Prime. How else could she have survived the ordeal? Dana had been an anchor of resolve for her. Meta had also been tough aboard the *Geronimo*. It was armor to hide the guilt buried deep in her heart.

These feelings of unworthiness had intensified after entering the strange room aboard the star cruiser. The teacher

328

had twisted her thoughts. Because of that, she had believed Kane's lies. She had lied for him. Ludendorff said her death would be a kindness. Maybe he was right. Why did Captain Maddox think he was always right? He would kill anyone who touched her. That meant…

"Ah, Meta. I'm glad you're here. Hurry to me."

Meta halted and looked up. She had become so lost in her thoughts that she hadn't been paying attention to her steps.

She stood in a corridor facing a New Man. He wore a silver suit, a tinted helmet and gripped a blaster in his right hand.

"Meta," he said.

She cocked her head. His voice was familiar, but why—

The tinting faded until she could see his features. It was Per Lomax, the golden-skinned superman who had spoken to her aboard the star cruiser.

"I have need of you, Meta," he said.

A smile curved onto her face. She wondered about her reaction. She felt glorious that a New Man, a superman, wanted her help. Maybe all these dreadful thoughts were wrong. If one of the New Men believed her important enough to need her assistance—

"I have given you an order," Per Lomax said.

Meta nodded. He had at that. But if that was so, why didn't she scurry to him as her mind told her to do?

"The teacher—"

"I remember," Meta said, interrupting the superior. "The teacher put me on a spinning table. He used pain to force thoughts into my mind."

Per Lomax cast what might have been a worried glance over his shoulder. Then, he strode to her, aiming the blaster at her stomach.

"Have I displeased you?" Meta asked.

"Yes," Per Lomax said. "You did not obey me fast enough. You do realize your mistake, yes?"

Meta nodded. He had golden skin. He was her superior. The teacher had explained some of that to her. Because of her Rouen Colony genetics, she would be superior to the lower order of humans. They were hardly above cattle. If she

329

faithfully served the New Order, there would be a place for her in it. She could thank her Rouen Colony genetics for that.

"Where are the others, sir?" Meta asked.

What might have been irritation flashed across the superior's ivory-like features.

"The storm assault has been a debacle," Per Lomax said. "The ancient starship's defensive features are unusually effective. It is up to us to reverse the situation. If we bring *Victory* to the Throne World, we will achieve greatness. Can you imagine how far we could climb in the hierarchy after that?"

Meta lowered her head in deference to his rank. She spoke to Pcr Lomax. He had been Kane's chief. He was also the New Man who had sent her to the teacher. There in that room, on the spinning table, they had altered her mind.

Meta hated them for that. She loathed how guilt swamped her feelings. She was tired of others using her as a tool. It had begun long ago in the mines of the Rouen Colony. Others had trained her to be an assassin…

As Meta walked toward Per Lomax, she decided it was time to change everything. Yes. She knew the New Man had steely strength. Per Lomax had dug his fingers into her shoulder on the star cruiser, causing pain. Kane had feared the man, and she had never been able to defeat the wrestler in hand-to-hand combat. She doubted, therefore, that she could defeat Per Lomax in that way.

The New Man lowered his blaster. Meta had the feeling he wanted to get behind her. Were others coming down the corridor? She wondered if Per Lomax thought to use her as a human shield. How many tactical moves did he have left?

As Per Lomax neared, Meta made her move. Maybe this had been her idea all along. She felt so confused, in turmoil. Whatever her mental state in the beginning of her walk, she had paused long enough somewhere to pick up a shock baton. She had tucked it in back between her belt and slacks.

Meta reached behind her back, gripped the handle and withdrew the baton from its location. She flicked on the device with her thumb. It was already at the highest setting. The baton

330

sizzled with power, and maybe it gave Per Lomax a moment to understand what she did.

This time, it didn't matter. Meta swung, swatting Per Lomax against the ribs. The shock baton sizzled a killing blast, discharging a trickle of smoke.

Through the bubble helmet, Per Lomax's eyes lifted in surprise. He actually looked down at her hand and could no doubt see the baton sizzling and bucking in her grip. The New Man's features remained placid, though, almost as if he didn't feel pain.

"Meta, Meta, Meta," Per Lomax said. "That was a treacherous blow. It would appear the teacher failed with you. I find that remarkable."

Meta frowned. She didn't understand. The damned silver suit must act as insulation against the shock baton's premier power.

Stepping back, Meta shifted tactics. She would have to do more than stroke the New Man with the baton. She would have to beat him down.

Before she could do that, Per Lomax lashed out with his left hand. The speed startled Meta. He chopped the side of her neck. Pain flared. He must have hit a nerve. Meta felt her limbs collapsing, her body flopping. Then she struck the floor, hitting it with the back of her skull.

With a groan, Meta tried to rise.

"Treacherous creature," Per Lomax said. He raised the blaster, aiming it at her.

***

Captain Maddox had left the antimatter chamber and the annex, attempting to sneak up on the last remaining New Man clutching a slam-rifle against his chest.

He wore a headset, and Valerie spoke into his ear.

"Sir," the lieutenant said, "the New Man is aiming a blaster at Meta. I think he's going to kill her."

Maddox broke into a sprint, coming around a corner, seeing them down the corridor. At a full run, with the rifle at his hip, Maddox pulled the trigger three times in quick succession.

The slarn rifle discharged a heavy .44 caliber slug. He wasn't used to the weapon, but he did know guns and rifles. The first shot went wide. The second was worse because of the bucking weapon. He almost shot Meta. The third slug missed the New Man's torso but obliterated the hand holding the blaster.

Maddox grinned and pulled the trigger again. Nothing happened. The weapon had jammed.

The New Man spun toward him, with anguish twisting across his features. With a start, Maddox realized he recognized Per Lomax. Oh, this was too good.

With his remaining hand, Per Lomax reached behind for his pack.

Maddox put on a burst of speed. As he did, he reversed his grip of the slarn rifle, holding it by the barrel like a bat. Per Lomax must have realized he couldn't reach whatever he tried for in time. The New Man set himself as intensity swirled in his inky eyes.

Maddox twisted his shoulders, faking a swing. Per Lomax ducked. Then, Maddox clubbed. Instead of striking the body as he intended—the New Man twisted like a cat—Maddox hit the bubble helmet with a *crack*. Per Lomax crashed to the deck. Maddox swung the rifle around for a second blow. As Per Lomax rose, Maddox connected against the ribs. The New Man grunted, but his good hand latched onto the rifle with snake-like speed and he ripped the weapon out of Maddox's grip.

"You are a fool," Per Lomax said. One-handed, he shifted his grip with phenomenal speed. Now, he had the makeshift bat.

Meta wasn't out, however. From on the floor, she swung a leg. It caught Per Lomax's ankles, sweeping them out from under him. The New Man crashed backward onto the deck plates, his helmet thudding.

Given this respite, Maddox drew his tri-steel knife. Per Lomax scrambled upright. The New Man was like a snake. Nothing seemed to slow him down. Maddox slashed. The blade sliced through the silver fabric, leaving a bloody slash along Per Lomax's side.

The New Man grimaced. "You have damaged me."

Maddox stabbed, going in for the kill. Per Lomax chopped with his good hand, striking the captain's wrist. Maddox barely kept hold of the knife-handle, letting the blade and hand swing away. Per Lomax's leg whipped out as Maddox jumped back. The toe of the boot grazed Maddox's chest instead of the New Man connecting with full force.

Stunned by the New Man's speed and toughness, Maddox back-pedaled, with the knife before him.

Per Lomax advanced, with his good arm swaying like a cobra ready to strike.

"You're bleeding," Maddox said.

Per Lomax's eyes tightened with anger.

"Given enough time, enough blood loss," Maddox said, "you'll collapse. Do you know what I'll do then?"

Per Lomax took three quick steps and kicked again. The amount of blood loss must have already taken effect, slowing the New Man. Maddox evaded the blow and slashed. Once more, the blade sliced through silver fabric and cut a gash, this time along the right thigh.

Three more times, Per Lomax lunged. The captain evaded each attack, cutting the New Man two out of the three tries.

"You're bleeding out," Maddox said. "Look at the amount. My, my, my, I never thought I'd kick your ass so easily."

Per Lomax's eyelids fluttered. He was starting to look desperate.

"I'm going to make you my prisoner," Maddox said. "Star Watch is going to study you. Can you imagine that? You'll be the first New Man caught alive. How did Captain Maddox take him, people will ask? Well, in hand-to-hand combat, man-to-man. Not only will you be our prisoner, I'm going to be a galaxy-class hero. Thank you, Per Lomax."

The bleeding New Man charged. He must have forgotten about Meta. As before, she leg-whipped him, and the New Man went down hard onto his belly.

Maddox struck, stabbing the knife into Per Lomax's kidney. Maybe he could capture the New Man and maybe not. The first thing would be to incapacitate the dangerous invader.

Per Lomax arched in agony, reaching back for the knife. Maddox stomped on the New Man's good hand until he felt bones break. Then, the captain began to kick the bubble helmet, cracking it and finally breaking off a piece. Maddox pulled out the knife and reached into the helmet with it—

"Captain Maddox!" Meta shouted.

He wasn't listening.

Meta rushed him—she had climbed to her feet. In a bear rush, the Rouen Colony woman grabbed the captain and drove him away from the bleeding New Man.

"Maddox!" she shouted.

He turned his head, staring into her face. She searched his eyes. Finally, she let go.

"Make him your prisoner like you said," she suggested. "That's more important than killing him."

Maddox realized he *had* meant to kill the New Man. He nodded and looked at Per Lomax. The captain half expected to see the golden-skinned adversary aiming a blaster at him. Instead, the lean man was unconscious.

"We did it," Maddox said. "You and I captured a New Man."

Meta smiled at him.

She looked so beautiful. Maddox couldn't believe it. "Meta," he said. "You're here. You're—" The captain hugged her fiercely.

Meta hugged him in turn, whispering, "I'm sorry we fought."

For an answer, Maddox kissed her. That seemed like a lifetime ago now.

"He is down."

Maddox reluctantly pulled away from the kiss. Still holding her, Maddox turned his head.

The holoimage of Galyan pointed at Per Lomax.

"Yes," Maddox said, "the New Man is down."

"My sensors tell me he's dying," Galyan said.

"Then we'd better patch him up," Maddox said. "He's more of a prize alive."

"I have news for you," Galyan said. "That is why I came. The star cruisers are attacking. Their long-range beams are even now striking our deflector shield."

-34-

"Which star cruisers are attacking?" Maddox asked.

"The two leaving Wolf Prime's orbit," Galyan said.

"Where are the other three?"

"Still accelerating from the outer system jump point."

"How far away are they from the starship?" Maddox asked.

"They cannot reach me in time, if that's what you're asking," Galyan said.

"Is the deflector shield holding against the two beams?"

"Yes."

"Can it hold for a while?"

"For quite some time," Galyan said.

"Then we should attack them," Maddox said. "Let's destroy two star cruisers while we can. These New Men must be acting out of desperation."

"They will have drones to launch," Galyan warned.

"Probably not enough to hurt *Victory*," Maddox said. "Engage the star cruisers and destroy them while you have the opportunity."

"Yes," Galyan said. "I will do it." The holoimage vanished from the corridor.

"Give me a hand," Maddox told Meta. "We have to carry Per Lomax to medical and see if we can save his sorry hide."

***

"Maddox said what?" Valerie asked Galyan. The holoimage had returned to the bridge, telling the lieutenant the captain's orders.

"Attack and destroy the two star cruisers," Galyan told her. "That's what he said."

Valerie had asked for clarification as the ancient starship began hard deceleration from its flight from Wolf Prime.

"We have Professor Ludendorff," Valerie said. "We've stopped the New Men's commando assault, and I presume we're far enough away from the planet to use the star drive."

"That is correct," Galyan said.

"So, what's the point of attacking two star cruisers?"

"To bring about their destruction," Galyan said.

"I understand that." Then, Valerie fell silent. She'd almost told the AI their plan. Galyan knew it, of course, but had become fixated on the idea of finding the Swarm homeworld.

Valerie studied her board. The two star cruisers left Wolf Prime's orbit. Their beams reached across the distance to strike *Victory*. The powerful rays reddened an area of the deflector shield, but it wasn't anything serious yet. So far, she didn't see any of the previous drones the New Men had used before in their first attack.

It was going to take time to get the starship into neutron beam range. Wasn't the better maneuver to leave the Wolf System altogether and let Ludendorff discover how to activate some of *Victory's* more exotic weaponry? Why risk the starship now? It was true *Victory* had faced and survived three star cruisers before. The alien vessel was in better repair than it had been over a year ago in the Beyond. Even so, engaging star cruisers was always a risk.

Lieutenant Noonan sat back and rubbed her chin thoughtfully. The Lord High Admiral had given her a secret set of instructions that would allow her to take control of the starship as its commander. Yet, that would mean supplanting Captain Maddox. Nothing would ever be the same between them if she did that. The Lord High Admiral had told her to give Maddox room. She had done that the entire trip. This last order of his, though...

It's the wrong order, Valerie told herself. *I know it is, and it jeopardizes the mission. Do I have the guts to follow my instincts and take command?*

Valerie's fingers tightened against her chin. Her first responsibility was to Star Watch. Yes, they were a team here, almost a family. Yet...

She leaned forward and tapped a control. "Captain Maddox," she said into the comm.

"Here," Maddox said.

"Sir..." Valerie hesitated, not certain what she should say.

"Spit it out, Lieutenant," Maddox said.

Valerie checked her panel. Maddox and Meta carried the unconscious New Man to medical. Before the AI had gone crazy back in the Oort cloud, Star Watch had installed a regular medical station on the ancient vessel.

"Sir," Valerie said. "I...*respectfully* wish to ask you a question regarding your last order." She'd grown up a little, Valerie realized. The months on the Lord High Admiral's Strategy Council had taught her how to properly address a superior officer.

"Ask your question, Lieutenant."

Valerie felt her face stiffen at the word "lieutenant," but she would resume her rank as captain after this voyage.

"Lieutenant?" he asked. "Do you have a question?"

"Yes, sir," she said. "I think— Sir, shouldn't we engage the star drive? We have Professor Ludendorff. Why risk *Victory* in a battle at this point in the operation?"

"To whittle down the odds for the Tannish System," Maddox said.

"Keeping *Victory* fully intact seems more important than whittling down odds, sir. Once Ludendorff fixes the exotic weaponry, the starship will be many times more powerful."

"You're working on several assumptions," Maddox said. "We don't know that Ludendorff can fix anything. We're hoping he can. But what if he can't?"

"Then this has all been for nothing, sir."

"I don't believe that. We fight one battle at a time. If the New Men have made a miscalculation here, we should exploit it and destroy two of their ships."

"What miscalculation have they made?" Valerie asked.

"I suspect they've just found out they have Lank Meyers, not Professor Ludendorff. Logic on their part would indicate that we have him. Thus, they attack us, hoping to reverse the situation. We're going to oblige them because we don't know if we have a joker or a joker who turns into an ace card with Ludendorff."

Valerie thought about that. Yes, she could see Maddox's point. But she still didn't think it was worth risking the only vessel that could save Fletcher's Fifth Fleet. Without that fleet, Star Watch would be too weak to do much more than sit and wait for the New Men to pick off one Commonwealth star system at a time.

"Thank you, sir," Valerie said, switching off the connection. She wasn't going to change Maddox's mind any time soon. So there was no use trying.

The lieutenant checked her panel. The deflector shield was redder than before and in a larger area.

"Warning!" Galyan said.

"What is it?" Valerie asked.

"Observe on the large screen," the AI said.

Valerie looked up at the main screen. She saw dark missiles moving at them. Galyan had outlined them in red. Beside the missiles in the void—on the big screen—were green numbers showing distance from the starship. The missiles would be in blast range in another fifteen minutes.

"Where did they come from?" Valerie asked. It wasn't from Wolf Prime.

"My computations suggest the other New Men launched the stealth missiles when we used the star drive to flee the outer system Laumer-Point."

"Wait a minute," Valerie said. "You're saying the New Men in the three star cruisers must have realized we would double back to Wolf Prime?"

"Correct," Galyan said.

"So…they launched them, and the missiles underwent massive acceleration while we left, and therefore we couldn't see them with our sensors."

"That is an excellent deduction," Galyan said.

"With these missiles coming," Valerie said, "we have to flee the attacking star cruisers. You have what you came for: Ludendorff. The professor must know how to find the Swarm homeworld, which is what you really desire. With these missiles coming, our chance of success against the star cruisers has significantly fallen. We should begin accelerating *away* from Wolf Prime so you can engage the star drive. Let's go somewhere safe so you can start questioning the professor. The starship's safety is too important to do anything else."

Galyan's eyelids fluttered, which meant the AI was in deep thought. For a pregnant second, the holoimage looked up and studied the main screen. Then, Galyan said, "You are correct. I am reversing course. We must flee from Wolf Prime."

***

Maddox felt a *bump* in the starship as they carried Per Lomax through a corridor. The captain didn't dwell on it, though. Soon, Meta and he entered medical.

Dana was already there. She sat on a med-station, finishing what must have been an examination of her broken ankle.

"Where should we put him?" Maddox asked the doctor.

"Use that bed," Dana said, indicating one with restraints.

Meta and Maddox did so, depositing the New Man on it. They engaged the leg and arm restraints, imprisoning the unconscious enemy soldier.

Dana hobbled beside the station on her crutches. She eyed him critically. "He's badly cut up."

Maddox nodded in agreement.

Balancing on her good foot, Dana began tapping the med-station's controls.

"You can't see it," Maddox said, "but I stabbed him in a kidney, too."

"Which now makes my task harder," Dana said. "Not that I'm blaming you. It is better he dies than to have gained control of the ship. But it would be a coup capturing a living New Man."

"Yes," Maddox said, staring down at the barely breathing, golden-skinned captive.

Maddox realized Dana could take a sample from the New Man, testing his DNA. That would tell the captain if he had some of their genetics. Maddox wanted to order the doctor to do so immediately. The need to know burned in him. Maddox hoped with everything he had that he had nothing to do with the New Men.

Stepping back, enjoying the feel of Meta's shoulder against him, Maddox watched the doctor. He also watched the automated medical station begin to work on the New Man.

"He has a higher core temperature than a normal human," Dana said, studying the readings.

"How much higher?" Maddox asked.

"More than you," Dana said.

I'm a half-breed, the captain thought. *Maybe that means I'm only half as good as he is.*

An intercom came on. All three of them looked up.

"Prepare for jump," Valerie said.

"What?" Maddox asked. "We should be attacking the enemy cruisers, not jumping anywhere."

There was no answer.

Maddox adjusted his headgear. It was on. Valerie should be able to hear him. "Lieutenant," he said.

That's when the star drive engaged, ending the conversation before it could begin.

***

Kane should have been elated. He had captured the fabled Professor Ludendorff, plucking him from the enemy's midst. Now, he was about to receive a commendation for his splendid performance.

Someone other than Per Lomax would give him the award, however. Per Lomax's assault against *Victory* had obviously failed. The ancient starship had escaped from the Wolf System. Did that mean Per Lomax was dead?

Kane waited in solitude, in a minimalist room aboard a star cruiser, with his hands on his knees. He analyzed his unease and realized it concerned Meta. She should have fought to join him aboard the shuttle. Instead, she had remained with Captain Maddox.

The door opened and a golden-skinned dominant regarded Kane with cold eyes.

"You abducted the wrong person," the dominant said.

Kane almost told the dominant, "No," which would have been a mistake. "I took Professor Ludendorff," he said evenly.

"He was an imposter," the dominant said. "His name was Lank Meyers."

Kane kept his face impassive, a difficult task under the other's stern gaze.

"Meyers slew our commander with deadly spores, dying in the process. It is possible you knew this would happen."

"I did not know," Kane said.

"That is a mere technicality, if true," the dominant said. "The critical point is that you failed in your assigned task."

Coldness tightened around Kane's heart. He debated launching himself at the dominant, forcing the other to kill him. Swiftly, Kane decided that life equaled hope. He would not attack the other.

"You will be punished for your failure," the dominant said.

Kane opened his mouth to argue. Quietly, he closed his mouth, realizing the futility of such an endeavor.

"Come," the dominant said.

Kane hesitated.

The dominant's eyes tightened.

Sighing, Kane rose. He would endure the punishment, hoping they would need him again at a later date. Without a word and without any resistance, Kane followed the dominant into the corridor, heading for a pain booth.

***

Maddox sat alone with Valerie in a conference chamber. He sat at the head of the table, and she was on his left, fidgeting with a cup of coffee.

At the captain's request, Galyan left them alone. Maddox was aware of the video setup in the starship and knew the AI likely eavesdropped on them. He could have used a scrambler so Galyan couldn't listen, but decided against it. The AI trusted him after a fashion. Why dabble with that now?

"You saw the stealth missiles and decided to flee without asking me," Maddox said. "Does that clarify the situation well enough?" They'd been talking about the combat circumstances for a few minutes already.

Valerie kept her gaze downcast, but Maddox wasn't fooled. She was anything but contrite. Her jaw muscles were quivering as she clenched her teeth. With the lieutenant, that was a sure sign of agitation. What the captain didn't know was her reason.

"Yes, sir," Valerie said. "That clarifies it."

Maddox recalled the bump as Meta and he had carried Per Lomax to medical. That must have been *Victory* shifting from deceleration back to acceleration. That meant Valerie had been acting on her own initiative for longer than he'd realized. She could have called him at any time, but had decided not to. Why would that be? What didn't he understand?

"Did Galyan override you?" Maddox asked.

Valerie shook her head.

"What happened then?" Maddox asked.

"I talked him into fleeing," Valerie said.

"Against my direct order to attack the two star cruisers?"

Valerie looked up. "It was the wrong order. *Victory* is too important to gamble with now."

"I appreciate that is your opinion, Lieutenant. But you—"

"Why did you do that?" Valerie asked.

Maddox raised an eyebrow. "Do what?"

"Why did you talk the Lord High Admiral into demoting me back to lieutenant?"

"Is that what this is about?" he asked.

Valerie's lips thinned as she stared into Maddox's eyes.

"Fair enough," Maddox said. *Something is going on here that I don't understand. Valerie is a rules stickler. She's not one to rebel against the chain of command. Yet she just did.*

"I asked Cook to do that because I didn't want any misunderstanding between us," Maddox said. "I'm not trained as a starship captain. You are. If we held the same rank, I wondered if that would hurt your efficiency, if you would attempt to second-guess me. I can see through this incident that I did the right thing."

"Is that what you believe, sir?"

"I'm not in the habit of making up reasons."

Valerie licked her lips. "You're an Intelligence officer first. Your kind *loves* making up reasons in order to slide through whatever they want to do."

Maddox stared at her, and he let the full force of his personality shine through. "What is this about?"

Valerie held his gaze for several seconds. Then, she looked down, and that seemed to make her angry. She gestured sharply.

"I know how to command a starship," Valerie said.

Maddox waited, wondering if this *problem* had been festering for some time.

"Instead of getting a line command," Valerie said, "what happened to me? I got stuck on the Lord High Admiral's Strategy Council."

"There are many Star Watch officers who would give their right arm for such a posting."

"Well, I'm not one of them."

"Cook has honored you," Maddox said.

"He knows I want an independent command. Yet—" Valerie hesitated.

"Yes?" Maddox asked.

"I don't know," Valerie mumbled.

I'm close to getting to the truth. She needs a nudge, but I'm not sure which way.

"Valerie," Maddox said, "it could be that Lord High Admiral Cook knows exactly what he's doing."

She looked up at him.

"I need an excellent executive officer," Maddox said. "One who knows how to run a starship. As you pointed out, my primary training is in Intelligence. Yet, I'm commanding the most powerful starship in our arm of the galaxy. Cook knows I need assistance, an executive who can help me during combat and other stressful situations."

"You're a sharp operator, sir. I don't think you need much help with anything."

"*Much?*" Maddox asked.

Once more, Valerie's jaw muscles tightened and she began shaking her head. "You don't understand. I've trained all my life for this. I've worked harder than anyone can imagine. Now...now the Lord High Admiral has put me in a terrible situation with an almost insurmountable temptation in front of me."

"I'm not sure I understand," Maddox said.

Valerie slapped her open palms onto the table. Her mouth opened and moved, but no words came out. The lieutenant hung her head.

Maddox waited. This was it. He was about to hear the truth, finally.

"Sir," Valerie said, without looking up. "I know you're the best person for the job. The Lord High Admiral knows that too. But there is a problem of trust, your origins specifically."

Maddox felt his chest go cold.

"I have secret orders, sir, and they've been killing me. Every night when I lay down, I wonder if I have the courage to use them. I wonder if in using them, I will destroy your career. I don't want to do that. I've learned to like you, even if I don't always approve of your ways. I want to open the secret orders and take over command of the ship so badly that it's giving me an ulcer."

Maddox waited, knowing there was more.

Valerie frowned and shook her head again. "Yet I wonder if that's not the greatest mistake of all. You have the makings of a sterling starship captain. I can see it. I see you improving all the time. I wonder…I wonder if the best use of *my* talents is in helping you achieve that. I believe I have many of those qualities myself, but not like you do, sir. Maybe the best way I can serve Star Watch and…"

Valerie's voice lowered to a whisper. "Maybe the best way I could serve my family—" she licked her lips. "We're a family, sir. Do you realize that?"

The idea shocked Maddox. He'd been adopted and had known peace for a time as a child. Yet, he had never belonged and had known that in his heart. Once he'd learned the truth about his mother… A family, the team of Meta, Riker, Keith, Dana and Valerie… Could the lieutenant be right about her idea? It was far outside his emotional thinking. He was a lone wolf, had been for so long now.

Valerie looked up.

Maddox turned away, embarrassed. He didn't know what to say.

"I'm going to give you this," Valerie said. "If you think I should use it, you can give it back to me. Otherwise, I don't want it anymore. I can't take the temptation, the pressure. I'd rather devote all my efforts to...to beating the enemy."

The lieutenant slid a slim folder across the table to him. It had a Star Watch stamp on it.

"These are the secret orders, sir. They contain my right to replace you as captain of the ship."

Maddox felt a stab in his heart. The Lord High Admiral hadn't completely trusted him. Out of the corner of his eye, Maddox glanced at the folder. In the end, he was still the outsider.

Maybe Valerie saw him scowl. Maddox stiffened a moment later. The lieutenant put a hand over the one he had on the table.

"We're a family, sir," Valerie said. "You're the captain. *Victory* had to flee once those missiles came. I did what I thought was right, but I did it as your executive officer. I did not do it to usurp your authority."

Maddox nodded. "I accept that."

Removing her hand from his, Valerie sat up, waiting.

Maddox's frown deepened. He felt as if he'd been stabbed in the heart. The Lord High Admiral—

The captain looked at Valerie. Maybe he was concentrating on the wrong thing. Here was a good officer, one who had come up the hard way. She trusted him. She was...was *family*.

Valerie is saying she will stick with me through thick and thin. If so, that meant he wasn't a lone wolf anymore. He wasn't the outsider, the half-breed. He belonged.

Maddox stood and held out a hand. Valerie took it, and Captain Maddox helped the lieutenant to her feet.

"We went to Wolf Prime and found the professor," Maddox said. "We escaped intact from the New Men. Every one of us did his or her part to defeat the enemy assault against the starship. Now, it's time to race to the Tannish System and make sure the Fifth Fleet gets past the enemy armada."

"Yes, sir," Valerie said, with enthusiasm.

Maddox released her hand and turned toward the hatch. As he did, Galyan appeared. The holoimage frowned.

"No, Captain," Galyan said. "We are not heading to the Tannish System. It is time for Professor Ludendorff to fulfill his bargain to me. I want to know the location of the Swarm homeworld. Then, we must hurry there and obliterate it as they did to my homeworld."

-35-

Maddox would have liked more time to prepare the professor. Everything seemed to be happening at once. It was maddening.

They had escaped the Wolf System. The starship was fully intact, and they had kept it out of the hands of the New Men. They had enough time to get to the Fifth Fleet, and Ludendorff could begin studying the ancient weapons systems that no one in the Oort cloud had been able to make work.

Unfortunately, Galyan had this fixation on the Swarm. Maddox supposed it made sense. He would have thought an advanced AI would be more logical, not this emotional monomaniac they had to deal with.

The door opened into the conference chamber and Ludendorff walked in.

"Ah, Professor," Maddox said. "I'm glad you could join us."

The older man nodded stiffly. It seemed he hadn't gotten over the manhandling in the shuttle. Ludendorff was proud. The professor had made that abundantly clear.

Behind him, Dana crutched in.

Valerie had gone back to the bridge. Keith slept, and Ludendorff had made it clear he didn't want Meta in attendance. Riker kept watch on Per Lomax, who remained in a deep sleep in medical. That left the handful of technicians they had taken along with the now deceased space marines and a few archaeologists and slarn trappers from Wolf Prime.

Maddox had told those people to remain in their quarters. Galyan didn't trust them, probably because their "patterns" weren't right.

"Professor Ludendorff," Galyan said. The holoimage stood on the other side of the conference table as the others.

Ludendorff stopped short, and his eyes widened.

It took Maddox a moment to understand why. The professor hadn't seen the alien holoimage yet. Galyan looked human enough except for the inordinately deep-set eyes and the ropy, dangling arms.

"You're an Adok," Ludendorff said.

Maddox sat up in surprise. Could the professor have recognized Galyan's race?

"A-dok?" the holoimage asked.

"Don't you know your own species name?" The professor turned to Dana. "You didn't tell me you had a living Adok. This is incredible."

"We don't," Dana said, unable to contain her grin.

"But—" Ludendorff looked more closely at Galyan. "Ah. You're a holoimage. Of course, you must be a replica…of whom, might I ask?"

"To save time," Maddox said, speaking before the AI could. "I'll give you a rundown on how Driving Force Galyan came to his present status."

The captain told Ludendorff about deification: the engrams of the last commander of the Adok fleet imprinted on the starship's AI core.

"That's clever," Ludendorff told Galyan. "I'm even more impressed with Adok technology than I was before entering the room."

"Are you certain about my race name?" Galyan asked.

"Perfectly certain," Ludendorff said. He pulled a chair out from the conference table and sat down, tilting the chair back as he eyed the holoimage.

Dana sat two chairs down from the professor.

"Adok," Galyan said, as if tasting the word. "I wish I could tell you I recognize the name, but I don't."

"That's odd," Ludendorff said.

"Why do you say that?" Galyan asked, sounding miffed.

348

"I find it even odder that you don't think it's odd," Ludendorff said. "It shows me something is off in your AI core."

"In what way?" Galyan asked.

"Now, *that* is a good question." Ludendorff turned to the captain. "Doctor Rich tells me the AI wishes to know more about the Swarm."

"I want the location of their homeworld," Galyan said.

"Why is that?" Ludendorff asked.

"They destroyed us," Galyan said, swinging one of his arms in agitation. "That was a monstrous crime. I wish to find their homeworld and obliterate the Swarm in retaliation."

Ludendorff tilted his chair even farther back so it looked as if he would topple over backward. He kept himself there with his feet, putting his hands on his chest as he twiddled his thumbs. Settling his chin on his chest, the professor eyed the table.

Everyone waited in silence.

Finally, Galyan stirred. "Well, where is this planet? I have gone to great lengths to retrieve you. I have endured many indignities, and I have suffered having rabble roaming through my corridors. The single reason for this was to gain you. I was assured you would know the answer to my question."

"If anyone would know," Ludendorff said, "I'm the person. Your faith in me is well founded. I'm not so sure I have faith in you, though."

"Clarify your statement," Galyan said.

"There's something abnormal in your actions," Ludendorff said. "I'm trying to perceive exactly what it is. Your desire to find the Swarm homeworld... Surely, the Adoks must have known more about the Swarm than others could now. Your people fought them six thousand years ago. I've had to decipher their psychology through cave etchings, fallen implements, the construction pattern of their hive and other clues."

"What is your point?" Galyan asked. "Are you saying the Swarm are dead?"

"Possibly," Ludendorff said.

"This is terrible news."

349

"Why would it be terrible?" Ludendorff asked. "It would mean the Swarm cannot harm other races. You wish them destroyed, and they are. Your desire has already been fulfilled."

"I want to be the one who destroys them," Galyan said.

"Now that's interesting."

"You said the Swarm is *possibly* dead. That would imply they could still be alive."

"True," Ludendorff said in an offhanded manner.

"Which is it?" Galyan asked.

"Exactly," Ludendorff said.

"Professor, are you trying to test my patience?"

"Not at all," Ludendorff said. "Consider. The Swarm did not have a homeworld as you conceive of it. They had an origin point. According to my studies, it appears the Swarm proved ultra-successful in taming their environment. Their problem was hunger. Let me explain. Human population growth slows once the baseline group achieves a certain amount of individual wealth. I don't believe the same was true for the Swarm. Instead, they increased growth as they gained wealth. Thus, the Swarm devoured their homeworld as a fire consumes its fuel, leaving ashes behind. It forced the Swarm to leave their star system in search of more wood."

"Wood?" Galyan asked.

"Please excuse the analogy," Ludendorff said. "The Swarm expanded into space in search of other worlds to consume. One branch invaded the Adok star system. You destroyed most of them."

"I destroyed all of the invaders," Galyan said. "Otherwise, *Victory* would not have existed."

"That's one possibility, I grant you."

"I am not interested in your theories regarding my holy task," Galyan said. "I want a target planet. I want to destroy the Swarm. If I must search the galaxy for them, so be it. I accept the task."

Ludendorff closed his eyes. He might have been trying to feign sleep, except that his thumbs kept twirling. Finally, he opened his eyes.

"Do you realize that if *Victory* attacks a Swarm star system," Ludendorff said, "you will approach your ancient enemy?"

"I do not care for didactic questions," Galyan said. "Instead, I want to know your point."

"The point is your intense desire to find the Swarm and attack them," Ludendorff said. "It makes me wonder about your last days. Could you describe them to me?"

"Last days in what manner?" Galyan asked.

"The Adok fight against the Swarm invasion, of course."

The holoimage's eyelids fluttered. Soon, Galyan spoke solemnly about the battle against the Swarm, the clouds of enemy craft, the viciousness of the assault. During those horrible weeks, he watched enemy vessels destroy one Adok ship after another. He witnessed the planet-busters obliterating his homeworld, so the planet became a vast field of drifting asteroids. Finally, the last Swarm attack-craft launched an assault against *Victory*. Galyan spoke about the conflict inside the corridors where his robots defeated the Swarm soldiers.

After Galyan finished, silence descended upon the conference chamber. Ludendorff put all four chair-legs onto the floor. The old man appeared to be thinking deeply.

"You have a theory, Professor?" Maddox asked.

Ludendorff looked over at the captain and nodded.

Maddox waited.

The professor inhaled, holding his breath for a long moment. Then, Ludendorff began to talk. "I have a theory, as Captain Maddox has rightly divined. The Adoks were a peaceful race. This was my conclusion about them from studying their ancient star system. Now, it has been confirmed."

"How did you reach your conclusion?" Dana asked.

A smile played on the professor's lips. "You wouldn't understand my how. That is both my gift and curse. I see connections that no one else can. It seems so obvious to me that I'm at a loss to explain how I know. That much makes sense to you, yes?"

Dana turned her head and rolled her eyes so the professor couldn't see her.

Maddox did, and he deciphered the meaning. Dana didn't care for the professor's smugness and intellectual arrogance. Maybe that was one of the reasons why she'd mutinied so long ago during Ludendorff's time in the lost star system.

"Are you saying the Swarm are extinct?" Galyan asked. "I would like a 'yes' or 'no' answer."

"I don't have that kind of answer," Ludendorff said. "There are no Swarm star systems nearby. That doesn't mean there aren't any in the Beyond. Frankly, I think there are."

"Then we must hunt for them," Galyan said with finality.

"That is an excellent idea," Ludendorff said. "Particularly for the Swarm."

"What?" Galyan asked. "That is illogical."

"Obviously it isn't," Ludendorff said, "as I spoke it."

"How can you state such foolishness?" Galyan asked.

"I can state the *fact* because I believe you're infected with a Swarm computer virus," Ludendorff said. "It would explain your hostile attitude and this insistence of finding them."

"I want to destroy the Swarm," Galyan said, "not aid them."

"That is the lie you're telling yourself," Ludendorff said.

"That is preposterous," Dana said.

"I agree," Galyan said.

"You're both wrong," Ludendorff said. "I see it clearly. Once you reach the Swarm—any Swarm world—the virus will metastasize, and you will give your ancient enemy the starship and all its accompanying technologies. Since you have a unique star drive and Laumer Drive, you will unleash the Swarm onto the universe in a way it can hardly conceive."

"You cannot be right," Galyan said.

"The professor cannot possibly know any of that," Dana added. "This is too much."

"I assure you," Ludendorff said. "I speak the truth."

"Just a moment," Maddox said, before Dana could rebuttal the professor. "This is an interesting theory. I don't believe we should discount it out of hand. We know Professor Ludendorff knows more about aliens than any human alive."

Ludendorff nodded.

"You believe him?" Galyan asked Maddox.

352

"The professor found your lost star system," Maddox said. "He knew who could board you. He has revealed your species name and told us something about your race."

"That we were peaceful?" Galyan asked.

"Lovers of peace," Ludendorff said. "You were unsuited for warfare. It's why you built such devastating battle systems. Terrorism is the tool of the weak. Warriors fashion swords to fight hand-to-hand because they love battle. The truly frightened mix poison and feed it to their enemy."

"That is a disgusting analogy," Galyan said.

"That is your peace-loving side talking," Ludendorff said. "The Adoks were a noble race. It would be a shame for you to gift your destroyers with the ability to unleash themselves upon the universe."

"Given that this Swarm virus exists," Galyan asked, "could you eradicate it from my core?"

"Indeed I could," Ludendorff said.

"How would you do so?"

"We would have to shut down your AI core," Ludendorff said. "Then, I could study your systems and eradicate the obvious Swarm protocols. I doubt anyone else in the galaxy knows as much as I do about the Swarm and their methods and could do this favor for you."

"You ask too much of me," Galyan said. "I cannot let you untrustworthy creatures turn me off."

Ludendorff shrugged. "It's up to you, of course."

"You seem to think this doesn't affect you," Galyan said. "But it most certainly does. You will help me find Swarm star systems. You can teach me what to search for. Then, I shall destroy them."

The professor pursed his lips.

Maddox wondered what Ludendorff was thinking.

"You have been deified," the professor asked, "is that not so?"

"It is," Galyan said.

"The Adoks perfected such a process for a reason," the professor said. "It was not for you to become an avenger, but for you to do something healthy and productive. You have a holy task to perform. Instead of doing what your people designed you to do, you follow a twisted course. The Swarm have corrupted your good nature. I cannot understand how the Adok part of you can agree to such a perversion of purpose."

"I have already stated why," Galyan said. "I cannot trust any of you to turn me on once you've turned me off."

"I can give you my word that we'll turn you back on," Maddox said.

The holoimage regarded the captain. "Those words could be an attempt to deceive me."

Maddox wondered how to appeal to an emotional AI. Maybe he should tell Galyan what Valerie had told him. Even as he wondered, Maddox realized it was the right course.

"We've become a family, Galyan," the captain said. "You were alone in the universe. I thought I was alone, a wolf stalking through life, using my superior talents in any way I saw fit. Lieutenant Noonan has taught me otherwise. Maybe I can teach you."

"I am not human," Galyan said.

"You're not flesh and blood either," Maddox said. "But you can become part of the family. Together, we can discover our purpose and carry it out."

"I already have a purpose."

"To kill and destroy," Maddox said. "That's not a purpose. That's just vengeance. There has to be more to life than that. Your people deified you. Your engrams were believed worthy of saving. Was that only to destroy or was it to build even though the Adoks had passed away? Why do you exist, Galyan? If a Swarm virus has corrupted you…"

"I am alone," Galyan said. "I can trust no one."

"You're wrong," Maddox said. "You can take a leap of faith. Trust me. See that you're not alone. If you wake up afterward and have regained your real purpose, I submit you will enjoy your existence more. You will have a true reason for being."

"Your words are a trick," Galyan said.

"If that's true," Maddox said. "Then self-destruct, and take us with you. What's the point of being alive if you're all alone in the universe?"

Dana stiffened, staring at Maddox in shock and shaking her head.

"I remember when we first boarded you," Maddox said. "Swarm carcasses littered your corridors. There were crusted slime trails everywhere. I think it's possible the Swarm gave you a virus. Maybe the virus moves extremely slowly. I don't know. I'm not the professor. But I think if I were you, I'd want to follow my designed purpose. That's the reason your people did what they did with your engrams."

Galyan studied Maddox. "You tricked me once before in what you refer to as the Beyond."

"I did," Maddox said. "But that was before we went to Wolf Prime together. There's another thing. Back in the Oort cloud, the humans did turn you back on."

"Because they didn't realize I still had an independent will," Galyan said.

"A Swarm virus is making you distrustful," Maddox said. "Once you're rid of it, we'll have much more in common with each other."

"You cannot know that."

"I'm taking it on faith," Maddox said.

"You are using an emotional appeal," Galyan said. "I resent that."

"It's up to you," Maddox said. "Trust me, and see that you're one of us, one of the team, part of our family. Or stay in your shell of distrust and remain alone for the rest of your unhappy existence. The choice is yours, Galyan. What's it going to be?"

The holoimage kept staring at Maddox.

"Even after six thousand years, the Swarm are using you," Ludendorff said. "The Adok part of you must deeply resent that."

"Yes," Galyan said.

"Then let me repair the damage and make you whole again," Ludendorff said.

Galyan looked at Maddox.

The captain nodded with encouragement.

"This is preposterous," Galyan said. "I find myself compelled by your words. I do not desire to live alone.

355

Therefore, I will risk and choose foolishly. I will trust you, Captain Maddox. I despise the Swarm and wish with everything I am to rid my AI core of their horrible influence. You may shut me down so Professor Ludendorff can scrub my core of the deadly enemy."

-36-

Later, as Maddox watched in the central computing area of the ship, Ludendorff and Dana turned off the AI core.

Using her crutches, Dana went backward, sighing with relief. "We did it. We finally turned off the damned computer. I can't believe it. Well done, gentlemen."

"It wasn't a trick," Maddox said.

"Of course it was," Dana told him. The doctor turned to Ludendorff. "I'm amazed you thought the AI would believe your cock and bull story about a Swarm virus."

"It's true," Ludendorff said.

"Supposing such a thing could be true," Dana said, "you couldn't know it on such slim evidence."

"But I do," Ludendorff said.

"How?" Dana asked.

"We've already been over that," Ludendorff told her. "I see connections. For one thing, an Adok would not seek a species' destruction with such vengeance."

"How can you know anything about the Adoks?"

"How can you ask me such a question?" the professor asked. "You were with me in the Adok star system."

"You collected space trash," Dana said. "I remember it very well."

"That 'trash,' as you call it, revealed much to me concerning the Adoks."

"Why didn't you ever tell me their name?" Dana asked.

"I must have sensed your venal nature," Ludendorff said. "You mutinied, after all. It is clear you do not want me to turn the AI back on."

"We'd be fools to trust the AI again," Dana said. "It almost wrecked the mission."

Ludendorff glanced at Maddox.

"Can you find a Swarm computer virus, if it exists?" Maddox asked.

"Words mean little in this regard," Ludendorff said. "I must begin working to see if it is possible. I will need time to familiarize myself with the ship's equipment."

"Fair enough," Maddox said. "We'll head for the Tannish System in the meantime."

"The star system will be full of New Men," Dana said.

"We won't enter the Tannish System," Maddox said. "We'll head there and bypass it, reaching Fletcher first."

"Using our star drive?" Dana asked.

Maddox nodded.

"And you're hoping Ludendorff can figure out how to fix the various weapons systems?" Dana asked.

"That was your original suggestion, if you remember," Maddox said.

Dana looked away, finally nodding. Was she having second thoughts?

"First, we should rid the AI core of the virus," Ludendorff said. "I believe a clean computer system will give you those weapons systems far easier and faster than trying to do it manually by ourselves."

"Turning the AI back on would be a mistake," Dana said.

Maddox laughed. "Doctor, we're trying to save the Fifth Fleet against a superior enemy force. The only hope of doing that is *Victory*. To win, we're going to have to become the greatest fighting vessel there is."

"We already are," she said.

"Not by a big enough factor to defeat massed star cruisers," Maddox said.

Dana stood quietly, finally shrugging and turning toward Ludendorff. "I'd forgotten how insufferable you are. You're brilliant, but not half as smart as you think you are."

The professor nodded. "I haven't forgotten that you've always been a pain in the ass. Still, you have a quicker brain than ninety-nine percent of the populace. We will arrive at a solution faster if we work together."

"Doctor?" Maddox asked, trying to forestall Dana from launching another round of insults.

Dana stared at the captain, finally sighing and nodding. She regarded Ludendorff. "I don't care for your arrogance, but I do respect your intelligence."

"Remember," Maddox said. "There are technicians here to help you two. I hope they can also be of assistance."

"We shall find out," Ludendorff said. "Now, I must eat, take a siesta and then we shall begin an exhausting task."

***

Starship *Victory* began a careful journey to the Tannish System.

"We shouldn't use the Laumer-Points," Valerie told Maddox on the bridge. "We don't know what's on the other side of each portal. We only have a few thermonuclear-armed missiles, and I don't think we should expend them for travel."

"You mean by sending a warhead through a jump point first?" Maddox asked.

"It's the only safe way to use a Laumer-Point in enemy territory," Valerie said. "We must assume there are star cruisers everywhere. That way, they won't surprise us at the worst possible moment."

"It will take us longer to reach Fletcher if we only use the ship's star drive," Maddox said.

"We have a small margin of time to spare. I think this is the best way to use it."

Maddox considered that, finally agreeing with his executive officer.

The days passed as the ancient starship made its way toward the Fifth Fleet by star drive jumps.

On the sixth day out from Wolf Prime, Ludendorff declared a breakthrough. He'd discovered Swarm protocols in the AI core. Maddox asked for clarification on how the professor

359

knew and sat through a detailed talk. It made almost no sense to Maddox.

"Do you understand?" he asked Dana.

"Enough to know that Ludendorff is right," she said.

"Can you purge the AI of the virus?" Maddox asked Ludendorff.

The hooked nosed Ludendorff didn't answer right away. "Maybe," he finally said.

"Considering our present goal," Dana said. "I believe you should stop work on the AI and concentrate on the weapons systems."

"I'm not ready to agree to that," Ludendorff said.

"You do understand the stakes involved?" Dana asked him.

The professor gave her a frosty stare.

"Can you spare the doctor?" Maddox asked Ludendorff.

"For half a day," the professor said.

"I need your assistance," Maddox told her.

"Very well," Dana said. "I could use a break."

Ludendorff soon returned to the AI, leaving Dana and Maddox alone in the conference chamber.

"What is this about?" she asked.

"Per Lomax," Maddox said. "He's healing fast. I think he's fully recovered."

"You want me to test his DNA?" she asked.

"Among other things."

She raised her eyebrows. "You want to question him?"

Maddox nodded. "First, though, I have to know the truth about myself."

"I understand, Captain. Let's do it."

***

An hour later—after Dana's examination of the New Man—Maddox and the doctor met in a side room near the medical station. The doctor wore her white lab coat. She sat in a cushioned chair, sipping a dry martini. There was a small bar in the room and a large screen showing a forest in the Appalachian Mountains. A recording of birds chirping and a hidden stream babbling gave the chamber a homey feel.

"Well?" Maddox asked from the door.

360

"Make yourself a drink and sit down," Dana said.

Maddox hesitated. She knew alcohol had little effect on him. Then, he moved to the bar and poured himself a shot of vodka. He slugged it back, enjoying the warmth of it going down. Pouring a second shot, he slammed that back too, filling his glass a third time.

"Why do you do that?" Dana asked.

Maddox drank the vodka as he moved to a chair. Then he slumped down. The alcohol had a slight numbing effect on his brain. He luxuriated in it, but the feeling began to fade almost immediately.

"Well?" he asked.

"You're not going to answer me?" she said.

"If you insist," he said. "I pretend once in a while."

"At being normal?"

"I suppose," he said. "Am I?"

Her brown eyes held his, and she shook her head.

"I have their DNA?" he asked, his chest turning cold.

"You do," she said. "It's conclusive. You are part New Man."

Maddox sat transfixed, staring at a bulkhead. He debated going back to the bar and guzzling the bottle of vodka, maybe opening another and draining it too. Keith was in the starship, and he had struck the ace once in order to help the man control his drinking problem. Wouldn't that make him a hypocrite if he now tried to drown his sorrows in hard liquor?

The captain turned to Dana.

"Let me forestall a few questions," she said. "There is absolutely no mistake. You are not fully New Man, but you have certain DNA similarities to them and to regular humans. Your mother must have been…normal. She must have escaped from a New Man breeding program. I don't know that for certain, though."

Maddox breathed through his nostrils. He was one of them, one of their experiments. It was the reason he could move so fast and heal so much better. Yet, he wasn't as good as the New Men."

"Are they of human stock?" Maddox asked.

"Yes."

"Meaning they had to originate on Earth?"

"That's what yes means," Dana said.

"The New Men had to be genetically modified, isn't that right?"

"I believe so," Dana said.

"How much of a difference is there between them and us? Well, between them and regular humanity?"

"Less of a difference than between us and chimpanzees," Dana said.

"That's not comforting."

"I don't believe offspring between a New Man and a regular woman would be fertile."

"I'm like a mule?" Maddox asked.

"Offspring," Dana said. "We don't know how your mother was impregnated."

"What does that mean?" Maddox asked, trying not to sound bitter.

"We don't know if New Men are fertile," Dana said. "We don't know how your mother was impregnated or if it was through natural means."

"You're talking about rape?"

Dana chose her words with care. "We don't know that."

"My mother fled the Beyond," Maddox said. "Would she have fled if she loved my father?"

"There's far too much we don't know," Dana said. "I suppose we could test Per Lomax and discover if he's…like a mule, as you so delicately put it."

Maddox shot to his feet, striding to the bar. He picked up the vodka bottle and hesitated. With a *clunk*, he set it back on the bar. He kept his back to Dana.

"You can't let this defeat you," she said. "You're still Captain Maddox of Star Watch. You've proven critically important in humanity's struggle against the New Men."

"I'm a mule," he said, "a freak, a—"

"No!" Dana said, crutching her way to the bar and sitting on a tall stool. "You are Captain Maddox of Star Watch Intelligence. Don't let DNA strands control your life. Make of it what you want, not what they wanted."

"Who are *they*?" Maddox asked.

362

"You have a prisoner. I suggest you start asking him for answers. I have some chemicals that might help loosen his tongue."

"Truth serum?" Maddox asked.

"A colloquial name, but apt enough."

"Per Lomax might shrug it off the way I do alcohol."

"We won't learn anything by sitting here."

Maddox faced Dana and saw the worry in her eyes. "You want me to do something so I don't brood over this."

"That's part of it. I also want answers. Ludendorff isn't the only one who figures things out. We were doing all right before he came along."

I've been the lone wolf for a long time. Now, I might be the sterile mule, a freak. Can I let what the New Men did conquer me? Or can I make them pay—pay for what, though? I have existence. I am the starship's captain and an entire species—humanity—may rise or fall depending on what I do. Isn't that enough of a purpose for me?

The idea of being an experiment bothered Maddox. Someone had fashioned the New Men. Someone wanted to eradicate humanity, or conquer them at the very least. Who had done this to him? Who had begun to fashion a superior race? What purpose did making a new race of people serve?

Maddox's gaze narrowed. He wanted answers. He wanted to know why. Then, he wanted to defeat the enemy. He wanted to make the people who had made his mother flee die.

Was that vengeance?

Maybe it was. Maybe, though, he wanted to save something worth fighting for: the existence of humanity, the right to live and—

I could be a mule, a sterile nothing.

A wolfish grin spread his lips. He didn't feel sterile. Seeing Meta again, feeling her against him…

Maddox faced Dana. "Thank you, Doctor. I appreciate your help."

"Go see Meta," she suggested.

"Not just yet," Maddox said. "I plan to interview Per Lomax. It would be good to know more before we face the New Men in battle again."

Dana hesitated, maybe wanting to say more.

"Go help Ludendorff," Maddox told her. "I think we're going to need Galyan again, but as a full Adok, not—" The captain almost said not as a half-breed.

"Keep things in perspective," Dana said.

Maddox nodded.

"I'm not sure I should leave you—"

"Doctor," Maddox said. "I'm fine. It's time to work. We can worry about these problems later. You do your task, and I'll do mine."

Dana slid off the stool and approached him on her crutches. She leaned in, maybe to give him a hug. In the end, she simply rubbed his shoulder before heading out the hatch and into the corridor.

-37-

Maddox considered the situation. Throughout the past few days, he'd spoken with Meta at great length about her journey with Kane and her time on the star cruiser.

Standing in front of a viewing port, the captain studied the stars. He didn't recognize any constellations. They had traveled a long way from Earth. They were in "C" Quadrant in the rim of Commonwealth territory. Heading outward in this area soon brought one to the Beyond, where only Patrol ships, prospectors and other daring souls traveled. The Wahhabi Caliphate was the nearest Commonwealth neighbor. Far away in the other direction was the Windsor League. The Spacers traveled back and forth within the Oikumene or Human Space. There were a few independent star systems with human colonists, less now with the invasion of the New Men. Taken altogether—the Commonwealth, Wahhabi Caliphate, Windsor League and free planets—this was the extent of known space for regular humanity. The Beyond held everything else, including, one supposed, this Throne World of New Men.

Meta had told Maddox about Per Lomax's words on the star cruiser. She'd told him about the silver pyramid—the Nexus—and about the great leap through space, crossing over one hundred light-years at once. Meta had also told the captain what she remembered about her kidnapping and afterward as Kane moved her through the underworld on Earth.

From Meta's description, it was clear Kane had kept her in the dark about much of what had been happening.

365

What do I know about Kane?

The man had been born on the Rouen Colony. He was a genetically modified human.

Maddox's eyes tightened.

Who ultimately controlled the Chabot Consortium that owned the Rouen Colony? Who controlled the Cestus Space Hauling Company that carried their ores? It would appear Octavian Nerva owned the latter.

After escaping from Earth, Kane must have traveled for a time on a Cestus hauler. When they reached the right star system, Kane had departed in his scout. According to Meta, the scout had been in the hauler for quite some time.

That's an important point. What does it tell me?

Maddox had believed Octavian Nerva aided the New Men. Speaking to the tycoon in Monte Carlo had changed his mind. After listening to Meta's story, Maddox began to wonder again.

There was something else. How could Kane have moved so effortlessly on Earth by himself? The man's ability to remain hidden, staying ahead of Star Watch Intelligence *and* Nerva Security, meant Kane had an organization, a good one. Such an organization would be difficult to hide completely. Star Watch Intelligence would have come up against it from time to time. Yet, Maddox didn't recall such an independent organization.

The captain frowned. *What am I missing? There's a clue here staring me in the face if I'm smart enough to see it. Maybe if I lay out all the pieces of the puzzle something will connect.*

Who controlled the Cestus Haulers? The title deed said Octavian did. Yet, the tycoon had claimed to have no knowledge of Kane. Given the extent of Octavian's holdings, it was conceivable someone could work from within like a mole, using various aspects of the Nerva Financial Empire. The question was: how big of an organization could hide from Octavian and for how long?

After Meta's kidnapping and during an interrogation session, Kane had allowed her to slay and injure some of his own people who had fronted as Nerva Security employees. Why would Kane have done that? How had Strand's people found the shot up members of the team so easily?

366

Standing in the starship's observatory, Maddox cocked his head. He could see his faint reflection in the glass.

It seemed as if an idea floated just out of his range of understanding. He wondered if that meant he was closing in on the truth. He needed to press forward and see what fell into place.

Apparently, there was a gargantuan silver pyramid in an unknown star system within the Commonwealth. Kane had hinted to Meta that meant something. How long ago had the builders of the silver pyramid constructed the relic? Were the builders aliens or humans? Was the silver pyramid the prototype for the stone ones on Earth, in Egypt? If so, did that imply that aliens had contacted Earthlings in the distant past?

Maddox's lips twisted with distaste. It felt as if he was getting colder now, not hotter. In these things, one had to trust his instincts.

Abruptly, the captain turned toward the hatch. Maybe he was avoiding what he knew he had to do. It would be a challenge. He came from the New Men…

Maddox inhaled deeply.

What was the origin of the New Men? If he knew, it might explain their purpose. Their purpose might explain their ultimate end for humanity. Did the New Men come as conquerors or as exterminators of the inferior species, the Neanderthals of the Space Age?

It's time to face my captive and force some answers out of him.

***

Maddox stood before Per Lomax.

The New Man lay on a cot inside a force field-shielded room. Per Lomax wore a Star Watch shirt, trousers and boots. He also had a steel band around his neck. It was a harsh device, able to shock its wearer. If the New Man could short the force field and escape the cell, the collar would shock him into unconsciousness.

The situation was too dire to let Per Lomax run free. On no account could they let the New Man render the starship inoperative.

367

Maddox gripped a small device with a dial. He could change settings if he wished to administer various levels of pain through the collar.

Under normal conditions, Maddox disliked torture of any kind. It wasn't an effective way of discovering truth and he believed the process was unethical.

Yet, here he stood before Per Lomax's cell. The stakes were huge. Humanity's future was uncertain. Should he let a few qualms stand in the way of using such a device if it helped him prod Per Lomax to talk?

For the moment, Maddox figured he didn't have to decide. He pocketed the dial device and regarded the New Man.

Maddox had faced Per Lomax on several occasions. The first time had been on Loki Prime over a year ago.

"You've healed rapidly," Maddox said into the intercom system. New Men did that, he knew. It was another feature of their superiority. The captain healed faster than normal humans did. Now, he knew why.

The New Man lay on his cot, seemingly oblivious to Maddox.

"You've healed quickly," the captain repeated.

Per Lomax still didn't respond.

"Do you prefer me to administer pain to make you sit up?" Maddox asked.

The New Man turned his head, regarding the captain. Maddox wasn't sure what he saw. Per Lomax's eyes had become like ice, his face a wooden mask. Had the man's capture stolen some of his insufferable arrogance?

Slowly, the New Man sat up.

"It's time we talked," Maddox said.

There was no response. This was how Maddox supposed Galyan should behave. Instead, the AI was the emotional being. The captive on the cot could have been a robot.

"I've just learned I have similar DNA to you," Maddox said. "I'm half New Man."

A flicker of something showed in the inky eyes. Briefly, Per Lomax looked at the captain. "You are an anomaly," the New Man said in a flat voice. "It is better you were destroyed."

"Why is that?"

368

Per Lomax's features became wooden again.

Frustrated, Maddox took out the dial device, raising it so his captive could see. The captain turned the dial to a lower setting. He made to press his thumb against the switch, and hesitated. Finally, Maddox shoved the device back into his pocket.

Per Lomax made an odd noise. It sounded like a cross between a snort and a laugh. "You cannot give me punishment shocks. I know what that device does." The New Man touched the collar around his neck. "Your inability to use the collar shows your weakness, your unfitness to rule."

"The New Men should rule us?"

"We will rule over you soon enough," Per Lomax said.

Maddox contained a grin. He was interrogating the enemy without having to use the shock collar.

"Observe your reaction at my news," Per Lomax said. "You have joy hearing we will rule you. This is indicative of your innate understanding of the Monarchical Principle. Your chaotic society has rendered you prone to the acceptance of our rule. The human spirit wants order above chaos. That means you will surrender initiative for safety."

Maddox hid his surprise, doing a better job of it this time. Per Lomax was quick and astute in observing minute reactions in others. The New Man's interpretation of what he noticed showed the supremely arrogant bent of his thinking.

"By initiative," Maddox said, "you actually mean freedom."

Per Lomax's shoulders twitched in what might have been a shrug.

Wait a minute. Per Lomax just said the New Men plan to rule over us. That means...

"You're suggesting this isn't an extermination campaign but conquest of our living space?" Maddox asked.

Per Lomax said nothing.

"If you're hoping to conquer us, why use thermonuclear warheads on planetary surfaces? That kills millions, if not billions of subjects, and demolishes the industrial base. You're destroying what you hope to make yours. That is illogical."

"You lack understanding of our true goal," Per Lomax said.

369

"You just implied that you're trying to conquer us."

"No," Per Lomax said. "We will *reform* you."

"What? Why?"

"For the best of reasons," the New Man said. "Your species has become weak, stupid and slothful. A precise eugenics program will weed out the useless among you, leaving the fit. With such material, the Throne World will build a mighty imperium pulsating with life force. Renewed with the surge of good blood, the New Order will expand at an exponential rate throughout the galaxy."

Maddox hadn't expected such an answer. It took him several seconds to adjust. Finally, he asked, "What percentage of humanity is useless?"

"Surely, you can envision that for yourself. You are superior to the common ruck. *Think*."

"I do not have the benefit of your training," Maddox said, dryly.

"You believe yourself cunning, trying to lead me with your questions. Instead, I learn more about you by the second. It leaves me saddened and surprised. It seems inconceivable you have restructured genes. You are more like them than you are like us."

Restructured genes. Maddox remained pokerfaced instead of allowing his lips to twist with distaste. "What percentage of humanity is useless, in your opinion or in the opinion of the Throne World?"

Per Lomax's shoulders twitched once more. What was he thinking? "I would estimate seventy-five to ninety percent, depending on the star system."

Maddox felt himself go cold. "Are you suggesting that…your side plans to eliminate eighty percent of humanity?"

"That is essentially correct. However, you must not think of them as humans, but as mongrels weakening the species with their befouled genes. We aid the human race, weeding out the sick and useless and strengthening what's good."

He thinks he's aiding us. Did I hear that right?

"By strengthening, you mean to take the remaining twenty percent and breed them like cattle to produce 'better' humans," Maddox said.

"Selective breeding will be one manner of improvement. The greater way will be direct genetic manipulation. That will produce change at a faster rate."

Maddox tried to envision what that meant in real terms. The idea was monstrous, a plan to change humanity on a gigantic scale. How had the New Men ever conceived of that as a doable goal? It would take decades to implement, maybe even longer. The death, the misery and corruption it would entail, the mass murder...

"I see your revulsion," Per Lomax said. "That means your mind is too small to encompass reality. You prefer your propagandistic lies that you tell each other. You cannot see the greater good we will achieve. The New Order brings a better life because it improves a warped animal weakened by the comforts of the modern age."

Maddox stared at Per Lomax, wondering if the New Man really believed what he said. Did Per Lomax see himself as good? It seemed inconceivable. Maybe his captive tried to bewilder him with these sick ideas. Yet, how could Per Lomax think that would help his plight?

"Let me explain a simple concept," Per Lomax said. "Perhaps you can understand then. In the earliest days of proto-humanity, survival of the fittest ensured that the hardy and clever humans passed on their genetic material to the ensuing generations. The slow and the dull-witted died out, weeding their genes from the collective pool of possibilities. Your modern society has reversed the process. The hardy and clever have few children as they use their time and energy to amass wealth and position. The slothful and ignorant have mass broods, filling your planets with sub-standard stock. It is killing the human race. This will all change under the Throne World's guidance."

"So...you're helping us get better?" Maddox asked.

"We are."

"By killing us?" Maddox asked.

"By eliminating the befouling genetic elements," Per Lomax said.

"Maybe we don't want your help."

"That is humanity's collective stupidity speaking through you. For no other reasons than sloth and foolishness, your race loves to hinder progress. We will no longer allow that."

"What gives the New Men the right to interfere with us?" Maddox asked.

"The Life Force Principle," Per Lomax said.

"What does that mean?"

"Successful and continuous expansion throughout the galaxy," Per Lomax said.

"We're already doing that."

After a moment, the New Man looked away.

"Humanity *is* expanding," Maddox said, pressing the point. "You're hurting us by standing in our way. Thus, we will have to eliminate the New Men to protect ourselves."

"You will fail."

"I beat you. I succeeded."

"Your victory was an anomaly, an absurdity."

"What one can do once," Maddox said, "one can duplicate."

"No," Per Lomax said. "Humanity will fail without our guidance. We have to come to save the human race from its own folly. You have restructured genes. You have the mental capacity to understand the truth of my words. Release me, and I will ask the teacher to reconfigure your mind instead of simply destroying your body."

"No thanks."

Intensity flared in Per Lomax's eyes. He became earnest. "You cannot defeat the New Order. That is an axiom derived from the power of our Life Force. Do not waste your genetic material on this folly. You were bred for better things than to stand in the way of progress."

My mother escaped from what, a breeding colony, a gene-splicing laboratory? What kind of monster would I be if she'd failed to escape? It killed her in the end. They killed her.

"I slaughtered the New Men sent against me on Wolf Prime," Maddox said, making a sweeping gesture. "We're going to do the same thing in the Tannish System to your invasion armada."

"If you are correct in that—you have this ancient vessel, after all—you will be responsible for retarding the uplifting of your species. That would be a crime of the highest order, demanding the harshest punishments."

"Wrong," Maddox said. "I'm the one punishing you. I will also enjoy smashing your armada."

"That is nonsensical."

"You used my mother in your Frankenstein experiments," Maddox said. "You made me a—" The captain bit his tongue, bottling his emotions. After a moment, he grinned.

Per Lomax cocked his head. "The Throne World granted you loftier genes. You are better than your compatriots are in every conceivable way. You should be grateful for this gift of superiority."

Maddox searched the New Man's face. He didn't detect madness or hypocrisy in Per Lomax. The other had a different philosophy, using words like *utility* and *good* in an opposite manner as the captain.

The evilest people often regarded themselves and their actions as good. How could Per Lomax, how could a nation of people, have come to accept such a monstrous viewpoint? Why had the New Men ever thought of the idea of "helping" humanity? It seemed like an odd concept to arrive at. What compelled the New Men to want to "improve" the human race?

Maddox considered the latest theory on the origins of the New Men. A utopian group of colonists—the Thomas Moore Society—had fled into the Beyond over one hundred and fifty years ago. The region where they fled was where the first known sightings of the New Men had occurred. Did that mean the New Men were the result of the colonists' experiments?

The idea made sense in a way, but how could the colonists have built a big enough industrial base to field the technologically advanced star cruisers? How had the colonists developed a superior beam and shield compared to Star Watch vessels?

I've looked into Per Lomax's thoughts. They're demonic. Maybe it's time to concentrate on the New Men's societal structure. Maybe I can find a weakness there to exploit.

"Who rules your Throne World?" Maddox asked.

Per Lomax seemed to lose interest in the conversation. "You will discover this soon enough."

"I'd like to know now."

"Patience is a virtue," the captive said.

Before Maddox could respond, a ship intercom beeped. "Captain," Lieutenant Noonan said.

Maddox turned around. "Yes?"

"We're about to make a jump," she said.

"How long until we do?" Maddox asked.

"Fifteen minutes, sir."

"Thank you, Lieutenant."

The intercom shut off.

Maddox faced the New Man. He would throw the other a curve, to try to play on the arrogance later. "You've given me much to contemplate. I hadn't realized until this moment you had such noble intentions for humanity."

"You have improved genes," Per Lomax said, "meaning your mind has a greater capacity than that of a mainline human. That is why I have revealed these truths to you. Gain the Throne World's good will. Release me, and help me bring the ancient vessel there."

"That's an interesting thought," Maddox said. "Where is the Throne World?"

Per Lomax's eyes went blank. Without another word, he retreated to the cot, laying down on it.

The interview was apparently over, so Maddox left. It was time to prepare for the jump as *Victory* raced to the Tannish System.

-38-

Several days passed as the starship journeyed through the void of "C" Quadrant.

Maddox spent the majority of his time with Meta. During their many hours together, he asked for clarification about Kane, searching for clues, for anything that might help him understand the enemy organization on Earth. He also wanted her to remember everything that had taken place aboard the star cruiser, especially with the teacher. That proved the most difficult for her to recall, making her frustrated.

"I don't know!" Meta cried one evening. They were in the armory, checking the remaining space marine combat suits.

Maddox sat on a stool, bent over as he checked an exoskeleton relay joint. He straightened, noticing the anguish on Meta's face.

Moving to her, he pulled Meta from a suit laid out on the deck. He kissed her gently, holding her.

There was one moment of convulsion, her arms tightening around him so Maddox found it difficult to breathe. Then, she relented, resting her forehead against the hollow of his throat.

"The teacher's voice," she whispered. "It was like he entered my mind, my very emotions. I could feel him twisting them, twisting *me*," Meta said, with a shudder.

Maddox tensed for another of her two G hugs. It didn't happen. "Did you try to resist?" he asked, softly.

"I used techniques I learned long ago in the Rouen Colony," Meta whispered. "I retreated into myself, verbally agreeing with him while building a citadel of self deep inside my ego. Sometimes I wonder, though. Am I still me, or am I a self-destruct bomb waiting for one of the teacher's commands?"

That was a critical question. Maddox kept trying to discern the answer. He recalled the spy he'd had to kill in New York City Spaceport. Had the New Men altered the man's mind? Had the teacher twisted Meta's thoughts long enough to make the damage permanent?

"The New Men are users," Maddox said, bitterly.

Meta looked up into his eyes.

Maddox grinned at her.

"Why do you do that?" she asked.

He shook his head, not understanding the question.

"You can feel me...bonding with you. Instead of saying something loving, you give me your cocky grin. It's like armor, as if you're afraid of becoming too close to me."

"Meta," he said, stroking her face.

"Now, you're avoiding the question, trying to sidetrack me."

He kissed her, keeping at it for a time.

Afterward, Meta asked, "Why don't you want to be close to me?"

"We are close."

"Physically, that's true. I'm taking about heart to heart."

He said nothing.

"I've told you what I fear," Meta said. "What do you fear?"

"That we won't make it to Fletcher in time," he said.

"No," she said. "I'm not talking about your mission. I mean inside you. What makes you stare up at the ceiling at night? What gnaws at your heart?"

He smiled sadly at her.

"You can't tell me what it is, can you?" she asked. "That's going too deep with you. You want to stay behind your armor so you can appear strong to everyone. You don't want to show any of your vulnerabilities to anyone, not even to me."

"We should finish working on the combat suits," Maddox said.

Meta searched his eyes, and she nodded. "You have to remain Captain Maddox even with me. You've built your armor around your soul and you refuse to let anyone all the way in."

He held her chin in his fingers.

Meta searched his face one more time and seemed to come to a decision. She smiled sadly.

"My strong Captain Maddox," she said. "Kiss me."

He did. Then he took her hand, guiding her through the hatch, down the corridor toward his quarters.

***

As Maddox spent the days with Meta, Ludendorff, Dana and the technicians worked overtime on the alien computer, searching, calibrating and finally purging pieces of the Swarm virus. It was hard work, and none of it would have happened without the professor's continuing insights.

Every time Maddox asked for an update, Dana told him about another half-miracle Ludendorff had pulled out of his sleeve to fix a problem.

"Ludendorff is good," Dana said. Maddox spoke to her in the cafeteria as they sipped coffee. "But I'd forgotten just how maddening he can be. The professor's arrogance makes me want to grab his throat and choke him until he admits he's insufferable. I'd also forgotten how he can pinpoint a problem with..." The doctor shook her head. "...with almost supernatural insights. It's uncanny."

"How much longer until you're ready to turn Galyan back on?" Maddox asked.

Dana looked down at her cup, shaking her head. Then, she stared at Maddox. "I worry about that. The AI has never acted how we've expected. Maybe we should keep running the starship on our own."

"Maybe," Maddox said, in a noncommittal manner.

Dana frowned. "Why am I the only one who can see the danger of trusting the AI?"

"Without Galyan, I doubt we'll figure out the more powerful weaponry. This is a matter of need."

"I hope you're right, Captain. I sincerely do."

✳✳✳

The hour of decision finally arrived. Maddox squeezed into a cramped AI chamber that buzzed with electrical noise. It felt as if ants crawled across his skin. The professor worked on a panel, tapping endlessly, looking up and checking a board and then tapping a new sequence. Ludendorff must have known he was here, but chose to ignore him.

Maddox endured the discomfort. He'd been thinking about something Dana had said regarding the professor's "miracles."

Ten minutes later, the professor straightened and glanced back.

"I've been wondering about something," Maddox said. "How did you know to search for a Swarm virus?"

Ludendorff hesitated before saying, "I doubt you would believe me if I told you."

Maddox didn't look any different, but he watched the professor more closely. "Tell me anyway," the captain said.

Ludendorff shrugged. "I discovered the possibility on Wolf Prime, deep in the hive. I won't bore you with a tedious rendition of the tale."

"I wish you would. I'm interested."

Ludendorff smiled, putting creases in his face. "It's time to reboot Galyan and find out if he can help me fix the starship's defunct weapons systems. Afterward, we'll have to rendezvous with Admiral Fletcher and devise an operational plan. He should be able to tell us interesting information. The admiral has faced the New Men in battle, I believe."

"The reports say Fletcher destroyed seven star cruisers."

"The admiral must be formidable," Ludendorff said.

"He's a bear," Maddox said, who'd had his share of run-ins with the man. Fletcher didn't like or trust him.

"Excellent," Ludendorff said. "Now, if you'll get out of my way, I can get out of this horrible chamber."

Maddox backed into the next room. The professor followed, sealing the access hatch.

"Much better," the professor said. He straightened his shirt and rubbed his arms, shivering. Then he turned to Maddox. "If

378

you're a praying man now's the time. We're about to reboot. I have no idea what a fully restored, deified Adok will give us."

"I'll get the doctor," Maddox said.

"Yes. That is a good idea. She can help me with the final calibrations."

The *final* calibrations took five more hours. They jumped once during that time. The Tannish System was less than ten light years away now. It would take three more star jumps to get in range and start searching for the sub-light traveling Fifth Fleet.

Ludendorff, Dana and Maddox stood in the AI control chamber. A tired-looking Doctor Rich turned to the professor. Ludendorff nodded.

Dana turned to Maddox, "This is our last chance to reconsider. Once we turn Galyan back on, I doubt the starship is going to let us turn him back off again."

"Do you have a specific worry?" Maddox asked.

"Of course," Dana said. "Galyan is an alien. He won't think anything like us."

"He is an Adok," Ludendorff corrected.

"What do we know about the Adoks?" Dana asked. "Nothing," she said.

"I beg to differ," Ludendorff said. "We know many things about the race."

"Name some specifics then," Dana snapped.

"They were intelligent, resourceful, thrifty—"

"You could say that about any intelligent species," Dana said, interrupting.

"The Adoks were peaceful," Ludendorff said. "You can't say that about the Swarm or about most human cultures."

Dana gave him a scornful look. "I know you think they were peaceful, but I can assure you, you don't know."

"You can assure me all you wish," Ludendorff said. "I'll still know I'm right."

"Professor Ludendorff—" Dana said.

"Wait a minute," Maddox said, holding up his hands. "Each of you has his or her theory on the matter."

"I have more than a *theory*," Ludendorff said.

"Fine," Maddox said. "My point is… Forget my point about you two. We need Galyan. That's all that matters now."

"We're taking a big risk reawakening the AI," Dana said. "I just want you to realize that."

"Without the use of the better weapons systems," Maddox said, "we're not going to defeat the enemy armada. After listening to Per Lomax's theories, beating the New Men means everything."

"Fine," Dana said. "Just don't come to me later and complain. Don't ask my help to shut Galyan off again. Don't—"

"I've heard enough," Ludendorff said. He sidestepped to another panel.

Dana watched the professor, holding her breath.

A spot between Maddox's shoulders grew tense. This was it. Could Dana be right? Would a fully Adok alien AI—without the Swarm virus—respond much differently than Galyan had been acting previously?

With an index finger, Ludendorff tapped a board.

Lights flashed on various panels. A chamber-wide hum began. It grew louder. Then, side vents opened and a blue mist hissed, billowing into the room.

"Retreat," Ludendorff said. "The system, or the AI, is gassing us. It must want out of this chamber."

Did we make the wrong choice? Was Dana right? Holding his breath, Maddox strode through the hatch. This reminded him of Dempsey Tower in New York City where the chief security officer had tried to poison him.

Ludendorff was the last one out. He closed the hatch and glanced around expectantly.

What's he looking for? Maddox wondered.

"There," Dana whispered, pointing. "Look."

Maddox followed her finger. Galyan shimmered into existence. The holoimage seemed sharper than before, the eyes a little more deep-set. The captain wasn't sure how, but Galyan appeared more noble.

The holoimage opened its mouth and spoke gibberish.

"Oh no," Dana whispered. "We've lost the language codex. In the Oort cloud, it took weeks teaching the AI English."

The holoimage cocked its alien head. Experimentally, it opened its mouth once more. "You did it," Galyan said, sounding less mechanical than before.

"Driving Force Galyan?" Maddox asked.

"Of course it's me," Galyan said. "Who did you expect?"

"Do you remember us?" Maddox asked.

"Your question is ridiculous," Galyan said. "I am part of the greatest computing system the Adoks ever designed. I have full access to the video recordings of the previous..."

The entire holoimage flickered in a bad reception sort of way.

"Let me back inside the control chamber," Ludendorff said. "I think I forgot to reengage a setting."

Nothing changed about the shimmering, flickering holoimage, nor did the hatch reopen.

Dana glanced at Maddox with an I-told-you-so look.

"The Adok must be accessing his six thousand years of history," Ludendorff said in a low tone. "He—"

"Interesting," Galyan said, peering at Maddox. "I have you to thank for this. I am whole once again."

"He did all the work," Maddox said, pointing at Ludendorff.

Dana made a "harrumph" sound.

"And her," Maddox added, pointing at the doctor.

"Mere technicians," Galyan said. "I am more interested in the broad scope. You convinced the infected me to take a chance, to trust...to have faith. I congratulate you on your heart, Captain Maddox."

"You're welcome," the captain said.

"I'm more than a *mere* technician," Ludendorff said, testily.

The holoimage of Galyan scratched behind his head. "Yes, you *are* more. It was a turn of phrase, a saying among the Adoks. Six thousand years...I find the timescale daunting in the extreme. I fear there has been entropy among many of my systems, particularly the disruptor ray. That would be the weapon system best suited to use against your enemy's shield."

"Before we get started," Maddox asked. "What is your feeling toward finding the Swarm homeworld?"

381

Galyan faced the captain. "Yes. I recall a faint desire in that regard. That 'faint desire' I sense through a recovery program tracing former wants. The Swarm virus instilled the desire." Galyan faced Ludendorff. "That was a remarkable deduction, Professor."

"Thank you," Ludendorff said, bowing his head.

"What is your chief desire now?" Maddox asked the holoimage.

"I find myself without a primary want," Galyan said. "I am in embryo. For six thousand years, the Swarm virus has surged through me, seeking to override my motivation centers." The holoimage waved one of its ropy arms. "That is the wrong way to speak about this. I am Driving Force Galyan, the deification of a valiant starship captain. In the end, though, my tactics failed to save my planet from destruction."

The holoimage studied Maddox, continuing to do so until Dana cleared her throat.

"I have reached my conclusion," Galyan announced.

Dana glanced at Maddox before asking, "Will you share it with us?"

"I will share it with *him*," Galyan said, pointing at Maddox. "The captain convinced my corrupted self to trust, to make the leap into the dark. I will be forever grateful for that. Thus, I have decided to follow the captain's lead. For now—until I decide otherwise—I will act on the captain's commands. During this instruction period, I will teach myself about this era."

"Excellent," Ludendorff said, as he rubbed his hands. "Captain, what are your wishes concerning the disruptor ray?"

"I would like it operational for the coming battle," Maddox said.

"Then with your assistance, Galyan," Ludendorff said, "we should head to the main combat chamber and see if the two of us can't bring the disrupter cannon back to its former efficiency."

"Let us go," Galyan agreed. "I find it exciting to envision greater combat power. I will become as I was in the beginning. That is a good thing."

"Indeed," Ludendorff said, heading for the exit.

***

Maddox returned to the bridge. From there, Lieutenant Noonan, with Keith's help, brought the starship closer to the Tannish System using star drive jumps.

Tannish was an unremarkable system with a single Laumer-Point near the K-class star. The yellowish-orange fireball had a surface temperature of 4,000 K. Because of the lone jump point, it was a dead-end system. Three terrestrial rocks made up the inner planets with a vast comet field the extent of the outer system. There were no habitable worlds, no science outposts or mining colonies. The star system was normally empty of life.

"Do you see anything so far?" Maddox asked.

Keith had taken over piloting. Valerie made the scans at her station.

The lieutenant shook her head.

That made sense to Maddox. They were three light years out still. From this distance, it was impossible to hide manufacturing planets or heavily mined asteroids. Starships and drones were another matter entirely. Such tiny-mass objects were less than blips in comparison to a planet or even a larger asteroid. There was another problem. A planet or asteroid remained in its orbit, radiating the information year after year. An enemy vessel moved into new positions all the time. Because *Victory* was three light-years out from the star system, any heat signatures they saw would be three years old. If enemy star cruisers had just used the Laumer-Point, they wouldn't show up on *Victory's* scanners until three years from now. To see what was going on in the Tannish System in the present, they would actually have to go there.

That was one of the potential dangers with the star drive. One couldn't see with total accuracy what one jumped toward. The odds, though, of popping into a grave situation were practically zero. Even with Jump Lag, they should have enough time to observe the situation—enemy warships—and make the necessary adjustments. With a Laumer-Point, the enemy knew where to wait, making the old way to travel much more dangerous to use.

383

Maddox sat in a chair, relaxing before the next jump. "It's hard to believe we've gotten this far," he said.

From her station, Valerie turned toward the captain. "You didn't think we could do it, sir?"

"We *are* facing a race of supermen with superior technology," Maddox said.

"Are you sure about the last part?" Keith asked.

"Ah...yes," Maddox said. "Do you remember how the New Men tracked the *Geronimo* through the void in the Beyond?"

"I remember," Keith said. "Was that with sensors, though? I don't think that would have been possible."

"Not with our technology, no," Maddox said. "Maybe the New Men have some super-advanced tech that allows them to scan in a star-drive sort of way."

Valerie shivered. "If you're right, sir—that the New Men can track across light-years of distance—they might be able to see us now."

"If some of them are already in the Tannish System that is," Maddox said.

The lieutenant nodded.

"What about their jumpfighters?" Keith asked. "Those weren't better than ours. In fact, they were worse."

"Those so-called inferior jumpfighters almost allowed the New Men to capture *Victory*," Maddox said.

"It was far from almost, sir," Keith said. "We stopped them cold."

"What if the shield hadn't gone up in time?" Maddox asked. "What if you hadn't raced outside in time in the shuttle? That would have meant three times the number of New Men inside the starship. Twelve New Men would have been enough so they would have captured us. Therefore, I'd call that almost."

"Fair enough," Keith said. "I'm still thinking of their jumpfighters. They weren't as good as ours."

"They were smaller," Maddox said. "Doesn't the same but smaller indicate better tech?"

"Sometimes that's true," Keith admitted. "But their jumpfighters couldn't do what ours could. At least, I don't believe so. They had crappy jumpfighters, sir, barely doing the job. And that's what I mean. They have selective advantages over us, not total."

"Better beam, better shield and better hull armor," Maddox said. "Just how selective is that?"

"Our collapsium hull armor is better," Keith said.

"It's also the most expensive in the galaxy," Maddox said. "Only *Victory* has it."

"Maybe only our starship needs it, sir."

Maddox raised his eyebrows. "You want to take on the entire enemy armada with just *Victory*?"

"I'm not saying that, sir."

"What then?" Maddox asked.

"I've been thinking about this a lot, sir," Keith said. "Fletcher has been out in the void for almost six months. How great of a repair can his people have done to the worst hit ships?"

"Not too well, I'd imagine," Maddox said.

"The Fifth Fleet is likely going to be badly beaten up," Keith said. "The New Men's star cruisers—not so much. How much firepower will Admiral Fletcher have left?"

"I take your point," Maddox said. "Our side is going to be weak, and the New Men are going to be strong. We already knew that at the start of the mission. It's why Star Watch sent us."

Keith nodded as he perched on the edge of his chair. He seemed excited. "Sir, I suggest we use *Victory* like a giant jumpfighter." The ace clapped his hands. "Boom, we appear among enemy star cruisers, blasting our weapons. Boom," Keith clapped his hands again. "We're gone, having used our star drive to get away. Bam. We come back, hitting the star cruisers again, and boom, out we go again."

"The New Men are going to start getting ready for our sudden appearance," Maddox said.

"True. So, you wait several days. Let the New Men get tired of waiting. After a while, boom, we do it again, hitting them, beaming, before taking off. That's how the Jumpfighter School envisions using jumpfighters. Hit and run raiders. With our star drive, we have the ultimate jump-ship."

385

"I appreciate your idea," Maddox said. "Yet, there's a problem. We're going to be disoriented when we first come out of jump. The enemy won't be. The New Men will hit us hard before we even have our shield up."

"I'll be at the controls," Keith said, "having juiced up so Jump Lag won't affect me as badly. I can start fighting right away, well, almost right away."

"Jump Lag will affect Galyan, and I suspect we're going to need the AI to run the starship efficiently."

Keith sat back, with his shoulders hunched. "Okay. Let me think about that a while."

"Sir," Valerie said. "I think we should start figuring out where to jump next."

Maddox made a show of appearing thoughtful. "Any suggestions, Lieutenant?" he asked.

"Yes, sir," Valerie said. "We should jump close enough to the main Tannish System to take a look around. But we don't want to get too close so the New Men can attack us, in case they have star cruisers there or drones ready to strike."

"Then?" Maddox asked.

"We almost jump to the Caria 323 System," Valerie said. "Again, not right into the star system, or we might find enemy drones lighting up, attempting to hit us."

"From there, we try to jump near where we expect Fletcher to be," Maddox said.

"Near enough so we can spot the Fifth Fleet," Valerie said. "Another jump will bring us among them. Once united with Fletcher, we can relay our scouting information of the Tannish System. That will help us make our battle plan."

Maddox sat back as if considering her idea. After an appreciable length of time, he said, "I like it, Lieutenant. Now, let's make it happen."

-39-

Captain Maddox raised his head as the aftereffects of Jump Lag wore off.

He was getting seriously sick of this part of it. He was tempted to raid the last jumpfighter in the hangar bay and confiscate Maker's Baxter-Locke hypos to ward off Jump Lag.

With an effort of will—making his head throb—Maddox pushed off his chair and staggered to Valerie's board. She sat slumped in her seat, moaning softly. Maddox began tapping controls, scanning the Tannish System. He searched close first. There was nothing but empty space. Next—

"I can do that, sir," Valerie whispered.

Maddox stepped back.

Like an old woman, Valerie lifted her arms. She began a more thorough sweep of the star system, tapping the panel as if she'd had the flu for a week.

Maddox turned to the main screen. The Tannish star shined its relatively cool light.

"There," Valerie whispered.

Turning back to her, Maddox saw the blips on her screen. More appeared. "How many star cruisers do you count?"

"Nine so far," Valerie said.

"Distance from us?" Maddox asked.

"Several hundred thousand kilometers," the lieutenant said.

"That's almost beside us in interstellar terms."

"It's closer than I would have expected," Valerie admitted.

"Are the star cruisers acting as if they see us?"

387

"Not that I can tell," Valerie said. "Ah. I'm counting five more, making fourteen enemy vessels."

Soon, Galyan appeared on the bridge as well. "Fourteen star cruisers are waiting between the inner and outer Tannish System," the holoimage said. "I have detected faint signs three hundred thousand kilometers before the flotilla, if one considers 'forward' to be closer to the Caria 323 System."

"I see them," Valerie said, "your faint signs. Those are enemy drones—missiles. The drones are facing the Fifth Fleet."

"I have not yet detected the Fifth Fleet," Galyan admitted.

"Neither have I," Valerie said. "It's a deduction. The New Men like to employ a massive drone fleet somewhere in their operational mix-up. The New Men have been waiting for the Fifth Fleet for almost six months. It makes sense the enemy would begin the battle with a massive missile barrage."

"Those fourteen star cruisers have waited an entire six months?" Galyan asked. "I find that interesting on two counts. Firstly, how do you know that to be true?"

"What?" Valerie asked.

"How do you know those star cruisers have been in the Tannish System nearly six months?" Galyan said.

"I have no idea," Valerie said.

"But you just said—"

"That's a figure of speech," Maddox told the AI. "The New Men as a group—the armada—have been waiting nearly six months to finish the battle. We have no idea when those fourteen star cruisers took up station in the Tannish System. Presumably, they have been watching the Fifth Fleet journey from Caria 323 for quite some time. Thus, they know where to put their drones: the likely point of entry for the Fifth Fleet into the Tannish System. Valerie meant to imply we can probably locate the Fifth Fleet more easily by studying the location of the drones."

"Yes, yes," Galyan said. "That is clever thinking, Captain Maddox. I can see why your people made you the starship captain of me. You have a quick and obviously intuitive grasp of the situation."

Valerie rolled her eyes, muttering under her breath before saying, "We should jump as soon as we can, sir."

"Must we attempt it right away?" Galyan asked. "I dislike the disorienting effect of these leaps."

"How close is the Fifth Fleet to the drones?" Valerie asked the AI.

"I do not know," Galyan said, "since I don't know the location of the Fifth Fleet."

"Which is why we should jump sooner rather than later," Valerie told him. "We need to coordinate now in order to make sure Fletcher isn't taken by surprise later."

"Yes," Galyan said. "I understand. It was wise of you, Captain Maddox, to make her the executive officer of me. I congratulate you once again on knowing your task to a nicety as a starship captain."

"Thank you," Maddox said.

"What about me?" Valerie asked Galyan. "Are you going to congratulate me on a task well done?"

"I would imagine Captain Maddox would remove you from duty if you failed in your task," Galyan said. "You are honor bound to perform the best you can. That you do so indicates the captain knew whom to choose for the post."

Valerie glanced at Maddox. He was already turning away to study the main screen.

"Get ready for jump," Valerie said. "We're heading for Caria 323."

***

There was no joking of any kind as *Victory's* sensors scanned the Caria 323 System. On the bridge, Galyan stood mute. Valerie manipulated her board, sweeping from one scene to the next.

Maddox sat straight in his chair, frowning at the destruction.

Hulks of starships or their pieces tumbled in the void. Some had taken up a highly elliptical orbit around the star, already becoming meteors. The extent of the space debris showed this had been a brutal battle. Not all the junk was from

389

Commonwealth vessels. Seven enemy star cruisers had died here as well.

"If we weren't on such a tight schedule," Valerie said, "it would behoove us to collect some of those pieces. Maybe we could figure out what the New Men use to armor their hulls."

"Show me Caria Prime," Maddox said. "I want to know if the New Men bombarded the planet."

Valerie nodded stiffly. "I'm scanning long-range," she said. The seconds passed, turning into minutes.

"Anything?" Maddox finally asked.

"I'm detecting high levels of radiation on the planet," Valerie said. "The New Men dropped hell-burners, sir. I've been searching for radio signals, something to show me if some of the population survived."

"Did the enemy carpet bomb the planet?" Maddox asked.

"I'm not reading planet-wide radiation levels," Valerie said. "But I don't think we're going to find too many survivors down there."

Maddox made a fist, tapping an armrest of his command chair with it. The New Men hadn't weeded out seventy-five or even ninety percent of the planetary population. It looked as if they'd taken down *one hundred percent*. Did that mean Per Lomax had been lying to him before?

"Wait," Valerie said. "I'm getting a signal."

Maddox leaned forward.

"I can't make it out," she said. "The interference is too heavy. Do we head there, sir, and help the survivors?"

Maddox's lips thinned. He considered the idea, but finally shook his head.

"You must help the survivors," Galyan said. "It is the ethical action to take."

"I know," Maddox said.

"But we don't have the time," Valerie said. "We have to save the Fifth Fleet, or there may be too many planets just like this in the coming year."

"You are a hardheaded, emotionless executive officer," Galyan told her in a scolding tone.

Valerie's mouth dropped open in surprise and shock.

390

"She's Space Academy-trained," Maddox said, staring at the lieutenant. "She's the chosen officer of Lord High Admiral Cook. He made sure the very best officer joined the venture. Her advice is golden, Galyan."

"Do you agree with her harsh analysis?" the holoimage asked.

"I'm afraid I do," Maddox said. "I also wonder if the New Men have set up a situation like this on purpose. If anyone goes to Caria Prime, will drones appear and attack?"

"Drones where?" Galyan asked. "I don't see any nearby drones."

"Maybe there are some hidden in the planet's lowest atmosphere," Maddox said, "ready to rise up and attack any relieving starships. Maybe the survivors are meant to lure us into a bad tactical situation."

"If true," Galyan said, "it would show that the New Men are without remorse."

"It's time to change our heading," Maddox told the lieutenant.

"Yes, sir," Valerie said.

The lieutenant began a long, curving half-loop. After spotting accelerating drones, *Victory* headed toward the Tannish System. The ancient starship traveled at a greater velocity than before, hoping to match speeds with Fletcher's vessels.

"Any sign of the Fifth Fleet yet?" Maddox asked Valerie.

"No, sir," she said.

"Galyan?" the captain asked.

"I may have something," the holoimage said. "Lieutenant, try scanning at twenty-three, six by seventy-two."

Valerie tapped her panel. She squinted at her screen, adjusted the board several times.

"What is it?" Maddox asked.

"I think I have some exhaust," Valerie said. "It's faint, and it has to be…" She continued typing on the panel. "Given the distance from us, the data I'm scanning is four months old."

"Configure the next jump at their present heading and velocity," Maddox said, "given that you've spotted the exhaust of the Fifth Fleet."

"Done," Galyan said, before Valerie moved any of her fingers.

"Put the flight data onto the lieutenant's board, please," Maddox said.

"Done," Galyan said.

Valerie nodded that she saw the data.

"Take us there," Maddox told Valerie. "But first warn the rest of the crew we're about to jump."

***

A half hour later, *Victory* made another star drive jump. The ancient vessel left the outskirts of the Caria 323 System, moving toward the Tannish System. It meant they appeared in the void between the two star systems.

For fifteen seconds, nothing happened on *Victory*. Outside, three *Titan*-class missiles accelerated toward the starship. The big drones moved away from a collection of scoured battleships, beat-up heavy cruisers, nearly empty motherships and a handful of destroyers and more plentiful missile boats.

On *Victory's* bridge, Maddox finally raised his head. He heard a warning blare from Valerie's board. Forcing himself to his feet, he still didn't beat her to her equipment.

Valerie opened bleary eyes, staring at her screen. "Missiles," she said. "They're coming at us. Wait. These are Star Watch missiles. What should we do, sir?"

"Open channels with Fletcher," Maddox said. "If those are Star Watch missiles, it's a good bet we should be able to see the fleet."

"Right, right," Valerie said. With stiff fingers, she tapped her board and scanned the void. "There," she said in a raspy voice. "I see them, sir. It's the Fifth Fleet. They're traveling straight to the Tannish System."

"Hail them," Maddox said. "We have to get them to turn the missiles off or redirect them."

"Yes," Valerie said. She rubbed her face before going back to her board. Finally, she said over her shoulder, "I'm getting a response."

Galyan appeared on the bridge. The holoimage opened his mouth.

392

"Just a minute," Maddox told the AI.

"It's Admiral Fletcher," Valerie said.

The captain turned to her. The lieutenant glanced at Maddox with worry in her eyes. She jutted her head, indicating the main screen.

Maddox faced it. The stars disappeared, and a big man in a scruffy uniform sat in a command chair on a Star Watch bridge. The man could have used a shave. He had white whiskers of several days' growth.

"Admiral Fletcher?" Maddox asked.

The big man on the screen ran a hand across his chin. It took a moment, as if his mind needed time to warm up first. Then, the man sat up. Suspicion swam in his eyes. Did he suspect a trick from the New Men?

"Who am I addressing?" Fletcher asked.

"You know me, sir. I'm Captain Maddox of Star Watch—" He almost said "Star Watch *Intelligence*." But that wouldn't be right. He was regular Star Watch out here.

"Maddox?" Fletcher asked. "The Iron Lady's pet maverick?"

"Yes, sir," Maddox said.

Fletcher blinked in confusion.

"You have three *Titan*-class missiles headed for us, sir," Maddox said. "We'd like you to redirect them."

The suspicion returned to the admiral's eyes.

The New Men had jumpfighters, or they had on Wolf Prime. Could they have some here in the Tannish System? Had enemy jumpfighters tried sneak attacks against the Fifth Fleet?

"We're here to help you, sir," Maddox said. "I've brought the ancient starship that Brigadier O'Hara sent me into the Beyond to find. We're here to beat the New Men when they try to take apart what's left of Fifth Fleet."

Fletcher pushed up to his feet. "Captain Maddox," the admiral said in a rough voice. "Star Watch sent you?"

"That's what I'm saying, sir."

The big man grinned, nodding. Fletcher laughed, and he clapped his hands. "I'd...I'd given up hope. You can't know what it is like— Yes! Missiles. I'll get those missiles stopped right away. Bring your ship in. We have a lot to discuss."

393

-40-

Second Lieutenant Maker inched *Victory* toward what was left of the Fifth Fleet.

"This isn't anything like the records of the fleet leaving the Solar System," Valerie said, as she scanned the ships. "Together with the Lord High Admiral, I watched the Fifth leave. I can hardly believe what I'm seeing, sir."

Maddox nodded as he viewed the main screen, the beaten ships passing before him. He'd read up on the Fifth Fleet and studied the various classes: the armaments, armor and shields. There were not gleaming warships here. This fleet had taken a pounding. The worst was a battleship with jagged wounds in its flank. A ribbon of atmosphere still leaked from the great rent. One of the destroyers lacked an exhaust port. Crumpled metal had pinched it off. A cruiser with a tractor beam pulled the destroyer along. Whatever repairs the damage control teams had managed to muster these past months, couldn't hide the major damage to each vessel.

Valerie pointed out individual warships, naming the vessel and class—mothership, cruiser, destroyer or missile boat. There were ten battleships, mammoth vessels, although smaller than *Victory*. The damage to some of the hull armor made Maddox wince. Clearly, the New Men had knocked out more than one laser cannon per warship. The one bit of good news was there were more *Gettysburg*-class battleships left than the older *Bismarck*-class: seven to three.

"Seventeen heavy cruisers," Valerie said.

Some of those cruisers left a lot to be desired. The *Quebec* looked like half a ship, with open levels showing in space. An enemy beam hitting there would shred the *Quebec* in seconds, as the ray would already be past the nonexistent armor. A few of the cruisers seemed undamaged. Seventeen of them, together with the ten battleships, made twenty-seven capital ships.

"Those look ready to fight," Keith said, indicting nine big motherships. In old parlance, they were carriers with strikefighters and bombers to launch. "That's some heavy striking power, sir," the ace said. "Nine of those mothers and their broods can do wicked damage."

"How many strikefighters do the motherships have left?" Valerie asked. "The number of their attack craft is what counts. I'm betting not all nine carriers have their full loads."

After crossing the void from Caria 323, thirty-six capital ships moved at high speed toward the Tannish System. Maddox knew the vessels represented a critical Commonwealth investment in labor, materials, money and time. It also represented a good portion of the remaining Star Watch fighting power. It was easier to repair a beat-up warship than build a new one from scratch. Some battleships-in-construction took four years to build. A heavy cruiser usually took two years.

The key industrial planets in the Commonwealth presently churned overtime to produce more warships. Those vessels-under-construction would still take several years before they were ready to fight. It would also take time to train new crews. That meant for the next two years, Star Watch had what it had to fight the interstellar war against the New Men.

So, even though some of the ships out there were little better than junkyard hulks, Star Watch needed them back home for refitting. If the New Men could finish off Fifth Fleet, High Command would be forced into an entirely defensive strategy. That would likely mean the enemy could eat up enough star systems in two years so the war would be lost by the time the new warships came out of the dockyards.

There were smaller destroyers, missile boats and escorts out there as well. Maddox wondered how many missiles the medium-sized boats had left—probably not too many.

"Seems like we're going to need more than just *Victory* to save them, sir," Keith said.

"Which is why we need the disrupter ray," Maddox said, turning toward Galyan.

The holoimage disappeared, presumably to find Ludendorff to help with the repairs.

Keith continued to ease the giant starship among the lesser vessels. Soon, Fletcher came online again, requesting a face-to-face meeting.

Maddox agreed.

An hour later, the captain left in a shuttle with Keith. They headed toward Fletcher's *Gettysburg*-class flagship, Battleship *Antietam*. Big blast marks showed where enemy star cruisers had shot through the wave harmonics shield to made direct hits on the hull armor. In two places, Maddox could see inside *Antietam*. Those holes needed new armor plates.

Docking procedures went well enough. Maddox wore his dress uniform as he exited the shuttle's hatch. Keith remained aboard the craft.

An *Antietam* aide approached Maddox in the hangar bay. It was smaller than *Victory's* hangar bays. The captain noticed the woman's uniform. It was scruffy, and she looked worn with hollowed-out eyes.

When they left the hangar bay and entered a main corridor, the smell shocked Maddox. It was stuffy with a hint of burnt electrical. In places, litter lay to the side. He could hardly believe it. No one saluted him either. A few people stared wide-eyed, amazed as he passed them.

Maddox kept his opinions internal. If he had to guess, he'd say the crew's morale had sunk to its lowest point. They must have all been realizing for months now that the fleet didn't have a chance at surviving the New Men. Maybe none of them had believed, or hadn't believed for quite some time, that Star Watch could do anything to help the Fifth in the Tannish System.

These people have faced the star cruisers and were shown in the most direct way possible that the enemy has superior ships. They fled into the void because they couldn't stand against the star cruisers and survive. All these months in the stellar emptiness, with no word from Star Watch, they must have come to accept that they were the walking dead, written off by High Command.

As good as *Victory* was, Maddox didn't think the ancient vessel could defeat twenty or more star cruisers even with the disruptor ray. He doubted *Victory* could take on ten. It would be more like four, possibly five if the disruptor ray worked after six thousand years of idleness.

What if it turns out I can't save the Fifth Fleet? Do I leave with Victory *to fight again another day? It would be folly to let the ancient starship die with the Fifth.*

Something in Maddox hardened. He didn't want to leave the defeated fleet to the enemy. There had to be a way to save these vessels. Yet, for that to be true, he needed the means. Could Ludendorff do it again?

The woman walking with Maddox cleared her throat.

The captain realized his mind had been wandering. "Yes?" he asked.

"The Admiral's quarters," she said, stopping before a hatch. Taking out a small pipe, she blew into it, making a high-pitched sound.

The hatch opened, and Admiral Fletcher stood there. He looked gaunter than Maddox remembered. Worse, the fire had gone out of his eyes. At least, the big man had shaved since he'd seen the admiral on the screen. Fletcher had a bloody nick on his chin. His uniform hung loosely, but it was clean.

"Captain Maddox," Fletcher said, holding out a big hand. "You have no idea how glad I am to see someone from Star Watch. I knew Cook wouldn't let us down."

The captain saluted first and then shook hands. At first, the admiral's grip was flaccid, but it tightened as Maddox applied pressure, forcing the other to respond.

"Come in, come in," Fletcher said. "Thank you, Ensign," he told the woman.

She turned more smartly than before, marching away. Afterward, Maddox entered the admiral's chamber.

Various items, including dinner plates, were piled against the sides, as if Fletcher had hurriedly shoved them out of the way. A smell of dust pervaded, as if someone had just finished cleaning up.

"Please," Fletcher said, "have a seat."

Maddox obliged, sitting at a small table with several chairs.

"Would you like a drink?" Fletcher asked, pressing a button. A small portion of the wall slid up, revealing a cabinet with bottles.

"Please," Maddox said.

Fletcher chose a green bottle, prying out a cork.

Aged brandy gurgled into Maddox's snifter. The captain swirled the glass under his nose, enjoying the aroma. He nodded in appreciation before sipping.

Fletcher sat down, took a gulp and let his glass *clunk* onto the table. "Haven't let myself drink for some time," he said. "I haven't dared."

Maddox nodded.

Fletcher's fingers tightened around the glass on the table. With an effort, he released it. He stared at Maddox with haunted eyes, and something seemed to bubble out of the man.

"I-I failed in the Caria System," the admiral said. "It's a galling admission. Maybe you wonder why I say this to you. It's because you're the Lord High Admiral's representative, and I know I have to give an accounting of my decisions. That's the hardest part of being in charge." Fletcher shook his head, and his eyes became staring and unfocused. "You have no idea how many times I've replayed the battle in my mind. The people who died— No one buried them. They're adrift in space, their spirits wandering the void. They come to me during the night cycle, plaguing my sleep. They ask me why I let the New Men fool me so easily."

"You killed enemy soldiers, Admiral," Maddox said. "Few people have managed to do that."

Fletcher's head turned as if rusted. He regarded Maddox. "You're like them, aren't you?"

The captain nodded. He was who he was. He couldn't change it and he didn't plan on trying or pretending.

"It's probably why you made it through to us," Fletcher said. He stared at his fingers. It was clear he was thinking hard. The old man looked up. "Is the human race doomed?"

"Not if you're ready to fight again, sir," Maddox said.

Fletcher scowled. "I'm confessing my mistakes. That doesn't mean you can throw a question like that at me."

"Admiral, if the rest of the fleet is like your ship, you've let your command go soft. These people have lost confidence in themselves."

Fletcher made a sour sound. "The New Men kicked our asses, son. They almost demolished my command. I thought I had them. I *did* have them. But they tricked me. The New Men are impossibly clever. We're doomed. You know that, don't you?"

"No."

"No, he says." Fletcher picked up the bottle and poured more brandy into his glass.

Before the admiral could grab the glass, Maddox swept his hand across the table, sweeping the snifter away. Brandy spilled on the table and floor as the glass bounced across the small room.

Fletcher stared at the table in shock. Then, his head whipped up. Anger flared in his eyes. With a grunt, he pushed back, standing.

"I could throw you into the brig for that," Fletcher said.

Maddox hadn't stood. He leaned back in his chair, tilting his head to look up at the bigger man.

Color appeared on Fletcher's cheeks. He balled his big fingers into fists.

"You..." Fletcher said, but the steam seemed to dissipate. Without a word, the admiral sank onto his chair. He shook his head. When he raised it, he asked, "Do you think we have a chance?"

"Yes."

"Because of your freakish vessel?" Fletcher asked.

"Yes."

The admiral's eyes narrowed. Then, he snorted. "Maybe you're right. By all that's holy, you have to be right. Otherwise—"

"Otherwise, the New Men will practice selective culling," Maddox said.

"What's that mean?"

Maddox told the admiral about Per Lomax and the enemy's plan for humanity.

"They're demons," Fletcher whispered.

Maddox said nothing.

"Why would they conceive such a plan?" the admiral asked.

"It's an interesting question," Maddox said. "The better one at the moment, though, is what we're going to do about the waiting drones and star cruisers in the Tannish System?"

"You've been there?"

Maddox told the admiral what they had seen.

"That's an amazing vessel, you're using," Fletcher said afterward. "You have an independent star drive. It's too bad we didn't all have that. The Fifth could just jump home."

"Admiral, how can I help you raise the morale of your people? Whatever we do, we're going to need your crews wanting to fight again. *Victory* can't win alone. We need the Fighting Fifth to help us."

Fletcher glanced at the glass on the floor before examining Maddox. "A good start is to tell me how we have a chance. If I believe we can win, I might be able to convince my senior officers. If they believe, they might be able to stir their crews."

"The trickle-down theory," Maddox said.

"Jokes won't help us. What can you do?"

Maddox leaned back, thinking. "Do you have a holo-imager?"

Without answering, Fletcher rose stiffly, moving near his bed, opening a small access hatch. He withdrew a holopad and control board, bringing them to the table and setting them before Maddox.

"I've sat here a hundred hours or more," Fletcher said, "setting up tactical situations and trying to devise a way past a picket of New Men. That's what sapped my morale the most. I've never figured out a method to win our way to the Tannish Laumer-Point. What can one more vessel— even a super-ship—do to change the outcome?"

Taking the control unit, Maddox began to make adjustments. The holopad lit up. He tapped the control. Soon, a holoimage of the void appeared above the pad. At one end of the holoimage, fourteen red triangle star cruisers waited. The Fifth Fleet appeared as small blue dots at the other end. A few more taps brought the waiting enemy drones into view. They were between the two forces.

"Where's the Laumer-Point?" Fletcher asked.

Maddox made one more adjustment. Far behind the star cruisers was the exit to freedom.

"What kind of firepower does your ship have?" Fletcher asked.

Maddox told him about the powerful but short-range neutron beam.

"Short range, you say?" Fletcher muttered. "That's the worst news of all. You'd have to use that star drive to jump right beside them. The only problem with that is the star cruisers would slice you into bits before any of you shrugged off Jump Lag."

Maddox nodded as he stared at the holoimage.

"Jump Lag nullifies the best use of your star drive," Fletcher said.

"Are you aware of the experimental jumpfighters they're practicing with on Titan?" Maddox asked.

"In concept," Fletcher said.

"Maybe I should summon my second lieutenant. He can explain their ramifications."

"Who is he?"

"A man by the name of Keith Maker," Maddox said.

"Never heard of him."

"He once fought against the Wallace Corporation during the Tau Ceti Conflict."

"A rebel miner? I don't know what he could bring to the table."

"He'll bring a keen understanding of jumpfighter tactics," Maddox said, telling the admiral about Keith's idea of using *Victory* as a giant jumpfighter.

Fletcher waved one of his big hands. "I'm out of ideas, and you're not Fleet trained to know what's best to do. Let's see if a damned mining rebel can come up with anything."

***

Second Lieutenant Maker walked into the Admiral's quarters with a grin on his round face. It was about time the commanders starting asking for his advice.

He'd moved briskly through *Antietam's* corridors. The stuffy smell and litter hadn't bothered him as it had the captain. Keith was used to bad morale and messes. The miners at Tau Ceti had been in hard situations far too many times. One day, people were up. The next, they were down in the sewer. The asteroid tunnels had held women and children, not just the fighters. Lots of people stuffed into small places had meant bad smells and litter.

"Admiral Fletcher," Maddox said, standing. "May I present to you, Second Lieutenant Keith Maker?"

"The captain tells me you're an ace," Fletcher said, as he shook hands with the smaller man.

"Yes, sir," Keith said. "There's no one better than me in a strikefighter."

The admiral raised an eyebrow. "I can see this man belongs with you. He has your humility."

"I'm just stating facts, Admiral Fletcher," Keith said.

The big man scowled.

Keith noticed the captain giving him the smallest of head shakes. Keith shut-up and stiffened to attention, staring straight ahead.

Fletcher eyed him, glanced at Captain Maddox and cleared his throat. "Bunch of damned mavericks. I can't believe this. But I'm not in a position to be choosy. Maybe that's why you people are here and no one else made it or even thought of trying. Look at the table, see what you can see."

"We're examining the tactical situation," Maddox told Keith.

"I see it," Keith said, who put his hands behind his back and looked down at the holoimage. "That's their fleet, their drones and our fleet. What's the question, sir?" he asked Maddox.

"*Victory* acting like a giant jumpfighter," Maddox said. "What could we do that wouldn't let the star cruisers destroy us while we're dull with Jump Lag?"

"That's easy, sir," Keith said. "We take out their drones."

"Their drones?" Fletcher asked. "No. You'd just be exchanging a thermonuclear blast for beam-fire. I don't see how that allows your starship to survive."

"Begging the admiral's pardon," Keith said, "but that's as simple as can be, sir." The ace sat down at the table. "Can I, sir?" he asked, indicating the control unit.

Maddox slid it to him.

"Here, sir," Keith said, making a green dot show up before the drones. "Our starship jumps to a position well out of their immediate blast-range. Then, we unload *Titan*-class missiles and jump away again. Our missiles accelerate for their drones. Both are still out of star cruiser beam-range. The enemy warheads begin detonating and so do ours. Soon enough, the enemy drones are gone, sir."

Fletcher sat down heavily, blinking at the holoimage. The admiral began to nod. "That should work."

"It *will* work, sir," Keith said.

Fletcher turned sharply toward Keith, grunting after a moment. Then, he faced Maddox. "I was wrong about your mining rebel, Captain. Your man knows his jumpfighter tactics after all."

"He does indeed, sir," Maddox said. "Now, I have to ask, will your people fight when the time comes?"

"They will," Fletcher said. "I'm going to see to that. How soon until you're ready to make the drone attack?"

"Several hours, I should think," Maddox said.

Fletcher rose to his feet. So did Maddox and Keith. The two men saluted the admiral. Then, the captain turned to Keith. "Let's go. We have a lot of work to do."

-41-

The next several days proved busy and physically grueling for *Victory's* crew.

First, Maddox collected seventy percent of the Fifth Fleet's remaining *Titan*-class missiles. Second, the ancient starship jumped near the accelerating enemy drones. The drones moved away from the waiting star cruisers, zeroing in on the Fifth. Through *Victory's* open bay doors, the crew cold-launched two dozen missiles at interspaced intervals. Maddox didn't want to hit the drones all at once, but in stages. Third, at Maddox's orders, Lieutenant Noonan engaged the star drive, jumping out of danger.

Maddox waited for the crew to recover from Jump Lag. Soon enough, Valerie monitored the situation, giving a running report.

Distances—this time, from the star cruisers to their drones and the battleships from their missiles—mandated computer controlled reactions aboard the drones and missiles.

From his chair, Maddox watched the main screen. The drones and missiles appeared as blips. The enemy's were red, and theirs were blue. They headed toward each other. The drones came in three big waves. The lesser number of missiles came in five staggered clumps. There was a reason for that.

The first *Titan* missile closed in on the first wave of drones.

"It should be any second now," Valerie said.

Maddox nodded, although he didn't speak. Space battle was so different, so long-ranged and slow. When the New Men had parachuted onto Wolf Prime, the captain had had to move fast, reacting in the moment. Out here in space, one could deliberate each move to death. Yet, what one had done hours or even days ago made the difference.

"There," Valerie said. She pointed at a splash of white on the screen. That indicated an exploding thermonuclear warhead from one of their missiles.

Drone or missile, each side's warhead was shape-charged. It meant the thermonuclear blast funneled forward in a cone shape instead of radiating outward in a circumference.

"Yes," Valerie said.

Maddox squinted, wondering what she meant—then, he noticed ten percent of the drones, those in the very front of the first wave. They went from red to gray, indicating the blast from the missile's warhead had rendered those drones inoperative.

For the next hour, the missiles and drones closed in on one another. Many exploded. Others imploded from enemy X-rays hammering them, frying the inner workings, turning them into inert warheads.

Despite the shape charging, the powerful nuclear reactions often killed the drones too close to the "friendly" explosions.

"We aren't giving the drones time to spread out," Valerie explained. "They would have done that against the fleet. Our missiles came at them before the enemy was ready to make his drones operational."

Maddox understood. It was the key reason the missiles came in staggered attacks. That way, the first warheads didn't destroy the other clumps of following missiles when they detonated.

By the end of the automated skirmish, eighty-three percent of the drones were gone or had malfunctioned. All the missiles were dead or exploded. That left a mere seventeen percent of the original drones heading for the Earth Fleet.

The fourth, fifth and sixth tasks *Victory* and her crew performed also involved the star drive jump. The ancient vessel moved around the star cruisers in a gigantic sphere. The starship stayed far beyond enemy beam range. At each location, the crew launched more missiles. Those missiles accelerated toward the enemy, timed to arrive all at the same time from various locations on the compass.

The jump maneuvering took its toll on the crew and on Galyan. It made everyone irritable and sluggish. One of the technicians died from a heart attack. A slarn trapper had an aneurysm, perishing on his acceleration couch.

Before any more fatalities occurred, the starship made its last jump for the moment, returning to the Fifth Fleet.

For the next several days, everyone aboard *Victory* rested. At high velocity, the Fifth Fleet approached the outer limits of the Tannish System. Continuing scans showed that another ten star cruisers accelerated from the Tannish Laumer-Point to the others. That made twenty-four enemy vessels against the Fifth's thirty-six capital ships, plus destroyers, missile boats and *Victory*. Once more, Star Watch had a greater number and tonnage of vessels. This time, however, it was even more lopsided for the New Men than it had been at the Battle of Caria 323.

From what Valerie could tell, each enemy ship came with fully repaired hull armor and with all weaponry intact. It would be a battle of "healthy" star cruisers against "wounded" battleships and cruisers.

"There's no turning back now," Admiral Fletcher told his assembled senior officers.

It had been six days since Maddox's meeting aboard the *Antietam* with Fletcher.

The Fifth moved against the enemy concentration with its heaviest, best-armored vessels in the lead. That meant the battleships, the least-damaged heavy cruisers and the empty motherships. Those carriers had good hull armor and shields, almost as powerful as *Bismarck*-class battleships. That was all the empty motherships were good for now. The others held the Fifth's remaining strikefighters and bombers.

As per the plan that Fletcher outlined to the senior officers, *Victory* waited with the most damaged warships in the back of the formation.

The idea was straightforward. The best-armored ships protected the rest as a shell protected an egg's yolk. The "shell" would take the long-range pounding from the star cruisers, hitting back with the heaviest-mount lasers once the Earth Fleet came within range. Once the Fifth reached within medium-range of the star cruisers, the rest of the ships—except for *Victory*—would come forward and unleash their firepower at the enemy.

At short range, as the two fleets moved into colliding territory, *Victory* would come forward to engage its neutron beam.

Admiral Fletcher stood in the conference chamber aboard *Antietam*. The senior officers sat around the long table, including Captain Maddox, with Lieutenant Noonan attending as his aide. She stood along the back wall where the other aides waited for their senior officers.

Fletcher still looked gaunt, but his eyes shined with a new intensity. "The Lord High Admiral sent us his best bet," the admiral said, indicating the captain. "Cook sent Captain Maddox into the Beyond to find an ancient ship that wasn't supposed to exist. It did, though. *Victory* holds ancient secrets. A mad genius named Ludendorff is still hard at work trying to figure out those weapons systems. Maybe he will before the battle starts, but it's beginning to look as if he won't."

"Well," Fletcher said, scanning the officers and aides. "Even though the professor hasn't succeeded yet, *Victory* does have its unique propulsion system. With it, Captain Maddox destroyed the massed enemy drones and seeded our own missiles to hit the star cruisers as the battle begins. Maybe the ancient Adok vessel can hammer the star cruisers into submission once it unleashes the neutron beam. I don't know if we can save the Fifth, though. But, by damn, we can help Star Watch win the bigger war by annihilating as many enemy vessels as we can. I say that's worth fighting for. I say that made our dash into the void a good gamble. We don't get to see the finished product of our handiwork, but neither did King Leonidas."

"Who is that, sir?" a commodore asked.

"Leonidas was an ancient Spartan king," Fletcher said. "He led his three hundred Spartans at the famous Battle of Thermopylae at the Hot Gates. Those hoplites bought their side time with their lives, and they showed the enemy what the

Greeks were made of. We're going to show the New Men they can't win this war. We'll go down swinging, and *Victory* is the sharp sword we're going to use to ram into their guts!"

Fletcher eyed Maddox. "Keep firing that neutron beam as long as you can, Captain. Then, when you know it's over, jump out of danger, race home and tell them how the Fifth Fleet fought to the very end."

"I will, sir," Maddox said.

Fletcher inhaled before smiling sadly. "We have another twenty-eight hours before this battle begins. Let's prepare to meet our end with dignity. Let's go into the next life with glory in our hearts. Let them speak for a thousand years of how the Fifth Fleet battled against adversity, buying life for their loved ones at home."

The senior officers at the table squared their shoulders. The aides along the walls stirred.

Maddox could feel the resolve building in them. Fletcher had a knack. The admiral had restored some of the lost morale. Dying wasn't so bad if one had a reason. No one got out of this world alive. It was how you went that counted.

Captain Maddox scraped back his chair, standing. He gave Admiral Fletcher the crispest salute of his life.

"It is an honor serving and particularly fighting with you, sir," Maddox said.

The admiral nodded, and then, he stared at Maddox. "*Attention*," the big man said in a loud voice.

Everyone jumped to his feet.

"Let us salute the man who came to rescue the lost command," Fletcher said. "He braved the enemy and took every dare to fight through to us. You, sir, have my respect. You, Captain Maddox, are a man."

Admiral Fletcher thereupon led the senior officers and aides of the Fifth Fleet in saluting Captain Maddox of Star Watch.

-42-

"I think I have it," Ludendorff told Maddox twenty-seven hours later.

"The disruptor cannon works?" Maddox asked. He stood on the bridge, speaking to the professor via the main screen. The older man was in the disruptor chamber.

"No," Ludendorff said. "The ancient cannon isn't working yet, but I think I understand the key principle."

"Sir," Valerie said, indicating her smaller screen.

"Show me," Maddox told her. "Split the big screen."

The lieutenant manipulated her board. One-half of the main screen showed Ludendorff with Galyan behind him. The other half showed the two fleets approaching one another.

A green number appeared on the fleet half. According to it, the New Men would be able to reach the leading elements of the Fifth Fleet with their long-range beam in approximately twenty minutes.

Ludendorff was still speaking. "The disruptor principle is an amazing use of applied physical—"

"Professor!" Maddox said, interrupting the man. "Show me how it works. Don't tell me things I don't understand anyway."

"That would be a problem," Ludendorff said. "Making the disruptor operational will take me three days of—"

"You must know we don't have that long," Maddox said, interrupting once more.

"You're not listening to me," Ludendorff complained. "You're too fixated upon saving these lost ships."

409

"You're right about that," Maddox said.

Ludendorff shook his head. "There is no saving them, Captain. It's a hopeless situation. Now we at least possess a new and powerful ray. We must concentrate on what we can achieve, not wish for a miracle."

"I want you to make the disruptor ray operational *now*," Maddox said.

Ludendorff stared at the captain. Finally, the professor said, "I could conceivably jury-rig—"

"Yes, do that," Maddox said.

"Let me finish," Ludendorff said, beginning to look annoyed. "I could jury-rig a system, but it might burn out the main component. If that happens, the disruptor ray is gone forever. There goes our chance of future victories over the New Men."

"That doesn't make sense," Maddox said.

"Of course it does. The jury-rigging would let us use the disruptor cannon for a few shots. Unfortunately, the cannon's interior mechanisms will heat up rapidly. Some of those unique parts will melt into slag. To use the ray effectively, I would need a de-atomizer and a heat bleeder to dissipate the build-up of surplus energy. Are you beginning to see the problem?"

"Spell it out for me," Maddox said.

"Not only could we lose the disruptor cannon. We might build-up such a surplus of energy that it all unleashes at once. In other words, we would blow up our prized vessel. We would die and—"

"No, no, no," Galyan said from behind the man. "I will not allow such an event. I will not risk my existence on such a haphazard scheme."

Maddox glanced at Valerie. She frowned severely.

The captain stood up, turned his back on the main screen and walked toward the hatch. What kind of decision was this? Future victories over the New Men rested on the ancient starship. Star Watch also needed the Fifth Fleet to fight the interstellar war. What was the best course to take?

His mother had likely fled a gene-splicing laboratory in the Beyond. She had run away to fight again another day. Unfortunately, she'd never had that day, although her action

410

had given him one. Could he throw his life away on a poor jury-rigging that exploded *Victory*?

Maddox faced the screen. Battles were risks. If the New Men faced a disruptor ray beaming the same distance that their weapons could reach, it could shake their confidence.

"Jury-rig the disruptor cannon," Maddox said.

"No!" Galyan said from behind Ludendorff. The holoimage vanished and reappeared before the captain on the bridge.

"The starship is the last legacy of the Adoks," Galyan said. "That is too precious to risk on a mad gamble."

Maddox searched for the right argument. Finally, he told the AI, "You trusted me once, and it came out in your favor. Now, I'm asking you to trust me again."

Galyan looked away. "You are making this difficult for me."

"Your people died a brutal death to the Swarm. Don't let mine die to these perverted idealists. We need the disruptor cannon, and we need it now."

Galyan bowed his head. The seconds passed in silence. Finally, the AI said, "Lead me, Captain Maddox. I will follow you into oblivion if this is to be our destination."

"We're going to win this fight," Maddox said. "I want you to return to the chamber and help Ludendorff fix your cannon."

Galyan looked up. Then, the holoimage disappeared.

"Put me through to Admiral Fletcher," Maddox told Valerie.

With a start, Valerie turned back to her panel.

A few moments later, the admiral appeared on the split-screen. He wore his slackly-hanging dress uniform as he sat in his command chair. Fire burned in his eyes, though.

"Trouble?" Fletcher asked.

"No, sir," Maddox said. "It's possible I can work the disruptor ray."

Fletcher's features hardened. "There's an 'if' with this."

"Yes, sir," Maddox said. "There is."

"What is it?"

Maddox told him.

"I'm not sure you're making the wise choice," Fletcher said.

"You could be right, sir."

"In fact, the more I think about it, the more I believe you should run away to fight again another day."

"Fortunately, sir, it's not your decision to make. It's mine."

Fletcher stared at Maddox. Impassively, the captain held the admiral's glare.

"You're a cheeky bastard," Fletcher told him.

"I've heard that before, sir."

"I pray you're right about this ray."

"Yes, sir," Maddox said. "That means I'm bringing *Victory* forward to join the battleships."

"You're taking a lot on yourself, Captain. Have you stopped to think you may...?"

"Sir?" Maddox asked.

Fletcher nodded abruptly. "I accept your decision, Captain. I'll admit wanting to live has something to do with it. But it's more than that. These New Men have snookered me every way to Sunday. I'm sick of it. I want to bash them hard. If we can destroy the invasion armada, then I say let's give it everything we have."

"We're on our way, sir. Captain Maddox, out."

***

The two fleets headed toward each other. The New Men moved slowly, heading out-system. The star cruisers began to merge into their deadly cone formation. Last time, they had combined the many beams into one gigantic force of annihilation. Could the colossal ray destroy *Victory* in a short amount of time?

The Fifth Fleet had fifteen times higher velocity than the enemy armada. The Fifth moved in-system toward the Laumer-Point near the star. The battleships, the best heavy cruisers and the empty motherships formed a front sheet of armored vessels. Now, Starship *Victory* headed toward the firing line. Waiting in the back were the worst damaged vessels, the smaller ships and the loaded carriers.

On the bridge of *Victory*, Maddox sat in the command chair. Valerie had communications and scanning, while Keith piloted the ancient starship.

"Professor?" the captain asked.

"It's set up," Ludendorff said on the screen. "But I have no idea how long the cannon will fire and how we'll dissipate the excess energy."

"Lieutenant?" Maddox asked.

Valerie made some quick adjustments on her board. "I have one of their star cruisers targeted, sir."

"Let's wait a few minutes longer," Maddox said.

Valerie didn't nod. She watched her board with total concentration.

Several minutes later, the massed enemy beams merged into one giant ray. It smashed out of the void and struck a battleship's new wave harmonics. The hellish energy turned the shield a bright cherry red. The affected area grew in a concave shape, showing the spheroid nature of the shield. Almost immediately, the spot nearest the hitting beam became brown, darkening every second toward black. If a big enough area became black, the shield would collapse. Once that happened, the hull armor would have to absorb twenty-four beams striking as one. It was a pitiless strategy on the enemy's part.

Victory reached the Fifth Fleet's forward sheet of vessels. It slid among the battleships, cruisers and empty motherships.

"Fire," Maddox said in a low voice.

The giant antimatter engines inside *Victory* began to howl as they built up power.

"What's happening, Professor," Maddox shouted.

"The disruptor beam takes fantastic levels of energy," Ludendorff said on the split-screen. "I can't talk. I have to monitor the board, judging this to a nicety."

The howl rose even higher.

Keith clapped his hand over his ears. Valerie hunched her head. Maddox sat straight, refusing to acknowledge the danger or the noise.

Ludendorff spoke on the split-screen. Maddox couldn't hear his words above the howl.

The captain understood though. He jumped up and strode to Valerie, squeezing her shoulder. She jerked in surprise, staring

413

up at him. He nodded sharply. She whipped back toward her board and pressed the firing button.

The howl weakened to a whine. A new sound started, growling like a hungry slarn. The growling intensified: building, building and then a release noise told Maddox the cannon fired its deadly disruptor ray.

With his right hand on Valerie's shoulder, Maddox bent over and watched her screen.

The disruptor ray did not beam like a laser in a continuous line. Instead, it ejected as a blob of force.

Was this even a beam at all? Maddox decided not to worry about it. He straightened, turning to the main screen. "Build up for another shot," he said.

"I don't recommend it," Ludendorff said.

"Do it," Maddox said. "We may need a second shot to kill the star cruiser."

"Right," Ludendorff said. "I hadn't thought of that."

At that moment, Valerie stiffened. Maddox turned in time to see the effect of the disruptor ray.

The blob of force struck a star cruiser's shield. The entire electromagnetic screen went black with overload, and then it went down.

Valerie blinked with amazement. "Do you see that, sir?" she whispered.

"I do. Ludendorff!" Maddox shouted.

The antimatter howl began anew.

"Track that star cruiser," Maddox said. "We have to kill it before it can retreat behind a different vessel."

At that moment, the enemy's intense, combined beam knocked down Battleship *Blucher's* shield. The massive ray now heated the hull armor, burning through the thick, toughened metal. It would be a matter of a minute or less before the beam destroyed the *Bismarck*-class battleship.

"Now," Ludendorff said. "The cannon is ready. You must fire at once, as I can't bleed away excess energy."

"Target the same star cruiser!" Maddox shouted.

Valerie did so, and the disruptor cannon fired again. It was a race of seconds as the ray moved at the speed of light, heading for the star cruiser trying to do a mouse down its hole—trying to hide behind another of its kind.

The enemy lost the race. The second disruptor shot stuck the star cruiser's hull armor, blasting through and starting a chain-reaction within the vessel. The enemy ship finally managed to sneak behind another star cruiser. Then, it must have exploded. A white flare of brilliance told of the vessel's end. The star cruiser's inner core must have blown.

"Look, sir!" Valerie shouted. "A dozen star cruiser shields are turning red. Now, they're brown."

"I suggest we let the cannon cool," Ludendorff shouted on the screen.

"Are you mad?" Maddox asked. "We have a weapon the New Men can't believe we own. Pound them hard. Don't give them time to think."

"The risk rises, Captain," the professor said.

"I understand," Maddox said. "Two more shots, Ludendorff. I want them."

As the enemy cone formation kept beaming, the giant ray burned through Battleship *Blucher's* armor. The beam turned interior decks into slag and struck the engine core. A titanic explosion told of the battleship's end. Mass—decking, engines, food, munitions, people and water—and billowing heat expanded, hurling the debris and energy outward in a giant sphere. The nearest Star Watch vessels took the brunt of the blast. Their shields went critical, but held just barely.

Victory was far enough away that none of the destroying blast reached the starship. The disruptor cannon fired its third and fourth rays in close succession.

The result proved just as fantastic as the first time. Another star cruiser blew up, turning more nearby enemy shields red and then brown. One of the previously stricken vessels lost its shielding.

That was too much for the cone formation. Each destroyed star cruiser did too much damage to its side-by-side neighbors. The cone broke apart. The New Men vessels drifted farther away from each other. That broke up the giant beam. Now, the enemy star cruisers fired their individual rays, striking various battleships and heavy cruiser shields.

415

"Captain," Ludendorff said. "My make-shift dissipater is going to blow. We have to wait to fire again."

"Yes," Maddox said, "wait. We've busted up the enemy cone. Second Lieutenant Maker, pull us back from the front sheet."

"Aye-aye, sir," Keith said.

"Sir," Valerie said, "the admiral is on the line."

Maddox faced the big screen. Fletcher grinned like a maniac.

"You royal son of bitch!" Fletcher shouted. "You broke the cone formation. Congratulations, Captain Maddox. You've given me a fighting chance. I'll never forget this. I owe you a debt I can't repay. Anytime, anywhere, ask me for anything. If I can give it to you, I'll do it."

"I'm asking right now, sir," Maddox said.

"Yes?"

"Destroy the New Men for me."

Fletcher's grin broke into a savage smile. "This is a death ride, son. You know that, right?"

"No, sir, I don't know anything of the kind. When I play, I play to win, not to draw and never to take second place."

"Right," Fletcher said. "Win." The smile vanished, leaving fierce determination on the admiral's face. "I hope you have some more shots left in that miracle weapon of yours, Captain."

"Yes, sir," Maddox said. "So do I."

-43-

The fleets converged on each other, the distance rapidly dwindling between them.

The big Earth missiles Maddox had unloaded earlier tried to reach the star cruisers. The enemy shot the Titans down, but that took time, targeting and beams. It meant those star cruisers didn't fire for those minutes at Fifth Fleet vessels.

Battleship *Blucher* was gone. The enemy star cruisers now collapsed Battleship *Chattanooga's* shield. Enemy beams burned deeper into the hull armor. Escape pods should have fled the stricken ship.

From Valerie's board, Maddox heard the admiral ordering the battleship's crew to flee. *Chattanooga's* commodore respectfully informed Fletcher to stuff the order. The battleship's personnel yearned to fire their lasers at the enemy. Soon, the vessel would be in range. They were dead anyway. It was time to enter the next life with glory in their hearts.

Thirty seconds later, *Chattanooga's* crew no longer had a choice. The vessel broke apart under multiple star cruiser beams. Fortunately, there was no fusion core reaction. The chief engineer had braved critical radiation poisoning to go inside to pull the rods. He made sure such a chain-reaction had been impossible.

There were lesser explosions throughout the hit vessel, though. Battleship *Chattanooga* broke into five uneven pieces. The biggest chunk tumbled end-over-end. Two destroyers moved up at the admiral's orders. With their lesser guns, the destroyers shattered the tumbling piece into smaller chunks, making sure it didn't smash against a front-line vessel's shield and weaken it.

The third lost battleship didn't even break apart. It went gray, hurdling through space with Star Watch corpses in its belly.

By that time, the fleets entered heavy-mount laser range. The remaining battleships began firing back. Thick rays of deadly light speared from the huge Star Watch vessels. They hit enemy star cruisers, chewing against the shields.

It would still be some time before the smaller SW heavy cruisers could strike the approaching enemy with their shorter-range beams.

"Captain," Ludendorff said over the screen. "I believe I can give you three more shots. That will be it then."

"Three shots will only kill one more star cruiser," Maddox said. "It takes two hits to destroy one of them. I need a fourth shot."

"Sir," Valerie said. "Maybe you can use the disruptor to just knock down an enemy shield. Let Fletcher know which star cruiser you're going to strike. He can coordinate the battleships to shoot all their lasers at it. With the shield gone, the heavy lasers might be able to chew through the armor before the star cruiser can hide behind a different vessel."

Maddox's eyes gleamed. "That's an excellent idea, Lieutenant. Get me the admiral."

In seconds, Maddox explained the idea to Fletcher.

"Which star cruiser do we hit first?" the admiral asked.

"Pick it," Maddox told Valerie. "Then tell the admiral your decision."

Lieutenant Noonan did exactly that.

In another minute, *Victory's* antimatter engines howled with build-up. Captain Maddox slid forward on his chair as he watched the main screen. His gut churned with anticipation. Would this work? Could they kill more star cruisers? The enemy was whittling away Fifth Fleet's best battleships one at a time.

"Now," Valerie whispered. She stabbed the firing pad.

418

Victory's disruptor cannon shot its blob of highly charged energy. The glob sped through the void and knocked down yet another enemy shield. Seconds before the shot, a spread of mighty Star Watch lasers beamed against it. As the shield blackened, overloaded and vanished, the heavy-mount lasers pounded against the hull armor. The star cruiser moved sharply, trying to get behind its nearest unwounded companion. The Star Watch lasers burned deeper, deeper into the armor. The enemy vessel increased speed—

A vaporization of matter and billowing energy told of the star cruiser's brilliant ending. One second, it was there. The next, debris showed that nothing, not even New Men-built warships, lasted forever.

Two more times, *Victory* used the disruptor ray, knocking down enemy shields. Two more times, the combined wattage of heavy-mount laser power destroyed their foe.

The New Men had annihilated three battleships. The Fifth Fleet with *Victory* had taken out five star cruisers. Amazingly, the advantage belonged to the regular humans fighting under the Star Watch banner.

"Captain," Ludendorff said. "That's it. We dare not risk another shot."

Maddox stared at the screen showing the enemy formation. Nineteen star cruisers yet faced thirty-three capital ships. How many star cruisers could the New Men lose before their resolve broke? How many reserve vessels did the enemy side have anyway? Winning this fight meant getting these Star Watch vessels back home to the repair yards. The Fifth Fleet had to reach the Tannish Laumer-Point.

In that moment, Maddox knew their lack of intelligence on the enemy keenly hurt Star Watch. How could one make informed decisions if one didn't have all the information? Maybe the invasion armada was the full extent of the New Men's manufacturing ability. They had these ships—and the others that hadn't made it for the fight—and that would be it.

It didn't make sense the New Men had huge fleets of star cruisers. If these star cruisers were the result of the Thomas Moore Society one hundred and fifty years ago, then the New Men did not have a vast number of planets behind them. They might only have the Throne World. That would mean the enemy couldn't absorb many losses.

Yes, once *Victory* got in short range, they could use the neutron beam against the enemy fleet. That beam lacked the disruptor cannon's firepower, though. The starship could work down a shield with the neutron beam, not simply swat it aside with one shot. There was another thing, once the star cruisers came in close range, they could annihilate the wrecks hidden by the present front sheet of heavy armored Star Watch vessels.

"I'm betting the New Men don't have a big industrial base," Maddox told the professor.

"Why would that matter to us here?" Ludendorff asked.

"The New Men's willingness to take losses might be dependent on how easy it is to replace destroyed star cruisers."

Ludendorff cocked his head, blinking rapidly. "Oh, I see. Yes, you're right. It could make a critical difference."

"Heat up the cannon, Professor," Maddox said. "We're going to shoot again."

The professor closed his eyes, shaking his head. When he opened them, he said, "You don't know when your luck has run out. We're past the danger zone, Captain. This is red zone, lose the super-ship time."

"Do it," Maddox said.

Ludendorff heaved an explosive sigh. "As you wish, Captain."

Once more, the antimatter engines howled. Once more, the disruptor cannon sent its package of globular terror at the enemy. Another enemy shield went down, and massed Star Watch heavy lasers burned into the hull armor. Another enemy vessel died to the Fifth Fleet.

Maddox's throat was dry. He wanted to order one more strike. He'd helped take down six star cruisers. That meant eighteen enemy warships were left. What was the enemy commander thinking? Oran Rva couldn't know each disruptor shot was a grave risk for *Victory*. The enemy commander might be computing the odds and what would happen if he kept the remaining star cruisers on an intercept course with the fleet.

"Look," Valerie whispered.

Like ink from an octopus, each enemy star cruiser sprayed a red cloud before its ship. The twinkling clouds merged into a bigger field, blocking the two fleets, hiding the enemy ships from view.

Maddox stood up, walking toward the main screen. "Explain what I'm seeing, Lieutenant."

Valerie studied her board, finally nodding. "The enemy is spraying some sort of crustal field, sir. As you can see, they're spraying the crustals before their ships in relation to our vessels."

"The enemy isn't beaming us anymore," Maddox said.

"Their rays mustn't be able to burn through the crustal field, or not easily, anyway," Valerie said.

"What do you mean by crustal?" Maddox asked.

"Tiny pieces of highly reflective matter, sir," Valerie said.

"To reflect laser light?" Maddox asked.

"To dissipate a laser's killing power," she told him. "Oh, no."

Maddox's stomach muscles tightened until it became painful. "What now?" he whispered. Had he come this close only to lose to a New Men surprise?

"According to my sensors—"

"You can see past the cloud?" Maddox asked.

"A dim outline of a view, yes, sir," Valerie said. "It looks like they're running away, sir."

"What?"

"They're trying to get out of our path, sir," Valerie said. "One half of their fleet is going right, and the other half is going to the left of us, sir. They engaged their engines. It looks as if the star cruisers are accelerating at full speed."

Maddox envisioned what that meant in terms of the battle.

"They don't want to go head-to-head with us," the captain said. "The New Men will try to set up and rake our ships at long range."

"Maybe," Valerie said. "Or maybe they're just trying to get the hell away from *Victory*. Sir, I think you've intimidated the enemy. The New Men don't like our disruptor cannon one bit."

***

421

The star cruisers fairly leapt away from their former position. Using the quickly sprayed crustal field as a temporary shield, they accelerated out of the Fifth Fleet's path.

Fletcher's ships moved fifteen times faster than the star cruisers. That meant it was many times more difficult for the Star Watch vessels to alter course. They still headed for the Tannish Laumer-Point. In another few hours, they would have to begin braking if they wanted to use the jump point.

The New Men vessels could alter course easily because they did not have a high initial velocity. Now, for the first time, Star Watch personnel saw how fast the enemy's vessels could accelerate. The star cruisers moved away from the crustal field, becoming visible again. The enemy ships *moved*. Not only that, but they moved beyond the battleships' long-range heavy lasers and beyond the star cruiser beam range. The enemy commander made it clear he feared the disruptor cannon.

I used it exactly right, firing just enough and not one shot more. Only as Maddox thought that did he begin to tremble. He realized how close he'd come to losing the ancient starship and his life.

Maddox stood on the bridge watching the star cruisers fleeing. The crustal field had been the enemy's surprise. It meant the New Men had eighteen of their twenty-four original vessels this time around.

During the last battle in Caria 323, Fletcher had destroyed seven star cruisers. This time, Star Watch killed one less. Last time, however, the enemy had brutally wiped out masses of Star Watch ships. This time, the New Men had destroyed three battleships. What's more, this time, Star Watch had beaten the enemy and driven him from the field of conflict.

That was what he was seeing, right? Maddox could hardly believe the New Men fled for safety away from the Fifth Fleet.

"Lieutenant," Maddox said. "Hail the enemy. Demand to speak to Commander Oran Rva."

"Are you sure, sir?" Valerie asked. "They're running. Maybe we should leave it at that."

"That isn't how an aggressive admiral would act," Maddox told her. "We're bluffing them. We've played the extent of our super-weapon. That means we have to speak like a victor to keep them running."

Valerie turned to her board and began to send the signal.

Was it the last disruptor shot that had decided it? Maddox wondered. If he hadn't taken the risk, would the star cruisers be among them soon? Would he now be fighting the last battle of his life? How strange that a single order might have tipped the scales and saved humanity, saved this wrecked fleet. Would these remaining warships be enough to shift the balance of the interstellar war in the Commonwealth's favor?

"Sir," Valerie whispered. "I have Oran Rva on the line."

Maddox squared his shoulders. A second later, the golden-skinned New Man in his silver suit stood before him on the screen.

"You run away like a beaten cur with its tail between its legs," Maddox said.

The New Man's inky eyes burned with intensity. The slit of a mouth tightened into a razor line. Then, the lips parted, and Oran Rva spoke:

"Ancient alien technology saved your paltry fleet," the New Man said in an arrogant voice. "It has nothing to do with your capabilities."

"Oh, sure," Maddox said. "Keep telling yourself that as we hunt you down throughout the galaxy. You tried a cowardly sneak attack against the Commonwealth. Now, your people will have to pay a bitter price. You have one hope left, Oran Rva. Surrender and save your people."

"You dare to say that to me?" the New Man asked.

"Did you watch your star cruisers blow up?" Maddox asked. "I did. It was beautiful. Even better, all those aboard the ship must have burned to a crisp. Your day is over, Oran Rva. The New Men picked the wrong people to mess with."

"You pitiful mongrel," the New Man said. "You cannot conceive what is in store for you. One small success doesn't a war make. You prattle on because you managed to use an ancient weapon. Yes, we know all about your starship. Maybe it will return home to Earth. The rest of your fleet will never survive the journey."

Maddox smiled.

Oran Rva scowled and made a sharp gesture. The connection ended.

"What was that about?" Valerie asked.

"He just gave his game away?" Maddox told her.

"What game?" she asked.

"The second way the New Men plan to destroy the Fifth Fleet," Maddox said.

"What way is that?" Valerie asked.

Captain Maddox told her, and he told her how they would defeat the last attempt.

-44-

Kane gasped as the pain booth cycled down. The restraints holding his wrists opened. His arms dropped to his side.

He had lost weight. The greatest difference, though, was to his eyes. Desperation shined in them.

The hatch opened. Kane staggered through and slumped onto a bench. He waited. Would they feed him, let him drink? Or would they order him back into the booth?

The outer hatch slid up. Oran Rva stepped within.

Surprise caused Kane's mouth to open. Hurriedly, he shut it.

The golden-skinned dominant stared at him. "I question your utility. Each time, you have captured the wrong person. A third failure means your destruction."

Kane struggled for self-control. They were going to let him live. He had made the correct decision after all. For some time now, he wished he had died trying to kill the one who had put him in the pain booth.

"You will return to Earth," Oran Rva said.

Kane did not close his eyes. That would be bad form. Returning to Earth would be painful, as it meant another long-distance jump.

"Will you succeed this time?" Oran Rva asked.

"I will," Kane said in a raspy voice.

"You do not even know your assignment yet. How then can you make such a boast?"

425

"Let me prove my worth to the New Order," Kane said. "Give me any task, and I shall succeed."

Oran Rva sneered. "You have failed twice, but you understand the Earthlings. I grant you that. Thus, the Throne World requires your services once again. Attend me well, Kane. I will only give you these instructions once. Are you ready?"

"Yes," Kane said.

"No. You will clean yourself first and eat. We have a little time still. It is possible the Fifth Fleet will fail in their next attempt. If they succeed, however, I will personally give you the assignment. Afterward, you will leave in a scout."

Kane nodded. He would get another chance. This time, he would succeed, doing whatever he had to in order to gain rank in the New Order. And if the chance came, he would teach Meta and Captain Maddox the price of having thwarted his will.

***

The surviving ships of Fifth Fleet waited before the Tannish Laumer-Point, having braked hard for over two days.

Oran Rva's eighteen star cruisers were in the outer Tannish System, waiting and no doubt watching. To escape the star system and escape the debacle of the Battle of Caria six months ago, all Admiral Fletcher's vessels had to do was jump through the Laumer-Point and begin the journey home to Earth.

Using the Laumer-Point was the rub, though. That's what Maddox suspected, at least. He knew about Commander Guderian's report of the Battle of Caria. Six months ago, the New Men had begun the battle with forty-eight star cruisers. Fletcher had destroyed seven enemy craft. His warships had damaged fourteen more. That had left twenty-seven star cruisers intact.

At the beginning of the Tannish Battle, the New Men had twenty-four vessels. That implied three other unaccounted for star cruisers. Now, it made sense that some star cruisers had sustained damage during the ensuing six months of New Men activity. It also seemed possible that out of the fourteen originally damaged craft from the Battle of Caria 323, some had managed to finish their repairs back at the Throne World. Those could have rushed back here.

Maddox suspected that some star cruisers waited for the Fifth Fleet at the other end of the Tannish Laumer-Point. The jump route led to the Markus System three and half light-years away. Oran Rva had cut and run here. The New Man had also threatened Maddox, saying the captain didn't understand the true situation.

Maddox felt that he did understand. The enemy would pounce on the Fifth Fleet at the worst possible moment. Waiting star cruisers in the Markus System would hit the Fifth while the crews were in the grip of Jump Lag as they came out of the Laumer-Point. The enemy vessels in the Markus System would likely be far enough away from the Laumer-Point to shrug off any thermonuclear warheads Fletcher sent through first. But those enemy vessels would also likely be close enough to use their long-range beams against the Fifth's vessels.

"Are you ready?" Fletcher asked Maddox.

It had been over two days since the New Men had sprayed their crustal field to help them escape. During that time, Ludendorff, Dana, Galyan and the remaining technicians had worked overtime on the disruptor cannon. The professor believed the cannon could fire two more shots, but not one extra. Maddox hoped two would be enough for what he had in mind.

"I'm ready, Admiral," Maddox said over the screen.

"Good luck, Captain."

"Thank you, sir."

"I hope you know what you're doing," Fletcher added.

"Sir, I have the best crew in the service. *They* know what *they're* doing."

"I imagine they do at that," Fletcher said.

"Give us a half-hour, sir. Then, start bringing your ships into the Markus System."

"No nuclear blasts first?" Fletcher asked.

"That's right, sir. We may be in a bad way and couldn't survive any nuclear warheads."

"This is the last risk," Fletcher said.

"For now, at least," Maddox said.

The admiral cut the connection.

Maddox stood up, moving beside Keith.

The ace unwound a cloth, revealing three hypos he'd taken off the last tin can in *Victory's* hangar bay.

"Even with these Baxter-Locke shots," Valerie said. "Some of our ship systems won't work immediately as we come out of the star drive jump."

"True enough," Maddox said. "But the New Men in the Markus System aren't going to know right away that we're there with them. They'll be watching the Laumer-Point. We're using our star drive instead."

"You hope they won't notice us right away, sir," Valerie said.

"It's always a matter of playing the odds," Maddox said. "Ready?"

Valerie and Keith nodded.

"Let's do it," Maddox said.

Each of them injected themselves with the experimental dosage to help them shrug off Jump Lag.

After Maddox was finished, he flexed his left hand. He felt disoriented. Then, his mouth became dry, and his eyes felt gritty as he blinked them.

"I don't feel one hundred percent," Valerie said.

"You never do," Keith told her. "It's better than Jump Lag, though. That's the point."

"Galyan?" Valerie asked.

"I'm ready," the AI said.

The lieutenant glanced at Maddox. He nodded. Valerie warned the crew to get ready for jump.

Thirty seconds later, as Keith piloted the ancient vessel, *Victory* made a star drive jump to an exact point in the Markus System.

Maddox felt the familiar sensations, but they weren't as strong as in the past. He felt woozy. Then, the starship landed inside the new system several hundred thousand kilometers from the Laumer-Point connected to the Tannish System.

The captain squeezed his eyes shut before opening them wide. He glanced at Keith.

The ace grinned. "Amazing, isn't it, sir?"

Maddox nodded. It was indeed.

"Ah," Keith said. "My controls are coming back online."

Maddox saw the pilot's screen flicker into normal usage.

"I see the enemy," Valerie said. "I'm counting four star cruisers...three hundred thousand kilometers away. They're on the other side of the Laumer-Point as us, sir."

"Use the star drive again," Maddox told Keith. "Come in behind them."

"At what distance should I do that, sir?" the ace asked.

"Make it twenty thousand kilometers," Maddox said.

"They're going to start pounding us almost right away," Valerie said. "There's no way they'll miss us if we jump that close."

"This is where the expensive collapsium armor is going to earn its pay," Maddox said. "We'll absorb their hits until the shield comes back online."

Valerie looked worried.

"It's going to take Ludendorff time to come out of Jump Lag for us to use the disruptor cannon," Maddox said.

The lieutenant used the intercom, warning the others they were about to jump again.

As she did, Keith's fingers began to play on his board. "I don't think the New Men see us yet," the ace said. "They're not looking here. They're watching the Laumer-Point." His board blinked green. "Get ready," Keith said. "Now!"

The jump sensations hit Maddox once more. Reality disappeared and reappeared at almost the same moment. The captain felt dizzy. He sat down hard on his chair. Then, a faint buzzing sound made him cock his head.

"Do you hear that, sir?" Keith asked him.

"Yes," Maddox said. "What is it?"

"That's the enemy beams chewing into our collapsium, sir."

The knowledge made the hairs stand up on Maddox's neck. The New Men hammered *Victory*. Just how long could the collapsium armor take this kind of punishment?

"Should I jump again?" Keith asked.

"Negative," Maddox said. "We can do this. We have to."

Lieutenant Noonan hunched over her board. A green light suddenly blinked. Valerie pressed a spot on her panel. The ancient starship's antimatter engines began to whine. Then, the purple neutron beam lanced outward and hit an enemy shield.

The seconds passed in growing violence. All four enemy star cruisers hammered the hull armor. Vaporized metal floated in droplets outside the giant vessel. Klaxons blared on the ship. The enemy beams threatened to rupture through into the interior.

Maddox felt his gut churn. Was he about to lose *Victory*?

Valerie laughed as she pressed a control. The shield appeared, absorbing the four rays. The enemy beams turned the shield red and then brown, the area growing larger by the second.

The starship's hull armor began to cool. Now, the targeted star cruiser's shield turned brown. The enemy vessel maneuvered to get behind another star cruiser.

"Pound that ship," Maddox said.

The purple beam poured against the enemy shield, turning it black. Another ten seconds passed, and the enemy shield collapsed.

"Yes!" Keith shouted. The neutron beam hit enemy hull armor. It began chewing through it. At that moment, the star cruiser slid behind one of its fellow vessels.

"I'm retargeting," Valerie said.

Keith swiveled in his seat, facing Maddox. "We can't win this one, sir. Those star cruisers are too close together. They're supporting each other. Our shield is starting to go critical."

Maddox said nothing. He waited.

Again, the purple neutron beam brought a star cruiser's shield down. As before, the stricken vessel hid behind a fully shielded star cruiser.

"I'm ready," Ludendorff said over the main screen.

"Do it," Maddox said.

Now, the battle entered a new phase. The disruptor cannon came online. The horrible whine built in power. Then, the cannon ejected of glob of unstoppable force.

It struck a star cruiser's shield, knocking it down. Now, the neutron beam chewed into the hull armor. The stricken vessel tried to flee. Unfortunately for it, the disruptor blast that took down the shield also weakened the hull armor. It gave the neutron beam an advantage. Before the star cruiser could escape behind a different vessel, the neutron beam stabbed into the star cruiser's vitals.

The enemy craft shuddered. Armor plates blew off it. In slow motion, cracks appeared in the star cruiser. The cracks widened and ship atmosphere and water vapor billowed out. Then, particles appeared in the volume. Those were New Men squirming and other objects.

Immediately, Maddox ordered the neutron beam against a different star cruiser. With three enemy vessels, the number of beams against *Victory* lessened. The newly targeted enemy shield blackened all too quickly.

"I can give you one more shot," Ludendorff said.

"Aim at the stricken star cruiser," Maddox ordered Valerie.

"Yes, sir," the lieutenant said.

The enemy shield collapsed from the neutron beam. Then, the disruptor fired and the glob of energy struck the star cruiser. The reaction was a fantastic and obliterating destruction. The force of the spheroid explosion—it was an expanding nova white flare—weakened the last two remaining enemy shields.

At that point, the battle turned sharply in *Victory's* favor. The New Men didn't try to flee. Instead, despite the distance, the two star cruisers started a run at the ancient vessel. Their exhaust plumes lengthened to an incredible degree as the enemy vessels accelerated hard.

"They're going to try to ram us, sir," Keith said.

"Good," Maddox said. "Let them try."

"Sir?" Valerie asked.

Maddox didn't reply to her question. The captain watched as the neutron beam destroyed first one and then both enemy vessels. The first kill caused an explosion, weakening the last enemy shield. Then, it was over. The last two star cruisers never even got close to *Victory*.

As the final enemy craft splintered into pieces, Captain Maddox slouched back in his chair. He grinned at the other two.

"Is that it?" Keith asked. "This battle seemed to end too fast, sir."

"Yes," Maddox said. "That's it. We did it. We beat the enemy flotilla waiting to destroy us in the Markus System."

"This is an amazing day," Valerie said, giggling as she spoke. "With these four gone, we destroyed ten star cruisers altogether."

"With Fletcher's kills in the Battle of Caria," Keith said. "That's seventeen star cruisers destroyed. What do you think, sir? Did we blunt the invasion? Did we buy Star Watch enough time against the New Men?"

For an answer, Maddox pointed at the main screen. The first surviving warships of Fifth Fleet began to appear at the Laumer-Point exit. Fletcher had made it out of the Tannish System and into the Markus System.

"It's time to get these warships home to Earth," the captain said.

-45-

The battered Fifth Fleet came through the Laumer-Point into the Markus System.

There were three Laumer-Points altogether in the system. As the crews shook off Jump Lag, the battleships, heavy cruisers, carriers, destroyers and missile boats accelerated for the point midway to the reddish star. The jump route led to the Ember System and from there linked to Caria 323.

Lieutenant Noonan stood alone on *Victory's* bridge with her hands behind her back, watching the disparate vessels on the main screen. Two years ago, she had escaped the death of Admiral von Gunther's battle group. She alone had survived the horrible debacle against the New Men. Once she had returned to Earth, she'd gone before an emergency session of the Star Watch senior officers in Geneva, Switzerland. There, Admiral Fletcher had berated her for surviving the butchery. He'd said she had fled in the face of the enemy.

Valerie would like to ask the admiral about his thoughts concerning the accusation now. The lieutenant frowned. The thought wasn't gracious, she knew. Fletcher had been through a terrible ordeal. For six harrowing months, the Fifth Fleet had journeyed through the void between the Caria and Tannish Systems. Fletcher must not have expected to win through to the Tannish Laumer-Point to the Markus System, yet he had.

Valerie's eyes narrowed as she observed the half-wrecked ships out there. The fleet had faced the New Men in two major battles. The first time, the crews had lost. The second time, they watched the star cruisers flee before them. Now, the crews were heading home. They would be able to tell others the New Men weren't invincible after all. Humanity could win this war.

We won one battle, but we wouldn't have done it without Victory *and without Captain Maddox leading us.*

Valerie thought about that. Before the present assignment, she'd wanted a line command. She'd wanted to show the universe that she was just as good—no, better—than the next person was. Yet, she had just helped save the Fifth Fleet. She had been in the right place, and in the right slot of command, to help Star Watch win its first critical battle against the New Men.

Maybe this is where I belong, not in command, but helping Captain Maddox defeat the enemy. Dana, Meta, Keith, Riker and Maddox are becoming my family.

Valerie frowned. Then, a grin appeared. She realized something else. She felt good about what she had done here. She felt very good indeed.

***

Captain Maddox hurried along a corridor. A smile kept appearing and disappearing. It appeared as he thought about the victory over Oran Rva and the destruction of the four star cruisers attempting to ambush the fleet. The smile disappeared as he wondered about what would happen next.

I'm half New Men. I'm like them. Yet, I don't think I'm like them at all. They have insane notions of right and wrong. They think nothing of contemplating the deaths of billions.

A troubled look swam in the captain's eyes. He owed his mother a fantastic debt. How had she escaped the New Men? How had she managed to commandeer a spaceship and leave their planet? She was gone. He couldn't repay her for her sacrifice, but he might be able to pay if forward.

Maybe that's what I'm doing. By defeating the New Men, I'm helping my mother's people, my people.

That was another thing. *Who am I really? I am Captain Maddox of Star Watch. Yet, I'm half New Man.*

"No," he said. He would not let his DNA decide his future. He had given his allegiance to Earth. He would fight for freedom and the right to choose in life. He would battle against tyranny and against the genetic manipulation of planets and star systems.

Maddox turned a corner and spied an open hatch. He smelled a faint perfume, recognizing it as Meta's scent. Her voice drifted down the corridor. Maddox smelled coffee.

He burst into the cafeteria. Meta, Dana and Sergeant Riker played cards. All three looked up, with cautious Riker putting his cards face down on the table, no doubt to hide their value.

Maddox stood in the hatch. He wanted to shout. He wanted to jump into the air and click his heels. He'd seen a holo-vid once where a hero had done just that. Yet, that wasn't like him. He was the cool and collected Intelligence officer.

The touch of a smile played upon his lips. He came into the cafeteria.

"You did it," Meta said.

Maddox liked the raspy tone in her voice. He nodded.

Meta let her cards spill from her hand. Two of them showed. They were an ace of hearts and a ten of diamonds.

The captain ran his fingers through his hair. Why did his throat catch? This wasn't like him.

There was something in Meta's eyes as she stared at him. Was it hunger? Yes, he thought it might be. Maybe she needed too. She needed someone to sweep her off her feet.

Maddox laughed and took two swift strides toward Meta. He hugged her and picked her off her feet. Then, he spun around, holding her tightly against him. The feel of her breasts against his chest felt glorious. Letting her feet touch the floor, Maddox stared down into her eyes. He kissed her lingeringly. Then, he put his lips by her left ear.

"We won," he said.

Her arms tightened around him. "We won!" Meta shouted.

Riker whooped with delight.

"I knew we could defeat them," Dana said.

Maddox kissed Meta again.

Afterward, Meta pushed out of his grasp and clutched one of his hands. "Sit down with us," she said. "Tell us what happened."

Maddox sat down at the table. He began to describe the last battle. As he did, the captain used his hands, showing the various positions of the star cruisers and *Victory*.

The sergeant got up, bringing the captain a cup of coffee. Riker refilled everyone else's cups and brought donuts from the dispenser.

Maddox continued the tale, enjoying the glow of delight in their eyes. Most of all, he appreciated Meta's smile every time he looked at her.

***

Second Lieutenant Keith Maker gripped a bottle of long-necked whiskey in his fist. He laughed, raising the bottle high. He had kept the whiskey in his cabin the entire time, a test to his resolve to remain sober. The small ace moved down a corridor with his eyes alight.

A second later, he put his head down and ran. He raced, laughing as he went. "We beat them bastards!" he shouted. "We shoved their heads in a toilet and flushed."

He had been worried. He could admit that to himself now. The journey to Wolf Prime had been wicked hard. Out here in the void between star systems, watching those enemy cruisers—

"You didn't get our starship, and you didn't kill the Fifth Fleet. We chased your asses so you had to piss a crustal field to escape."

Keith gulped air, his side beginning to ache. Instead of slowing down, he ran harder. With his fist clutching the long-necked bottle, the second lieutenant moved the whiskey up and down like a baton. He'd raced from the bridge to his room to grab the bottle. Now, he sprinted to the cafeteria to join the others. He heard their voices.

"I love you all!" Keith shouted, leaping through the open hatch into the cafeteria.

Maddox, Meta, Riker and Dana sat at the table. Steam rose from their coffee cups.

"We paddled their bottoms!" Keith shouted, raising his arms in a victory salute.

"You're drunk," Dana said.

Keith laughed. And he noticed the captain's frown of disapproval. Last voyage, the captain had threatened to toss him off the starship if he ever got drunk again.

"Oh no," Meta said.

Maddox still said nothing.

Before the captain could get too upset, Keith marched to them, slamming the unopened whiskey bottle on the table. It shook their coffee cups. Some of the black liquid sloshed over the rim and splashed into a waiting saucer.

"I'm not drunk," Keith said. "I haven't tasted a drop, even though I'd like to. I've sworn off drinking. And I keep my word."

Maddox glanced at the bottle's top, and his eyebrows rose.

"Right," Keith said. He tore off the wrapper, took out a jackknife and unfolded a blade. He worked the cork up. Finally, he brought the bottle near and used his teeth, removing the cork and spitting it onto the floor. He put the bottle back onto the table and went to a cupboard, grabbing four glasses.

"I can't drink," Keith said. "But that doesn't mean you lovely people can't toast our victory over the New Men."

He put the glasses in a row, picked up the bottle and let whiskey gurgle into each one. Keith's eyes shined as he glanced at each person in turn.

Sergeant Riker leaned forward, grabbing a glass. "Well, I don't mind if I do."

"Very well," Dana said, taking another glass.

"Yes," Meta agreed.

Silently, Maddox took a whiskey.

"Raise them high, mates!" Keith shouted. "You're making a victory toast."

Again, Riker led them, raising his glass into the air. Each of them did likewise.

"To defeating the enemy," Keith called.

"To defeating the enemy," Riker agreed. He clinked his glass against the others.

They each did likewise. Then, everything gulped.

Meta began coughing. Riker put his whiskey down easily. Dana sipped, while Maddox simply drank. The captain didn't seem to enjoy the whiskey, but watched Keith.

The ace eyed the bottle. Seeing the others enjoy the whiskey put a pang in him. He licked his lips. And he lifted the bottle. Part of him wanted to put it against his mouth and chug. They had done it. But this wasn't the last battle. This was the beginning of the war. He would need to stay sober for more battles to come.

With a sigh, Keith set the bottle on the table and made his fingers release the neck. Afterward, he stepped back.

"Congratulations," Maddox told him.

"On how I piloted *Victory*?" Keith asked.

"Yes, on that too," Maddox said.

Keith understood the captain congratulated him on remaining sober. He appreciated that. Maybe that's why he'd brought the whiskey here: to show Maddox he could do it.

"Sit down with us," Meta said. "The captain is telling us how he—"

"How *we*," Maddox corrected her.

"How you people defeated the New Men," Meta said.

"I'd love to," Keith said. "First, let me take care of this." He grabbed the bottle, walked to a sink and upended it, pouring the lovely whiskey away. For yet another mission, he had remained sober. That made two terrific victories.

As Keith thought about that, he grabbed a cup of coffee and a donut and joined the others at the table,

***

On the bridge, Valerie finally got tired of viewing the ships of Fifth Fleet. She went to her station and sat down.

Galyan appeared and moved to her. "What are you doing?" the holoimage asked.

"Keeping watch," she said.

"You won a great victory," Galyan said.

"We all did," Valerie said, "you included."

"I suppose I should come right out and say it. The others are celebrating. You should go to the cafeteria and join them."

"Someone has to stay on guard," Valerie said.

"I will do that," Galyan said. "I have done it for six thousand years. I am used to the post."

Valerie wanted to join the others, but she hesitated. Why hadn't someone asked her to come down there? She almost told Galyan that.

The intercom buzzed.

"You see," Valerie said. "There's a reason I'm on the bridge." She tapped the comm unit.

"Lieutenant," Maddox said.

Valerie's features twisted with surprise. "Yes, Captain?" she asked.

"Your presence is requested in the cafeteria."

"Sir, someone has to keep watch—"

"Lieutenant," Maddox said, interrupting. "Must I make it an order, or will you come down here and unwind with us? You have done excellent work, and we should celebrate that before we start on what could be a long voyage home."

Valerie blinked several times and smiled. "I'm on my way, sir."

"Good, and make sure you hurry, Lieutenant." The connection cut.

Valerie stood, and she studied the holoimage of Galyan. "Did the captain send you here to get me?"

"The bridge is where I belong," Galyan said.

"You're evading the question."

"It is possible the captain suggested it," Galyan said. "Then he must have decided I was taking too long."

The alien AI still seemed lonely. What did Galyan think? What did he feel?

"Come down to the cafeteria with me," Valerie said. "You belong with us there."

Galyan smiled. It was the first time Valerie had seen that.

"You are kind to suggest it, Lieutenant. I can watch the celebration through the interior ship sensors. Thus, I will be there in spirit. Someone should remain on watch, however, and I am the right candidate for the post."

Galyan had a point. They had won a battle, driving off the star cruisers. The warships of Fifth Fleet could go home for massive repairs. But they were still in a war zone. The starship had to be ready for anything.

439

Realizing *Victory* was in safe hands with Galyan at the post, Valerie hurried through the hatch. She hurried for the cafeteria to join the others in a hard-earned celebration.

The End

Printed in Great Britain
by Amazon